idea
Library Learning Information

To renew this item call:

0115 929 3388

or visit

www.ideastore.co.uk

TOWER HAMLETS

Created and managed by Tower Hamlets Council

EVERY MOTHER'S SON

Harriet and Fletcher Tuke have worked hard to raise their children well. Daniel, the eldest son, has always accepted that his birth father died shortly after he was born, and Fletcher has brought Daniel up as his own. But as Daniel comes of age and falls in love with childhood friend Beatrice Hart, he can't help but wonder about his heritage – his olive skin and dark eyes reminding him daily of the difference between him and his siblings, and between him and Beatrice's families. Meanwhile, shocking truths about Fletcher's own family line are suddenly brought to the surface, revealing a connection between the two families...

EVERY MOTHER'S SON

by

Val Wood

Magna Large Print Books
Long Preston, North Yorkshire,
BD23 4ND, England.

British Library Cataloguing in Publication Data.

Wood, Val
    Every mother's son.

    A catalogue record of this book is
available from the British Library

    ISBN   978-0-7505-4157-2

First published in Great Britain in 2014 by Bantam Press
an imprint of Transworld Publishers

Copyright © Valerie Wood 2014

Cover illustration © Johnny Ring

Valerie Wood has asserted her right under the Copyright, Designs and
Patents Act, 1988 to be identified as the author of this work

Published in Large Print 2015 by arrangement with
Transworld Publishers

Magna Large Print is an imprint of Library Magna Books Ltd.

Printed and bound in Great Britain by
T.J. (International) Ltd., Cornwall, PL28 8RW

DEDICATION

For Peter Wood and George Silvester

On 24 June 1956, after finishing their National Service and before beginning their separate business careers in the print industry, my soon-to-be husband Peter and his friend and former army colleague George Silvester began a three-month tour of Europe on a Lambretta scooter.

They began by boarding a ship from Hull docks and the following day celebrated their arrival in Copenhagen by visiting the Carlsberg brewery.

From my late husband's diary I have learned of their route through Denmark, Germany, Austria, Switzerland, Italy and Spain. Their adventures were many and varied and included sleeping on beaches when hostelries were either full or not within reach, cooking spaghetti in sea water, and having to push the Lambretta up and down mountains when it refused to start. They also celebrated their twenty-fourth birthdays during the month of August.

The diary lists the fellow travellers they encountered: Americans, British and Canadians, as well as hospitable local inhabitants who welcomed them as they progressed on their journey. Quite unexpectedly they chanced upon one of Peter's work colleagues as they rode over the Alps and, best of all for me, he and I were able to meet for a brief and lovely day while I was on holiday in Interlaken.

Although the route they travelled was not the same as the fictional one that Daniel and the Hart twins took, I had this tour very much in mind as I began this novel and I dedicate it to two enterprising and enthusiastic young men whose friendship lasted until Peter's death in March 2009.

IN THE BEGINNING

January 1864

The very first words that Beatrice Hart had chortled were *'Danl, Danl, Danl,'* clapping her chubby hands in delight. Her twin brother Charles, much more sombre and not yet talking but at twelve months old already staggering purposefully from one chair to another, dropped down on his hands and knees. He did a fast crawl towards two-year-old Daniel, who glanced up at his mother, standing by his side, and on seeing her smile clapped his greetings back to them.

'They're going to be such good friends, Harriet,' Melissa Hart had remarked. 'The twins love Daniel.'

'Their lives will be very different, ma'am,' Harriet replied.

'I suppose so,' Mrs Hart agreed. 'But I hope their friendship remains durable, and there is no reason why it should not.'

And although Harriet had nodded in agreement as the children sat down to play on the fine wool Oriental carpet, she could think of two exceptions, the first being that despite Melissa Hart's liberal views she and her husband Christopher were rich landowners whilst she, Harriet Tuke, had worked in their laundry room and her husband-to-be was a small farmer just starting out on his own land.

'Do sit down, Harriet,' Melissa had said, 'and I'll ring for tea.'

Harriet sank down on to a brocade chair. She loved this room, which overlooked the garden; it was Melissa's own and one she was familiar with, for several times when she had worked in the manor laundry room Mrs Hart had called her in here to ask her advice. Advice from me, she had wondered at the time, me from 'back streets of Hull who knows nothing; but she did know about life and the complications of marriage, and those were the subjects that Melissa Hart had wanted to discuss.

Neither of them, in the few short years they had known each other, had ever crossed the wide social line that divided them, but they had a friendship of a kind, for both had suffered difficulties they could discreetly share and both knew instinctively that the other would not divulge their secrets.

Alice had brought in a tray of tea, not showing by her manner that she had ever known Harriet, and then Mary, the twins' nanny, knocked and came in. She had given Harriet a wide smile for she knew her well, not only from the laundry where they had worked together, but also from the time when Harriet had lodged with her in her cottage near the Humber. She told Mrs Hart that she'd take the children to the nursery so that they could have their tea in peace, and picked up the twins, one in each arm. Daniel put his small hand on Mary's skirt and went off with her without a backward glance at his mother.

Harriet had shaken her head and said wryly, 'That's sons for you: love you and then leave you.' She hesitated for a second as her hostess poured the tea. 'I came to tell you something, ma'am.'

Melissa's eyebrows rose, then she lifted the milk jug. 'Milk?'

'Please, just a drop.'

Melissa handed her the cup and saucer and then poured her own. She gave a small sigh as she slid a slice of lemon into her cup. 'Something momentous?'

Harriet had felt a rush of happiness. 'Yes, and I wanted you to be 'first to know, ma'am. We're getting married at last, Fletcher and me. Our house is almost ready and we're getting married in June at St Mary's in Elloughton.'

'I'm so pleased for you, Harriet. I have met Mr Tuke a few times and he seems like a good man – not,' Melissa added hastily, 'that I'm saying your first husband was not. But – Fletcher, is it? – seems charming.'

In spite of her pleasant words Harriet could hear the strain, the tension. 'He is, ma'am. He's nice and he's honest, and a hard worker. He will always provide for us; for me and Daniel, and...' she added hastily, 'and any other children that we might have together. And trustworthy,' she said in a hurry. 'He'd never do or say owt – anything – untoward that might hurt anybody else.'

Melissa pressed her fingers to her lips and gently tapped them. 'Yes, of course,' she breathed. 'That's – very reassuring.'

And that was the other exception; the subject they hovered around as delicately as a butterfly's wing on a nettle, that had never been broached, never spoken of or alluded to in any way, that they had learned through different sources yet never acknowledged, lest it tear both families apart.

CHAPTER ONE

Autumn 1874

The old ash tree had been standing on the prow of the dale for as long as anyone could remember. Some said fifty years, some said one hundred and fifty, though the latter declaration was laughed at, for who could remember so far back?

To Daniel, sitting on the lowest branch and surveying the scene below him, it didn't matter how old the tree was, although he admitted it creaked like old bones as he climbed it, for it was *his* tree, on his father's land.

Below their boundary hedge, the meadow land was a haze of golden buttercups, dotted with bleating sheep and deep dark wooded dells and divided up by ditches and drains stretching right down to the Humber estuary, which meandered like a glistening snake through the channel of salt marsh on this warm autumn day.

He wrinkled his nose. It was a pity it wasn't all his father's land, but a farmer would have to be very rich to own all of this, even richer than Christopher Hart, the father of his friends Charles and Beatrice.

Daniel was thinking. He had to make a decision, and he could only do that whilst sitting up in his tree, which had been his special place ever since he was a child and his father, Fletcher, had first lifted him up into it and pronounced that it was his very own.

The question was, when he was grown up to be a man – which wouldn't be long as he would be thirteen in December, and had left school this summer to work on the farm – should he stay and become a farmer or should he pack a rucksack with essentials, like meat pie and cake and clean socks, put on his sturdy boots and walk down the dale towards the Humber in order to board a barge or a ship and sail away to foreign lands?

Daniel's grandmother Rosie had told him several years ago that his grandfather had been a seaman and had come to England from some far-off land; when he'd asked her which country, meaning to ask his teacher if she would show him where it was on a map, Granny Rosie had been rather vague about it and said she wasn't sure.

He flipped a backward somersault over the branch to the ground and set off back up the rise. Life was a mystery, he thought. There were a lot of questions to be asked, but when he did ask some of them the answer was always 'when you're old enough to understand'. But surely he was old enough now.

One of the questions had come up on a Sunday last year when the Harts had invited the farming families of the area to a summer party in the garden of Hart Holme Manor. Charles Hart was a year younger than Daniel – he was ten then to Daniel's eleven – and they had been friends since they were infants; Charles had come across to him and murmured that he had heard an old farmer's wife say that Daniel was a throwback.

'What did she mean, Daniel?' he'd asked. 'What does *throwback* mean?'

Daniel hadn't known, so the two of them went across to Daniel's mother Harriet, who was talking to Mrs Hart and Charles's twin sister Beatrice, and asked her.

She didn't seem to understand at first when he asked, 'Ma, what's a throwback?' but when he explained that someone had called him that, she blinked and gazed at Mrs Hart as if she might know the answer. But Mrs Hart seemed suddenly angry and Daniel wondered if he'd said a rude word, like *dammit* or *blast,* which he did sometimes if he thought no one was listening, but then she drew herself up very regally and said, 'Come with me, boys, and I'll get you some lemonade. Beatrice, dear, stay with Mrs Tuke until I come back.'

Mrs Hart had led them towards the tables where ale and tea and lemonade were being dispensed, stopping to talk to several people on the way. Presently, though, she asked Charles to point out the woman who had made the remark about Daniel, and had taken them right up to where she was standing with another cluster of guests.

'Good afternoon,' she'd said graciously. 'I don't think we've been introduced; you are...?'

The women in the group, who were from tenanted farms in the district, had dipped their knees and given their names. Mrs Hart had nodded and introduced her son, Charles, who gave a polite bow of his head, and then she had put her hand on Daniel's shoulder and said, 'And this is Charles's friend, Daniel Orsini–Tuke.'

Daniel had glanced at them all and, taking his cue from Charles, he too had given a short polite bow and touched his forehead.

He heard one young woman murmur, 'What a handsome boy.' Mrs Hart had smiled at Daniel, who had blushed, and said, 'Indeed, he'll be breaking several hearts before long,' before moving away to another group.

Now, as he ran up the steep daisy-covered bank towards home, he wondered why Mrs Hart had taken him and Charles to greet the woman, who had seemed rather uncomfortable and startled by the encounter, and what Mrs Hart had meant when, on their return to his mother and Beatrice, she had said in a low voice, 'I am so sorry you should have been embarrassed while a guest at our party, Harriet. I'm afraid there will always be curiosity. But let them speculate, and in time Daniel will answer their questions himself. However, you should prepare him.'

It was something to do with the grave in the churchyard, he was sure. They went to lay flowers every Christmas. In the grave was someone called Noah Morley Orsini Tuke, his mother's first husband, who had died when Daniel was only a few weeks old. His mother had told him that this man Noah was his father and that Fletcher wasn't, even though he called him Da. She must have meant that Noah had sired him, he thought, with a country lad's innate knowledge, and perhaps that was what the old woman had meant, but why had Mrs Hart been so cross?

'Where've you been, Daniel?' His mother was in the kitchen preparing food when he arrived home. 'Your da's been looking for you. He wants you to help clean up 'field hosses cos Uncle Tom's had to go down to Brough. When you've done you can both come in for supper.'

'Where's Jack? Can't he help?'

Harriet flourished her thumb for him to get going. 'He's probably feeding 'pigs, I don't know. Come on, look sharp, and find Lenny,' she called after him as he headed for the door, 'and tell him to come in.'

Daniel's sister Maria, who was nine, was setting the big wooden table with plates and cutlery for supper, and eight-year-old Dorothy, whom everyone called Dolly, was sitting on the floor playing with two kittens. She looked up at Daniel as he passed and put her tongue out at him. He put his thumbs in his ears and waggled his fingers at her, then lifted the door sneck and went out.

He found his young brother Leonard in the pigsty, helping Jack the hired help feed the pigs and their young. Although he was only seven, Leonard had already announced that he was going to be a farmer and help Da and Uncle Tom. Tom Bolton wasn't their proper uncle, but Da's longtime friend and partner. Between them they had scraped enough money to buy the land over ten years before, and they were at last making a small profit, earning sufficient for them all to live on. Tom was still a bachelor and lived in a small cottage in the lower dale, whilst Fletcher

16

with Tom's help had built the farmhouse for Harriet and Daniel and now their own growing family and called it Dale Top Farm.

Fletcher was in the stable yard removing the gear from one of their four working horses. 'There you are,' he said. 'Did you give Johnson my message?'

'I did. He said he'd be up first thing on Monday and give you a couple more days in 'week.' He hesitated. 'Sorry I took so long, Da. I, erm, came back by 'meadow instead of 'road and sat in my tree.'

Fletcher shook his head but gave a laconic smile and said, 'So what was more important than coming straight back home? Here,' he added, handing him the reins. 'Check her over while I bring Duke out.'

Daniel ran his hands over the mare, checking her feet and legs for bites or wounds. 'I needed to think,' he continued, when Fletcher came back leading the stallion. He knew that Fletcher would always want to know his motive before telling him that he should have come straight back from an errand.

'About?' Fletcher asked.

'Well, about my future I suppose.' He thought it sounded very grown up when he said it. 'Because it's nearly here. I'll be thirteen in December so I ought to be mekking plans.'

'I see.' Fletcher glanced at him. 'And does your future include us, your ma and me, and your sisters and brothers? Or is it summat you're planning for yourself?'

'Well, that's just it, you see.' Daniel took a stiff-

17

bristled brush from a bucket and began cleaning the mud from the mare's feet and checking her hooves. 'I can't decide. Do I stay here and work wi' you and Uncle Tom, or do I become a seaman like my grandfather?'

'But you didn't know your grandfather,' Fletcher said mildly. 'You never met him, so what meks you think you'd like to be a sailor like him?'

'I don't know.' Daniel wrinkled his forehead. 'It's onny that Granny Rosie told me he came from somewhere else – somewhere not England, I mean – and I thought it would be interesting to go there.'

Fletcher smiled. 'And so it might. But first, let's finish here and go back to the house for our supper, or your mother will be feeding it to the pigs.'

CHAPTER TWO

Fletcher turned to Harriet in bed that night and said, 'We're going to have to speak to Daniel about his beginnings. About Noah and Rosie, I mean, and my mother.'

She snuggled up close. 'He knows about Noah. We visit his grave every Christmas. I don't think he's concerned about it. We've never concealed the fact that Noah was his father.'

'I don't know.' Fletcher sounded dubious. 'He's growing up and thinking more. When he was little he probably didn't understand what we meant. But Rosie has been telling him about his grandfather ... Marius.'

18

'Marco,' Harriet interrupted. 'You mean Marco.'

'Well, yeh.' Fletcher exhaled. 'Him. But I don't want Rosie telling Daniel about her former life. I think it's better coming from us. You,' he told her. 'It has to be you.'

Harriet sat up, leaning on her elbow, and gazed down at him. 'Are you serious? Are you worried about it?'

'Yes, I am,' he said emphatically. 'I don't want him getting to the age where he thinks he knows everything, like lads do, and then discovering it from somebody else. And 'other bairns should be told too,' he added. 'I know they're young, but we could tell Maria and Dolly at least, though mebbe not Lenny.'

Harriet put her head back on the pillow and stared up at the ceiling. 'Perhaps you're right.' She turned and kissed his cheek. 'You usually are.'

It was not going to be easy, Harriet thought the next day. In fact, it was very complicated. How would she explain to a boy not yet thirteen that his father, not Fletcher but Noah, had had such a strange upbringing and hadn't known the truth about his own background or parentage until he was a grown man and a father himself?

I needn't tell all, she decided as she hung washing on the line in the paddock and stood with her hands on her hips, watching the sheets and shirts flap in the breeze. No need to say too much about Fletcher's embittered mother, Ellen Tuke, who had been compelled by her husband to bring up a child who was not her own, and the part she had played in turning Noah into such an angry, hostile man.

19

Harriet often wondered how Ellen, a resentful and uncaring woman, had given birth to a son as mild and loving as Fletcher, a man of strength and reasoning; it was a puzzle she could never understand.

She walked to the edge of the garden and looked down the fertile valley. She folded her arms and pondered on how lucky she was. Sometimes she couldn't believe it, to have a loving husband, a clutch of beautiful children and a home of which she was so proud.

Behind her sat her house, their house, hers and Fletcher's, who had built it brick by brick, stone by stone. Built it for her and Daniel and the children who had come later. Double-storeyed, of brick and limewashed stone, its windows gazed down the valley towards the Humber, the river that she had known all her life, from her poverty-stricken birthplace in Hull to the farm at the edge of the estuary salt marsh near Broomfleet where Noah had brought her as his bride, and where a year later the waters had claimed his life as he tried in vain to save Nathaniel, the man he had thought was his father.

Harriet's marriage to Noah had been a convenience and a necessity for her at a time when she was desperate and at her wits' end. She had lost her job at the mill and was working part time in a Hull hostelry, which was where she had met him. Her mother was sick; dying, although Harriet hadn't realized it. Noah's offer was the result of an arrogant bet with his brother Fletcher that he would find a wife before he did, and came shortly after her mother had died, leaving her all alone.

Her father Joseph and her brothers had died at sea many years before, except for Leonard, her favourite, who had gone off to seek his fortune but had never returned, which had left her with feelings of anger as well as loss.

What would have happened to me if Noah hadn't made me that offer? she thought now, as she so often did. I'd have gone into 'workhouse, I expect; no work, no home, no family. She gave herself a shake and turned to go back inside to prepare the midday meal. Then she smiled. Who'd have thought that such a bad beginning would have turned out as it did: meeting Fletcher, Noah's brother as they'd assumed he was before knowing the truth, and falling instantly in love. A love that they never imagined could be fulfilled. And it never would have been but for poor Noah's death. A shadow of sadness fell upon her; she understood Noah's anger and bitterness so much better now than she ever did when she was married to him.

As Harriet served up their dinner, Fletcher said to the children, 'I thought I'd go to Brough on Sunday to see Granny Tuke. Who'd like to come with me?'

No one answered immediately until Lenny said, 'Can we go fishing in 'Haven?'

'Erm – no, not this time,' his father answered. 'I shan't stay long. I've to prepare for 'harvesters coming on Monday.'

Maria shook her head. 'No thank you,' she said. 'I'm going to help Ma with Sunday dinner. I'm going to mek an apple pie.'

21

'Oh, very nice,' her father said, trying not to sound disappointed. 'Daniel, what about you?'

Daniel finished what he was eating. Then he looked down at his plate. 'I don't think Granny Tuke'd want me to go. She doesn't like me very much. She doesn't talk to me.'

Harriet drew in a breath of anger. How dare her mother-in-law give that impression to her beautiful boy? She glanced at Fletcher and thought that Ellen Tuke didn't really like anyone except her own son.

'I'll come if you like, Da,' Dolly said quietly. 'We could take Joseph; he likes to ride in 'trap.'

'You'd watch him, wouldn't you, Dolly?' Harriet interrupted hastily. 'I wouldn't want him going near 'water.'

She knew that Mrs Tuke wouldn't bother to watch over the toddler, and thought that the woman would probably like the children more if they had been born to someone other than her. Ellen had never forgiven Harriet for marrying Fletcher.

'Well, we'll see.' Fletcher pushed his chair back from the table. 'No need to decide now. Come on, Daniel, let's get back to it. We'll turn 'sheep into 'hayfield to graze.'

'Where's Tom today?' Harriet asked. 'I thought he'd be up for some dinner.'

'He will be. He's in 'threshing yard.'

'I'll keep it hot for him.' Harriet set about plating up meat pie and vegetables for Tom and putting them in the side oven.

'Right then, Da.' Daniel rose from the table. 'Thanks, Ma. See you after.'

22

Harriet smiled. Daniel never failed to thank her for a meal. It was as if he knew that cooking and keeping them all well fed was her job of work just as his was helping Fletcher.

Fletcher nodded and mouthed his thanks too, and put his hand on Daniel's shoulder as they went out into the yard.

'Sorry, Da, you know, about not wanting to go to see Granny Tuke,' Daniel murmured.

'What meks you think she doesn't like you, Daniel? Has she said summat? I know she can be a bit crabby sometimes. I think it's because she spends so much time on her own.'

Fletcher was making excuses for his mother; he couldn't ever recall a time in his life when she had seemed pleased or happy to see them. Maybe occasionally if he called by himself she might greet him with a nod, but she never asked about the welfare of his family and always grew silent again when he made his departure.

Daniel shrugged and his voice dropped even lower. 'She – erm, she once said I was nowt to do wi' her. It was when Joseph was just a little babby and we took him to show her, an' I said, you've got three grandsons now.' He stopped as if unsure whether to go on. 'And she said, *two*, I've got two. You're Rosie Gilbank's grand-bairn, not mine.'

Fletcher cursed beneath his breath at his mother's insensitivity. How could she be so cold and cruel? It's because I treat Daniel as my own. He's just 'same to me as those born to me. She's so unforgiving; she thinks life has treated her badly, but it hasn't. There are others who have had a harder life than her, but they don't hold grudges in the way that she does. He thought of Rosie Gilbank, Daniel's grandmother by blood. She had had a much worse life, but she was loved by all the other children and considered to be their grandmother too, and it made her happy to be treated as part of their family.

His own mother had never visited his home, never seen how successful he had become, and she never would, because of her animosity towards Harriet.

'Why isn't she my gran?' Daniel asked. His smooth forehead creased into a furrow and he pushed away a lock of dark curly hair. 'Is it because of Noah in 'churchyard being my father? But he was your brother, wasn't he, so wouldn't she still be my grandmother?'

Fletcher opened the gate to the recently cut hayfield, and closed it behind them before they walked down towards the bottom end to let the sheep in.

'Erm, no, not really. It's quite complicated to explain,' he said. 'But your ma and me were onny saying last night that we should talk to you about it again, cos you've probably forgotten what we told you when you were a bairn.'

'I have,' Daniel said. 'And I'd like to know. Is it why Maria and Dolly and Lenny and Joseph have all got fair hair and I haven't?' He frowned again. 'A lad at school once said that I was a foreigner.'

'So what did you say?'

'I didn't say owt,' Daniel replied. 'I just put my fists up and told him to say it again.' He gave a sudden grin and Fletcher thought what a handsome lad he was. Large dark-brown eyes with thick long lashes that any girl would envy and olive skin that browned in the summer sun. 'And he ran off,' he added triumphantly.

On the following Sunday Fletcher decided that he wouldn't visit his mother after all, but would invite Granny Rosie to come for Sunday dinner with them instead. She came often, having moved to Elloughton Dale from her home in Brough to be closer to the family; she loved her charming cottage and enjoyed the walk up the dale to help Harriet with the children.

Harriet had first met Rosie when she was seeking out Noah's birth family and Daniel's forebears. She often reflected that Rosie was almost her surrogate mother, Harriet's own mother having died shortly after she had met Noah. Rosie, a widow, living alone, was delighted to be included as part of the family.

Fletcher and Daniel went in the trap to fetch her and save her the walk.

'Granny Rosie,' Daniel blurted out. 'We're going to discuss our family.'

Rosie turned to Fletcher, who raised his eyebrows. 'Are we?' She chewed on her bottom lip. 'What sort of discussion?'

'Nowt too daunting, Rosie,' Fletcher answered before Daniel could reply. 'Daniel wants to know about Noah. He's forgotten most of what we told him.'

Rosie looked anxious. 'But you know that I was – well, you know about my circumstances, Fletcher?'

He patted her hand. 'Don't worry,' he said. 'Har-

25

riet will explain only as much as is necessary.'

'Oh,' Daniel leaned forward, 'but I want to know everything. I'm old enough.'

Fletcher nodded. 'Of course.' He cast a pacifying glance at Rosie. 'But some of it will keep.'

When they arrived back Daniel and Fletcher took themselves off somewhere and Lenny ran out to join them after shouting a quick hello to Rosie, and she reflected that for a farmer there was always a job to be done, even on a Sunday. In the kitchen, where Harriet and the two girls were busy, there was a good smell of roast pork; Dolly was beating up a Yorkshire pudding and splashing the batter all over her apron, and Maria was rolling pastry for the apple pie.

'What a hive of activity,' Rosie said. 'Is there anything I can do?'

'Yes, you can sit in a chair with a cup of tea and give Joseph some milk, if you will,' Harriet said. 'Then mebbe he'll settle down a bit.'

Rosie picked up the child and kissed his round and rosy cheek. 'He's as plump as a chicken,' she smiled, thrilled to be given such a task. She sat in a fireside chair with Joseph on her knee, and took the milk from Harriet, whispering to her as she did so, so that the two girls wouldn't hear, 'Daniel said we're going to have a discussion about the family. You won't tell him everything, will you, Harriet? About me, I mean. I don't want him to despise me if he finds out what a terrible person I was.'

'You were not a terrible person, Rosie,' Harriet said gently. 'You were a victim of circumstances, and you were young,' she added, 'and not in control of your life.'

Rosie gazed at her, this woman who had become the daughter she had never had. A tear rolled down her cheek. 'I was young,' she agreed huskily, 'but I should never have tekken 'step that I did. How different life might have been.' She took a deep breath and peeped at Joseph, who was looking back at her from his blue eyes. He giggled at her and wriggled on her lap.

'How did I come to do it?' she whispered. 'What kind of woman would give a child away as I did?'

CHAPTER THREE

Rosie saw that Joseph's eyes were beginning to close. It wasn't wholly my fault, she thought. She put her head back on the chair and closed her own eyes. It was a life-changing occurrence. She felt Harriet take the cup from her limp hand as if she thought that Rosie and Joseph were both asleep.

I'm not asleep, Rosie thought. I'm just thinking of how it was.

There was just me and Ma and my father. I was fourteen and had started work a month before in a fabric shop in Whitefriargate, which was just round 'corner from where we lived in Hull. Da worked on the New Dock clearing out the ships when they came in from abroad and Ma worked in one of 'flour mills. We were not rich, but we had a nice little terrace house with clean curtains and a well-scrubbed doorstep and we allus had food on 'table and paid our rent regularly.

I remember that day so well. Ma was already in and cooking a meal when I got home at about seven. Da got in about an hour later, dead beat because he'd been working all day in 'bilges of a military ship. The soldiers had been put off at the garrison and the ship had been directed round to 'New Dock as there was a berth available.

'Oh, God, what a stink down there,' Da said. 'You just wouldn't believe it. I had to put a scarf over my mouth or I'd have thrown up.'

'We don't want to know about that,' my mother said. 'Go and wash your hands afore you sit down at 'table.' She was fussy like that, was my ma.

I could smell 'stink on his clothes, though, and moved away from him. 'Da,' I said, 'you're going to have to change your clothes, they stink horrible.' So he got up from 'table and took his jacket and shirt off and sat in his trousers and vest and I noticed that he scratched a lot as if he had lice.

We blamed that ship when he got ill a few days later, and Ma spoke to one of 'neighbours who told her that her son had travelled on the same ship and was taken off sick and put in quarantine. I didn't know what quarantine meant until someone at 'shop told me. And then Ma got sick too and couldn't go to work so I had to stay at home and look after them both.

I went to 'dock office to tell them why my father was off work. 'He's picked something up off that ship,' I told the clerk. 'He'll be back as soon as he can, and can I have his wages up to date, please.'

He said he'd have to ask a superior and would I wait, which I did, and another man came out to talk to me, but he stood well back and asked what

Da's symptoms were and why did we think he'd picked up a disease from the ship.

'Cos he was working in 'bilges, and he said that they stank,' I said, very bold I was, 'so it stands to reason that it was 'stink that's made him sick. And,' I added so that he would think I knew what I was talking about, 'we know that a soldier off 'same ship has gone down wi' summat and is in *quarantine*.'

'It's called ship fever,' he said. 'Or sometimes workhouse fever. Are you well fed and clean?' He looked me up and down and said, 'You look as if you're healthy.'

I was very put out when he said that, as it seemed to imply that I might not have been, but 'next day a doctor knocked on our door and he had a black bag with him and said that he'd heard from the ship authorities that someone was probably carrying an infectious fever.

He looked at my father, who by now was in a very poor state and quite delirious, and then at my mother lying next to him. 'Who else lives here?' he asked. 'Do you have any other family?'

I told him that we hadn't, that there was onny me, and he said that Ma and Da would have to be moved to 'Infirmary where there was a special room for patients like them, and that I would have to move out of the house because it would have to be fumigated. And then 'worst blow of all was that my father probably wouldn't last 'night out.

When I recovered my senses, I asked him what disease had they got and he said he couldn't be totally sure but probably typhus, which was deadlier than typhoid. And he said that it was endemic in Hull and I didn't know what that meant either but it didn't sound very nice.

Rosie's eyes flickered and she saw Harriet still busy at the stone sink and Maria putting something into the oven. She felt the warmth of Joseph on her knee and remembered how it had felt when Noah had been a small boy.

I had to leave home after Da and then Ma died. I couldn't afford 'rent on my wages. When I explained that to Harriet she said she understood as she'd been through 'same thing after her mother died. I had an aunt who lived in Brough so I decided to sell up everything we owned and get a lift wi' carrier and ask Aunt Bess if I could stop with her for a bit until I got another job. But I hadn't reckoned on nobody wanting to buy any of 'furniture because of us having an infectious disease in 'house, so I onny just scraped enough money together to buy some food and pay 'carrier's charge.

I had Aunt Bess's last known address but when I got there and knocked on the door, the woman who answered said there was nobody of that name living there.

I didn't know what to do and I wandered around 'town asking various folk if they knew my aunt but nobody did. I hadn't enough money for lodgings so I sat on a garden wall just to think what would be 'best thing to do.

And then a woman came out of 'house and asked what was I doing. I told her and started to cry, and she asked if I'd like to go in for a cup of tea. What an angel she seemed. She said her name was Miriam Stone and I didn't know then what her occupation was, which was just as well as I'd

30

never have dared to go inside otherwise. As I didn't know, I went in, and my life changed from then on.

I'd heard of brothels; there were a few in Hull, some quite well known ones in Leadenhall Square, for instance, where the respectable neighbourhood wanted 'houses pulling down; my ma had always told me to keep well clear of that area.

Rosie shifted a bit in the chair and Joseph sleepily protested. I was innocent then, she thought, but not for much longer. Mrs Stone was very kind to me and made me comfortable, gave me supper and offered me a bed for 'night, and she had a lovely home. It was when some of her girls started to arrive that I became suspicious, but it was getting dark by then and I'd no means of getting back to Hull that night or even 'following morning, so I stayed and then 'next day she put the proposition to me.

Rosie breathed deeply. I sometimes think it all happened to somebody else, but I can't deny it, it was me, and I stayed with her for a couple of years and it was there that I met Marco and fell in love with him and had his child, which foolishly I thought I could keep. But of course I couldn't; Mrs Stone wouldn't allow it. She said it wasn't a suitable place to bring up a child, and it wasn't, but I thought that one day Marco would come back for me, as he said he would. But he didn't.

Nathaniel Tuke had been a regular visitor to the house. Poor man, we felt sorry for him, although some of the meaner girls used to laugh at him. But I didn't. I felt sorry that his wife Ellen kept him from her bed and he had to visit such a place as ours. But unbeknown to me, he'd asked Mrs Stone if one of us would give him a child, a son. He told her it was what he wanted, and that he was willing to pay and 'child would be well looked after and given a good home, so after I'd had Noah Mrs Stone suggested that we say Noah was his, even though I knew very well he wasn't. I didn't want to part with him, I wept over him but Mrs Stone said that he couldn't stay, and I'd have to leave if I didn't agree.

Rosie stirred herself and opened her eyes; the dinner smelled good. She sighed again. It was difficult reliving the past, and it would be even more difficult explaining to her grandson Daniel, the son of Noah who hadn't lived long enough to know him, just what had happened. And I can't tell all, she thought, it wouldn't be right; it's not 'sort of discussion for such a young lad. That would have to come when he was grown up and able to understand.

But some good has come out of it after all, for me at any rate. Noah married Harriet and she gave birth to Daniel, but 'saddest thing was that Ellen Tuke hadn't treated Noah as her own as I thought she would, and he was never told that he didn't belong to them, or that Fletcher wasn't his brother, not until it was too late, and so he never knew he'd been born to someone who had really loved him.

'We're about ready to eat, Rosie.' Harriet bent over her and picked up a sleepy Joseph. 'You've had a nice nap, haven't you?'

'No, I wasn't asleep. Just dozing, you know, and thinking.'

'What were you thinking about?' Harriet smiled down at her.

'Well, about what I was going to tell Daniel about his father – about Noah. I don't want him to think 'worst of me,' she added in a whisper.

'He won't do that,' Harriet said gently. 'Not my boy. And besides, we won't tell him everything.'

They all sat down at the big wooden table, which was covered in a large white cloth: Fletcher and Harriet, Rosie and the four older children, and Tom Bolton, who often had Sunday dinner with them. Elizabeth sat in a high wooden chair and banged the tray with a wooden spoon.

The pork was tender and the crackling crisp and succulent. Dolly had done well with the Yorkshire pudding and apple sauce, and Rosie commented that Harriet had taught her daughters well.

Harriet nodded. 'It's so important,' she said. 'My ma never had enough money to buy food for cooking or baking and we didn't have an oven anyway. We ate ready-made bread and pies, which were 'onny things we could afford.'

Maria and Dolly gasped at the thought and Daniel too raised his eyebrows.

'Were you very poor as well, Gran?' he asked. 'As poor as Ma, I mean.'

'Not when I lived with my ma and da,' she said. 'But after they died I was. It wasn't until I married Mr Gilbank that I had a house of my own and a bit of money to spend.'

Rosie could see that Daniel was chewing this over as well as the pork, and waited for the inevitable question.

'So how is it that Noah's got Morley, Orsini and

Tuke on his gravestone?' he asked after a moment. 'But not Gilbank? Was it because there wasn't enough room for another name?'

'There are rather a lot of names, aren't there?' she said. 'But no, that's not 'reason. Rosie Morley was my name and Marco Orsini was Noah's father's, but Marco went away and didn't come back, you see, and after some years had gone by I met Mr Gilbank and he asked me to marry him. I didn't want to live by myself so I said I would.'

Dear man, she thought. He saved my life if he did but know it.

'So,' Daniel's forehead creased, 'why wasn't Noah living with you? And why was his name Tuke?'

Rosie hesitated, unsure of what to say, and Harriet jumped in. 'When your grandfather went away, Granny Rosie didn't have any money and had to go out to work, so your Granny and Grandad Tuke looked after him for her.'

Daniel thought about that for a minute, and then turned back to Rosie. 'Yes,' he said, 'but couldn't you have asked for Noah back when you married Mr Gilbank, instead of leaving him with Granny Tuke?'

'Oh, but he was quite grown up by then,' Rosie said, 'and...' She was looking pink and flustered, and this time it was Fletcher who came to her rescue.

'And besides,' he interrupted, 'I'd have missed Noah if he'd left Marsh Farm, just as Lenny and Joseph and 'girls would miss you if you went away.'

Daniel tucked into the rest of his dinner, and said, 'Yeh, but I'm not going anywhere. Not yet

34

anyway. I might later on, mebbe when I'm grown up, say,' he paused as if calculating, 'fifteen.' He thought for a moment, and then said, 'Tom, can we go out in your boat sometime, just to get 'feel of the water?'

Tom grinned. He'd been a barge man on the estuary before taking up farming with Fletcher, and he'd been primed that there might be a question and answer session at this meal. He knew as much about Noah as any of the other adults round the table.

'Yeh,' he said. 'Course we can.'

'And then, Gran,' Daniel continued, 'if I'm all right, not seasick or anything, then I might get a job on board ship for a year or two and go off on voyages, and mebbe...' He took another forkful of pork and chewed it thoughtfully. Daniel did nothing without considering it carefully first. 'And mebbe I'll go and try to find Marco Orsini and tell him who I am, and ask him if he'd like to come back home wi' me and see Rosie again.' He grinned at the company seated around the table and then turned his attention back to Rosie. 'What do you think about that?'

CHAPTER FOUR

Below Elloughton Dale and nearer the estuary, in the vicinity of Broomfleet, sat Hart Holme Manor, the home of landowner Christopher Hart, his wife Melissa and their four children.

Melissa was Christopher's second wife, his first wife Jane having died many years before he met Melissa, who was twenty years his junior. Jane had given him a daughter, Amy, now married and living in London with children of her own.

He and Melissa had been married for five years before she had the twins, Charles and Beatrice. Stephen was born two years later and George followed a year after, and that was quite enough sons for any man over fifty, Christopher thought, though with a wife only in her early thirties they might not be the last. But it was very tiring looking after a large estate, even with a bailiff to organize the general running of it, and an early evening in bed, to read or sleep, was very desirable. Charles would not be twelve until December, and even supposing he begins helping out on the estate as early as eighteen, when he finishes school, Christopher thought, sighing, I will be sixty, with little chance of retiring early.

Charles had gone away to school when he was ten, much later than his father had wanted, but Melissa couldn't bear to part with him and had said adamantly that eight was far too young for a boy to be sent away from his mother. Melissa liked to have her children at home and hadn't entertained any thought of sending Beatrice away to school even though she was the one who was always climbing trees and had been the first to ride a pony; having taken her first tumble when she was five, she had run after and caught her pony and climbed back on again, whilst Charles after his first fall had gone hopping to Nanny Mary to have his knee bandaged.

36

School, however had toughened Charles up, and although he didn't get into fights with other boys he refused to be bullied and often went to the aid of those who were, and could fell his opponents with a glare or a few well-chosen words; when it was time for Stephen and George to join him, Melissa was quite sure they would be looked after by their older brother.

Charles was like his father in looks, tall, fair-haired and slim, but whilst Beatrice was also fair she was beginning to develop curves like her mother and had her angelic features, which hid much mischief. Both children had a special friendship with Daniel even though they saw less of each other now that Charles was at school and Beatrice wasn't allowed out of the grounds on her own; but unbeknown to either set of parents the twins and Daniel met frequently during the school holidays, and if Beatrice could have sneaked away from her governess to trek up the dale on her own and find Daniel at home she would have.

Harriet was awake an hour earlier than usual and knew as soon as her feet touched the floor, as soon as she felt the nausea rising, that she was pregnant again. Well, she thought philosophically, at least there'll be a reasonable gap between Elizabeth and the next one. Elizabeth will be nearly three by then and able to do more things for herself. She swallowed hard and hoped that she could manage to get outside before she was sick and so keep the news from Fletcher for a little longer. It would have to be today of all days to discover it, she thought; one of our busiest weeks of the year.

37

She knew she could rely on Maria to help out, but she wanted her eldest daughter to enjoy her childhood and not be tied to the kitchen chores or looking after the younger children. Nor be like me at that age, already trying to find work to help out with 'family finances ... and then she laughed at herself: listen to me, *finances,* a pittance more like, that my mother brought home from the mill.

Fletcher had raked the ash beneath the fire and set the kettle over it to boil. She loved him for those little touches and for the fact that he didn't expect her to do everything for him. She stood by the open door and breathed in the fresh morning air and thought that perhaps she wouldn't be sick after all, that the nausea was subsiding, so maybe, but only maybe, she wasn't pregnant after all.

'Good morning, my lovely.' Fletcher crossed the yard and came towards the house. 'Did I wake you?' He kissed the tip of her nose, and then, with his hands on her shoulders, said, 'You look beautiful this morning.'

She smiled. 'You allus know how to get round a woman.'

'Not just any woman,' he said. 'Onny one.' He smacked her rump. 'Now get inside,' he joked, 'and cook my breakfast.'

It was as she was cooking the bacon and sausage that she felt queasy again, and moving the pan off the heat she rushed outside. Fletcher's gaze followed her, but he went to the bottom of the stairs and called up, 'Maria! Daniel! Time you were up.'

They were both downstairs in ten minutes and by then Harriet was back inside. She'd swilled her hands and face under the outside pump and was back cooking again, but she knew without doubt that she wouldn't be eating any of it. She saw Fletcher's eyes upon her and he raised his eyebrows questioningly, and so she nodded. He would guess anyway; no need now to try to keep the news from him.

There was no further chance to talk as Tom Bolton arrived as she was dishing up and sat down to join them for breakfast; then they heard the clatter of wheels, the rattle of carts and the sound of men's voices, and the first day of harvesting began.

Although Tom's working life had begun as an apprentice on the barges that plied the estuary, whenever he was able to he had worked on the local farms at harvest time or filled in as a general labourer to earn extra money. He had known the farmers in the district since he was a lad, and they regarded him as reliable; it was through one of them that he had heard of the piece of land that was coming up for sale in Elloughton Dale. At a hundred and fifty acres it was too small and too far from his home farm to be of use to the farmer who had told him of it, but to Tom, who, having no wife or dependants, had managed to save some of his earnings, and Fletcher, who was desperate for a fresh start away from the waterlogged marshes where his parents had scraped a living, it was a gift from heaven. Fletcher too had saved money during a period when he'd worked in America.

After laying drainage pipes on the land they had decided on a mixed farm, growing some crops and keeping livestock, and what Tom didn't know about cows, pigs or sheep he more than made up

39

for with a head for figures and a practical knowledge of building barns, sheds or fences, as well as understanding the workings of the new machinery which was being invented week by week, but was at present beyond their reach. They had paid good money for a plough, and the next thing on the list to buy when they could afford it would be a manure spreader, which would save them much time and effort. Meanwhile, with one or two exceptions such as the harvest which they couldn't tackle without the help of friends and neighbours, the two of them could manage just about everything else.

At midday, Harriet and Maria came out with baskets containing bread and beef, meat and potato pasties, some sweet cake and jugs of cold tea. Many of the local men brought their own dinner or *lowance* as they called it, an expression that had amused Harriet when she had first heard it, and Fletcher had laughed and called her a townie.

When they had distributed the food and were turning to go back to the house, Maria said suddenly, 'What's Dolly doing, Ma? I thought she was looking after Elizabeth and Joseph.'

Harriet looked across to where Maria was pointing towards a dozen or more horses that had been resting and drinking from a wooden trough, but were now shuffling and stamping their big legs and feet.

'What's she doing? She'll get trampled!' Harriet raised her voice. 'Dolly! Come away! Don't disturb 'hosses.'

Dolly looked up. 'Help me,' she shouted. 'Joseph is under 'hosses' feet. He can't get out.'

Harriet gave a startled cry and began to run. 'Fletcher!' she screamed. 'Fletcher!'

Fletcher, standing with Tom and Daniel and taking a drink of cold tea, looked up. 'What's happened?'

'Summat wrong wi' hosses,' Tom said.

But Daniel, being shorter, had spotted somebody or something in the melee beneath the horses' legs. 'Come quick, Da,' he shouted. 'It's our Joseph. He's under 'hosses' feet.'

CHAPTER FIVE

On the track above the dale and looking down on the harvesting scene were three figures on horseback. Beatrice, Charles and the apprentice groom Aaron were out riding. The twins were not allowed out of their home grounds without someone older and responsible in attendance.

'Which is not fair,' Beatrice had argued with her mother. 'Aaron is no better on horseback than either of us, and besides...' she'd hesitated, as she liked Aaron and didn't want to say anything against him, 'he's only sixteen and rather slow.'

'You're not going out for a gallop,' her mother said. 'You must keep to the tracks and bridleways.'

'I didn't mean slow at riding,' Beatrice muttered.

'She means he hasn't got much in the top attic,' Charles grinned.

'Do not let me hear that kind of language,' Melissa said sharply. 'Aaron hasn't had the benefit

41

of an education as you have, but he's perfectly capable, and if there should be any kind of accident he'd be able to ride for help, whilst one of you would stay with the other.'

'But Mama,' Beatrice protested. 'There isn't going to be an accident.'

But now, as they looked down on the men and women scurrying across the fields, they both wondered if there was and whether they should send Aaron home for help.

'That's Daniel!' Charles said. 'Look how he runs. He's so fast.'

'There's something under 'hosses feet that's scaring 'em.' Aaron narrowed his eyes. 'Looks like a nipper, a young bairn.'

'Oh!' Beatrice moaned. 'I hope it's not one of Daniel's brothers. But he's calming them; look, he's trying to settle them. Should we go down, do you think?'

'No, miss,' Aaron said quite firmly. 'Not yet anyway. There're plenty o' folks to give a hand. We'd onny be in 'way. Besides, we ought to–'

'Oh, I'm sure we wouldn't. Do you think we'd be in the way, Charles?'

'Don't know. Maybe we should wait, but Daniel's gone between their legs. Goodness,' he exhaled. 'They're such big brutes, he could get trampled on.'

'They're not brutes, Master Charles,' Aaron intervened. 'They're gentle animals, but they'll be scared–'

'I didn't mean that – oh, but look! Daniel's got the boy out. Is he all right, do you think? I think we should go down. Come on!'

Charles dug his heels into his mount's flanks and was off down the hillside with Beatrice behind him before Aaron could stop them.

They dismounted when they reached the scene and handed their reins up to Aaron, who had reluctantly followed, then went towards the small crowd gathered about Harriet, who was kneeling on the ground and cradling the toddler.

'I hope everything is all right with the boy, Mrs Tuke. Can we help?' Charles asked.

'Can we ride for a doctor or someone?' Beatrice was eager to be involved.

Harriet looked up at them, screwing up her eyes against the sun. 'He's fine, thank you,' she said. 'He's just had a bit of a fright. He loves horses, don't you, Joseph, and went charging in and scared them. Is it Miss Beatrice? How you've grown since I last saw you, and you too, Master Charles. You've overshot Daniel.'

'Yes, I know.' Charles straightened his shoulders to make himself even taller. 'And he's a year older than me.'

'Daniel was very brave,' Beatrice interrupted, looking round for him and spotting him talking to some of the horse lads. 'We were watching from the top of the dale and thought we ought to come and give a hand or something.'

'That was very kind of you.' Harriet got to her feet. 'But Joseph will be all right. I'll tek him home and he can have a sleep.'

'Can we stay?' Beatrice asked. 'I mean, can we stay and help with the harvest? We'd love to, wouldn't we, Charles?'

'No, miss.' Aaron spoke up from atop his horse.

'Mistress said we'd to be back for luncheon an' it's just about that time already. We'd best be getting back if there's nowt to be done here.'

Daniel came over to join them. 'Hello. What 'you two doing here?'

'We saw what happened, and came down to help,' Charles said again.

'You were very brave, Daniel,' Beatrice said, and then tried out a joke. 'Daniel in the horse's den.'

Her brother and Daniel looked at her. Daniel grinned but Charles said, 'Ho, ho, ho! Is that supposed to be funny, Bea?'

Beatrice sighed dramatically. 'Well – it obviously wasn't.' She turned her back on her brother. 'We wondered if we could stay to help with the harvest, but Aaron says that we can't because we have to be home for luncheon. I'm not in the *least* hungry, so I don't see why we should have to go back yet!'

'You'll be hungry by 'time we get back, miss, an' if we don't go now, we'll be late and missus'll be mad at me.'

'You don't want Aaron to get into trouble, do you, Beatrice?' Daniel said. 'And besides, you're not dressed for harvesting. Why don't you ask your mother if you can come tomorrow?' He looked at her in her green riding habit and matching hat, and then at Charles in his tweed hacking jacket and riding breeches. 'And come in your oldest clothes, cos you'll get covered in dust.'

'Oh, very well,' Beatrice said sulkily. 'But we might not be allowed to come. We're not allowed to do everything we want, you know!'

'None of us are,' Daniel told her. 'I'd rather be

44

fishing down at Broomfleet lock but I can't cos it's harvest time and all hands are needed.'

'Broomfleet lock?' she said. 'But that's a long way. Nearer to our house than yours.'

'I know.' Daniel glanced towards the gangs of men who were moving back up the fields. 'But there's good fishing. Anyway, I'll have to go, we're ready to start again.' He raised questioning eyebrows at Charles. 'Might see you tomorrow?'

Charles shrugged. 'Don't know if I want to come; but if I don't, then Bea can't either.'

'Oh, Charles!' Beatrice broke in, exasperated. 'You're such a spoilsport!'

'Got to go,' Daniel broke in before he sped off, and he heard Aaron say, 'Best be going, miss. I'll bring you tomorrow if Mrs Hart says it's all right.'

The first thing Melissa said when they told her about the incident at the harvesting was, 'Is the child all right?' and the next, 'And how did you come to be there? Wasn't that out of your way?'

'We saw something going on from the top of the rise,' Beatrice said swiftly before Charles could speak. 'So we rode down to see if we could give assistance.'

'Really! Surely there were people about?'

'It was Beatrice who wanted to go down,' Charles said.

'But then you rode off before me,' Beatrice interrupted. 'You said you thought we should go. You just wanted to be first. Aaron said we shouldn't, because there were plenty of folk there.'

'You only wanted to go so that you could see Daniel.' Charles forked a slice of chicken into his

45

mouth and chewed, and when he'd swallowed it said, 'She's sweet on Daniel.'

'No I am *not*,' Beatrice said hotly. 'He's your friend just as much as he's mine.'

'Children!' Mrs Hart warned. 'No quarrelling at table.'

Her husband looked up and smiled. 'Who is this Daniel?' he asked. 'Do I know him? Should I be making lists of eligible young men for my daughter?'

'Charles is being stupid,' Beatrice said crossly. 'He thinks he's so grown up since he went away to school.'

'You do know Daniel, dear,' Melissa told their father. 'Daniel Tuke. You remember? Fletcher and Harriet Tuke? He's the eldest son.'

'Oh, yes, of course.' Christopher's expression closed, as she had known it would. 'Not a contender, then.'

Daniel was shaken by the incident, although he didn't show it. Joseph had started to scream and he'd been sure that the horses would bolt, which would have meant real trouble, but he'd managed to scoop up the child, pressing his face into his jacket to muffle the sound so as not to disturb the horses further, and murmuring, 'You're all right, Joseph, you're all right now,' until his cries had turned to a whimper.

When Harriet came back later with more freshly drawn water in a pail for the men to dip their cups and take a drink, she told him that she'd put Joseph to bed and Dolly was staying with him. 'Little monkey,' she said. 'He'd wandered out to

46

follow Maria and me, and poor Dolly hadn't noticed he'd gone. She's very upset.' She smiled shakily at Daniel. 'But I told her that her brave brother had saved the day.'

Daniel shrugged. 'I just happened to get there first, Ma, that's all.'

'Young Beatrice from the manor thought you were brave. They were a long way from home, weren't they?'

'Beatrice gets bored riding on their own land and she's not allowed out on her own,' Daniel said. 'She can only go out when Charles is home from school, and even then someone has to go with them.' He gave a grin. 'He thinks he's so grown up and gets mad when I say I can go anywhere I want!'

'Except that you have to work now,' his mother reminded him. 'You can't go wandering off in 'way you used to.'

'I know,' Daniel admitted. 'But I'm a year older than Charles,' he added, 'and on a Sunday I can. I can go fishing in 'lock and streams and even go down to 'river bank if I want.'

'No!' Harriet said sharply. 'I don't want you larking about down there. 'Estuary is deep and 'tide runs fast and if you got on to 'salt marsh you'd never get out. You mustn't go there, Daniel, do you hear?' She was agitated, not her usual self. 'Daniel! Are you listening to me?'

'Aye, Ma, I'm listening. I hear what you're saying.'

It was another piece of the puzzle and he couldn't quite make it fit. It was something to do with the old house down by the estuary. There were only a few broken-down walls left and they were covered in ivy. He and some of his pals had found it when they'd headed down towards the river one day a couple of summers back. He'd asked his father if he knew who it belonged to and Fletcher had said it was private land belonging to Master Hart.

'It's where I lived when I was a boy,' he'd said. 'With Granny Tuke and my father and Noah.'

He too had said he didn't want him to play there. 'The walls are dangerous,' he'd said. 'They should be demolished.' He'd also told him that the land had been allowed to flood. Warping, he'd called it; drains had been put in and sluice gates built and in a few years it would be good land for growing. 'But don't go there again, Daniel. There are bad memories of a drowning and you mustn't tell your ma that you've been.' Fletcher hesitated, then took a breath and said, 'It was Noah who drowned. My father Nathaniel got into difficulties on 'salt marsh and Noah tried to save him. They both died.'

Daniel nodded his understanding. It was all becoming much clearer now and helped to explain why his mother had been so agitated when she learned that he thought he could go down to the river bank by himself. He realized now that he couldn't, that it was totally out of bounds.

CHAPTER SIX

It dawned on Daniel when he was seventeen that not everyone was equal. He had long realized that some folk were richer than others, that some only scraped a living and others such as his father and Tom – he'd stopped calling him Uncle when he overtopped him at fourteen – had good years and poor years like most farmers, and that there were others who owned land but didn't farm it themselves, like Charles and Beatrice's father for instance, who let his farms and land to tenants.

But until then he hadn't considered that there was a difference in status or prestige; he touched his forehead or doffed his cap, as his father did, out of respect, or because the other person was older or wiser, or politely to a female, not because he thought that he or she was superior to him. But at the twins' sixteenth birthday party, to which he and Maria had been invited, he became aware that he had been under a misapprehension.

Maria hadn't wanted to go to the party. Her mother thought she had been invited to be company for Daniel. At thirteen she was quite shy, unlike Dolly who wasn't, but who hadn't been invited.

'Maria doesn't have to come if she doesn't want to,' Daniel protested. 'I don't need company. I know Charles and Beatrice well enough to go on my own, even though I'm not bothered about

49

going either.' His forehead creased. 'Why do you think they're having a party anyway?'

Harriet considered. 'Not sure,' she said. 'Perhaps they've something special to announce. Although they've had parties before. You used to go to them when you were little.'

'Did I?' Daniel said. 'I remember the summer parties on 'manor lawn. I've never been in their house.'

'You have,' his mother said. 'Lots of times, but not since you were a bairn.'

'Did I go?' Dolly said, anxious not to be left out.

'We all went to 'summer parties. The Harts used to hold one most years if 'weather was good. All 'local farmers and tenants were invited.'

'I remember them,' Maria chipped in. 'But I haven't been inside 'house. I won't know what to say to Mrs Hart and I hardly know Beatrice. If ever she calls here it's only to see Daniel.' She cast a significant glance at her brother.

'Will there be cake?' Joseph piped up. 'Cos if there is I'll go 'stead of Maria.'

'You haven't been invited,' Dolly said peevishly. 'So it's not a children's party. It must be for them who are nearly grown up. Like Daniel.'

'Aye, mebbe,' her mother said vaguely. She too had wondered why Daniel and Maria had been invited to this gathering, which surely must be more formal than those they had attended previously. When Harriet was widowed and before she and Fletcher were married, the twins' nanny, Mary, often called to see her, bringing the children, and on several occasions she and Daniel had been invited to the manor where Daniel played in the nursery with Charles and Beatrice.

'You must tek 'trap, Daniel,' she said now. 'It's too far for Maria to walk in her best dress and shoes and it'll be dark when you come home.'

'Oh, Ma! Do I have to go?' Maria said again.

'It'd be churlish not to, Maria,' her mother said, 'and it's good to mix with other young folk.'

Fletcher offered to drive them. The party was on a Sunday, and although there were the animals to attend to as usual there was little fieldwork that could not wait another day.

'Can we leave early?' Maria begged. 'Please, Da. Can we leave at seven?'

'Eight,' he conceded. 'Daniel has to be up early 'following morning anyway.'

They drove down the dale towards Broomfleet and the estuary and up the long drive of the manor, taking note of the carriages and gigs depositing the guests outside the house, after which some of the vehicles were driven round to the yard at the back whilst others set off down the drive again.

'Looks as if there are some local folks and others from out of 'district,' Fletcher commented. 'D'you see that some of 'drivers have gone round 'back to 'servants' area?'

'Mm,' Daniel murmured. 'I mebbe won't know many people then after all.'

Maria gave a small moan. 'I'll die of fright, Da. Can Daniel say I'm not well and I'll come back home with you?'

'No,' her father laughed. 'Don't worry; you're as good as anybody else if that's what's bothering you. Don't forget that I'm a farmer with my own

51

land. Just like Master Hart,' he added. 'Though not as big.'

He pulled up at the front steps and Daniel jumped down and then helped Maria. 'See you at eight o'clock then, Da,' he said. 'Come on, Maria, nobody's going to bite you. You look very nice,' he said warmly. 'You'll have all 'lads after you, but look for me if you have any bother wi' them.'

'Oh, but stay by me, Daniel,' she whispered. 'Don't leave me.'

He kept hold of her arm as they mounted the steps. The door opened and a maid bobbed her knee and asked if she could take Maria's wrap. Maria's eyebrows shot up as she recognized the girl, who was a little older than herself and had been at the local school; she didn't say hello, although Maria was sure that she knew who she was.

'That's Meg Hall,' Maria murmured to Daniel as they followed her across the floor. 'Why didn't she speak to me?'

'Cos she's working,' he said softly. 'She's probably been told not to speak to 'guests even if she knows them.'

'But why?' she asked, but Daniel was saved from answering as Charles and Beatrice came out of the drawing room to greet them.

'Oh, Daniel! And Maria, I'm so glad that you've come.' Beatrice was exuberant in her enthusiasm. 'You're the ones I know best!' She lowered her voice. 'Some of the others are sons and daughters of friends of our parents and we hardly know them at all!'

'What a relief that you're here,' Charles confided to Daniel. 'Some of the chaps from school are staying the night, and they're not getting on very well with the locals. I need you as a sort of go-between.'

'Me?' Daniel was astonished. 'But do I know them? Are they local lads?'

'Erm, well sort of, and their sisters. One's from Swanland, and there are some from South Cave and Market Weighton and North Ferriby; you know, all in farming or agriculture. I need you to help me out, Daniel.'

And all gentlemen farmers' sons, I'll bet, Daniel thought, and knew how Maria felt. He guessed, rightly, that he would know none of them.

Beatrice whisked Maria away so that she might change her shoes, chattering as she did so. 'It's all very well, Maria, but some of the girls, sorry, *young ladies,*' she said, wriggling her eyebrows, 'are expecting dancing, and we aren't doing that, only party games, which I adore, don't you? You look very pretty,' she added, barely pausing for breath. 'How fair you are. We could almost be sisters. You're so different from Daniel.'

'That's because we have different fathers,' Maria ventured. 'Daniel's father died when he was just a bair– a baby,' she corrected.

'Oh.' Beatrice looked at her. 'Did he? I can't remember if I knew that.'

'I don't know,' Maria shrugged, wondering if she was letting slip a family confidence. 'Ma's always saying that she'll tell us 'full story one day, but she never does.'

'Oh, well when she does you must tell me *immediately,* because I intend to marry Daniel one

53

day and I need to know *everything* about him.'

Maria stared at Beatrice, as did another girl who had just entered the room.

'Really, Beatrice?' the newcomer said pertly. 'Is this what the party is about? To announce an engagement? Are you not too young? You're only sixteen, after all.'

Beatrice huffed out a breath. 'Not a word to Mama or Papa,' she urged. 'I haven't told them yet and no, that's not what the party is about. My parents wanted us to have it; they said that sixteen is a milestone.'

'And – and does Daniel know?' Maria asked, and thought that it was odd that Daniel hadn't said anything about it to anyone. He wasn't usually secretive.

'Oh, heavens no!' Beatrice exclaimed. 'Of course not, and please don't say anything to him, not yet anyway. I haven't formulated a plan. Come along, let's go back to the other guests, or Mama will say I'm neglecting them.'

Charles had led Daniel into the drawing room to meet the other boys and Daniel drew in a breath. They're all togged up in waistcoats and cravats, and I don't possess such things. He'd thought when he dressed in his newly ironed shirt and best trousers and jacket that he looked smart, but he realized now that he looked like a country lad going to Sunday morning service, and knew immediately that this was how the other guests perceived him.

But he nodded at them and said 'How de do' and turned to the young ladies. Some of them were about Maria's age, but others were older,

54

and he smiled and gave a small bow of his head, as he knew Charles would have done, and was gratified when some of them smiled shyly back and then hid their faces behind their fans. One or two of the older ones looked him up and down, assessed him quickly, nodded and then turned away to continue their conversations.

'Well,' Charles commented. 'You've given them something to talk about.'

'Have I?' Daniel turned to him. 'What? I've barely opened my mouth.'

'No,' Charles said laconically. 'You don't have to, old fellow.'

Daniel laughed aloud. 'Old fellow! You're forgetting, Charles, who you're talking to. I'm not one of your school chums!'

'No,' Charles said, 'you're not. Thank heavens.'

'So why have you invited us, me and Maria I mean? We've nothing to talk about with these swells.'

'Well, don't you see? Our parents invited most of these people and we said we wanted to invite our real friends, those we're comfortable with. Some of the fellows from school are all right, I'll introduce you in a minute, and then we're going to set up some games. That's what Bea wants to do, anyway.'

'What sort o' games?' Daniel asked suspiciously.

'Charades,' Charles said, 'and Consequences. Bea's in charge of those, then someone will play the piano and we'll all sing, and then we'll have supper.'

Daniel suppressed a groan as Charles marched him across to a group of his school friends, or chums as he described them. This was much worse than he'd anticipated and he looked round for Maria, but smiled when he saw Beatrice holding her firmly by the arm as if to stop her running away.

'Daniel, I'd like you to meet Toby Hanson, and George Meldrick,' Charles said. 'Edward Pickard and Clifford Roxby. We're all in the same year. Chaps, this is my good friend Daniel Tuke.'

They all bowed stiffly and two of them, Hanson and Pickard, put out their hands to shake Daniel's. 'How do you do,' Hanson said in a drawl. 'I gather you're one of the locals?'

'I am,' Daniel replied. 'We farm up in 'next dale.'

Hanson rubbed together the fingers of his right hand as if to wipe off the imprint of Daniel's hand. 'Ah, yes, I'd put you down as a farming boy.'

'Hardly a boy,' Daniel answered drily. 'I'm seventeen and a working man. And you're still a schoolboy, I gather?'

Hanson flushed. 'I'm almost seventeen and I'll be going to university next year.'

'Where are you from?' Clifford Roxby asked him. 'Not locally bred, are you,' and Daniel heard Hanson snigger.

'I am as a matter of fact,' he said slowly, and thought that had they been anywhere else he might have been less polite than he was being now. 'But I have more exotic forebears than most.'

'A Roman plebeian, I bet!' Hanson laughed. 'And do you intend going back?'

'Yes, I do,' Daniel confirmed. 'Possibly in a year or two.' Well, he thought as he realized what he had just said, I always told Granny Rosie that I would, so why not?

'And I'm going with him,' Charles interrupted. 'I've always wanted to travel.'

Daniel grinned. They would discuss it later. He was fairly sure that Charles wouldn't be allowed on such an adventure.

'Going where?' As if on cue, Beatrice appeared behind them with Maria in tow. 'You're not going anywhere without me.'

'We'll discuss it later, Bea,' Charles told her. 'Are you going to start the charades?'

'Hold on,' George Meldrick said pleasantly. 'You haven't introduced us to your other sister.' He gave a short bow in Maria's direction. 'I'm George Meldrick, one of Charles's school friends.'

Charles and Beatrice turned to Maria. 'I'd never noticed the likeness before today,' Beatrice exclaimed, 'but as I said, you could easily be mistaken for our sister.'

'Maria is Daniel's sister,' Charles explained, turning back to his friends. 'I'd like you to meet Miss Maria Tuke.'

CHAPTER SEVEN

Someone else had remarked to Melissa Hart on Maria's likeness to Beatrice and Charles, but not to Stephen, whose hair was a mid-brown colour and who had strong facial features; at fourteen he had not wanted to be at the party either, unlike their youngest brother, George, who did, but after a brief appearance to say hello was sent up to have supper in his room. Daniel commiserated with him as he sulked and told him that Joseph had wanted to come too but hadn't been invited either.

'I don't think I know Joseph,' George said. 'Would he come over sometime, do you think?'

'He's younger than you, George,' Daniel told him. 'Leonard is nearer your age, but he's already busy on 'farm when he's not at school.'

'Everybody has a better time than me,' George grumbled as he climbed the stairs.

From the open doorway of the drawing room Melissa Hart had watched Daniel as he talked to George and then turned to look again at Maria. Although she had appeared to be shy when she first arrived, under Beatrice's wing she seemed to blossom, and although she didn't want to play charades she agreed to help the other young ladies into their various disguises – masks and fans and shawls to hide their faces – and some of the young men into top hats or bowlers and scarves and greatcoats to play the parts of villains or heroes, and clapped her hands in delight when she succeeded in concealing their identity.

It had been Anne, one of the young ladies from South Cave, who had remarked on the likeness. She was from a family Christopher had known when he was young and with whom he had recently become reacquainted. She was a child born to an older father and younger mother in a second marriage, just as the Harts' children were.

'I had thought that Beatrice was your only daughter, Mrs Hart,' she had said confidently. 'I was sure that Mama said you were lucky to have

58

three sons and a daughter, whereas they only have me and no heir.'

There will be no shortage of suitors then, Melissa considered, for she will be worth a fortune. 'I do have only one daughter, Anne,' she told her. 'Why do you think otherwise?'

'Then she must be a cousin,' the young woman went on artlessly, 'for she is so like Charles! Maria, is it? She's been by Beatrice's side constantly.'

'A neighbour's daughter,' Melissa said. 'No relation whatsoever. Will you excuse me?'

She had seen that Stephen had sought Maria out and was taking her to the anteroom where the supper table had been laid, and she was filled with a sudden misgiving. The evening had been deliberately informal so that the young people could come and go as they pleased, to the supper room, or to sing by the piano or play chess or cards in the library, but now she decided to make the short announcement as planned. The party was to be the forerunner of similar events over the next few years, for although Melissa believed in love in marriage above all else, she also believed that young people should have the chance to mingle before deciding on their future life partner and to this end she had chosen the guests carefully.

She signalled to Christopher, who had kept very much in the background, disappearing into his study from time to time, and he came across to her. She picked up a silver teaspoon and tapped it gently on a crystal celery vase to bring everyone back into the drawing room.

'I wanted to say how very pleased we are to see you all, and trust you are enjoying yourselves.

59

Beatrice and Charles are today celebrating their sixteenth birthday, a time that bridges the line between childhood and adulthood, and we hope that today you will have made lasting friendships.

'We also wanted to tell you that in January, Beatrice will be going away to school in Harrogate, which will prepare her for finishing school in Switzerland.'

Delighted applause broke out from some of the young ladies, and then Christopher spoke up.

'Charles will continue at school in York,' he said, 'and then go on to university, after which I sincerely hope he will join me in running the Hart Holme estate. With three sons,' he joked, 'I will soon be able to retire.'

Daniel glanced at Charles from across the room. Charles caught his eye and gave him a negative look, and Daniel realized that Charles's father had no idea that his son wanted to travel first. As for Beatrice, he thought that a few feathers might fly in Switzerland if any attempts were made to turn her into a lady. He saw her looking his way and couldn't read anything into her expression, but he grinned at her and put his thumb up.

She came over to him when the speeches were finished. 'What was that supposed to mean?' She put up her own thumb. 'Will you be pleased to see me go away?'

'No!' he protested. 'Of course not, but I suppose it's what you want.'

'I told them I was bored,' she said petulantly. 'I'd grumbled about still having a governess and so Mama said I ought to see some of the world and she sent off to Switzerland for a prospectus.

But where are you going, Daniel? I heard Charles say he was going somewhere with you.'

'Oh, it was nothing,' he said. 'One of Charles's pals was being stupid and asked if I was going back to Rome; he called me a *plebeian*. I think he thought I didn't know what it meant, so I told him that yes, I was going there.'

'To Rome?' she said breathlessly. 'Oh, Daniel!'

He shrugged. 'I only said it to shut him up, but then I thought that perhaps I might. Not to Rome especially, but somewhere,' he added. 'When I've given it some thought.'

'But that will ruin my plan,' she said.

Daniel raised his eyebrows. 'Surely whatever you're planning, Beatrice, it won't mek any difference where I am?'

Her cheeks turned pink. 'It might, and you know that Papa won't let Charles go with you.'

'I never supposed that he would,' he said drily. 'It was Charles who said he was coming with me, and I only mentioned it to score over that toffee-nosed idiot Hanson. It wasn't something I'd really thought about.' Although, he realized, I suppose the idea was planted in my mind a long time ago.

'So you might not?' Beatrice persisted. 'You might still be here when I come home again?'

Daniel gazed at her curiously. She seemed to be held in suspense, not full of bounce and vigour as she usually was but waiting expectantly for his answer.

'Will it matter if I am or not?' he hedged, and wondered why it should. Their lives were not intertwined; whatever one of them did would not make any difference to the other. They had been childhood friends but they were from different worlds; that much was becoming more apparent as they grew older. Sooner or later their paths would separate, and thinking of that made him feel quite melancholy.

'It will matter to me,' she said quietly. 'But seemingly not to you.'

It was as if she had suddenly become older than her years and he wondered why. He thought that he liked the old capricious Beatrice, the girl who was full of energy and wild foolish ideas, better than the solemn one in front of him now. Was this what happened with young girls? Would Maria and Dolly and Elizabeth change when they reached sixteen? Was this womanhood? Perhaps he should ask his mother, for surely she would know.

'I don't understand what you mean, Beatrice,' he said, and she turned her back on him and walked away.

Christopher Hart broke off from speaking to the young men from Charles's school and sought out his wife, who was watching the proceedings rather pensively, he thought.

'Melissa,' he said, 'everything seems to be going splendidly. I think you and I could slip away to my study and enjoy a quiet brandy.'

'I think you have had one or two already,' she remarked, and glanced around at the young people, who seemed to have formed themselves into groups of compatibility. The schoolboys were hovering on the edge of the young ladies' circle, except for one who was in conversation with Daniel Tuke.

Christopher had questioned Charles's insistence that Daniel should be invited, pointing out that although he was an old friend he might feel out of his depth; but Beatrice had also wanted him to come and had suggested that they ask his sister so that together they'd be more comfortable. But I was wrong, he thought. He's perfectly at ease.

Melissa was looking about her to make sure that no one was alone or not mixing with the others, and she noticed that Maria Tuke and Stephen had disappeared once more into the supper room. She bit on her lower lip. I'm being foolish, she thought. They are still children, and Stephen will be going back to school in January. But still, there was an anxiety in her mind that she couldn't dispel.

Christopher poured her a brandy, adding a little soda water as she requested, and sat down in his favourite leather chair opposite her. He sighed.

'I suppose this was a good idea? Mixing and getting to know the sons and daughters of families in our circle?'

'I think so,' she said. 'It was how you met Jane, wasn't it?'

'Mm, yes, a similar way, that's true,' he mused, swirling his brandy in the glass. 'Except that my parents had already earmarked several possibilities.'

He smiled, and Melissa thought that he was still very handsome, although he'd been looking rather tired lately. She thought, rather sadly, that there was little possibility of her having any more children, and she would dearly have liked another daughter. But I've given him three sons, she told herself, and he's pleased about that.

He lifted his head and continued, laughing, 'My father looked at their income and my mother at the suitability of the daughters.'

'Well, it does work quite well, I suppose,' Melissa agreed, and although I didn't realize it at the time, I dare say my parents arranged that I should meet Albert, even though we were very young.' As Beatrice and Charles are now, she reflected. But Albert died of influenza before they could marry, and it was a chance meeting with Christopher several years later, after he was widowed, that drew them together, for love rather than convenience.

Her thoughts ran back to their guests, to the young men and women who might be attracted to someone here tonight and so begin the precarious process of courtship. Enquiries would be made; families and fortunes would be looked into to assess their quality and durability. Again her thoughts ran back to Stephen and Maria. She must, for her own peace of mind, put a stop to any developing friendship.

Casually, she remarked, 'Daniel Tuke and his sister Maria are mingling very well. It seems your fears that they would be ill at ease were unfounded.' She took a sip of brandy. 'Tell me again, darling, because I forget the detail, how did you come to meet their grandmother, Ellen Tuke?'

CHAPTER EIGHT

Maria couldn't wait to tell her mother about the party. She'd given her father a potted version of it as they drove home, but he seemed to be rather sleepy. He was usually in bed by this time, and she didn't think he was listening.

Harriet had waited up for them although she was ready for bed and in her nightgown, with a warm shawl round her shoulders and her hair hanging down her back.

'Oh, Ma,' Maria burst out as soon as they went into the kitchen, where her mother was making hot drinks for them. 'I'm so pleased that I was persuaded to go. It's been lovely. I'd such a good time. We had lots to eat, didn't we, Daniel, and I tried some fruit punch, and although I didn't play any games I helped with 'dressing up.'

'And spent time with Stephen Hart,' Daniel grinned. 'Don't forget that, will you?' He shook a finger at Maria, and turning to his mother joked, 'You'll have to watch her, Ma or she'll be 'lady of the manor afore you know it!'

Harriet turned sharply. 'What! What do you mean?'

Maria blushed. 'He's being silly.' She gave a little shrug. 'Stephen hadn't wanted to be at 'party either, or play games, and so we talked about what we did like to do. He wants to farm. He doesn't want to go to university after he's finished school but his father expects him to.'

Harriet exchanged glances with Fletcher, then, looking at her daughter's glowing cheeks and sparkling eyes, said softly, 'Don't get any ideas above your station, Maria. His parents will have mapped out his future and it won't include you.'

Daniel protested. 'That's a bit unfair, isn't it? If Stephen–'

Fletcher cut in. 'It might be unfair, but that's 'way it is. We're all equal, but there're some who are more equal than others. I'll tek my drink upstairs, Harriet.'

Harriet handed him his mug of cocoa. 'I'm coming up too. Turn 'lamp down whoever's last to bed.'

Daniel finished his drink. 'I'm going up, Maria. Are you staying?'

'Yes,' she said. 'I'm going to sit by 'fire for a bit. I'll see to 'lamp.'

She sat by the banked-down fire and cradled her cup between her hands. Of course Daniel was only joking, but why had her mother been so swift and negative, and then her father, rebutting any suggestion of friendship between her and Stephen? They had only had a friendly talk, which she had found quite easy, and she hadn't been shy with him, which she often was with people she didn't know very well. But he was down to earth, she thought; quite ordinary, and unlike Charles who, although he treated her kindly, always seemed superior.

She gave a little smile as she thought of the moment when her father had arrived to fetch them home and Daniel had come to find her.

66

Stephen had put out his hand to say goodbye, and as she bobbed her knee he had taken hers, and given it a little squeeze. 'It's been very nice to see you again, Maria,' he had said. 'I hadn't realized that it had been so long since we last met. Perhaps I could call at your farm next time I'm home from school and we can talk again? Would your parents mind, do you think?'

She'd said that they wouldn't, and then thought that maybe he wanted to talk to her father about farming and wasn't coming to see her at all. But he had kept hold of her hand and only dropped it when he saw that Daniel was watching.

Daniel was climbing into bed in the room that he shared with Leonard, who was asleep and gently snoring, when he heard his parents talking next door.

'You'll have to speak to her,' his mother was saying. 'Ask her. If it can happen once it can happen again.'

'Nowt can come of it.' Fletcher's reply was muffled. 'Lad's away at school for most of 'year. Besides, I don't believe her. We know that she can lie.'

Daniel drew in a breath. Surely they weren't speaking of Maria, who was as honest as the day was long? But then he knew they weren't when his mother answered irritably, 'You must tell her we need *truth,* that our children's lives depend on it. They have three sons and we have three daughters.'

He lay on his bed thinking. They're talking of the Harts, but who else? And why have they mentioned the Harts' sons and not Beatrice? And

67

why not my brothers and me? He turned over and thumped his pillow to cradle his head. Another mystery to solve.

A few days later Charles rode alone to Dale Top Farm to talk to Daniel but he had forgotten that his friend would be busy; Harriet told him he was repairing fences somewhere nearby. 'You can go and talk to him, but don't hold him up. Remember that he's a working lad and he has to earn his keep.'

'Oh, sorry, Mrs Tuke.' He looked repentant. 'I should know, shouldn't I? Daniel is always reminding me that he's a man and I'm still a schoolboy!'

Harriet laughed. She'd always liked Charles; she enjoyed his ironic humour and although he was obviously a young gentleman, he wasn't overbearing or pompous and she could see why he and Daniel got on so well.

Maria came into the kitchen whilst they were talking and blushed when she saw Charles, who gave her a polite nod. 'Hello, Maria,' he said. 'I told Stephen I was coming over to see Daniel and he sent his regards to you. I think he would have liked to come too but he'd arranged to go out with the bailiff to visit the farms.'

Maria blushed even more, and Charles, seeing her discomfiture, said awkwardly, 'Well, I'll go and have a word with Daniel if I may.'

'Come back and have a bite to eat if you're still here in half an hour or so,' Harriet told him. 'That's when 'men come in.'

'Oh, thank you, I will. I'll make sure I'm still

68

here! Do you want me to round everybody up?'

'No.' Harriet smiled. 'They'll know; they won't need reminding.'

Charles could see Daniel and Tom Bolton in one of the fields. Daniel was wielding a hammer whilst Tom held the fence steady.

Daniel looked up as Charles approached. 'Well, it's all right for some folks wi' nowt to do but disturb them that's working.'

Charles grinned. 'Sorry,' he said. 'I'd forgotten what day it was. The last of the visitors have gone today; they seem to have been here for ever. Not that I'm grumbling; they're good company.' He saw Daniel's wry expression. 'Well, some of them!'

'I heard your party had gone well, Master Charles,' Tom said.

'Yes,' Daniel grinned. 'I gave a good report on you youngsters.'

Charles sighed. 'We were all very well behaved, Tom, especially in front of old gentlemen like Daniel, otherwise we might not have been.'

'You clear up here, Daniel.' Tom collected his tools. 'I'm going down to 'bottom field to fix 'gate. I'll see you up at 'house in half an hour.'

Charles gazed after him. 'Your mother said that no one would need reminding when it was time to eat.'

'That's because we start work so early,' Daniel remarked. 'It's onny just getting light when we come outside. So what brings you here?'

Charles hesitated, then said, 'Do you recall the conversation we had at the party about going to Rome? Were you serious? Bea said that you were not. That you'd only said it because of Hanson.'

69

'I did.' Daniel buttoned up his jacket. 'But I've been thinking about it since and I would like to go. I promised Granny Rosie when I was young, although I don't suppose she'd hold me to it.'

'Promised her what?' Charles bent down and picked up a bag of nails.

'To go and look for my grandfather. It's complicated. She said he was a seaman, from abroad, but she doesn't know where. Somewhere hot, at any rate.'

'But if she doesn't know where, how will you ever find him? The world is huge!'

'Don't know,' Daniel said. 'But if I needed an excuse to travel, then I have one, and,' he wrinkled his nose, 'I'd like to know more about my birth father's family. He wasn't really a Tuke – my ma said that Granny Ellen brought Noah up because Granny Rosie wasn't able to. I think,' he said confidingly, 'that she probably wasn't married to my grandfather.'

'Ah!' Charles said meaningfully. 'So what you're saying is that your birth father was born out of wedlock to an unknown foreigner?' They set off up the field towards the house, and he murmured, 'How very interesting. So you think that you might travel to look for him?' He glanced at Daniel, who appeared to be pondering on the subject, and added, 'And if you decide that you will, do you think you could wait until I've left school, because I really would like to come with you.'

Daniel blew a silent whistle. 'Would your parents allow it? To travel with me?'

His face broke into a grin and Charles felt a fleeting surge of envy. He was so handsome,

70

dammit, even he could see it and he was sure that Beatrice did; she was always dreamy after being with him. 'Why not with you?' he asked.

'Well, I'd have thought that they'd rather you went with some of your *chums* from school,' Daniel answered. 'Not a farmer's labourer like me.'

'I thought you were a farmer's son, just like me,' Charles said laconically. 'Is there a difference?'

'You know very well there is. Your father isn't a farmer, he's a landowner. Come on,' Daniel urged. 'Let's get a move on, or there'll be no grub left – sorry, *old fellow*, I mean luncheon.'

'Wouldn't it be marvellous if we could go together?' Charles continued. 'We'd have such a great time, no parents to say what we should be doing or what path we should be taking.'

Daniel frowned. 'Mine don't,' he said. 'Although I suppose they took it for granted I'd join Da and Tom at the farm, as I did too. But don't mention it yet. I need to think it through and talk to Granny Rosie.'

Charles was curious about Daniel's natural father, probably more than Daniel was. 'Are you like your father – in looks, I mean?'

They opened the gate into the yard and secured it behind them. Daniel leaned on it and looked back over the meadow. There was still a rime of frost shimmering on the surface, which probably wouldn't clear all day. 'I don't know,' he answered. 'I was only a week or so old when he drowned in 'estuary. I suppose I look like him; I don't look like 'rest of 'family, do I? You've onny to look at my sisters and Joseph to know they belong to Fletcher. Lenny looks like Ma, though,'

71

he added. 'Although she says he's the spit of one of her brothers.'

'I didn't know you had any uncles,' Charles remarked. 'Do you ever see them?'

Daniel shook his head and turned towards the house. 'I think they were lost at sea when she was young.' An idea struck him. 'I'd never thought o' that. Mebbe that's why I've got this feeling about going to sea, cos of Ma's family and nothing to do wi' my grandfather at all.'

'How lucky you are to have such a diverse family,' Charles said. 'Mine is quite ordinary in comparison.'

CHAPTER NINE

Fletcher took the horse and trap down Elloughton Dale early one Sunday morning, heading towards Brough. He hadn't asked any of the children if they'd like to come with him. If they had asked him if they could, he would have made the excuse that he was only going to check that his mother had plenty of provisions as more snow was threatened; but they didn't ask, as they were all busy with things to do of their own.

They were all growing up so fast, he thought; the older ones, if they wanted to, could visit either of their grandmothers on their own without having to be taken. They saw Rosie regularly, except in winter when she only walked up the dale to see them if the days were fine and dry. 'I'm not walking up that track in 'teeth of a gale,' she asserted. 'I'll see you all in 'spring.' But someone, Harriet or Daniel, Maria or Dolly, always called at least twice a week.

But they don't visit my mother, he brooded. She doesn't make them welcome and they have to search for something to talk about. But he had something to talk about, or at least ask about, which was the real purpose of his visit today.

The wind was whistling across Brough Haven, whipping the waters up to a froth as he turned down the lane that led to the waterfront and the cottage where his mother now lived. She hadn't wanted to leave Marsh Farm; when Fletcher returned from America on hearing of the double loss of his father and Noah, she wanted her and Fletcher to run it together. 'I can stop here as long as I want,' she'd said. 'Master Christopher allus said so.'

She had such plans for him, she'd told him, and he remembered his shock and the gleam in her eyes as she'd whispered the devious schemes she had nurtured for years; but those plans didn't include Harriet, whom he loved, or Daniel either, and since that time, after his rejection of her propositions, even after so many long years, Ellen had never again spoken to or even asked about Harriet.

The water was surging against the path outside the cottage as he approached. The property belonged to the Hart estate and was once the home of Mrs Marshall, a former cook, after her retirement from the manor. It was to Mrs Marshall that Ellen had gone scurrying in pique and defiance when Christopher Hart had told her that he had changed his plans and she could no longer stay at Marsh Farm, that he had another purpose for the land. She had never left, even after Mrs Marshall's death, and Christopher Hart, feeling guilty for turning her out of the farm, charged her only a peppercorn rent.

She'd have been better accepting the cottage in Brough that Hart had first offered her, Fletcher considered as he climbed down from the cart and made the horse fast. She'd have been more comfortable, and safe from the estuary waters if they should flood over the path and into the cottage. But some devilment within her had made her defy them all and choose to live a lonely life by the Haven; it's so that we'll worry about her, Fletcher concluded as he tapped on the locked door. It was a challenge, he'd decided long ago, but a challenge that no one had taken up.

He was kept waiting as always; it was as if she wanted whoever was disturbing her to go away. But she would know his familiar knock; it was just another idiosyncrasy that she deployed, another eccentricity to show that she didn't care a jot about anyone.

After waiting a few more minutes, he walked round to the back of the cottage and found his mother standing by the open back door with an axe in her hand. 'In God's name, what 'you doing!' But he knew what she was up to. She had heard him at the front door and intended giving him a fright.

'Chopping wood, what does it look like? I need to keep a good fire. It's cold by these waters.'

He looked towards the log pile that he had chopped the last time he was here. There was plenty of wood, enough for two weeks at least, and Christopher Hart often sent a sack of coal.

'You don't need to do this, Ma. You've plenty of fuel. Put the axe down and I'll split some more before I leave.'

She grunted but leaned the axe against the wall. 'Talking of leaving as soon as you get here,' she grumbled.

He didn't retaliate. He needed her in a reasonable humour. If they ever argued he always left feeling disgruntled and frustrated. He followed her into the small porch and then into her only room, where a pan of stew was bubbling over a bright fire. At least she cooked, he thought. She wouldn't starve. He unfastened his coat and unwrapped his scarf.

She sat down in the chair that had been his father's when they'd lived at Marsh Farm. Her bony hands rested on the worn upholstered arms as she gazed at him. He had often noticed that she seemed to take a perverse pleasure in sitting in that chair, as if by doing so she was claiming victory over Nathaniel, her long dead, much maligned husband.

'Are you all right?' he asked, sitting opposite her.

'Have to be, haven't I? There's nobody to care if I'm not.' Her voice was forthright, her straight back uncompromising. 'And to what do I owe 'pleasure o' this visit?' There was no delight or joy at seeing him and he knew that she was hoping for some indiscretion or misunderstanding that she could pounce upon.

75

'Do I have to have a reason to come? Am I not welcome?'

She blinked. 'In my experience folk who call generally have a purpose in mind. They don't come to talk about 'weather.'

I won't argue with her, he decided. It'll spoil my day. 'Well, I didn't think that I counted as *folk,*'he said genially. 'Who else has been who wanted summat?'

She gave him a sharp look. 'So you do want summat?'

He shook his head and sighed. 'It was a figure o' speech, Ma. A joke.'

She turned her face away. 'I don't understand jokes,' she muttered. 'Never did. Life isn't funny.'

'You spend too much time on your own,' he told her. 'Why don't I look for a cottage in Brough or Elloughton for you? You'd see more people, have–'

'I don't want to see more folk,' she snapped. 'Nosy busybodies most o' them. I'm all right here. I'll decide when I want to be somewhere else.'

'I've brought you some eggs and a bacon shank, and bread,' he ventured. 'I think we're in for some snow.'

'Who baked 'bread?' she demanded.

'Maria,' he lied, knowing that she'd throw it out for the ducks and geese on the Haven waters if he'd said that Harriet had baked it, which she had.

She nodded. 'It'll save me baking,' she said grudgingly. 'And my hens have gone off lay so I'll use 'eggs. Now tell me why you've really come.' The question was sudden and he was taken aback.

'Next time I'm coming I'll send you a postcard with a list o' reasons on it,' he said tersely. 'Then

76

you can be prepared.'

She didn't answer and Fletcher drew in a breath. 'If you don't want me to come, I won't,' he said abruptly; the only time his temper rose was when he was with his mother and it was rising now. 'So if this is to be 'last time, then yes, there are some things I want to ask you.'

He saw by her expression that she knew she had gone too far in her cat and mouse game; if he didn't come to see her there would be no one she could use for her whipping boy, no one else who would tolerate her moods, her bitterness and resentment that life had treated her unfairly, for the fact was that no one else did come, not even his children, although they would have done if they'd thought she was glad to see them.

She waited for him to continue and he in turn waited to order his thoughts, to decide on the best approach, knowing already that there wasn't a best way or a right way; she was going to be angry however he said it.

'My children,' he began. *My* children, not *our* children; she wouldn't tolerate even a vague reference to the mother of his children. 'My children are growing up, and as you might know they have been friends of Christopher Hart's children since they were very young.'

He had her attention now: her eyes narrowed, and her forehead creased into a frown. 'You mean Noah's son, not your bairns,' she corrected. 'She used to tek him to 'manor.'

'No,' he said softly, 'all of them. Mostly Daniel, I agree; he's a similar age to 'twins. But lately Maria too; she went with him to 'twins' sixteenth birthday party up at 'manor.'

'And?' she said. 'What's that to do wi' owt?'

He held her gaze. 'It's to do with what you once said. About me. About my parentage. I want to know if what you said back then is really true.' Or if you were speaking out of spite, he thought. As we know that you can and do.

Her mouth twisted and she grunted. 'Why would I lie?' she muttered. 'What would be 'advantage o' that?'

'But can you be sure?' he hedged. 'My father, Nathaniel – surely he would have guessed?'

'Of course I'm sure!' Her voice was strident, outraged, censuring him for such an unseemly suggestion. 'Huh! Mr Tuke believed me all right. He was that proud that he'd sired a son.' She paused, and then smirked. 'At least he was at first. He might have had doubts as you got older cos you looked nowt like him. But it was too late by then.'

Fletcher closed his eyes, defeated. What was to be done? He opened them to find her staring at him.

'You've spoiled your chances, o' course,' she muttered.

'What?' Baffled, Fletcher stared back at her.

'Spoiled your chances. You should have gone to him – Christopher – like I said all them years ago.' Ellen nibbled her nails. 'You should have told him afore his wife gave birth to them twin babbies, you'd have been 'eldest son then, seeing as his first wife onny gave him a daughter. It might still work,' she rumbled on. 'You'd still be heir to 'estate even if from 'wrong side o' blanket, but she might mek trouble; his second wife, I

78

mean. She'll want it for her sons.'

'Mother!' he shouted, and stood up. 'Don't you understand? I'm not talking about *me*. I'm talking about my *children* and what it means to them!'

She looked up at him. 'They'll be way down in 'pecking order,' she sneered. 'Especially with a mother like they've got and wi' knowledge that she was once married to Noah.'

He lifted his hands in exasperation. 'Are you being obtuse or do you really not understand what I'm saying? I'm telling you, Ma, that *my* children are friends of Christopher Hart's children. What if they should form an attachment?'

He thought of Maria's animated conversation when he had collected her and Daniel from the party. He'd pretended he wasn't listening as she described the talks she had had with Stephen, but he was, and he'd grown afraid. Nothing would come of it, he had persuaded himself. They are way out of our class, but then so had his mother been, and Christopher Hart had gone dallying where he should not.

'They'd not,' she said. But her voice trembled.

'They have three sons,' he exploded, his voice breaking. 'And I have three daughters! And are you telling me, once and for all, that their father Christopher Hart is also my father? Is it true or not?'

She looked at him for only a moment before turning her head away so that he could only see her profile, which told him nothing. She lifted her chin, in pride or defiance he couldn't tell, but there was no shame, no regret for what had gone before or the future consequences of her actions.

'It's true.' She turned back to face him. 'I knew he couldn't marry me, but I didn't care about that. Men like him don't marry for love, but they can marry to please their family and take a mistress elsewhere, and that's what I wanted and expected.'

Fletcher saw his mother's face slump and crease and she suddenly looked very old. 'I loved him,' she whispered. 'And I thought he loved me and mebbe he did, but he's such a principled man.' Her voice grew bitter. 'And his principles meant more to him than I did and so he didn't betray his wife. Men!' she scoffed. 'You're all 'same in 'long run. You tek what you want and then leave. Even you,' she added scathingly. 'You said you wanted 'truth but what you really wanted me to say was that I lied 'first time I told you. But I didn't lie. You are Christopher Hart's son and every time I see you I'm reminded of him and it's like a knife driven through my heart.'

CHAPTER TEN

Fletcher said nothing to Harriet about his mother until they'd gone upstairs that evening and then he sat on the edge of the bed with his chin in his hands. Harriet was propped up on her pillow waiting for him to speak.

'She's confirmed that it's true,' he muttered. 'She thought that Hart would keep her as his mistress after he married. I can't–' he stopped. 'I can't ... think of her in that way. She's my mother,

80

for God's sake!' he said bitterly. 'I can't think of her being – being–' He broke off.

'You can't think of her being young or willing to consider being a gentleman's sweetheart when he was married to someone else?' Harriet murmured.

A doxy we'd have called her in 'streets of Hull, she thought. A drab, a young man's bit on the side. But I know how devious she can be, I've had a taste of it, and I wonder if Christopher Hart saw through her too, perhaps even realized that she would want more of his time, more commitment than he could ever give. And did he ever guess or did she tell him that her child was his?

'No,' Fletcher said at last. 'I can't. And yet for all those years he gave her 'tenancy of Marsh Farm.'

'To keep her quiet,' Harriet said, and saw Fletcher's pained expression. 'I'm sorry, Fletcher, but that would be 'way it was.'

He gave a wry sigh and climbed into bed. 'You women.' He kissed her cheek. 'How is it that you know everything there is to know about men?'

They lay sleepless for an hour, murmuring about what to do, and finally decided that there wasn't any real threat. Maria wasn't likely to see much of Stephen after he went back to school, and, Harriet thought, Melissa Hart has her suspicions. I don't know how or why she does, maybe she's questioned her husband about his life as a young man and Ellen Tuke's name cropped up more than once, or more often than a servant girl's should, but she knows something, I'm convinced of it; and that's why I went to see her all those years ago before Fletcher and I got married. I have no doubt that she'll keep her sons away from our daughters.

81

'Tom,' Daniel said, 'seeing as we've got a quiet spell, can we go out in your boat one day?'

'Fishing?' Tom asked. 'It'll be a bit choppy to go out of 'estuary.'

'I didn't specially mean fishing, but I suppose if we caught some supper it'd be a bonus. No, I meant to find out if I could spend time in a boat without being sick again!'

Tom had taken him out on other occasions and Daniel had thrown up over the side of the boat as soon as they'd hit rough water.

'Mine's onny a small boat,' Tom said. 'That's why you're sick. In a bigger boat or a ship you might not be. Are you still considering being a sailor?'

'Well, mebbe not, but I'd quite like to travel – onny don't tell my ma yet – and wherever I go, if I want to travel abroad I'll have to go across water at some time.'

'Unless you climb aboard a herring gull's back,' Tom laughed. 'Aye, all right. But have you thought that if you do go away we'll be a man short on 'farm?'

Daniel nodded. 'I've thought of that but it won't be yet, not for a couple of years, and by then Joseph will be able to do a few jobs to help Lenny, won't he?'

'Aye,' Tom said thoughtfully, 'so if you're not careful, Dan, you'll be mekking yourself redundant!'

'I've thought of that too, and I've wondered if 'farm is going to keep all of us.'

'Ah, I get it, so you'll go off and mek your

fortune and come home and keep us all in luxury?'

'That's it,' Daniel agreed. 'So you don't need to worry about your old age, Tom. I'll tek care of you.'

'Will you find me a nice little wife as well?' Tom asked. 'One who can cook and keep house just like your ma?'

'That'd be impossible,' Daniel said. 'She's one in a million. There's nobody in 'world like my ma.'

In January at Hart Holme, Charles and Beatrice were preparing to go away. Charles was looking forward to being back at school; he enjoyed the company of his schoolfellows and was doing well with his studies, but when he thought of his future here on the estate and eventually taking over from his father he had a few misgivings as to whether he would settle down in the country. He thought often of the conversation that he and Daniel had had about travelling abroad together and considered that they'd be ideal companions. Daniel was practical and easy-going, optimistic and always ready with a quip to lighten a conversation, whereas he regarded himself as more serious, with an interest in people, history and art. Above all, he spoke French and had the option next year of taking another language. As yet, however, he had said nothing to his parents of any of this.

Beatrice knocked on his bedroom door and he called for her to come in. They both had a special knock to indicate who they were, but they never ever barged in; they'd respected each other's privacy since childhood.

Beatrice stretched out on his bed and unfastened her long fair hair from its plait, arranging it across the counterpane. 'I've been sorting out what to take with me,' she said. 'I hope I'm doing the right thing. Will I like school, do you think, Charles?'

'I think you will.' He turned from where he was kneeling looking through his school books. 'You won't be bored, at any rate, as you are now with just you and Miss *whatsername*.'

Beatrice went through governesses rapidly. None of them could understand her whims, or her desire to be somewhere other than sitting at a desk when the weather was pleasant.

'Can't be worse, can it?' she murmured. 'And I'll have other girls to talk to and it's only until the summer, and then I'll be off to Switzerland to be *finished off*.' She laughed at the thought of it. 'It's a pity I can't go straight there, but the Academy insisted I had experience of general schooling rather than just a governess. I wish I'd thought of it before.' She sighed.

'I suppose they want to be sure you can mingle with other young ladies,' Charles said vaguely, packing his books into a trunk. 'Being only with a governess all these years you could be a timid little thing or an unsociable outcast.'

'Which I am.' She sighed again, and turned sideways so that her head hung over the side of the bed and her hair fanned out like a waterfall to the floor.

'As it is,' he said, glancing at her, 'they're going to wonder who on earth has arrived and turned them upside down.'

'Do you think I'll ever be considered beautiful?'

84

she asked, her face turning pink as the blood rushed to her head.

'How would I know?' he retorted. 'I'm your brother. You'll have to ask somebody else. Ask Daniel the next time you see him. He'd tell you.'

Beatrice hauled herself up again. 'He wouldn't know!' she said scornfully. 'He wouldn't notice. No, really, if you were looking at me as if you'd just met me and I were not your sister, what would you think? I mean, would you think, erm, for instance, she'd be quite lovely if her nose were longer or ... shorter or, erm, if her eyes were larger or she were a little fatter – you know, that sort of thing.'

Charles rocked back on his heels. 'Well, for one thing, I wouldn't be attracted to you because you and I look quite alike, and I'd probably choose someone dark-haired and exotic, whereas you are the typical English woman with your fair skin that burns in the sun, just as mine does.'

He eyed her as she pouted crossly. 'But I suppose you're all right. Your hair's nice, blonde and shiny. I don't know! How am I supposed to know? I don't know any other girls.' He paused thoughtfully. 'I suppose that's why we were encouraged to have the party. Maybe our parents were sizing up the contestants for our eventual nuptials.'

Beatrice shot off the bed and crouched beside him. 'You're not serious?' And as he nodded, she teased, 'So that's you married off to Anne Mason and I to the – what did Daniel call him? The toffee-nosed idiot Hanson.' She folded her arms in front of her. 'I think *not!*'

'I'd gamble that it's the start,' Charles maintained. 'We'll be encouraged to go to parties and

85

balls and suppers to meet the right people.' He closed the trunk. 'Do you think that Father and Mama had to do this? Do you think that when Father was young he was invited to meet young ladies to discover if he got along with them and if they were suitable for marriage? I can't imagine it, can you?'

Beatrice considered. 'Yes, I can. I can imagine Papa being quite a catch. I think that all the eligible young women in Yorkshire, and,' she added darkly, 'even those who were not, would have fallen in love with him; and he's still quite handsome. You'll look like him, Charles, when you're old.'

He wasn't sure if he was being flattered, but he commented, 'Well, nevertheless, when I've finished school I'm not going straight to university as Father wants me to; I'm going on a tour of Europe with Daniel. He wants to find out about his background and I want to see life as it really is. We won't take a Grand Tour with Mr Thomas Cook, we'll make our own way; we'll cross France and Switzerland and travel into Italy, where, I suspect, Daniel's forebears are from. I shall plan a full itinerary nearer the time.'

Beatrice had been listening silently until then, but now she said, 'Italy? You think that's where his family is from? Because he's so dark-haired, you mean?'

'And his eyes,' Charles emphasized. 'Have you never noticed them? So dark, almost Arabian.'

'Yes,' she said softly. 'Of course I've noticed them. Will I still be in Switzerland when you come through, I wonder?' Her eyes gazed dreamily into the distance as if she were looking into the future. 'I think ... no, I'm sure, that I most certainly will be.'

CHAPTER ELEVEN

Daniel always eagerly awaited the return of Charles during school holidays, but one Easter, instead of coming home, Charles sent a postcard from the Lake District to tell him that the whole family was staying in a lodge near Lake Windermere and would be walking the fells and sailing, but he looked forward to seeing Daniel again in the summer.

'Lucky beggar,' Daniel said, after reading the card to his mother and sisters. 'Look at those mountains.' He showed them the sepia photograph. 'How high they are! Have you ever seen such high mountains, Ma?'

'Me!' Harriet laughed. 'No. Nor likely to. Top of this dale is as high as I'll ever get.' She looked closely at the picture. 'You'd have to have strong legs to get up those hills.'

'Maybe they'll ride mountain ponies.' Maria looked over Daniel's shoulder. 'Did you say that 'whole family have gone?'

Daniel glanced at her. 'Yes, all of them.' He gave her a smile; he knew who she was really asking about.

Maria nodded, and then Dolly said, 'They must be really, really rich for all of them to go off on holiday, especially to somewhere so far away.'

Harriet cast her eyes over her daughters. Seeing Maria's downcast face and Dolly's envious one, she hoped that neither of them would develop expectations beyond those that could be realized.

'Let me tell you what being rich means,' she said, drawing Maria close and reaching for Dolly's hand. 'Being rich is having someone to care for you; being rich means not having to worry about paying 'rent or wonder where 'next meal is coming from. We are lucky. We have our own land, our own house; we owe nothing to anybody. We are rich. It's hard work for your father and Tom, and Daniel and Lenny too – for all of us,' she added, smiling at Elizabeth and Joseph. 'We all have to pull our weight, but we're doing it for *us,* so that we can have a comfortable living. And most of all we're lucky to have each other.'

'Do you think, then, Ma,' Dolly said, 'that if we work really hard, one day we might have a big house like the Harts and be able to go away on holidays?'

Harriet gave a small sigh. 'Is that what you want, Dolly? To have servants to look after you, to only mix with people who have 'same kind of house as you do?'

'I'd still keep my friends,' she said. 'I'd invite them to come to my parties.'

'I don't think they'd come,' Harriet said softly. 'I think they might be envious of you.'

'I'm not envious of Charles or Beatrice,' Daniel said. 'Charles is still my best friend, and so is Beatrice.' As he spoke her name he realized that he had missed her chatter and exuberance since she went away to Harrogate.

'There's always an exception, Daniel,' his mother pointed out, 'and you and Charles are lucky to enjoy and keep your friendship, even though your lives are so different.'

'But what about you and Mrs Hart?' Maria asked. 'You're friends, aren't you?'

Harriet paused before answering. It was true she and Melissa Hart had a special relationship, but friends? No, she thought, we just have some things in common. 'We are friendly,' she agreed in compromise. 'And I know we could share a confidence. But no, we aren't friends in 'proper meaning of the word.'

'Well, I think it's silly,' Dolly pouted. 'We're all 'same, aren't we? Does it matter who's got 'most money?'

'No,' her mother said. 'It doesn't, except to the person who hasn't got any. And it's not just about money, Dolly. It's a different kind of life, and you're either born into it or you're not.'

Dale Top Farm continued to make a reasonable living for them all. The winters had been bitterly cold and ice was seen in the river near Goole, but the spring Maria turned fifteen Harriet suggested that she should try for service in one of the larger houses in Brough. She was a hard-working girl with many skills in the home, and she helped Harriet with the milking and the egg production, but her mother thought that her personality might flourish if she was in the company of more people. Maria didn't want to go and cried at her mother's proposal, but she saw the sense of it.

'I can come home if I'm unhappy, can't I?' she asked, drying her eyes.

'Of course you can, but try it for six months,' Harriet implored. 'You need to know what it's like to be out in 'world, instead of up here with no one to talk to but us. On your days off you'll meet other young maids, and lads too I shouldn't wonder, which will be a good thing as long as you're careful and mind what your employer says.'

Harriet had another reason for wanting Maria to move away. When Stephen Hart was last home from school he had ridden over to talk to Fletcher, ostensibly to discuss farming, but he also spent time talking to Maria, and Harriet worried when she saw how dewy-eyed Maria became.

Dolly, on the other hand, said that she would like to work away from home; Harriet knew very well that she wanted her freedom, but Dolly was giddy and still had to learn some sense, and her mother considered that she was not yet mature enough to leave her care. Harriet had seen plenty of children and young girls and boys working long hours in mills and factories, as she herself had done as a child in Hull. It wasn't right, she had said to Fletcher, as she pondered on the plight of young mothers who had to work to feed their families, and so put their babies and young children into the dubious care of unscrupulous childminders.

I am so lucky, she thought for the hundredth and more times. How very lucky I am.

In the summer Charles sought out Daniel. 'I haven't spoken to my father about going abroad,' he admitted. 'But I've dropped a few hints about some of the chaps doing the Grand Tour before they go on to university. A party of them are setting off for Switzerland this summer with one of the tutors; they're visiting Geneva, Lucerne and some of the other alpine districts. It's very well organized, but I think you and I should start out next spring and just go where our feet tell us. What do you think, Daniel? I'll be nineteen by then and I'm really excited about the idea of travelling. I've done well with my French lessons, although my Italian is a bit scratchy. I can't seem to roll my r's,' he laughed.

Daniel was anxious. He hadn't mentioned the proposed excursion to his parents either, at least not since some time back when he'd gone out on another trip with Tom and hadn't been sick, not even when they went out of the Humber mouth and into the German Ocean and along the coast as far as Bridlington.

Since then they had been too busy for him to even think about it; they'd bought more sheep and cattle, and at market had sold bullocks and heifers for between six and ten pounds, lambs at a good price and half-bred ewes for between thirty-eight and forty-six shillings, which made up for the hay crops which hadn't done so well as the summers had been wet. In addition, they had bought a small plot of land from a neighbouring farmer who was retiring, to use eventually for pig breeding.

Lenny had said he'd like to leave school and specialize in pigs and build up a herd. Harriet had raised objections, but Fletcher had said mildly, 'He can read and write and add up, and if pig farming is what he wants to do, what's 'point in him staying on at school? He's keener on farming than Daniel is – Daniel's love is his hosses. Has he mentioned anything more about travelling to find his grandfather?'

'No.' Harriet smiled. 'I'm sure it was just a childish whim. It was Rosie who put that idea in his head. I think he's got over it.'

Fletcher wasn't so sure and reminded her that Daniel had been out again in Tom's boat. 'Tom said he's got over his seasickness and is still talking of going abroad.'

'That was ages ago,' Harriet maintained, hoping that Daniel was content on the farm; she couldn't bear to think that he might leave and never come back.

Fletcher gently patted her cheek. 'Mother hen,' he smiled. 'Your chicks will fly eventually, you know.'

'Yes,' she murmured, catching his hand and squeezing his fingers. 'I know. But not yet, and I hope 'girls will stay close to home when they marry, and then we'll have grandchildren!'

'Not yet,' Fletcher begged, 'please!'

'No, of course not yet,' she teased. 'But they're all growing up so fast it's frightening.'

As she gazed at him so close to her, at his soft grey-blue eyes and full warm mouth smiling back at her, she thought that they were not yet too old to have more children, who would fill the gap if their older children did leave home. She wistfully remembered the baby she had lost a few days after Joseph's mishap with the horses – there had been no more since.

Tom stretched his back at the end of a busy harvesting day; they had turned the horses into the fold yard to drink and tomorrow at six would start another field. He and Daniel had been mending a broken spoke on a cartwheel whilst Fletcher and Lenny went back to the house. He looked up. 'Hello?' he said. 'Who's this come visiting?'

Daniel followed his gaze. Two women on horseback were on the road above them, looking down. 'Don't know,' he muttered, slightly uncertain; there was something familiar about one of them. 'Just riding by. Or is it...'Yes, he thought, it could be – but mebbe not. Then she waved, and he waved back. 'It's Beatrice!'

'Miss Hart, you mean,' Tom murmured as he watched the two young ladies turn their mounts down on to the stubby grass and come towards them.

Beatrice hadn't come straight home from Switzerland at the end of term but had been in France for several weeks visiting a friend, and he hadn't seen her for some time.

'No,' Daniel said, watching their progress, 'Beatrice. Unless she's changed.'

'Bet you she has,'Tom grinned. 'I'll leave you to it. Some of us haven't time for entertaining.' He touched his hat to the approaching young ladies and started walking towards the house.

'Hello, Daniel.' Beatrice gazed down at him. She was dressed in a blue riding habit with her fair hair tucked under a jaunty feathered hat and was mounted on a dark chestnut thoroughbred, not one he had seen before. Some Arab breeding, he thought, stroking the horse's neck and nodding his

93

head in admiration. Beatrice's companion was slightly behind her.

'Hello, Beatrice,' he said, suddenly awestruck by the change in her. Her skin had a golden glow and an escaped lock of hair seemed lighter, maybe bleached by the Swiss sun. 'Is this a new hoss? I haven't seen him before.'

Beatrice lifted her chin and gave a deep sigh. 'Mademoiselle Babineau, may I introduce my friend Daniel Orsini-Tuke. Daniel, Mademoiselle Agathe Babineau.'

Daniel cast a surprised glance at Beatrice. Why did she give him two surnames? Why not just Daniel? he thought, before turning his attention to her companion, who had moved her mount forward, and touched his hot and sticky fore-head. 'Happy to mek your acquaintance, miss. Are you here on holiday?'

Miss Babineau's forehead creased. 'I am. Yes. I am visiting Miss Hart at her parents' kind invitation.'

Her accent was attractive and Daniel smiled. 'Good riding country round here,' he said, running his hand over the mare's nose. 'This is Tilly, isn't it?' he asked Beatrice. 'The mare you used to ride?'

'I still do,' Beatrice said. 'Prince here belongs to Charles; an early birthday present from our parents so that he can get some riding in before the summer is over. I've borrowed him and loaned Tilly to Agathe.' She changed the subject abruptly. 'Did you know that Charles wants to finish school next spring? Is this what you and he planned all that time ago?'

94

'Oh! Has he asked your father?' Charles should have talked to me first, he thought. I've got to plan what to say to Da and Ma.

'No, but he let it slip to Agathe that he might be travelling through France in the spring.'

'Did he?' He gazed back at her, and spoke without thinking. 'You look nice. Erm, I mean ... you look well...' He stumbled over his words. 'You look very well.'

She didn't reply but simply arched her fine eyebrows, so he turned to her companion. 'I hope you enjoy your stay, miss.' He knew he couldn't manage her name without making a fool of himself.

'I 'ope so too,' she said, and smiled at him, showing small white even teeth. 'Per'aps when you come to France we might meet again?'

Daniel's mouth parted. What on earth had Charles been telling her? Some tale anyway. 'Aye,' he murmured. 'Mebbe so.'

They left then, turning their mounts to ride back up the meadow. He watched them go, and when they were almost at the top Mlle Babineau turned her head and looked down, lifted her hand and gave a little wave. Daniel laughed and gave a hearty wave back. Mmm, he thought merrily, I might have to ask Charles to teach me some French phrases before we go away.

Agathe gave a little giggle as they rode along the path, ducking their heads beneath the overhanging tree branches. 'He is very 'andsome, is he not? But his manners are not those of a gentleman, and you are right, he 'as some foreign blood, and 'is name – Orsini, I think you said? – it is Italian, yes? Or

95

per'aps Sicilian? He is – erm, how you say, attracted to you, yes?'

'No,' Beatrice said emphatically. 'I'm just a friend; he doesn't notice me.'

'I think you are wrong,' Agathe said mysteriously. 'He 'as noticed you but doesn't yet know why. But,' she shrugged, 'it is no matter, for he is not for you. He is a peasant, I think. A labouring man, 'andsome but quite unsuitable.'

CHAPTER TWELVE

Charles appeared at harvest the next morning wearing his oldest clothes. 'I've come to give you a hand,' he announced. 'Beatrice said you were harvesting.'

'Another hour and we'll be knocking off for our lowance.' Daniel wiped his forehead with his shirt sleeve. 'We've been out here since six.'

'Oh, good.' Charles grinned. 'I'm just in time, then. Has your mother been baking?'

'Yes, but not for you,' Daniel countered. 'Onny for 'workers. Why don't you help at your own harvest? Not that I'm saying we don't want your help, we're allus glad of an extra labourer, but–'

Charles clicked his tongue. 'I would,' he sighed, 'but Father's not keen. He says the men would feel awkward if I offered to help; you know, their employer's son. They'd have to watch their language and so on.'

Daniel eyed him. 'Well, that wouldn't be a bad

thing, would it? The casual labourers who come to help us don't use bad language if Ma and my sisters are around. Tom and Da wouldn't have them here if they did. Or is there another reason why you don't want to be there?'

'There is actually.' He followed Daniel to where the stocked sheaves were set out in neat rows to dry. 'It's Agathe; she keeps following me about. I'm sure that my parents asked Beatrice to invite her to stay for my sake as much as hers. In fact I don't think that Bea likes her all that much; she seemed to be cool towards her yesterday evening – in a polite sort of way, you understand.'

'And yet you told her – Agathe – that you might be visiting France next spring.' Daniel continued working, binding up the sheaves with twine to keep them secure, whilst he was talking.

'I know.' Charles pulled a face. 'I don't know why I did. Making conversation, I suppose.'

'Look,' Daniel said. 'Why don't you go up to 'house and help Ma bring out 'food and drink? She's more to do now that Maria's away.'

'Yes, all right.' Charles turned as he was bid. 'But we need to talk later. And I want to hear what your parents have to say about our jaunt before I tell my father.'

Tell him? Daniel queried under his breath as Charles walked away. Doesn't he mean *ask* him? Mightn't he have to wait until he's twenty-one before he can *tell* his father anything? And, he suddenly realized, so will I with Ma and Fletcher.

When the men knocked off for their break, Charles appeared carrying a tray balanced high like a waiter or serving footman, and calling out in a pseudo-affected manner, 'Come along, gentlemen, luncheon is served. Will you take wine or water, sir?' he asked a harvester from a neighbouring farm.

'I'll tek wine, m'lud,' the man answered. 'A large one.'

Charles handed him a jug of water and a large beaker. 'The best from the cellar,' he declared, before moving on to the next man, who was sitting on the ground and leaning against a sheaf with a chunk of bread in his hand.

'I'll tek 'same, sir, if you please.' The labourer squinted up at him; the sun was now high in a cloudless blue sky. 'An' you can come an' work alongside o' me any time you like.'

Charles bent down to murmur, 'I might well have to if my father finds out what I've been up to.'

'Don't you worry 'bout that, sir.' The man took the water. 'Your father probably got up to mischief just 'same as you when he was your age, like we all did. When we were young and free and had no encumbrances.'

Harriet called to Charles to come and eat. She had brought thick slices of bread stuffed with beef and spread with mustard, pork pie, apple pasty and jugs of steaming tea and cold fresh water from the pump.

Charles sat down by her side and took the offered sandwich. 'Don't tell Daniel I've been eating his lowance, will you?' he said, munching enthusiastically. 'He'll say I haven't earned it.'

'There's plenty,' she said. 'I always do too much.' She looked thoughtful. 'I think it's because of my upbringing. There were times when there wasn't enough to eat, so now I mek enough for 'next day too, and I don't ever waste it. If we don't eat it then 'pigs have it–'

'And then you eat the pig.' Charles smiled, and rolled over on to his stomach. 'Did you–' He stopped speaking and put a hand to his eyes to blot out the sun, the better to see Daniel and his stepfather coming towards them.

'Did I what?' Harriet said.

Charles rolled over again, his back to Daniel and Fletcher. 'Erm – I've forgotten what I was going to say. The sun has addled my brain.'

'Didn't know you had one,' Daniel quipped as he sat down next to him. 'Hope you haven't eaten all 'pork pies.'

'I'll have some beef, please, Harriet,' Fletcher said, adding, 'How do, Master Hart. Come to help 'workers, have you?' He took a gulp of water.

'They wouldn't let me play,' Charles joked. 'I did offer but I was sent to the kitchen as a scullion.'

'Well,' Fletcher said. 'Nowt wrong with learning how ordinary folks live out their lives.'

Charles gazed at him intently. 'I wouldn't say that any of you were ordinary, sir. You're earning an honest living, which is more than I'm doing.'

'Ah, but you're gaining an education, which will prepare you for greater things.'

'Like running a country estate,' Charles muttered. 'There's no great esteem in that, surely? Not when it's handed down to me as my right.'

Harriet looked away, eyes averted from Fletcher.

'You'll be giving people work,' Fletcher told him. 'If people like your father didn't employ them, what would country folk do? Not everybody can afford to buy a smallholding the way Tom and I did.' He pointed to Tom, who was coming over to join them. 'We run this farm to feed us and our livestock and mebbe share a small profit at 'end of 'year. Some folk would think that riches.'

'And if we don't get on with it,' Tom interrupted, 'we'll not get this crop cut afore 'end of 'day.'

'We've onny just sat down,' Daniel objected.

'Five minutes then.' Tom joined them on the ground and Harriet handed him a pie; she knew he had an appetite like a sparrow and would only finish half of it. He thanked her, cast a glance at Fletcher and then at Charles, and nodded amiably.

'I'll have to go home,' Charles told Daniel. It was well past six o'clock and the men were still working; Charles's face and neck were sunburnt. 'Mother will send out a search party if I'm not back in time for dinner. Can I come back later so that we can talk to your parents?'

Daniel shook his head. 'We won't be finished for another couple of hours and Da will be too tired to talk. We want to get this field finished and dried off ready for threshing. Let's leave it for now. There's no hurry, is there?' He was anxious about his mother's reaction to the news that he really would like to go away; he knew how she felt about the brother who had never returned and would have to reassure her that he would always come home. He looked sideways at Charles, wondering whether this would be a good moment to broach a subject which had been worrying him for some time, and decided that it would.

'There is summat to think about,' he said awkwardly. 'I don't have much money, onny what I've saved over this last year. If I am allowed to go I'll be travelling on a shoestring.'

'I'll have my allowance–' Charles began.

'No!' Daniel was adamant. 'I'm not borrowing or allowing you to pay. If we're travelling together we should start out wi' same amount o' money.'

'Right,' Charles agreed after only a slight hesitation. 'That's fair enough.'

At nine o'clock, Fletcher and Tom were the last to finish. The casual workers had gone up to the house to collect their wages from Harriet, Lenny had already had his supper and gone upstairs, and Daniel was checking on the horses before he finished, tired and aching and ready for his bed.

'I, erm, I feel I should just mention...' Tom began as the two men set off towards the house. 'It's nowt to do wi' me, but...'

'What?' Fletcher asked. Tom wasn't usually reticent in coming forward with a question. He and Fletcher were boyhood friends and knew most of what there was to know about each other.

Tom paused at the field gate. 'Young Hart,' he said. 'When he was here today.'

'What about him? I thought he worked all right,' Fletcher said. 'For a young gent.'

'He did,' Tom agreed. 'I'm not disputing that.'

'Well, what then?'

'I'll tell you if you give me a chance,' Tom admonished him. 'Just listen. I might be wrong but I think 'penny's dropped wi' him. Didn't you notice how he kept glancing at you as if he was puzzled over summat?'

Fletcher frowned. 'No. Like what?'

Tom sighed. 'Are you not right sharp at 'minute? Or...' he hesitated as if embarrassed, 'is it because you didn't think I knew?'

'Knew? Knew wh–' Realization struck him like a hammer blow. He took a deep inhaling breath. 'You mean...'

'Yeh.' Tom looked away into the distance. 'About your ma, and... I've allus known. I heard when I was just a nipper, playing under 'table at Aunt Mary's house. Not from Mary,' he added quickly, 'she wasn't there and wouldn't have allowed that sort o' talk if she had been. I can't remember where she was, out in 'garden fetching her washing in or summat, but I heard 'other women whispering about your ma and Master Hart, and you.'

'All that time ago?' Fletcher was astonished. 'You've known all these years? Ma didn't tell me till I was a grown man just back from America!'

'Yeh, I reckon she decided to tell you after Mr Tuke and Noah drowned in 'estuary. There was nobody to dispute it then, was there?'

'And you're saying that young Charles spotted the likeness between his father and me? Never!' he said. Then: 'Is it so obvious?'

'As plain as 'nose on your face,' Tom said. 'I suppose I've allus seen it because I knew, but as you've got older you've got more like him.'

'I didn't believe her the first time she told me – too shocked to tek it in, I suppose – but Harriet allus believed it, and that's why Maria's gone into service. She and Stephen Hart became friendly and Harriet was nervous about it. If Christopher

Hart is my father, and my mother insists that he is,' he said reluctantly, 'then I'm their brother, or half-brother or summat, and my bairns are... I don't know, related, anyway. What I don't understand,' he blurted out, 'is if Ma thought she'd kept it such a big secret, how is it that other folk knew about it, like those women you heard talking?'

'I don't know,' Tom admitted. 'But that's 'joy of living in a country district. Everybody knows everything about what's going on, but it goes no further and they all pretend that they know nowt.'

'But now,' Fletcher said slowly, 'young Charles Hart has noticed 'likeness.'

'He has. I've no doubt about it, but he's not going to ask his father, is he? And he's certainly not going to question you. But I thought you ought to know.'

Later that night, Fletcher told Harriet what Tom had said. She suppressed a cynical smile at the idea that Ellen Tuke thought she had kept her secret; in a small community like this, somebody was bound to put two and two together. And, wide awake with a harvest moon shining though their bedroom window, she recalled Tom's Aunt Mary once telling her how Ellen Tuke hadn't always been truthful, and of how she had cried when Fletcher was born. 'I'm sure your mother and Christopher Hart thought that no one knew of their liaison,' she said softly, knowing how hurt and embarrassed Fletcher was over the whole sordid affair. 'But how wrong they were.'

CHAPTER THIRTEEN

Daniel turned twenty in December and during the long Christmas vacation Charles rode over to visit. He said that Beatrice was confined to her bed with a cold and was in a filthy temper because of it.

'She's not been made into a lady, then?' Daniel asked.

'Not that you'd notice,' Charles grinned. 'How's everybody here?'

'We're all well,' Harriet answered. 'Fletcher took Lenny to 'market and bought a pig in litter, so he's happy. Dolly's got a new dress.' She smiled at Charles as she gave him all their doings. 'I've got some new kitchen curtains, but best of all, Maria is coming home tomorrow and staying for Christmas.'

'Hurray,' Daniel cheered. 'We've really missed her.'

'I'm sure you have,' Charles agreed. 'I miss Beatrice too whilst she's in Switzerland. I've seen more of Stephen this year, and astonishingly George's tutors seem to think he has an outstanding future in front of him.'

'Really!' Harriet said. 'In what?'

'Well,' Charles said, 'apparently he's very bright and really brainy.' He laughed. 'I can't imagine it; my little brother! And the opinion is that he should eventually go into law or medicine, or science.'

'Goodness!' Harriet exclaimed. 'Your parents must be very pleased to hear that?'

'They are.' He hesitated and then glanced at Daniel. 'And – so it rather takes the edge off their disappointment in me.'

Fletcher and Lenny came in as he was speaking, and after greeting Charles, they took the other seats at the kitchen table.

'Why?' Fletcher asked. 'What have you been up to? Are you in trouble at school?'

'No, no, not at all,' he speedily assured him. 'It's just that I've asked my father if, rather than going to university as he wants me to, I might travel to Europe for a few months.'

Daniel inhaled; he still hadn't broached the subject with his parents and he was sure that that was what Charles was leading up to.

'And he's said no?' Fletcher asked.

Charles sighed. 'He has, and I don't understand why. He didn't go to university – he went straight into the estate to help his father.'

'Perhaps he always regretted it,' Harriet suggested.

'Maybe,' Charles said. 'But I know that Stephen will want to do exactly the same. He wants to farm and ideally he'd like to start now, but Father won't hear of it.'

He paused for a moment, and then said, 'But I'm not giving up yet, and what I was going to ask, if you would consider it, is, if I am allowed to travel, would you permit Daniel to come too?'

Harriet gave a small gasp and put her hand to her chest, whilst Fletcher turned his gaze on Daniel, who looked stunned.

'Daniel?' Fletcher said. 'Is this what you'd like to do?'

'W-wait,' Harriet said, clasping her fingers tightly together. 'Don't rush into anything.'

'I won't, Ma,' Daniel said quietly. He knew what she was thinking of, or rather *whom* she was thinking of: her brother who went away and never came back and left her not knowing whether he was alive or dead. 'But you know I've been thinking about it.'

Harriet sank into a chair. My firstborn, she thought. When he was onny a babby I often wondered what I would do if ever I should lose him. But that had been when she was at a low ebb, recently widowed with no one to turn to. Now she was a happily married woman with a husband and a family of children who loved her in return, and she knew in her heart that Daniel would never completely desert her.

'I went away travelling when I was a young man,' Fletcher told Charles. 'Older than either of you, though, and my circumstances were very different. And although I wasn't away for very long, I saw things that I could never have imagined, and I never regretted it.' He looked across at Harriet, who gave him a wistful smile. 'But I allus knew I'd come back when 'time was right.'

They all sat in silence, even Lenny and Joseph and Dolly, who was looking enviously at Daniel, whilst Elizabeth stood by her mother's knee and gazed at them all.

Fletcher cleared his throat. 'I think you should go, Daniel, if that's what you want to do, but it's your ma who should mek 'final decision.'

'We don't need to decide now,' Charles said hurriedly. 'There's no rush, but I wanted to ask so that you could mull it over.' He glanced at Daniel. 'It's something we talked about when we didn't realize there was a possibility of its happening. But if there is, if he can, I'd choose Daniel above anyone else as a companion.'

'What?' Daniel found himself strangely moved by this show of friendship. 'Rather than any of your *chums* from school?'

'Yes, rather than any of them. I know that you would always get me out of a hole that I'd dug for myself rather than leave me in it,' Charles joked.

'Ah! Now we have it,' Daniel retaliated. 'He onny needs a strong labouring man to carry his bag.'

Harriet gave a sudden laugh. Why would she deprive Daniel of such an adventure when he and Charles were so perfectly suited to travel harmoniously, when they complemented each other so well? Daniel with his whimsical humour and practicality, Charles with his gentlemanly ways which hid a warm and witty personality that would surely get them out of any scrapes.

She found that her throat tightened as she started to speak. 'I wouldn't hold you back from doing owt you wanted to do, Daniel, provided it was honest and legal, of course.' She smiled, but had to blink back tears at the thought of her son leaving home.

Daniel got up from his seat and gave her a hug. 'Thanks, Ma,' he said huskily. 'I'd like to travel and this might be my best chance ... knowing that I've got a fine gentleman to look after me and find our way home again.'

Charles raised his eyebrows in mock irony, and said enthusiastically, 'That's great. Now all we have to do is persuade my father. I don't think my mother is against the idea, but I wondered...' he paused and looked at Fletcher, 'I wondered whether you and Mrs Tuke would help me out over this and explain to them that Daniel is keen to come too?'

So whose idea was it? Harriet asked herself. Charles has made the first overture but has Daniel put him up to it with his thoughts of searching out his elusive grandfather?

'Yeh, that can be arranged,' Fletcher said calmly. 'Mebbe when Christmas is over? That'll give us a chance to discuss all 'possibilities.'

It will also give Fletcher time to think up an excuse not to call on them, Harriet thought. He won't want to be face to face with the man he now knows to be his father.

Daniel walked alongside Charles and his horse out of the farm and up on to the top road. 'I can't believe that was so easy,' he said. 'Nor could I believe my ears when you asked! I just wasn't ready for it.'

'I couldn't believe I'd said it either,' Charles said. 'It seemed to pop out when I mentioned Father's disappointment in me. Which was perfectly true, by the way, and I think that your mother was probably right when she suggested that maybe he regretted not going to university himself.'

'But that's unfair, if he expects you to do summat just because he didn't do it when he was young.' Daniel frowned. 'Does it mean that older people want to live their dreams through us? Like

Granny Rosie, for instance? Is that why she would like me to find her long-lost...'

'Beau?' Charles suggested. 'Lover?'

'Yeh,' Daniel said. 'Except in her case, I don't mind at all if it gives me an excuse to travel and see some other countries.'

'You're going to have to ask her again where she thinks he might have come from.' Charles mounted Prince as they reached the top road. 'The world is a big place.' He grinned and lifted his hand in farewell. 'So we might be gone a considerable length of time!'

Christopher Hart paced the drawing-room floor, a brandy glass in his hand. 'It's such a missed opportunity,' he said. 'Charles will regret it. He would be mixing with the top young men, his peers, people of influence.'

Melissa sighed. 'And after that? You'd still expect him to come home and run the estate. He'd lose touch with all these so-called people of influence.'

'But don't you see, Melissa, he's doing what I did, which is why I know that by refusing a chance of university life he's missing out on a great advantage,' he insisted. 'He should do what I didn't – go to university, not go gallivanting all over the Continent. Dash it all, if he wants a holiday there's nothing to stop him. We could all go,' he added, as if it had just occurred to him. 'We could go to Switzerland, to France. Why not?'

'We could,' Melissa agreed. 'But Charles doesn't want to come with us. Haven't you noticed? He's grown out of us, like a suit of clothes. He's nineteen, Christopher, not a child. He wants to go on an adventure of his own.'

Christopher stopped his pacing and sat down. 'I don't understand young men of today,' he said. 'I'm too old to understand them.'

Melissa gazed at him. So you are, my darling, she thought. 'Why don't *we* go away?' she said suddenly. 'When the boys have gone back and Beatrice has returned to Switzerland, why don't we take a trip to Paris? It will be cold but we could see the sights; take a boat trip on the Seine. There won't be many tourists in January or February. Oh, do let's! We could visit the Louvre; see the Mona Lisa and Venus de Milo. I've never seen them.' She became quite excited at the thought of it and the expectation that it might give her ageing husband a new lease of life.

'Mmm,' he said non-committally. 'Well, we'll see. But what to do about Charles?'

'Let him go,' she said, and as something else occurred to her she added, 'Why didn't you go to university after school? Why were you so keen to come home?'

'Mmm?' he said again, and scratched his beard. 'I was the only son. I suppose I felt it my duty to come home, although I really did want to help run the estate.' He looked vaguely into the distance. 'But it was a mistake. I should have gone. It would have broadened my vision.'

They heard the clatter of hoofbeats and shortly afterwards the bang of the front door. 'Charles,' Melissa murmured. 'Home for supper.'

Her eldest son put his head round the drawing room door. 'Not late, am I? I'll just slip up and change; won't be long. Will Beatrice be joining us?'

'No,' his mother said adamantly. 'I'd rather she didn't. I don't want your father catching her cold and being ill at Christmas.'

Charles quickly washed and changed his riding clothes for a pair of grey trousers, a clean white shirt, cravat and a black jacket and then knocked and slipped into Beatrice's room.

'How are you, old thing?' he asked. 'I hear you're not coming down to eat.'

'No,' she sighed, and blew her nose. 'I was going to, but Mama said she'd rather I rested so that I'd be all right for Christmas. It is only us for Christmas, isn't it? We're not entertaining?'

'Only drinks after church on Christmas morning,' Charles said. 'I expect it will be the vicar and his wife and one or two others, but that's all. I wish you were coming down for supper,' he added. 'I wanted your support over this proposed tour. Daniel's parents have said he can come, so that's one hurdle over.'

Beatrice yawned and slid down below the sheets. 'When?' she asked. 'When will you go?'

Charles shrugged and then, hearing the supper bell, headed for the door. 'I haven't been granted permission yet,' he pointed out.

'You'll get it,' she said. 'Just seem really disappointed if Papa is negative.'

'Which I will be.'

'Mama will agree,' she assured him. 'Just gaze pleadingly at her, and tell them you wish you were as clever as George!'

He shook a fist at her and hurried downstairs to join his parents and Stephen at the dining table. George followed him in. George seemed to have grown in stature since the school's report on his academic qualities, no longer the baby brother but on an equal standing with his brothers.

After soup and a light fish course came roast haunch of venison with redcurrant jelly, and as the dishes were being cleared away Christopher announced, 'Your mother and I have decided that you can travel, Charles, if you are really fixed upon it and providing you have a suitable travelling companion. One of your chums from school, for instance.'

'Oh! Thank you, Father, Mama!' Charles looked gratefully at his mother, knowing that she had probably pleaded his cause. 'That's simply wonderful. I've suggested it to some of the other fellows, as a matter of fact, but none of them have the necessary spirit of adventure, so I've asked Daniel Tuke. He's very keen and his parents are willing too. He's very sensible, of course, and he'll be a good sort of chap to have along.'

'Oh!' His father seemed flummoxed at the decision already made. 'Really?'

'Yes. He'd been thinking of travelling abroad in any case, so it's quite opportune.'

His mother gave a little smile. 'Where is Daniel thinking of going?'

'Oh, well, his plan is to search out his grandfather, if he's still alive,' he said. 'So somewhere in the Mediterranean.' He grinned triumphantly at his brothers. Stephen raised a laconic eyebrow, whilst George gave a little frown and said that he'd look on a map first thing in the morning and suggest places where they could start.

'Thank you, George,' Charles acknowledged.

'That's most kind of you.' He felt the most tremendous surge of elation, and couldn't wait to return to visit the Tukes and tell Daniel the amazing news.

CHAPTER FOURTEEN

At lunch the next day Charles suggested to Christopher and Melissa that maybe they could have a discussion with Daniel's parents and decide on the best time to travel abroad. 'I was going to suggest setting off in the spring,' he said nonchalantly. 'As I'm not going to university I could finish school at Easter. Or...' he paused, 'I don't really need to go back after Christmas.'

'Yes, you do,' his father said, and by the tone of his voice Charles knew that that was the end of the matter. 'What would you do at home if you didn't go back?'

Plan the itinerary, Charles was going to suggest, but saw his mother's raised eyebrows and a negative shake of her head and decided not to mention it. 'Unless there's anything I can help you with, Father?'

'Not a great deal to be done in winter,' his father mumbled. 'Bailiff's got everything in hand.'

'You won't need a bailiff when I finish school,' Stephen ventured. 'I'll be able to do what he does.'

'Nonsense,' his father said. 'There's always a need for a bailiff at the helm on an estate of this size.'

Stephen didn't comment. Now wasn't the time; there were enough kettles on the fire with Charles planning on going away. He was pretty sure that Charles wouldn't want to come back to farming, but it was all he wanted. In a few years he hoped to be running the estate, and when his father retired he would choose his own workers and do things quite differently from him.

'So when will the Tukes come?' Beatrice asked innocently; she had been allowed downstairs as she felt much better, but wore a warm woollen gown and a shawl as the day was sharp despite the sun. She was thinking that when the Tukes did come she might wear her new dress of pale-blue muslin, which nipped in her waist and showed off her neck and shoulder line.

'I don't know,' Charles said. 'I thought I might ride over to see them this afternoon. Anybody want to come?' he asked generally. 'It's not a bad sort of day.'

'I might,' Stephen said, and Beatrice said she'd love some fresh air after being cooped up in bed over the last few days, but George rather studi-ously said he would look at a map of the Medi-terranean.

The three of them changed into their riding out-fits, the two young men into breeches, long boots and greatcoats, and Beatrice in her winter riding habit of navy blue with a top hat and veil. Hidden beneath the ankle-length buttoned skirt and jacket she wore a pair of chamois leather breeches.

After leaving their land they decided to quit the roads and were soon climbing the track towards Brantingham village, up the meadow land to

Elloughton Dale. They paused at the top of a steep rise and looked down over the Humber.

'I love it up here,' Beatrice said softly. 'See how the estuary glints in the winter sun, and look at the wildfowl, thousands of them! Do you know what they are, Stephen?'

Stephen narrowed his eyes. 'I can see waders, widgeon, teal and mallard for sure, and I can hear curlew calling. Look.' He pointed. 'See them? Long legs – downward-pointing beak? They're searching out shellfish and worms, and there are redshanks, too – there, with the long red legs; they're part of the same family as the curlew, with similar characteristics.'

'I'm impressed by your knowledge, Stephen,' Charles said, and as he spoke a large flock of geese flew overhead, making their distinctive croaking cry.

'Pink-footed!' Stephen cried out joyously. 'They come from Iceland, you know, to spend the winter here.'

'Come on,' Charles told them. 'Let's be going. We don't want to be travelling back in the dark.'

'It's getting colder, too,' Beatrice said, giving a little shudder, and dug in her heels to urge her mount on.

They clattered into the farmyard and Harriet came to the door. 'Oh, come in, come in,' she said. 'How good to see you, but you're one missing!'

'George,' Beatrice said, unwrapping her scarves and hat as she entered the house. 'He's become a swot since he was told how clever he is, but I expect he'll get over it.'

'Cup of tea?' Harriet offered. 'Or cocoa?'

'Cocoa,' they all chanted. 'How lovely.'

'Where is everyone?' Beatrice asked. 'Is this not a convenient time, Mrs Tuke?'

'They'll be in any minute for a hot drink,' Harriet said. 'They're onny doing jobs round about 'barn and sheds. Sit down, do. Ah, here's Dolly.'

Dolly dipped her knee and glanced curiously at Stephen. Maria had told her how friendly he'd been when she had met him at the twins' party and she wondered if maybe she would be invited to the next one.

'How do you do, Dolly. Have we met before?' Stephen asked, leading up to a question about Maria, but her mother interrupted.

'Not for a while, I think,' she said.

'And where's Maria?' Stephen asked determinedly. 'I haven't seen her in ages.'

'Maria works now,' Harriet said. 'She has a position as a parlourmaid in Brough. She's coming home tomorrow.'

She saw the disappointment on Stephen's face. Charles saw it too and gave a small frown. 'I hope she's enjoying her independence, Mrs Tuke?' he said.

'She's not,' Dolly butted in. 'She'd rather be at home and I'd rather be there!'

'Can't you swap, then?' Stephen asked.

'No,' Harriet said for her. 'Dolly's not leaving home just yet. She's too giddy,' she added affectionately. 'I need her where I can keep an eye on her.' She smiled as Dolly shrugged.

Daniel came in as they were sipping their cocoa and expressed surprise and pleasure at seeing them all, his gaze resting on Beatrice as he said he

116

hoped she was feeling better. 'And George?' he enquired as his mother had done. 'Didn't he want to come?'

'He's plotting our route,' Charles laughed. 'But as we haven't said where we're heading I rather think he's choosing somewhere for himself. But the real reason why we're here is that I wanted to tell you that my father has given his consent to my travelling!'

'And did you tell him that I was going?' Daniel asked; he was certain that Mr Hart would rather have one of Charles's school friends accompany him.

Charles beamed. 'I told him that under a great deal of pressure and persuasion you had agreed to come along as bearer.'

'No, he didn't!' Beatrice exploded. 'Don't be such a terrible snob, Charles.' She stopped. 'Even if you were joking,' she added, wondering if she'd made a complete fool of herself.

Daniel laughed. 'It's all right, Beatrice, I know Charles's warped sense of humour.'

'Even so,' she muttered, embarrassed now. 'Other people might think him serious.'

'I didn't mean to–' Charles stopped. What had got into Beatrice? She knew him better than anybody. She surely knew he wouldn't ever, nor let anyone else, make a snide remark about Daniel. He glanced at her flushed face and then at Daniel looking awkward and he suddenly understood.

He recalled her asking if he thought she might be considered beautiful and he'd told her to ask Daniel – and she'd got cross. She's more than fond of him as a friend, and he is more than fond of her. Golly, he thought. What's Father going to make of that?

Charles was wise enough to acknowledge that any infatuation between his sister and his friend could quite easily fizzle out as she met more people and potential admirers; as for himself, he couldn't wait to be away from home and meet young ladies simply for the pleasure of their company, rather than have his parents size them up as suitable marriage partners. It surely should be possible, he thought, to have conversation with females without there being any implication or significance construed.

Charles listened to the chatter going on around him, but darker thoughts were running through his mind for he had worries of another kind. They became stronger each time he came to visit Daniel and saw Fletcher, who had just now appeared through the kitchen door. I'd never noticed the likeness before, but my eyes were opened that day at the harvest when I saw Fletcher Tuke coming towards me and thought I saw a younger version of my father. A pure coincidence, I expect; but his height, his fair hair – although Father is very grey now – his eye colouring and most of all his bearing, his way of walking tall and proud, is the same.

He could be related to someone way back, I suppose, maybe coming down the family line from one of my grandfather's brothers or cousins. I don't recall any being mentioned, but that's what it will be, he decided, nothing more than that, for families often look alike. Nevertheless, he was a little anxious about Stephen's taking an interest in Maria Tuke, for if there was a link

118

between Fletcher and the Hart family then any liaison, no matter that it came to nothing, was better nipped in the bud.

He shifted in his chair and glanced round the cosy kitchen and all of them clustered around the table. But then, my father and possibly my mother wouldn't think any relationship between our families would be suitable, not Beatrice and Daniel, not Stephen and Maria. Quite out of the question, I should imagine. And could Daniel keep Beatrice in the manner to which she is accustomed? Could Maria become the wife of a country gentleman? How ridiculous you are, he chastised himself. None of this is going to happen. You're thinking like a fool.

The conversation had drifted along without him and he had simply nodded his head from time to time as if listening, until Beatrice said, 'I think we ought to be leaving, it's getting late.' She stood up and put on her hat and scarf. 'I hope we haven't held you up, Mrs Tuke. Thank you so much for the hot drink; we're well fortified for the journey home.'

They all stood up. 'It's been very nice to see you all,' Harriet said. 'I hope you can come again before you return to Switzerland, Miss Beatrice.'

'That would be lovely,' Beatrice said. 'But will you not be coming to us to discuss the arrangements for Daniel and Charles's journey? Please do.' She smiled. 'I want to hear about it before I go. I don't want to be left out. Charles, you'll arrange it with Papa, won't you?'

Charles cleared his throat. 'Yes, yes of course. Some time in January. Will that be all right?'

Fletcher amiably agreed. 'Perfect,' he said. 'Couldn't be better. We'll be able to think about it over Christmas, eh, Daniel?' He put his hand on Daniel's shoulder. 'Mek plans?'

What's going on? Daniel thought. Why's Da so hearty and Charles so uncomfortable? 'Yes, good timing,' he nodded. 'We'll fix a day afore you all go away.' He glanced at Charles and grinned. 'Spot on, old chap!'

CHAPTER FIFTEEN

The families celebrated Christmas in their different ways. Harriet cooked the Christmas goose, helped by Granny Rosie and Maria, who was pleased to be at home. Her mother told her to take it easy and put her feet up, but she insisted that she wanted to help.

'I'm comfortable now with Mrs Topham,' she said. 'She's used to me and I am to her; she's very kind and I'm more of a companion than a maid, for I sometimes read to her, or serve her tea and cake, and her cook and 'other maid do most of 'other jobs, although I always offer.'

Harriet was delighted to have Maria at home, even for a short time, but thought that she had been right to send her into service. Maria seemed less shy and reserved and was more mature than she had been.

There were ten of them around the table, including Rosie and Tom, and once more Harriet gave silent thanks for her precious loving family. She gazed at Fletcher and, not wanting to cast a shadow over the day, didn't mention his mother Ellen, alone in her cottage by Brough Haven, who had once again refused an invitation to spend Christmas Day with them.

The Harts managed with a smaller staff than usual. Melissa believed that everyone should have a chance of going home at some point during the holiday if they wanted to. Cook prepared and cooked Christmas Eve dinner and Christmas Day luncheon; she said that she couldn't trust anyone else to do it as well as she could. After luncheon she was taken by trap to visit her sister who lived in Brantingham and came back on the following day. Two young maids had Christmas Day off, returning late that evening, but Dora, Melissa's personal maid, had no family in the district, so she, a kitchen maid and the housekeeper, who had known Melissa since she was young, stayed behind and kept Nanny Mary company.

'Everyone in service should work for a family like 'Harts,' Mary said over her second glass of sherry. She took a small sip. 'I feel quite guilty sometimes that there are no small children for me to look after.' She sighed. 'But not so guilty that I should ever consider leaving. I think I earn my keep with supervising 'laundry and doing 'patching and stitching and ironing mistress's gowns, although I admit I haven't got as good a hand as Harriet Tuke. I've never seen such beautiful collars and ironed tucks and pleats as she used to turn out. And of course I listen to the young folk who come to ask me things that they wouldn't ask their mama.'

'Like what?' Dora asked curiously.

'Ah, well.' Mary took another sip. 'That'd be telling.'

Charles considered her to be a sort of cosy grandmother, for he hadn't known either of his own. Nanny Mary had a warm and welcoming room. There was always a fire with a rug in front of it, where as a small boy he used to stretch out without any censure, either drawing or reading or even just lying on his back daydreaming with his hands clasped behind his head. Her kettle was always simmering on the fire and she made the children drinks, and magically always had cake or biscuits ready and waiting in a tin.

'Have you heard that I'm going travelling, Nanny?' Charles asked her on Boxing Day morning. He took up too much room now to lie on the floor but she had a squashy armchair that he favoured.

'Aye,' she said, taking a cake tin out of a cupboard whilst waiting for the kettle to boil. 'I reckon I did hear a rumour.'

'It's no rumour,' he declared. 'It's official. I'm being allowed to go. I've decided not to go to university just yet and I'm going on a European tour, and do you know who else is coming?'

'I can't imagine,' she said, pouring the boiling water on to the tea leaves, although in fact she had already heard through Beatrice. 'Am I allowed to know?'

'Oh, it's no secret. Daniel Tuke and I are to be travelling companions. It's not that he is tagging along with me or that I am joining him, but that we are travelling together.'

He had, as he often did with Nanny, reverted to the younger self who had felt a compulsion to explain each situation, knowing that she would listen patiently to every word.

'Very sensible,' she said, offering him a slice of cake. 'You'll be able to tek care of each other, and Daniel is a level-headed young man as well as a merry one.'

'He is, isn't he?' Charles agreed, licking his fingers free of crumbs. 'Oh, I can't wait. We're going to have such great fun. I suppose you know him really well, don't you, seeing as you know his mother?'

'Oh, yes.' Mary settled herself into the other chair by the fireside. 'I've known him since he was a babby. I delivered him, just as I did all of you.'

'So did you know his father? I don't mean Fletcher Tuke, but–'

'Noah,' Mary said. 'Yes. The Tuke boys played wi' my nephew Tom Bolton. I knew most of 'bairns in 'district – and delivered 'em.' She chuckled.

'Did you?' he said, sounding impressed. '*All* the Tuke boys?'

'Have another slice of cake,' she said, successfully changing the subject. 'Or will it spoil your lunch?'

'It won't,' he said, taking another slice. 'But not my father?' he said cheekily. 'You won't have delivered him?'

'Get away wi' you,' she admonished him. 'I'm not so old! But I remember your father when he was a youngster, about your age I suppose, and wanting to finish school, just like you.' She gazed into the fire. 'I worked in 'laundry room at 'manor; I knew everybody. We were a very close community, and I was allus called upon to deliver 'babbies.'

And then she realized that she had been channelled back to the same subject and said deftly, 'So tell me where you and Daniel are off to on this travelling malarkey.'

When Beatrice came to see Mary she had sighed dramatically and asked her if she thought anyone would want to marry her and would it matter if she chose someone who might be considered unsuitable.

'Well, I've never been married, Miss Beatrice, so I'm not sure if I'm 'right person to ask. Your mama would be 'best person for that, but in my opinion you should enjoy your freedom while you can. Once you're married and tied to someone for life you might wish you hadn't been in such a hurry to tie 'knot.'

'I'm not in a hurry,' Beatrice said. 'But I know that once I've been *finished*, word will get out that I'm available and I hate the thought of that. I want to marry for love, not money or prestige.'

Stephen and George had no such worries, Mary reflected. George was still too young and not yet considering females and was assured, in his own mind, that he was destined for higher things. Stephen, Mary was quite sure, would decide his own destiny. He was different from Charles, and not only in his features, which favoured his paternal grandfather, whom she remembered. He was broad-shouldered and square-jawed like him, and had a manner that proclaimed he would make his own decisions.

He did, however, come to her during that Christmas holiday to communicate to an ear that would listen to his thoughts on his future.

'What I've decided, Nanny, is that I'd like to go to an agricultural college and learn about what's happening in farming not only in this country but also abroad. You see,' he went on thoughtfully, 'I need to do that in order to survive in farming – because you might not be aware that agriculture has seen some very dark days.' He didn't notice her sighs as he told her of the things that had come to his attention, convinced with the surety of youth that she must benefit from his insight.

'But how to convince my father,' he ended, a trifle despondently. 'Because I would like to go this coming year.'

When he put the proposal to his father he was told that he was too young; but Christopher's growing realization that his children had minds and ideas of their own was strengthened when Beatrice and Charles told him that they didn't want a birthday party this year.

'I don't understand our children,' he complained to Melissa. 'They don't want to follow our advice, but only to do what they want. My goodness,' he said, exasperated. 'My father would be turning in his grave if he knew.'

'Then it's as well that he doesn't know,' Melissa said mildly. 'And isn't it good that they all have some idea of what they want to do with their lives? I didn't; I only knew that I was expected to marry well. So we should be glad for them, and admit that the reason why Charles and Beatrice don't want a party is that they think we will only invite suitable people that *we* have chosen rather than those they would like to come.'

Christopher harrumphed. 'Which of course we will.'

A thick fall of snow at the beginning of January stopped the meeting of the two families and it was just a few days before Beatrice was due to depart for Switzerland and her brothers for school that a meeting was hastily arranged.

'I'd like to listen in, Charles, if I may,' George said. 'I've written an itinerary for you.' He handed Charles two sheets of paper with suggestions of countries they might like to visit and the proposed length of time they would spend there.

Charles was astonished that his young brother would take so much trouble. 'That's very kind of you, George, but Daniel and I have yet to decide on where we are going and how we will get there.'

'I know,' George nodded. 'But this is a starting point. You can add to it or subtract as you wish. I propose that you start from a southern port rather than a northern one.'

'Thank you,' Charles said wryly. 'I'll discuss it with Daniel.'

Harriet came with Daniel. As she had rightly predicted, Fletcher had some very urgent business on the farm that couldn't possibly be left. 'They'll understand,' he told her, 'and I don't see that I'll be needed in any case. Daniel is able to make his own decisions. He knows how much money he'll have to manage on, and we can give him a bit extra

126

for emergencies, can't we? I'd hate to think he'd be stranded in a foreign country.' He'd kissed her cheek. 'Don't worry about him. He'll have a tremendous time, something to look back on when he's older.'

'So,' Harriet had had to ask, 'you're sure that he'll come back?'

'Course he'll come back,' he said, heading for the door, and then turned and grinned. 'Even if it's to tell you that he's going away again.'

They were shown into the manor's downstairs sitting room, where Beatrice, Charles and their mother were waiting. Melissa greeted them warmly and coffee and biscuits were served. Harriet apologized that Fletcher wasn't able to come as some of the sheep were lambing and he needed to be there. She thought that Melissa seemed relieved by his absence, but she simply answered that she quite understood and that her husband had also been held up but would be along very shortly.

'As will George,' Charles told them. 'I hope you don't mind, Daniel, but he asked if he could come in to listen. He's written us an itinerary.'

'Really? That's decent of him.' Daniel was impressed. 'Where does he suggest we travel to? I haven't discussed it with Granny Rosie yet. Every time I start to ask her she changes 'subject. I think she's putting off talking about it.'

Melissa caught Harriet's glance, and smiled. 'Maybe it's difficult for her to dredge up old memories,' she said. 'You have your grandfather's name, Daniel; perhaps that will be enough. Orsini might be a regional name.'

'It's Italian.' George had come in without their noticing and had seated himself on the wide windowsill. 'I looked it up,' he said, giving a secret and satisfied smile. 'You need to visit Rome.'

CHAPTER SIXTEEN

'Why Rome?' Daniel asked.

'Because it's the capital,' George said.

'We know that,' Charles butted in.

George looked at his notes. 'Since 1871,' he continued, as if his brother hadn't spoken. 'It's a very poor country. Oh, and another thing. The person you're looking for might not be there; he might have left Italy and gone to live somewhere else, like America, because there's been mass emigration in the last few years.'

'Well, thank you for the history lesson, George,' his mother said, pleased with her clever son, but knowing that he loved to impart his knowledge and if he were allowed to continue no one else would get a word into the conversation.

'It won't matter, will it?' Charles said sotto voce to Daniel. 'We can still travel there.'

'I don't think 'person I'm looking for will have emigrated,' Daniel said. 'He'll be Granny Rosie's age.' Then he frowned. 'But I suppose a seaman could have landed up anywhere. I might not ever find him.'

'But if you start in Rome, the authorities will be sure to know which district the Orsinis come

128

from,' George said.

Charles conceded that he might be right. 'But we need to talk about how we'll get there.' He wagged a finger at George to shut him up. 'We'll wait for Father to come in and see what he thinks.'

Daniel thought that this meeting wasn't turning out to be such a good idea. It would be better if Charles and I discussed it on our own rather than having to listen to everybody else's opinion.

Christopher Hart came in at that moment, murmuring his apologies. He bowed and said, 'How do you do,' to Harriet, and shook Daniel's hand when he stood up to greet him.

'So how are you getting on with the travel arrangements? Ah,' he said, looking around. 'Mr Tuke not here?'

'Fletcher sends his apologies, sir,' Harriet said. 'He couldn't get away.'

'There's always a job to be done in farming,' Christopher commented, 'but I expect that these two young men would rather make their own decisions in any case?' He raised his eyebrows in query, and first Charles and then Daniel nodded.

'What I was going to suggest, however, if I may,' he went on, 'is that perhaps you would allow me to drive you to whichever port you decide to leave from. It might be quicker travelling by road rather than having to change trains several times.'

'Unless we sail from Hull, sir,' Daniel said, 'and across 'German Sea to 'Netherlands.'

There was then a discussion of the various options for getting across from England to the Continent, and Beatrice put in her opinion that travelling by road wasn't all that pleasant when the weather was bad. By the time they'd reached stalemate it was nearing midday and Harriet had to get home to attend to the men's food, so the meeting was abandoned.

'Let's both make an itinerary,' Charles suggested to Daniel before they parted, 'and swap notes. You put down your ideas and I'll put down mine. That way we'll know what the other wants.'

'Yes,' Daniel agreed. 'But I'll discuss it wi' Fletcher and Ma first. I haven't travelled before, so I'll need advice.'

His mother hadn't travelled either, but Fletcher said he considered that a Kentish port would be the best option as it was a mere hop across the English Channel, and if they intended to aim for Italy it would be a shorter journey than going from Hull and across the Netherlands.

'Although,' he mused, 'looking at the dykes that the Dutch built would be interesting.'

Charles dropped in to see Daniel a few days later, bringing an atlas. 'I've made notes of where we might disembark if we go from the south, and to some extent I've followed Mr Thomas Cook's footsteps when he takes his travellers to Switzerland. We could go via Le Havre.'

Later that evening, Daniel traced the journey from Le Havre across France, Switzerland and Italy and felt sick with excitement and trepidation. 'It's such a long way,' he said to his mother. 'Look at 'size of France!'

'I'm looking.' She was peering over his shoulder at the map. 'Would you go through Paris? There was a lot of trouble some years ago. News even came through to England.'

'There's always trouble somewhere, Ma.' Daniel continued tracing his finger across the Continent. 'It was a revolution of 'workers. It's all quiet now. Well, fairly quiet,' he added. 'I'd like to go there. I'd like to see Napoleon's Triumphal Arch. We had to draw it when I was at school.'

He looked at her. 'You're not to worry, Ma. We'll keep out of trouble; keep our heads down as much as possible. You don't mind me going, do you? You don't think I'm letting everybody down by going off on this jaunt? It's not just about finding my grandfather – I think 'chances of that are fairly slim – but it's a good excuse for going travelling.'

'I don't mind.' She stroked the back of his head. 'I think it's exciting. Such an adventure for you. I'm just anxious that you won't come back.'

'Like your brother, you mean?' He shook his head and smiled. 'I'll come back, Ma. I promise.'

'No,' she said urgently. 'Don't promise. I don't want to be 'sort of mother who'd hold her bairns back from what they wanted to do. But write and tell me where you are. Not knowing would be 'worst of all.'

Later, Daniel told Fletcher that he'd rather travel by train to the port of departure. 'We'll have to stop over somewhere on 'way down if Mr Hart takes us, and there's no need. We're not bairns. We're going travelling abroad; we can manage between here and Dover!'

'Then say so,' Fletcher told him. 'Tell Charles that's what you want to do. This is your journey as much as his.'

Charles was sorting through his books, deciding

131

which he would need for his final term, when his mother knocked and came in. 'Getting ready?' she asked wistfully.

Charles nodded. 'Yes.' He sat on his bed. 'Just think – I won't be needing these any more after this term.' He hesitated. 'Mama?'

Melissa raised her eyebrows; she always knew when something was bothering her eldest son. 'Yes?'

Charles bit on his lip. It was time, he thought, to assert himself. 'When Daniel and I set off in the spring, I don't want Father to take us. I want to travel by rail and Daniel does too, but he's too polite to say so. The journey by road is too long to do in a day, but if we travel by train we'd be at the port by evening.'

'And I would rather you did.' She smiled. 'It's just that your father has never trusted trains. He's always said they are dangerous.'

'He's stuck in the past, Mama. Trains have been running for forty years! They're quicker and safer than travelling by potholed roads, and Father would want to break the journey somewhere.'

Melissa gave a small sigh. It was true. Christopher was ageing; he took longer to do everything nowadays, but he took his duties seriously and she knew he would want to see Charles and Daniel safely on board ship, just as he insisted on taking Beatrice to London to meet her escort for the journey to Switzerland. He would take her all the way if he could.

'I'll speak to him,' she said. 'I'll persuade him.'

'No,' Charles said. 'Sorry, Mama, but I'll *tell* Father. It's what we want to do. And,' he added,

'Beatrice would rather travel by train to London. She says she's nervous when Father takes the reins to give Benson a rest. She travels across France to Switzerland by train, after all.'

'Why has Beatrice not said? She's usually quick to give her opinion.'

'She doesn't want to upset him. She knows how he worries.'

'Well, it's too late now. She travels tomorrow. I wish she'd told me,' Melissa said. 'I might have persuaded him. I could have gone with her to London, stayed a few days, done some shopping,' she added pensively.

When Charles brought up the subject with his father, he thought there was a sense of relief in Christopher's manner when he agreed that if that was what they really wanted to do, they should do it. 'I'll admit that I wasn't looking forward to the long journey – but,' he added swiftly, 'if you should change your minds...'

'We won't, sir,' Charles said equally swiftly. 'And I think I should mention to you that Beatrice would prefer to travel to London by train. I suppose it's too late for tomorrow, but perhaps next time?'

'Oh, dear,' his father sighed. 'I hate travelling by train, noisy smelly things. I fear I'm becoming redundant. By the time you come home again from your travels – how long are you likely to be away, do you think? – you'll be itching to take over the estate and I shall be ready for my rocking chair.'

I won't, Charles thought. It's the last thing I want. Stephen will suit the role better than I. But he answered amiably, 'You're a long way off the

133

time for your rocking chair, Father,' and avoided the question of how long he would be away.

Beatrice wished that the subject had come up earlier. 'I'm stuck with travelling by carriage,' she groaned. 'But I'll return by train when I come home in the summer.'

'Easter, you mean,' Charles said. 'Or are you planning on being in Switzerland when Daniel and I come over?'

'Yes,' she said, her cheeks flushing. 'I certainly am, so you'll come straight there, won't you? Sail to Le Havre as I do, and then take the train to Paris and make your way to Switzerland. By the way,' she said casually, 'I'm going to say that Daniel is my cousin, otherwise I might not be able to come out with you.'

'Out with us?'

'Yes. I'll say that we're going out for lunch or tea or something. If there are any girls staying at school for the holidays I might ask one of them to come, and then I won't need a chaperon.'

'Not Agathe, *please*,' Charles begged. 'Anyone but her.'

'No, not her,' Beatrice said contemptuously. 'We don't mix so much any more. She's become very pompous.'

'Will you go back after the summer hols?' Charles asked, and he laughed as he spoke. 'Or will you be *finished?*'

'As much as I'm ever likely to be.' Then she said despondently, 'I don't know. No, I hope not, but Mama and Papa will decide. But what do I do then? I'm nineteen. Must I do the rounds of partying and balls and wait for someone suitable to ask for my hand in marriage?'

'Poor you.' Charles patted her shoulder. 'I'm so pleased that I'm not a girl.'

She pouted. 'If no one desirable asks for me, then I might travel too. Women do, but not at my age. I'll have to wait until I'm mature enough to go on my own or with a female companion, otherwise I won't be classed as respectable.'

'But would you mind not being considered respectable?' Charles asked teasingly. 'Except, of course, that you realize it would rebound on us, your brothers and our parents?'

'Well, you wouldn't mind,' she said crossly. 'You don't care what anyone thinks.'

'No, I wouldn't.' Charles grinned. 'Unless you do something really reckless and stupid and then I might.'

'Like what?'

'Well, I don't know, running off with a bounder. Ruining our name and your reputation.'

'Ha!' she said. 'The chances of my finding a bounder are exceedingly slim.'

Daniel went over to the manor that evening. He'd spruced himself up and slicked down his unruly hair. He'd come to say goodbye to Beatrice before she left the next morning, and the boys too, he said awkwardly, in case he didn't see them the following week.

'I wish I could stay at home,' Stephen told him out of his father's hearing. 'I'd much rather be working outside or going to agricultural college.'

'Maybe next year?' Daniel suggested. 'They

135

might not take you yet in any case.'

'Perhaps not,' Stephen said thoughtfully. 'I hadn't considered that, so maybe I'd better buckle down and be sure of being accepted.'

'I like school,' George said, and his brothers groaned and called him Swot. Beatrice went up to him and gave him a hug and he squirmed and looked sheepish.

'I'd better be off,' Daniel said. 'I hope you have a good journey, Beatrice.' He could feel his neck flushing and he hunched into his jacket. 'I'll, erm, see you in Switzerland.' He laughed. 'I can't believe I said that. Pinch me, somebody!'

They all rushed to oblige, even Beatrice, and they were all laughing and jostling when Mr and Mrs Hart came into the room. Mrs Hart raised her eyebrows in her inimitable way, but Christopher Hart gave a small puzzled frown and Daniel wondered if he had ever had any rough and tumble with friends when he was young.

'Daniel was just saying that he couldn't believe he's going to Switzerland,' Charles explained ineptly. 'And asked us to pinch him.'

And although Mr Hart murmured 'Ah!' Daniel knew that it was Beatrice he was looking at, not him, unless – and more likely – it was at both of them.

CHAPTER SEVENTEEN

Over the winter period and towards the Easter season, Daniel fitted in as many jobs as he possibly could. Ever since he was old enough to yoke a horse to a plough, it was considered and accepted that his role in the farming year was the ploughing, harrowing, sowing and reaping. He loved his horses and took great care of them, checking their health and their feet and feeding, watering and grooming them, and he knew he would miss them almost as much as he would his family.

Fletcher would take over their care whilst he was away, for he was the one who had taught him; Tom, who was able to turn his hand to most work, would fill in wherever he was needed. Lenny had his beloved herd of pigs, which had produced several litters of piglets, some of which he had sold on after they were weaned; and whereas Joseph was still rather nervous of horses since his encounter with them when he was a toddler, he liked to tend the sheep, and helped Fletcher repair and reassemble machinery.

Yet Daniel still said he felt guilty at leaving.

'Tell you what, then,' Fletcher said one evening after they had finished their supper. 'When you come back home, Lenny can go off adventuring, and then when Joseph is old enough he can go.'

Lenny looked up. 'I can't go. I'm too busy to go anywhere. I intend building up an even bigger herd than I've got now, and I'm going to try out different breeds to find 'best meat for pork and bacon.'

'But what about me?' Dolly complained. 'I'd like to travel too.'

'You'll have to find a rich man to marry you, Dolly,' Tom said. 'I'd marry you myself, but I'm done wi' travelling.'

'But you're too old, Uncle Tom,' Dolly objected. 'You're as old as Da!'

'Your da and me have been having a discussion, Dolly,' her mother broke in, 'and we've decided that you and Maria can swap jobs. We think that you're ready to start work. Maria has already asked Mrs Topham and she's willing to tek you on. You can start after Easter.'

'Oh, Ma! Really?' Dolly was ecstatic. 'And you mean that Maria will come home?'

'Yes, she'd like to, even though she says she's been happy enough at Mrs Topham's.' She smiled at Elizabeth. 'And it'll be nice to still have two girls at home, won't it, Lizzie?'

Elizabeth, still scraping her bowl of custard, nodded.

The weeks sped by. Harriet worried about Daniel sleeping rough, and decided to sew him a sleeping sack in case there were nights when he couldn't find accommodation. Fletcher drove her to Brough station, where she caught the train into Hull. There had been many changes in the town since she had last been and she wished she had more time to look round some of her old haunts. She located a draper's shop and bought waterproof material, a pair of fustian sheets and some strong cotton thread, and returned home well pleased with her purchases.

When she had finished tacking it all together she asked Joseph to find her some sheep's wool from the meadow. She washed and dried and teased it until it was soft and fluffy, filled the sack and stitched it up.

Daniel climbed into it to try it for size and declared it perfect. 'Charles is going to want one, Ma. You ought to have bought enough material for two.'

'I never thought,' she said. 'Surely Charles will have something similar already? But if he hasn't, I think there's enough material left, and I only used one of the sheets.'

'Mek him one, Ma,' Daniel said. 'He'll be as pleased as Punch.'

So she did, and Daniel continued to plan their route and build up his list of what he would need for the journey. Granny Rosie knitted him thick wool socks, a scarf and a brightly coloured hat to cover his ears, which he gazed at in dismay even though he thanked her; he polished his best good strong boots and put aside several pairs of laces, because, as he told Elizabeth who was watching him, 'The best boots you can buy are no good without laces.'

'I'll miss you when you've gone, Daniel,' she said plaintively. 'I don't understand why you have to go.'

He gave her a squeeze. 'I don't *have* to go, Lizzie, but I want to. It's important to me.' He had already explained that he was going in search of his grandfather; when he came home again he

139

would explain further if he had discovered any answers.

Easter fell in early April that year and Charles, Stephen and George Hart arrived home the week before. Charles was euphoric at leaving school for the last time, for as he explained to Daniel when they met, 'Although I've left my options open for going to university later, and that is what my father expects of me, in all honesty I don't think I will. I'd like to study art and maybe literature, but mostly art, and I think this journey through France and Italy will open my eyes, allowing me to see what is possible.'

'I'd like to go to Paris,' Daniel told him. 'I'd like to see 'palace gardens and 'River Seine.'

'Yes, I would too,' Charles said eagerly. 'And the Louvre. Not that I want to be an artist, I'm not good enough, but I'd like to see the works of art that I've read about.' He lowered his voice. 'And particularly Montmartre,' he murmured. 'Don't tell your mother we're going in case she's heard of it.'

'Why?' Daniel whispered.

'It's where the artists and their models live,' Charles said in an undertone. 'There's a lot of drinking and, erm, other things going on. Struthers, our art master, told us about it; he's a very liberal-minded sort of fellow and spends his summers there. Have you heard of Camille Pissarro?'

Daniel shook his head, and Charles continued, 'He's one of the artists who live there and apparently he gathered a group of other artists together, including Monet and Cézanne, to create the Impressionist school of painting. There are other artists and writers living there too because accommodation is cheap and most of them struggle to earn money, but,' his voice dropped even lower, 'the area is considered to be very decadent.'

'Oh,' Daniel breathed in. 'I can't wait! Write and tell Beatrice we might be held up,' and they both laughed with glee at what was to come.

The day before they were due to depart, Daniel decided to visit Granny Tuke. He was apprehensive, in view of her attitude towards him, but he felt he should. Her door overlooking the Haven was open and she was sitting inside in her easy chair looking out. He gave her a wave as he drew up in the trap and fastened the mare's reins to the fence post.

'I've come to say goodbye,' he said awkwardly as he stood on the doorstep. He never knew what name to give her. Plainly not Granny, as she had told him that she wasn't, but Mrs Tuke seemed far too formal, so he didn't call her anything. 'I'm off on my travels tomorrow,' he explained. 'I'm hoping to find 'whereabouts of my grandfather, or some relative at any rate.'

'And then what?' she said dispassionately. 'Will that mek a difference?'

'I don't know,' he said. 'I don't think it'll change anything, but I'd like to know about his background; it's important to me.'

Ellen Tuke grunted. 'I can tell you a thing or two about your grandmother, if you want to hear it.'

I don't understand why she's so vindictive, Daniel thought, but he said, 'I know about Granny Rosie. She was very sad about losing her son; any

141

mother would be, wouldn't they?' His question was searching. Surely she would understand. When she didn't answer, he added, 'I hope I've made up to her for 'loss of him.'

Ellen's lip curled and he was sure she was about to say something cutting, so he said quickly, 'So I hope you keep in good health and I'll see you when I return,' and turned to unhook the reins. She hadn't invited him in but had kept him standing on the doorstep; nor had she enquired about his travels. 'Goodbye.' He nodded and, leading the horse, turned the trap and climbed in, and as he passed her door he raised his whip.

He had driven only a few yards when he heard her shout. 'Hey!' He drew on the reins and turned his head.

She was standing in the doorway and raised her hand. 'Look after yourself,' she said, and he felt exhilarated as if he'd scored a small victory.

The following day, Daniel said his goodbyes to his mother, his brothers, Elizabeth and Maria; Dolly had already said farewell when she departed to her new job in Brough.

Harriet had tried her best not to mention all the things he should avoid, but she couldn't help but tell him to take care not to lose his belongings, not to get into any trouble with roughnecks, and always to stick close to Charles. And then she had handed him some postcards so that he could write as soon as they'd landed in France.

He'd hugged her and promised to do all of those things and repeated that she shouldn't worry about him. Fletcher was driving him to the manor to collect Charles before taking them both to Brough railway station, but on the way there they were calling on Rosie.

From Dover to Le Havre was their final chosen route, and then they were going by train to Paris. Rosie eagerly asked when he thought they'd get to the Mediterranean.

'Not for a while, Gran. We'll be staying in Paris first and then going on to Switzerland to see Charles's sister. We want to see 'Swiss Alps and maybe climb 'Jungfrau ... well, not to 'top, of course, it's too high for us, but we'd like to go up part of the way.'

'Ooh, what's that, then?' Rosie asked. 'Is it a mountain? You'll need a deal of breath, won't you?'

He laughed and said that they would, and then gave her a hug and promised he would find out as much as he could about Marco.

'Just one thing, Daniel,' she murmured. 'He's most likely a married man, if he's still in the land of 'living, which I hope he is, and I wouldn't want you to cause any trouble with his family.' She gazed at him anxiously. 'Assess 'situation, won't you? Mebbe you could say that you know somebody who knew him when he was a lad, summat like that – you'll know what to say, won't you?'

He kissed her cheek. How gentle she was, not wanting to upset anyone, unlike Granny Tuke who didn't care about anyone else's feelings. 'Don't worry,' he said. 'I'll be tactful.'

He waved goodbye, a sudden thought possessing him. He hoped she would still be here on his return. 'How old is Granny Rosie, Da?'

Fletcher glanced at him quickly. As a child Daniel had always called him Da, but in recent years he had taken to calling him Fletcher. Fletcher hadn't minded, had understood that for Daniel it was part of growing up, but the fact that his stepson had reverted to the childhood designation today of all days touched him deeply, and he cleared his throat. 'Not suré. Not all that old – sixtyish maybe. She's very spry, anyway.' He glanced again at Daniel as they trotted along. 'Hale and hearty, so if you're worrying about her you know we'll look after her, don't you?'

Daniel nodded and murmured, 'Yeh. I'm just thinking that everything will be going on as usual while I'm away, but I won't know about it and nobody will know where I am to tell me.'

'True,' Fletcher agreed. He paused. 'But, you know, you'll think of us even when you're having adventures and seeing new sights, so don't forget to write things down to tell us about when you come home again.'

'Did you do that, Da, when you went to America?' There it was again. Fletcher swallowed, and knew how much he would miss him.

'Some,' he said. 'But my reasons for going away were different from yours.' His voice dropped. 'I went away because I loved your mother and she was married to your father; I thought of her every day and wanted a reason to return home, so I didn't enjoy the experience as much as I should have done. Your father's death brought me back again.'

Daniel remained silent until they reached the manor gates and then said in a great rush, as if it were important to speak before they reached the house, 'You know, don't you, Da, that I allus think of you as my father? And that–' his voice cracked, and he lowered his head, 'that I've never ever wished that anybody else was? I'm sorry that Noah died and that we never knew each other, but he could never have been a better father than you've been.'

Fletcher put his hand on Daniel's arm. He couldn't speak for a moment, and then he said, 'When I came home from America and saw your mother with you in her arms, it was 'loveliest sight I'd ever seen and I knew then that even though Noah had sired you, I wanted you in my life as much as I wanted your mother. I loved you as my own, and even with other bairns that remains true to this day.' Tears ran down his cheeks. 'You've been 'best son any man could wish for.'

Daniel sniffed and put his hand in his pocket for a handkerchief. 'Thanks, Da.' He risked a glance at his stepfather. 'I know I've been calling you Fletcher for a while, but I think if you don't mind I'll go back to calling you Da.'

Fletcher laughed and brushed his hand across his nose. 'We'd better perk up or 'Hart family'll think us a couple of old women.'

Charles's departure from home was not as traumatic as Daniel's had been, for his parents were used to their sons and Beatrice leaving for school, but Charles's mother took a deep breath before giving him a gentle kiss on his cheek and then doing the same to Daniel.

'Take care of each other, won't you,' she said

145

huskily, 'and have a wonderful time.'

Charles kissed the top of her head and murmured, 'Don't worry about me, Mama. Daniel will look after me!'

Daniel raised a wry eyebrow. 'I'll mek sure he doesn't get into hot water, Mrs Hart.'

Melissa gave a wide smile and gestured to her husband, who seemed rather bemused, but came and shook hands with both boys, and patted Charles affectionately on his shoulder. 'Send a telegram or a letter if there are any difficulties,' he said. 'And you know arrangements have been made with the Swiss bank if you should need money.'

'Yes, thank you, Father, but I'm sure we'll manage.' Charles glanced at Daniel. He hadn't told him that his father had arranged this backup and hadn't intended telling him, knowing that Daniel had wanted them to be financially equal. But Daniel's expression didn't change as he buttoned up his coat.

'Goodbye, Da.' Daniel put his arms out to hug Fletcher. 'I promise I'll write.'

'Goodbye, sir.' Charles proffered his hand but Fletcher gave him a hug too. 'Thank you for bringing us, and I promise I'll keep Daniel out of mischief.'

Fletcher watched the train steam away and two hands waving until out of sight. Then he turned to climb back into the trap. How lucky they both were, he thought. Not only to be able to go off on such a journey, but to have such a special friendship in spite of their social divide.

CHAPTER EIGHTEEN

Daniel staggered down the gangplank at Le Havre, muttering and groaning.

'What are you saying?' Charles asked cheerfully from behind him. 'Can't hear a word. What a glorious morning. Smell that French air!'

Daniel dropped his rucksack on a nearby bench and sat down. 'Dry land! Thank heaven.' His face was grey. 'I know now that I definitely haven't got 'sea in my blood. That voyage was much worse than any I've made on 'Humber.'

'Not rough in the slightest,' Charles said. 'And it's not that far. Look.' He put his hand to his forehead in an exaggerated manner and gazed into the far distance across the sea. 'You can still see England.'

Daniel groaned again, uttering, 'And to think we've to do that crossing again when we go home.'

'Don't talk of home already,' Charles complained. 'We've only just got here. Come on.' He hauled Daniel to his feet. 'Beatrice said there's a café along here where we can get hot coffee and fresh bread. We've time before we catch the train.'

The café was a mere wooden hut but in it was a stove with a fire burning beneath it and, sitting on top, a metal jug filled with fragrant-smelling coffee; on a wooden table were several *batons* of fresh bread and a dish of butter. The proprietor swilled out two cups in a bucket of dubious murky water and poured thick black coffee into them. He pointed to the bread with one hand and held out the other for payment. *'Avez-vous faim?'*

'Oui!' Charles patted his stomach in confirmation, and then fumbled in his pocket book for coins and handed them into the man's grubby hand. *'Merci.'*

'What did he say?' Daniel blew on the piping hot coffee. 'I don't suppose there's any milk?'

Charles turned to the man again. 'Erm, *du lait, s'il vous plaît.'*

'Non!' The Frenchman turned his gaze on Daniel and handed him a bowl of sugar cubes.

Daniel put several lumps into his coffee and nodded his thanks. *'Merci,'* he mumbled. 'Thanks very much.'

The sweetened coffee revived Daniel, restoring him to something like normal. They took a *baton* of bread to share and sat on a bench outside the hut to eat and drink, and then to their surprise the café owner came and brought them some change from their money. He touched his forehead and murmured, 'Good day. *Bonjour, messieurs!'*

Charles heaved a sigh. 'Well, that's a good start to the day.'

'Yes,' Daniel agreed. 'It is. I must admit that when I got off 'ship I was wishing I hadn't come, but I feel fine now.'

They finished the coffee and Daniel stood up. 'I'll take 'cups back. I'm going to practise my French.'

He handed the cups back after first throwing the dregs into a flower tub. *'Merci, monsieur,'* he said haltingly.

148

The Frenchman took them from him and asked, *'Parla Italiano?'*

Daniel frowned, then said, *'Non.* English.'

He was nonplussed by the garrulous Gallic response, none of which he understood except to gather that he looked like an Italian. He shrugged and raised his eyebrows, grinning as he did so, and the Frenchman patted his shoulder and said something else equally incomprehensible.

'I've had a great conversation,' he told Charles when he returned and shouldered his rucksack on to his back. 'Who needs a foreign language?'

They had a one-mile walk into Le Havre for the train to Rouen, where they would change for the Paris train. They were able to find seats together, and as the train rumbled, rattled and whistled through the green and undulating countryside, suggestive of the Wolds above his home village, Daniel relaxed, listening to the hum of voices around him. Not being able to understand any of it, he closed his eyes momentarily and drifted off to sleep, waking only when Charles shook his shoulder to say they had arrived.

They had an hour to wait for the Paris train so Charles suggested they take a walk into Rouen. 'I believe there's a fine cathedral here.'

Charles had done his research into what there was to see and Daniel thought the Rouen cathedral was the most beautiful building he had ever seen. 'Not that I've seen many,' he admitted. 'Only 'local church and once Holy Trinity and St Mary's in Hull. Ma took me when I was little and they seemed huge, but nothing compared with this.'

'It makes me wish that I could paint,' Charles

said as he too gazed up at the soaring towers.

'Can we buy postcards of it, do you think?' Daniel said. 'Ma gave me postcards to send home when we arrived in Paris, but if I could send one of this cathedral she'd be flabbergasted.'

They went inside to look round and found a stall where picture postcards of the cathedral were displayed next to a box for payment. Daniel dropped in a coin of roughly the equivalent of twopence, and Charles followed his example.

'They'll stop worrying now,' Daniel said as they sat in a pew and wrote to their parents. *Dear All*, he wrote. *We are sitting in R –* 'How do you spell Rouen?' – *ouen Cathedral as we wait for our train to Paris. Your loving son and brother, Daniel.*

'My parents won't be worrying,' Charles said as they came out into bright sunshine. 'They're used to me being away.'

'They must miss you, though,' Daniel said. 'We need to find a post office.'

A passer-by directed them to a place where they could buy stamps and post the cards. Then they made their way back to the railway station to wait for the train.

'Don't you think your mother misses you?' Daniel asked, reverting to their earlier conversation. 'And Beatrice?'

'Not Bea,' Charles said. 'She's too busy to think about it, although she used to when we were young.' He laughed self-consciously. 'We only ever liked to be together. I suppose twins have a special relationship, and when I first went away to school we both cried for the other. She needn't have gone back after Christmas; I don't know why she did. It seemed as if, as soon as she heard *we* were coming abroad, she wanted to stay on for another couple of terms.'

'Why's it called a finishing school?'

'Young ladies are taught how to behave in elite social circles where they'll be invited to attend parties and will then meet suitable contenders for their hand in marriage,' Charles said derisively.

Daniel remained silent for a moment, and then said, 'Like your friend Hanson?'

'Oh, no!' Charles exclaimed. 'Certainly not him. He's rich, but not a candidate. He's rather a boor, in fact, and Beatrice wouldn't consider someone like him.' He pursed his mouth. 'She'll decide for herself in the marriage stakes, will Bea. We both will.' He jumped up from the bench where they were sitting. 'Come on! Here's the Paris train!'

Gare St Lazare was a railway station unlike any other they'd seen. A classical façade fronted platforms covered by a huge glass canopy that allowed the sunshine to light up the whole station. The interior was full of steam and smoke and noise, of engines shunting and people shouting and carriage doors banging, making the atmosphere impressively potent, yet mysterious and ethereal.

'It's nothing like Paragon Station in Hull,' Daniel said in astonishment. 'And I can't compare it with anything else, except King's Cross.'

'Which doesn't compare at all,' Charles agreed, gazing up in rapture at the iron and glass structure. 'I feel – I feel so excited!' His voice was eager. 'Monet completed several paintings of it only recently,' he said. 'Or so my tutor told me; I

151

'haven't seen them, of course.'

'What? Someone painted a railway station, as a picture?' Daniel said.

'Artists will paint anything that appeals to them,' Charles explained. 'They aim to show the true beauty of an object or a landscape by giving an impression of how they see it: in light reflected by water, for instance, or even filtered through smoke and steam as we're seeing now.'

Daniel followed Charles's gaze up to the glass roof. 'I'd never have noticed if you hadn't pointed it out,' he said. 'I feel very humbled by your knowledge.' He wasn't mocking or being satirical, but genuinely impressed by his friend's perception.

Charles grinned. 'I'm showing off. I'm only parroting what I've been taught. You know so much more than I do about farming and animals, and you probably see more beauty every day from your land than I ever do from my schoolroom.'

'It's true that I see a new sunrise every morning and every morning it's different,' Daniel agreed. 'And it's like my tree, an old ash that Da said was my very own. He used to lift me up on to a branch and tell me to imagine I was on a ship or flying in 'sky like a bird, and I did, but I also saw 'Humber from up there and it was like a bird's eye view; is that 'same thing?'

Charles nodded. 'I think it is.'

As they both wanted to spend a few days in the capital, they decided that the first thing they must do was find cheap lodgings, but spring in Paris was a popular time for holidaymakers and by midday they had tramped up and down innumerable streets and been turned away at every

152

pension or *logement* door they had knocked on.

'We must eat,' Daniel said at last. 'I'm famished. We've not had anything since first thing this morning. Let's watch out for a family who might be going out for food and follow them.'

So they stood against a wall of a square and waited. They had not been there long before they were approached by two young and shabbily dressed girls, who put out begging hands; when they shook their heads, the girls came closer, touching and stroking them on their arms, murmuring something.

'What are they saying?' Daniel asked.

Charles was blushing. 'I can't possibly say. But don't look at them, and if they don't go away we must move on.'

'American?' one of the girls said to Charles. 'I speak ze American. You see dancing, monsieur? Can-can? Oui?'

The other girl sidled up to Daniel making kissing sounds and said, *'Je m'appelle Maria.'*

He finally understood what this young girl, with the same name as his sister, was suggesting and he pushed her away. 'Come on,' he said to Charles. 'Let's be off.'

As they strode away, the girls, laughing and not in the least offended by their rejection, called out, *'Adieu.* Good night, messieurs,' even though it was the middle of the day.

'That was a close thing,' Charles said as they turned a corner. 'We must take care. They might well have had a couple of ruffians close by protecting them.'

'Oh, but look here!' Daniel exclaimed. They had

153

come to the entrance of a narrow street and on each side of the street were cafés, many of them filled with families: fathers, mothers and children. 'These might be all right. Gosh, what a lovely smell!'

By the door of one of the cafés was a blackboard with a menu written in chalk and Charles quickly calculated that the food was within their means. A waiter came towards them and Charles indicated that the two of them would like *'le déjeuner'*.

'Certainly, gentlemen.' The waiter took them towards a table with a checked tablecloth set with cutlery.

'Oh, you speak English,' Charles said. 'What a relief. My French isn't very good.'

'I worked in London for two years, but then I came 'ome. The food isn't as good in England as in France.'

'We'll try it,' Daniel said. 'I can smell soup.'

'Les potages.' The waiter nodded. *'Bouillabaisse? Potage à la reine?* Fish or chicken?'

'Chicken,' they said simultaneously. 'And bread,' Daniel added. 'Lots.'

They were each given a deep bowl of piping hot chicken soup sprinkled with herbs and crisp croutons and a plate of crusty bread, and they ate without speaking apart from murmurs of pleasure until they were finished and the bowls scraped clean. The waiter cleared away and then brought them a plate of cheese and ham and a carafe of red wine and two glasses.

They glanced at each other and Daniel shrugged and grinned and poured the wine. 'When in France,' he said merrily, 'eat and drink as ze

French do!'

'Yes,' Charles agreed, taking a sip. 'But after drinking wine we'll need an afternoon nap.'

'A siesta! Or is that Spain?'

The waiter came back to chat with them and they guessed that he wanted to polish up his English. He told them his name was François and asked them where they were from; they told him they were travelling and were looking for somewhere to stay for a few days.

'We can't afford a great deal,' Charles explained. 'We have to make our money last.'

'What you want? Just a few nights?' the waiter asked. 'No more than three?'

'Three will be about right,' Charles said. 'We want to see the sights: the Louvre, Notre-Dame, the Tuileries ... Montmartre...'

'Ah, ah! You are artists, yes, or you want to see how the poor people of Montmartre live?'

'We know how poor people live,' Daniel broke in. 'My mother used to be very poor. But Montmartre–'

'You want to climb ze 'ill and see the view, yes?'

'And I'd like to see the artists' work too,' Charles said.

'Then you may stay with my mother,' François said. 'She can have you for three nights only. She will say that you are friends of mine if anyone asks. She doesn't speak English, but she will feed you and give you ... erm, *logement* for a franc or two. Come back 'ere at two o'clock and I will take you to look at ze room; she lives in Montmartre.'

'How absolutely wonderful,' Charles said as they paid the bill and walked back to the main street.

155

Daniel agreed. 'Right in the heart of Montmartre. Couldn't be better. Let's just wander now, shall we?'

Charles looked at the map. 'It's nearly one o'clock, so we've only an hour to kill before we go back to the café.'

'And then a siesta,' Daniel declared, 'and I don't mind if it's a French or a Spanish one as long as I can lie down and sleep!'

Charles slapped Daniel on the shoulder. 'I'm having a most wonderful time and this is only our first day!'

'Me too,' Daniel said. 'I can't believe we're here, and so far from home.'

CHAPTER NINETEEN

The house François led them to was down a narrow alley at the bottom of the Montmartre hill. 'Look,' he said. 'You see the building work at ze top? That is to be the finest church in Paris. The Sacré-Coeur.'

The boys looked up and saw men working from wooden scaffolding around a white stone building that was nowhere near finished, but would eventually have the finest position overlooking the whole of Paris.

'It will be a basilica,' François explained. 'A Roman Catholic church. My *maman* will be so pleased when it is finished.' He crossed himself. 'If she should live so long.'

'That's a very steep climb,' Daniel commented. 'I hope she has 'strength for it.'

François laughed. 'She say that God will give her strength to get to ze top. But,' he went on, 'there are many who do not want it there and try to stop ze construction. Politics; always politics.'

Madame Boudin, a small thin woman with sharp features and piercing dark eyes, was dressed in black. François spoke to her and she waved her arms about, letting out a stream of voluble language that was quite incomprehensible to Daniel and Charles. He turned to them, smiling, and said, '*Ma mère* says that you are very welcome to stay in her humble home.'

'Did she really say that?' Daniel asked.

'*Non,* but she need ze money.' He shrugged. 'Then she will be pleased.'

They were shown upstairs to a small neat and clean room with two beds squashed into it with one chair; a washstand with a jug and bowl on the marble slab was pushed under a small window.

'This'll do me,' Daniel proclaimed, throwing his rucksack on the chair and himself on to a bed.

Charles gazed round, unused to such a small space. Then he lifted the lace curtain and looked out of the window. 'We're in the heart of Montmartre!'

He could see houses with low roofs, many with their window shutters closed for the afternoon, men trundling wheelbarrows along the cobbled alley, women hanging out washing on balconies filled with tubs and pots of plants that he couldn't name, bassinets with muslin draped over sleeping babes. If only I could paint, he thought. There is a whole world outside this window.

He turned to say as much to Daniel and smiled when he saw that his friend was already fast asleep. Charles lay down on the other bed, folded his arms across his chest and heaved a deep breath. Here, he thought, closing his eyes, was freedom.

Daniel woke first, the aroma of food tantalizing his taste buds. He blinked and for a moment couldn't recall where he was; he could still feel the motion of the ship but no longer felt exhausted or as if his stomach had been turned inside out. The soup at midday had revived him, as had the sleep.

The sun had dipped below the hill and there was but a dusky glow coming though the small window. How late was it? He sat up and leaned over to lift the curtain. On the other side of the narrow alleyway, shop and house windows were lit by gas and oil lamps and the street seemed to be coming to life; he could hear people talking, someone laughing and dogs barking. He heard Madame Boudin calling to someone, then footsteps on the stairs, and he realized that she was calling to them.

He got up and went to the bedroom door. Madame Boudin was standing outside with a steaming water jug. *'Bonjour, madame,'* he said haltingly, hoping that he had the right time of day, and thought of the young girls calling out 'good night' in the middle of the day.

'Bonsoir,' she said. *'De l'eau.'* She lifted the jug. *'Chaude.'*

'Merci.' He took the jug from her and felt the heat.

'Avez-vous faim?' She patted her middle and he remembered that the café owner at Le Havre had

said the same.

'Yes,' he said. *'Oui.* Very hungry.'

She indicated that they should go downstairs and again he thanked her, feeling pleased that he had been able to communicate with her.

Inside their room he poured half of the water into the bowl and stripped off his shirt and underwear and washed in the hot water, then put on clean clothes. 'Wake up, Charles,' he said. 'Supper's ready.'

'Mmm.' Charles rolled over, his eyes still closed. 'How do you know?'

'Oh, I've been having a little chat with Madame Boudin,' Daniel said airily. 'She said that we should go down.'

Charles opened one eye. 'And what did you say, *monsieur?'*

'I said we'd be down in two ticks. Here you are, I've saved you some hot water. *Eau,'* he said, grinning. *'Chaude.'*

'Excellent.' Charles sat up and unbuttoned his shirt. 'You have a charming accent. *Charmant!'* he added and ducked, but was still hit by the wet flannel that Daniel threw at him.

A large tureen of onion soup with a ladle so that they could help themselves sat in the middle of the kitchen table with bread rolls and a slab of butter on a wooden board. There was also a bottle of red wine without a label.

The soup was delicious, thick with onion and very filling. Madame Boudin cleared away and brought out a selection of cold meats, ham, chicken, sausage and terrine. *'Charcuterie,'* she said, and then produced another plate, this one

159

displaying various cheeses. She raised her hand and indicated that they should eat.

'I say,' Daniel murmured in an undertone. 'Do you think they always eat this kind of supper, or is this put on especially for us? And,' he added, 'can we afford it?'

'Not sure,' Charles said. 'I think it might be traditional. It's delicious, anyway.' He picked up the wine bottle. 'A glass of wine, old chap?' and poured two glasses.

'I don't mind if I do.' A grin escaped from Daniel's lips. 'This is a whole new world for me.'

'Well, I occasionally drink a glass of wine at home.' Charles took a sip and then drew in a breath. '*Whooo,* but not as potent as this.' He took another taste. 'I suspect this is a local brew.'

He saw Madame Boudin watching him and lifted his glass to her. She nodded and smiled and pointed her finger at her chest, indicating that she had made it.

'Golly,' he said. 'Go steady with it.' He smiled back at their hostess. 'It *is* home-made.'

Daniel too lifted his glass in a toast. 'It tastes like my ma's home-made bramble wine. That's pretty strong too; if you drink enough it can lay you out.'

François came in just as they finished eating and sat down at the table with them. He poured a glass of wine and his mother brought him a plate and he took a helping of bread and cheese and some of the meat.

'Would you like to see Montmartre by night?' he asked. 'It is my night off from the café and I can take you. We can climb to ze top of ze 'ill if you would like to.'

160

'Yes, please,' they both said.

'And, erm, girls? You want to meet girls?'

They looked at each other. 'Erm,' Charles shrugged and made a moue. 'Do you mean dancing girls or...' He left the question hanging in the air.

François glanced from one to another. 'You like girls, yes?'

'Yes,' Daniel said quickly, 'but we're not here to meet girls. We want to see Paris and all the sights.'

'And art,' Charles butted in. 'Galleries and such. Girls might be a distraction.'

François nodded, pursing his lips. 'They would. They are. I will show you Montmartre, which is separate from Paris; we don't pay Paris taxes here, you know. I'll show you where the artists live and then tomorrow in ze daylight you will find your way; tonight I will also show you dancing, and you may join in if you wish.'

He took them up the hill to view the scene below, and told them that when the Russians occupied Montmartre they'd used the hill for artillery bombardment. 'Montmartre means mountain of the martyr,' he told them. 'And his head, St Denis's head, they say is buried in ze hillside.'

It was not quite dark and they could see the whole of what was little more than a village on the edge of Paris. Lights shone from the buildings, the cafés and houses, and the street stalls selling their wares. Then they walked round the basilica, which was already being used as a church even though it was not yet finished and was not likely to be for several years.

'It seems as if we're looking at history in the making,' Charles remarked. 'Perhaps if we come

161

back in twenty years it might be finished.'

'It'll be another century,' Daniel responded. 'We'll be middle-aged men!'

'I'll be an *old* man,' François said. 'I'm almost thirty now.'

'You'll have children of our age,' Charles laughed.

'First I must catch me a wife,' François said ironically. 'Then I shall make my *maman* very 'appy.'

They walked down again into the streets and he took them through several dark alleyways, where he said the artists lived in near poverty, to a basement where they could hear music and people singing and clapping.

It was an airless room with tables and chairs surrounding a small dance floor where a number of athletic men were dancing in a group, kicking up their legs and turning somersaults, while the audience cheered them on and hooted blandishments. The music was coming from a piano, a tambourine, an accordion and a fiddle.

François went to a bar counter and brought back three glasses of wine, putting them down on an empty table. Charles took out his pocket book and offered François money to buy a bottle of wine, which the Frenchman took.

'I daren't drink much more,' Daniel said as they sat at the table, whilst François went again to the counter. 'I'm already well oiled with Madame Boudin's wine. I want to remember where I've been.'

'It's late already,' Charles murmured. 'I shouldn't think François would want to stay much longer if he's working tomorrow.'

François came back a few minutes later with a bottle of wine, another glass and a dark-haired girl of about twenty clinging to his arm. She was dressed in a white frilly dress with black stockings peeping beneath it. 'This is my sweetheart, Claudette,' he said, giving them a sly wink. 'She's going to dance for us in a minute.'

Charles and Daniel had both stood up as she approached. 'Mademoiselle,' they said in unison, giving a short bow.

'I thought you hadn't yet caught a wife,' Charles enquired, when François told them that Claudette couldn't understand or speak English.

'I haven't,' François said. 'She's not ze kind of girl to take home to your *mère*.'

Claudette looked questioningly at him and then at the two young men. Charles smiled at her and said softly, *'C'est une belle femme,'* and she blushed prettily.

'Did you say she was pretty?' Daniel leaned across the table. 'Cos she is, she's beautiful.'

François grinned and said something to her and she glanced coyly at Daniel and then kissed François's cheek. *'Je t'aime,'* she said softly, before moving away.

'She loves you,' Charles said. 'Do you not love her?'

'Of course.' François shrugged. 'But I can't marry her. She is a dancer, she can't cook or keep house or any of ze things that would be expected of her. I love ze wrong kind of girl.'

The music started again and a group of young women rushed to the central floor, shrieking and catcalling as they began to dance just as the men

163

had done, kicking up their legs and turning somersaults, all seemingly competing with the others. Some of the men in the audience put on their top hats and the dancers vied with each other to kick the hats off their heads. When they succeeded the men pressed a coin into their hands. François went to lean on the bar counter to watch.

'I can see why François can't take Claudette home to meet his mother.' Charles's voice was strained as he attempted to be heard above the noise. 'She's rather wild.'

Daniel nodded. The girls were dancing without restraint, and he had a sudden memory of his sister Dolly turning somersaults out in the paddock and not minding if her brothers saw her with her skirts over her head and showing her cotton drawers; but I wouldn't like to think she was doing that in front of strangers, he mused. Men will get 'wrong message. They'll think the women free in their ways even though there's nothing to see but black stockings and suspenders.

When the dancing was over, François returned to the table with a girl on each arm. Daniel and Charles stood up again. One girl was dark-haired, plump and vivacious and he introduced her as Nanette. Daniel could see that Charles was attracted to her black hair, olive skin and brown eyes, a complete opposite to his fair colouring.

The other girl was blue-eyed, fair-haired and slender, and smiling at Daniel. She whispered something to François. He laughed and shook his head.

'What?' Daniel said. 'What's funny?'

François shrugged. 'Chérie thinks you are very

'andsome. She asks, are you Italian?'

'What else did she say?'

'They ask, can they sit at your table?'

'Of course,' Charles said, pulling out another chair for Nanette. Daniel did the same for Chérie. She sat down and crossed one leg over the other, showing rather a lot of black stocking, but when Daniel sat down beside her she transferred herself neatly to his knee.

'I don't think you need an interpreter,' François smiled, 'so if you will excuse me I will go to find Claudette. I come back in a short time.'

Daniel found himself blushing as Chérie made herself comfortable and then scratched under his chin with her forefinger. She murmured playfully into his ear and he guessed that she might be commenting on his bristles. He hadn't shaved since he'd left home and was now quite bearded.

'It's getting very warm in here,' he told Charles over the top of Chérie's head. 'Do you think we ought to be leaving?'

'It might be a good time, for I have had an invitation to go upstairs and I think that is what your mademoiselle might be suggesting to you too. Do you want to?'

'Want to what – go upstairs? Do they mean–'

'I rather think so!' Charles laughed. 'And I'm not sure if I'm ready for love.'

'They're not suggesting love.' Daniel tipped Chérie off his knee and stood up. He gave a short bow and indicated that they were leaving. Chérie pouted and purred, patting his cheeks with her fingertips and pretending that she was heart-broken. He blew her a kiss and turned away. 'Are you coming?'

Charles was kissing Nanette on her cheek and she also was trying to persuade him to stay. 'It's a pity,' he murmured as he too turned away to leave. 'But yes.' He gave a sudden laugh as they walked out of the door and into the busy street. 'Oddly enough, my father warned me to watch out for seductive young women.'

'Did he?' Daniel was surprised. Charles's father seemed to be such a sobersides. Fletcher hadn't warned him away from women. He probably thought I could make up my own mind about them, and of course I can; and it isn't that I didn't find Chérie attractive. She was beautiful and no doubt experienced in the seduction of men, but he didn't want to go upstairs with her for the simple reason that he felt it would be a betrayal.

Chérie was fair-haired and blue-eyed and he guessed that if he could have understood her she would have been charming and witty, but when he looked at her he saw someone else, someone who had similar colouring, a wide smile and eyes that sparkled with humour, and was completely unattainable. Beatrice.

CHAPTER TWENTY

They became lost, but eventually found their way back to Madame Boudin's house. She was sitting on a stool outside her door, smoking a small clay pipe, with a glass of red wine on the ground beside her. Her neighbour was with her. They seemed to have had a pleasant evening for they were very convivial.

'*Bonsoir, mesdames,*' Charles greeted them, and Daniel followed suit.

Madame Boudin asked if they would like a glass of wine and Daniel suggested to Charles that they should accept, to be sociable. When she went inside to fetch the bottle and glasses they sat on the doorstep.

It was a dry mild night, the sky full of stars and the air smoky from fires; they could hear the low murmur of voices coming from some of the shops that were still open, and laughter from nearby taverns.

They were both silent until Charles said softly, 'I have no experience with young women. I don't really know many, except for the daughters of my parents' friends.' He hesitated. 'Tonight was the first time I have kissed a girl.' He turned to Daniel. 'What about you?'

'Onny lasses at school 'year afore I left, and really...' He laughed. 'They were 'ones who were doing 'kissing. I'd rather have kissed my hosses, to be honest, until...' It was Daniel's turn to pause. 'I didn't want to kiss anyone until I was seventeen, but then I'd have liked to.'

'So who was that? Whom did you want to kiss?'

'Mmm, nobody you'd know.'

'Someone living nearby?' Charles insisted.

'Yeh,' Daniel said. 'A farmer's daughter. But she wouldn't look at me.' Then he added, giving Charles a clue, 'She looks rather like Chérie.'

'Well, you can have your pick here, it seems.'

Charles didn't notice the lead. 'But I think I'd rather wait until someone special comes along.' He turned his head as Madame Boudin came back holding a bottle and two glasses and they both stood up again.

They sat for another half-hour, drinking wine, looking up at the stars and listening to the sounds around them, and then someone nearby began to play an accordion and their hostess and her neighbour started to sing, and although Daniel didn't understand the words, the plaintive elderly voices and the evocative music seemed wistful. A longing for something unattainable ran through it, reflecting Daniel's mood.

When the music and singing finished he turned and smiled at Madame Boudin, gently clapping his hands, and she patted the top of his head understandingly.

They said good night to the two women, and Daniel added *'Merci, madame'* to Madame Boudin, who nodded affectionately at him.

The next morning they ate a hearty breakfast of eggs and ham and drank strong coffee, and clutching their street maps they set off towards Paris and their day of culture and sightseeing. They headed down towards the Louvre and the Tuileries, but the Louvre wasn't open yet so they wandered off to look at the gardens.

Daniel read in the guide that the Tuileries had had a chequered history. The gardens had been designed in the sixteenth century and continued to be developed right up to the time of the French revolution, when Louis XVI was imprisoned in the

Tuileries Palace with his wife, Marie Antoinette, and their son. In the present century the Emperor Napoleon I carved up some of the land to make a new street and used the lawns for military parades, and following the Franco-Prussian War the Communards flew their red flag over the palace. When the army arrived to move them out, the Communards burned down the palace, leaving it in ruins, which was how it was now as Daniel and Charles stood gazing at it.

'They didn't want anyone else to use it and so they burned it to the ground,' Daniel said. 'Sacrilege, wouldn't you say?'

Charles agreed that it was. 'But it will be rebuilt eventually. The people will speak, surely? It's their garden now and open to everyone.'

They returned to the Louvre. Charles was excited to be visiting, Daniel less so; he had little knowledge of art but was prepared to be open-minded. He was astounded by the size of the building, and had thought it would be filled only with paintings; he hadn't expected to see displays of Greek, Etruscan and Roman antiquities in such good condition in their glass cases.

Charles was overawed by the collection of drawings and paintings and pointed out to Daniel a picture by the English artist, Reynolds, of a small fair-haired child depicting Innocence, and another of young ladies in a garden. Then: 'Look here, Daniel. That could be you. *Man with a Glove*. By Titian. There,' he said triumphantly. 'I always knew you were of Italian stock.'

'I don't think so.' Daniel stared hard at the portrait, which he admitted was very fine. 'He looks like a gentleman.'

'The eyes,' Charles said. 'His eyes are like yours. He is an aristocrat, it's true, or at least that's what it says in the catalogue, but it could be you!'

Daniel grinned and shook his head, and they moved on to look at other paintings until they came to da Vinci's portrait of the *Mona Lisa*. Charles was in raptures over her beauty. 'Look at how the artist has captured her stillness, her calm, and that soft sweet smile. She's the kind of woman I want to marry. I know now what I want to do with my life.'

And I know what I want to do with mine, Daniel thought as he followed Charles up and down the galleries. Or at least I know who I'd like to have in my life, but I also know it's impossible. Charles is wrong about that portrait of a man with a glove. He's nothing like me; he's not even like those schoolboys who came to Charles and Beatrice's party and thought they were such gentlemen, although they weren't. This man with a glove is cultured; he's got breeding. Charles has it too but doesn't know it, and I'll never have it. Not in a million years.

After several hours they became tired and hungry and Daniel eventually said, 'Enough! We'll never see everything in one day; it's so big, and I'm starving!'

'So am I,' Charles said. 'Let's go, but I'll come back one day.'

'We've onny one more day in Paris,' Daniel reminded him, 'and we must walk along 'Champs-Elysees to see Napoleon's arch. Then 'next day we're off to Switzerland and Beatrice.'

'Oh, Beatrice won't mind if we're a day or two late,' Charles said airily.

'She will,' Daniel contradicted him.

'Do you think you know my sister better than I do?'

'As well as,' Daniel answered back. 'I've known her as long as you and you know she'll be waiting for us.'

'You're right, of course,' Charles said gloomily, adding, 'but she won't begrudge us a few more days sightseeing in Paris, surely?'

'She will,' Daniel repeated with a grin. 'Don't underestimate her or you'll get 'sharp end of her tongue. She's waiting.' And besides, he thought, I can't wait to see her again.

CHAPTER TWENTY-ONE

Beatrice paced up and down her room. What was keeping them? She had been sure that they would be close behind her and already in Switzerland. But then she recalled that Charles had proposed that they might go to Paris first, and that, she decided, must be where they were. They wouldn't want to miss it, not two young men on their own.

It's not fair, she thought. Men have so much more freedom than women. She heaved an exasperated breath. But I'm going to change that. I have only one life and I'm not going to miss any opportunity just because I'm a woman. She opened the window, letting in a cool draught of mountain air, barely noticing the view of meadows and mountains and the blue of the sparkling River Aare below her, which she had come to know so well. Down on the left bank of the river, Interlaken would be warmer, but in this mountainside château the residents felt the effect of the snow still lingering on the peaks.

It was her own fault that she was waiting; there had been no need for her to be here. She had finished her course of deportment, the art of conversation, the appreciation of fine art and its history. Staying on hadn't been Beatrice's original intention, but on hearing that Charles and Daniel's plans were fact and not merely pipe dreams she had asked her parents if she might continue for another term. The academy principal, Madame Carpeoux, had been surprised but wasn't going to turn down the extra fee, and had written to say that Beatrice was very welcome to stay on and that any new young ladies would benefit from her accomplishments and experience.

She stopped her pacing and sat down on the easy chair by her window. One of the perquisites of being older than most of the pupils was that she now had a room of her own rather than having to share. To a certain extent she had more freedom, too, and this was what she was considering now.

I must try to stay calm and not be as hot-headed as I tend to be, she thought. If I'm to contemplate freedom then I must take into account that whatever I decide to do must not reflect badly on Madame Carpeoux or the academy.

She gave some consideration to the question of

how Charles and Daniel would come. Would they travel by rail from Darlingen and then by steamship on Lake Thun? Interlaken was situated between Lake Brienz to the east and Lake Thun to the west and was mostly German-speaking. It's no use worrying, she told herself. They'll come as and when they choose and I must be ready.

The bell rang for afternoon tea, and she paused at the top of the staircase to watch the chattering young women who had recently arrived hurrying down or hesitating as if unsure what to do or where to go.

One of the uncertain ones, a girl of about sixteen, looked about her as if searching for a companion and caught Beatrice's eye. *'Bonjour, mademoiselle,'* she said in halting French.

'Hello,' Beatrice replied. 'Have you just arrived?'

'Oh, yes.' The girl seemed to be relieved to be speaking English. 'Only today. I wasn't able to come for the start of term as my grandmother was ill and there was no one available to bring me earlier. My French isn't very good, I'm afraid.'

'It will get better,' Beatrice assured her. 'As will your German.'

'Oh, dear. I don't know any German.'

'I'm Beatrice Hart. What's your name?' Beatrice asked, leading the way down to the sitting room where tea was being served.

'Anne Percy. I'm very pleased to meet you, Miss Hart. Are you a tutor here?'

'No, no. My brother and cousin are travelling in Europe, so I decided to stay for another term and perhaps join them for a few excursions.'

They found a vacant table and sat down. Anne

Percy looked around nervously. 'I don't know anyone,' she said. 'Everyone will have paired off by now.'

'I'll introduce you,' Beatrice told her. 'And you may always come to me if there is anything you don't understand.'

Tea was served in the English style with a silver teapot, a milk jug and a sugar bowl; there was sliced lemon on a china plate, and a selection of small sandwiches, bread and butter and cakes.

'You see, just like at home,' Beatrice told her. 'Would you like to pour?'

'Oh! Mama does it at home.'

Beatrice smiled. 'But your mama isn't here now, so pretend that I'm your guest. Everyone takes it in turn to be hostess, to pour the tea and offer refreshment. It's all part of the tuition.' I'm astonished that they don't know how to do it, she thought. Mama taught me at an early age. We used to play that I was she and I rang the bell for afternoon tea and poured the tea and offered cake when it was brought.

'I've slopped it into the saucers,' Anne said in an anguished whisper.

'Then ring the bell,' Beatrice pointed to the little silver bell on the table, 'and ask for clean ones. You're not the only one; listen.'

Tinkling bells were being rung at several tables as flushed young faces turned towards the maids for assistance.

For a few days Beatrice cultivated Anne, becoming her mentor and introducing her to other young ladies, and then she approached Madame Carpeoux with a suggestion.

174

'My brother and cousin will be calling on me very shortly, as I mentioned, madame. They are travelling through Switzerland, and I would like to go into town and buy presents for them. Would it be possible, rather than having a *compagnon* from the teaching staff with me, for me to *chaperonner* a small group of young ladies into Interlaken? We could walk by the lake and perhaps take tea in one of the hotels or restaurants.'

'Excellent!' Madame Carpeoux enthused. 'You must insist that they speak French between themselves and to shopkeepers unless German is spoken.'

'I wasn't thinking of taking the young ladies shopping,' Beatrice said innocently. 'But yes, it would be excellent tuition for them,' she agreed, as if it hadn't been her idea all along.

'But you must take a maid, to carry parcels if nothing else. How many *mesdemoiselles* were you thinking of?'

'Four would be a good number and it would mean that they would also become better acquainted, *n'est-ce pas, madame?*'

'Indeed they would. Excellent! When would you like to go?'

'Tomorrow,' Beatrice said firmly.

The following day was sunny and warm, and after luncheon the little group stepped into the open-topped carriage for their journey down the hillside to Interlaken.

They alighted by Lake Thun and Beatrice gave instructions to the driver to collect them at a certain hotel at five o'clock. He fingered his top hat and drove away.

The town was full of visitors come to enjoy a cruise on the water and the view of the Jungfrau, visible from the lakeside; even in the warm weather it was still covered in pristine snow that glistened so brightly that some eyes had to be averted.

'Can it be climbed?' Anne Percy asked. 'It's very high.'

'It can be climbed, but we haven't the time today, mademoiselle,' Beatrice joked, adding, 'I understand that it was climbed for the first time about seventy years ago. Does anyone know what Jungfrau means?'

The young ladies shook their heads, but the maid Jeanne, whose English was limited, said, 'Maiden, mademoiselle.'

'Yes, *bravo*, Jeanne. Well done.' Then she added impishly, 'Or virgin,' and smiled as they all giggled and blushed.

She led them along the lakeside, where one or two young gentlemen strollers tipped their hats at the group of young ladies, and then she steered them towards the shops and hotels.

'I'm going to give you an hour to yourselves,' she said. 'You may look in the shops and purchase items if you wish. Keep together and do not speak to any gentlemen who might approach you. Jeanne will come with you and you must be back here by three o'clock. No later, do you understand?'

They were all eager for freedom and promised that they would be on time. They trotted off chattering animatedly, and when Beatrice had seen them on their way she entered the establishment that sold climbing equipment and outdoor wear.

She was greeted by a shop assistant and told him that she would like to look at walking boots and socks. She sat down on a stool and un-buttoned her boots.

'For yourself, Fräulein?'

'*Ja, bitte.*' She spoke little German, but enough to make herself understood, and told the assistant that she needed sturdy leather boots that were soft inside and several pairs of woollen socks, plus a rucksack. He looked at her curiously, as if this was an unusual request, and as she looked around she saw only gentlemen trying on boots. Surely, she thought, there are women who walk up the moun-tains even if they don't attempt the Jungfrau.

She said as much to the assistant, who assured her that they did sell outdoor clothing for ladies as well as men, and then added graciously, 'But not normally to such elegant young ladies as yourself.'

She smiled, realizing then that her time at the academy had not been wasted after all. She had grown up considerably since leaving home for her finishing education.

The boots and socks, together with the gloves that the assistant recommended, were wrapped and put inside the new grey rucksack, and then the assistant said, 'Ah! Fräulein, you must have a hat to keep your ears warm. When you climb the mountains the air is much colder than down in the valleys.'

'Of course,' she said, and, flirting a little, asked, 'What would you suggest?'

'For you, Fräulein, silver fox. I have just the thing.' He went to a shelf and lifted down a hatbox, opened it and gently took out the most beautiful fur hat. Beatrice took it from him, handling it carefully.

'Poor fox,' she murmured. 'It would have suited him better than me. I'm not sure if I would be comfortable wearing it.'

'If not you, Fräulein, then someone else will,' he said, adding softly, 'Herr Fox, regrettably, will not be needing it any more.'

She bought it and left the shop with her purchases, thanking the assistant. *'Danke schön,'* she said. *'Auf Wiedersehen.'* When she looked back, she saw him standing in the doorway watching her. She smiled and then set off in another direction. She had one more important call to make.

The young ladies, unused to such freedom, were exhilarated by the outing. Anne Percy had become friends with the other three, and poured the tea at the hotel where a table had been booked for them. They all thanked Beatrice for suggesting the occasion.

'Perhaps Madame Carpeoux will allow it again,' Beatrice said, 'since it has been such a success.'

Back at the academy she hid her purchases at the back of her small wardrobe, and after supper she excused herself and went to her room. She unfastened the hatbox and placed the hat on her head, admiring herself in the mirror before putting on socks and boots and walking up and down in them for a while. Well satisfied, she kept them and the hat on whilst she wrote a letter home.

Charles and Daniel have not yet arrived, she wrote.

I assume they are still in Paris, or on their way from there. I will probably ask Madame Carpeoux for one or two days without tuition so that I might enjoy some excursions with them when they get here. Perhaps we might take a steamer along the lake, or visit the foothills of the Jungfrau. I hear that mountain walking is very popular with ladies now and that the local shops are stocking up with suitable clothing. The weather is beautiful and it is such a shame to be inside. You know how much I enjoy the outdoors. I do miss Tilly; this is such lovely riding country.

She went on to ask how everyone was at home, and said how much she was looking forward to seeing Charles and catching up with news. Deliberately, she didn't mention Daniel for a second time.

They wouldn't understand, she reflected. Well, Mama might, but Papa wouldn't, and I don't want to worry them by saying that I can't wait to see him again.

CHAPTER TWENTY-TWO

Daniel and Charles stayed with Madame Boudin for another day, to accommodate Charles's desire for a second visit to the Louvre. Madame Boudin raised no objection; her son François said she seemed to have taken a liking to the two young English *messieurs*. 'She said you are perfect gentlemen.'

179

'There you are,' Charles grinned as he and Daniel set off sightseeing again. 'You're a gentleman after all.'

'She's lovely,' Daniel said. 'She reminds me of Granny Rosie.' He hitched up his rucksack. 'Mebbe I'm a gentleman of the road, or one of nature's gentlemen,' he joked. 'Not a born and bred one like you.'

They split up when nearing the Louvre, as Daniel wanted to walk along the Champs-Elysées again, preferring to be out in the fresh air.

He had read in his guide book that the Avenue was considered to be one of the most beautiful in the world. And as he strolled and admired the impressive houses, the horse chestnut trees and lovely gardens, he thought that whoever had said it must be right. At the statue of Napoleon Bonaparte he walked on towards the Elysée Palace, once the home of princes, counts and royal mistresses, and finally, at the very end of the Champs-Elysées, stood the monument he had been hoping to see, the magnificent Arc de Triomphe.

Open-topped carriages drawn by fine horses and carrying well-dressed visitors clip-clopped past him as he strolled, followed by a pair of white Arab mounts ridden by an elegant young couple, and Daniel sighed jealously. What I wouldn't give to be on horseback, riding such superb animals, with a certain lady friend by my side. Then he heard the thud of boots and turned to see a contingent of foot soldiers approaching. Following hard behind them came another detachment, marching alongside a gun carriage, and finally another smaller company of fusiliers pacing in time to a drummer.

I wish that Lenny and Joseph could be here to watch them, he mused, and that Maria and Dolly and little Lizzie could see 'young women in 'carriages with their pretty dresses and parasols. Wouldn't they just love them! He took out a notebook and pencil and scribbled notes of what he had seen to remind him to tell them when he returned home.

He met Charles at midday as arranged, and they went off to find something to eat. In one of the smaller streets they sat down at a table outside a café, ordered bread and cheese and coffee, and animatedly discussed the highlights of the morning.

'I've decided,' Charles said, 'that I'm going to apply to university to study art. I know I can't paint or draw, or at least not very well, but I'd like to appreciate what others do.'

Puzzled, Daniel said, 'But why do you need to study it? Surely you can appreciate art just by looking at it? You know what you like.'

'I do, that's true.' Charles took a bite of bread and chewed. 'But I'd also like to know what the paintings mean to the artist and why one is so different from another.'

'Ah,' Daniel said. 'You mean like 'difference between a pure Arab and a draught horse? Both are beautiful animals but they have different characteristics.'

'Mmm.' Charles paused to ponder. 'I suppose that's what I mean. But that's what I want to learn. Do the artists notice things that the average person doesn't?'

Daniel considered what he was saying. 'I saw a contingent of soldiers this morning. Would an artist see them differently from me? I thought how splendid they looked in their uniforms–'

'Exactly,' Charles enthused. 'Would an artist see them as if in training for war?'

Daniel nodded, and thought of the Arab horses ridden by the young couple. I imagined myself and Beatrice riding like that and I suppose if I were an artist that's what I would paint. But he didn't say so to Charles.

Energized by the food, they set off to visit the Notre-Dame cathedral and both were awed by its magnificence. They found the strength to climb almost four hundred steps of spiral staircase and agreed that the effort was worthwhile as they gazed over the whole of Paris from the top.

They packed their rucksacks that night, and after supper they sat outside Madame Boudin's house for the final time and gazed up at the stars. She came out presently, bringing them cups of strong black coffee and a plate of *pâtisserie*.

Daniel tried a rich chocolate tartlet filled with orange cream whilst Charles chose a vanilla and walnut one. Both licked their lips and gave a groan of delight.

'Madame,' Daniel murmured, 'we will never forget you!'

Charles translated and she patted them both on their shoulders. *'Bonne chance!'* she smiled, wishing them good luck.

Very early the next morning they caught the train from the Gare de Lyon for the long ride to Montreux where they would break their journey.

Madame Boudin had packed them a parcel of bread and cheese and ham and several pastries, for which they were very grateful. They were travelling third class, as Daniel insisted that they couldn't waste money on train travel when they would have an even longer journey in front of them after leaving Switzerland for Italy, or wherever else they might go in search of his grandfather.

There were no other English-speaking travellers in the carriage. Daniel unfastened his sleeping sack from the top of his rucksack and folded it into a large cushion to sit on, which made the wooden seats much more comfortable.

After half an hour of bumpy travel Charles did the same with his. 'What a brilliant idea of your mother's,' he said. 'She should go into business with these.'

Daniel took out his pack of Paris postcards and a pencil. 'I'll tell her. Are you going to write home and say where we are?'

'Mmm, shortly,' Charles gave a yawn. 'I'm so comfortable now that I might have a snooze. Why don't you do the same?'

'Not me,' Daniel replied. 'I don't want to miss 'scenery. I might not come again and I don't want to miss anything. Has Beatrice told you what it's like? Though I suppose she does 'journey so often she mebbe doesn't notice it any more.'

He couldn't believe that she might not bother to look out of the window as the train gathered speed after leaving the outskirts of Paris, but his reason for asking was that he wanted to mention her name. 'Will she be anxious about us, do you think? We're later than we said.'

'She won't be anxious,' Charles said sleepily. 'But she might be annoyed.'

I hope not, Daniel thought, smiling. Beatrice doesn't mince her words, although she's never sharp with me – or at least I haven't noticed.

They changed twice en route and it was dark by the time they crossed the border into Switzerland and reached Montreux. Stiff and tired, they were dismayed to discover that there weren't any trains to Interlaken until the next morning.

'However does Beatrice manage such a long journey?' Daniel said. 'And why does she come all this way at all? Surely there are suitable schools much nearer?'

'I don't know.' Charles was puzzled too. 'I don't think our parents can have realized how far it is. They're not very well travelled, you know. They generally take holidays in England; Father doesn't really like being away from home, and I think Mama perhaps gives in to him.'

The ticket office was closed and only a very elderly porter who didn't speak any English was on duty. Through sign language they conveyed to him that they needed a bed for the night; he raised both hands and shook them in a negative manner, then pointed in the general direction of what they thought might be the town. Then a fellow traveller called out 'Messieurs,' and he too pointed in the same direction.

They followed him out of the station and found themselves in a long street of houses and restaurants and a few hotels that on a swift glance they knew they couldn't possibly afford.

'It's a lovely night,' Daniel remarked, pausing in

his stride to glance at the dark shimmering water of the lake. 'I wouldn't mind sleeping out.'

'What? Are you serious?'

'Perfectly. Have you never slept outside?'

Charles shook his head. 'Can't say I have. Never had the need to, I suppose.'

'I've never had 'need to,' Daniel said, 'but I have slept out; 'first time I was onny a nipper and I asked my da if I could sleep in 'barn. He said no as it was just after harvest and I'd be sneezing all night, but then he fetched a couple o' blankets and two pillows and we both slept under my old tree in 'bottom meadow. Do you know 'one I mean?'

'Yes, yes I do, but I didn't know that you'd slept under it.' Charles gave a wry laugh. 'I couldn't imagine my father sleeping outside, not unless he brought out his feather bed.'

'I suppose Fletcher was humouring me that time, but I've slept out since, especially when it's been hot. Tonight would be perfect; there's not a breath o' wind and barely a ripple on 'lake and there's a new moon. What do you think?'

'All right, we'll give it a try, but just this once and only because we've got our sleeping sacks.'

Daniel searched about for a sheltered place and found a grassy area away from the hotels and close but not too close to the water; they could hear it lapping as it washed against the bank. He breathed in. 'Smell them pine trees. And there's something else, sweeter than pine, some kind of blossom mebbe. They're much further on weatherwise than we are. This'll do us fine.'

'If you're sure?' Charles peered about him. 'Difficult to see when the moon is over the water

185

and not the land, but I'm so tired I could sleep anywhere.'

Daniel climbed into his sleeping sack and then rummaged in his rucksack. 'I've got some food left from Madame Boudin. It's rather squashed but it'll taste fine.'

'So have I.'

They sat quite snug in their cocoons, eating the remains of their bread and cheese, gazing at the shimmering water and the outline of what looked like a castle with the dark mountains behind it. Then, sliding down into the sacks and pulling the hoods over their heads, they immediately fell asleep.

Daniel woke once and put his head out to look at the lake and the backdrop of snow-tipped Alps tinged with the rosy hue of dawn. 'It *is* a castle,' he mumbled, before turning over and falling asleep again. He was awakened what seemed only a short time later by Charles shaking him vigorously by the shoulder.

'Daniel!' he hissed. 'Wake up. Wake up!'

He grunted. 'What time is it?' Sleepily he propped himself up on one elbow to look about him. The brightness of the sky and the lake dazzled him and for a second or two he couldn't see; then in front of them he saw a group of people laughing and pointing. A horse-drawn carriage had slowed so that the occupants could look out and they were all looking at them, at him and Charles.

'What–' He looked at Charles, who had his hand over his mouth, his eyes creased with laughter.

'We're in a flowerbed,' Charles croaked. 'A municipal garden, by the look of it.'

Daniel looked about him. The grassy area he had found in the dark was actually a green lawn dotted with circular flowerbeds, statuary and fountains, and he and Charles had made their bed in the middle of it.

They were being observed by the morning traffic, riders, trades-people delivering their wares to the hotels and houses, pedestrians on their morning walk along the esplanade by the lake, some of them raising their hats or whips in greeting, others calling out, *'Guten Morgen'* or *'Bonjour'* or *'Buongiorno!'*

'Crikey,' Daniel said, struggling out of his sack. 'At least they don't know what nationality we are! We'd better get out of here before *'gendarmes* arrive. We might be committing an offence by sleeping out.'

'I hadn't thought of that.' Charles quickly climbed out of his sack too. 'What a good thing we slept in our clothes. That could have been serious. Come on – we'd better be quick or we might miss our train.'

'It's a pity,' Daniel said as they hopped over a low wall and headed back towards the train station. 'It would have been nice to stroll by the lake. That was a castle we saw last night – did you see? But I suppose we'd better be moving on. Isn't it hot for so early in the morning? And yet there's still snow on top of 'mountains.'

'It must be very cold up there. You know, we could walk up a mountain when we get to Beatrice's place. She's within sight of the Jungfrau. Wouldn't that be splendid?'

'I reckon it would be a miracle,' Daniel said

drily. 'Do you know how high 'Jungfrau is?'

'No, do you?'

'No, I don't,' Daniel answered. 'But I do know that you've to climb up other mountains to reach its base, so I think we'll wait for some other time. Or, better still, until a railway has been built to 'top.'

Charles sighed. 'You have no sense of adventure.'

CHAPTER TWENTY-THREE

It was two days before they finally boarded the steamship on Lake Thun. They had travelled by train from Montreux to Bern, where they spent a day, and from there, with several changes in between, they reached Darlingen and the last lap of their journey. They had again slept out under the stars, this time making sure they were not in a public place.

They were enraptured by the towering Alps of the Jungfrau region and the fresh clean mountain air, and even Daniel wasn't sick on the steamship as they crossed the tranquil waters of Thun.

Night was descending by the time they reached Interlaken. When they enquired as to the whereabouts of the academy, they were told that it was too far to walk as they would get lost in the dark, not to mention risk falling over the edge of the steep and winding road.

'I can't sleep out another night,' Charles groaned. 'Shall we try to find an *auberge*, or perhaps hire a carriage? It surely won't cost very much.'

Daniel too was tired, but he said, 'Will anyone drive us in the dark if it's a bad road? And besides, we might not be allowed to stay overnight. It's a school for young ladies, isn't it?'

Charles groaned again. 'Surely? I'm Bea's brother, after all, and you're – well, practically a brother, aren't you?'

'Let's ask if anyone will drive us there first, and then we'll cross 'problem of accommodation when we get to it.'

Some of the shops were already closing their shutters for the night, but by good fortune they found a chandler's shop still open and the owner spoke a little English.

'No carriage,' he said. 'Only a *Fuhrwerk* – er – horse and cart.'

'That's fine,' Daniel said quickly, knowing that he'd be more comfortable in a horse-drawn cart than a carriage. 'Can you drive us there, and how much will it cost?'

The chandler nodded and grinned. *'Nichts.* No charge.' He indicated that they should wait, locked his shop door and strode off round a corner.

They sat down on his doorstep. 'That's a bit of luck,' Daniel said, 'but I think we should pay him something.'

'I agree, but we might offend him by offering.'

The chandler came back in about ten minutes and their spirits dropped when they saw not a horse but a donkey pulling a rickety wooden cart.

'Erm, is he strong enough to pull the three of us?' Charles asked hesitantly.

189

'Oh, *ja*. He is strong as *ein* – what you say?'

'As an ox?' Daniel offered.

'*Ja, ein Ochs*. But he is a – erm – *ein Maultier*.'

'A mule!' Daniel said triumphantly. 'I'm really getting to grips wi' this language!'

'Why's that, do you think?' Charles asked as they stowed their rucksacks in the back of the cart.

'It sounds a bit like English – you know, slightly guttural, from 'back of 'throat, not like French from up your nose!'

The mule didn't want to go out, that was quite obvious from his stance and the noise he was making, a mixture of neighing and braying with his feet firmly locked on the ground. The chandler cracked his whip and shouted to no avail, and after a few minutes Daniel jumped out of the cart, took hold of the snaffle and spoke gently to the animal, who then walked meekly on.

'*Bravo*,' the muleteer applauded.

'How did you do that?' Charles asked, when Daniel climbed back into the cart.

'He's part hoss, isn't he, and they respond to firmness. He was jumpy, probably because he didn't know us, so I just told him that I was 'boss.'

'I think you're kidding me,' Charles laughed. 'But at least we're moving at a fair pace now.'

The fair pace slackened when they left the valley and the road became steeper, but when they glanced back they saw they had already climbed a considerable distance from the town, which now lay in shadow with only the lights glinting from windows showing that it was there.

'Do you know this place, the academy, *monsieur*? Erm, *mein Herr?*' Charles asked the driver.

'Have you been before?'

'*Ja,* I know it. I go sometimes to deliver, or to drive ze *mesdemoiselles.* But not in this cart.' He laughed. 'In ze carriage.'

'That's a relief,' Charles murmured to Daniel, sinking back into his seat, 'because I noticed a couple of side roads back there and I wondered if he really knew the way.'

Daniel grinned. 'And you were afraid we were going to have to spend 'night on 'mountainside.'

It was now totally dark apart from the silvery moon and countless stars that only served to make the blackness even more impenetrable. They travelled on in silence, broken only by the wheezing of the mule, the clatter of the cart and the muted whistling of their driver. Charles was wondering whether they would be able to get a bed for the night, and Daniel how Beatrice would react to their late arrival. It's not so late, he thought, it's only that it seems to be because it's so dark. I hope she's pleased to see us, and not annoyed that we've taken so long to get here.

'Soon we come,' their driver said after another fifteen minutes and a long haul round several bends in the road. 'Five minutes only.'

There was nothing ahead to indicate any kind of dwelling place, but the mule brayed and seemed to pick up his feet; they turned another bend and ahead of them were several lighted windows that by their position suggested a large establishment.

The driver steered the animal to the front of the wooden building, which they now saw had three storeys, with short stubby chimneys rising from the low-hanging roof.

'Oh, this is nice,' Daniel said, climbing down and retrieving his things as their driver rang a bell at the side of the solid wood door. 'I hope they let us stay.'

A young woman wearing a dirndl skirt and a white blouse with puffed sleeves under a striped apron opened the door, and was nodding her head as Daniel and Charles approached. The driver turned to them. 'You are expected, yes?'

'We don't – erm, yes, probably.' Charles smiled at the young maid, who dipped her knee.

'Mademoiselle Beatrice, she say you come,' she said. 'I will fetch her.'

'Sir,' Daniel said to their driver, 'please, will you let us pay something? We have some money.'

'*Nein,*' he replied. 'Ze academy, they give me custom. It is enough.' He winked. 'It is a *gut* turn, *ja?*'

'It is,' Daniel agreed. 'Thank you. *Danke schön. Merci.*' He didn't know which language to use and as his command of any was limited he thought he would use the only words he knew.

The driver patted his shoulder, wished him good luck and climbed back on to his cart, and Daniel thought that if they couldn't stay here they were in for a sleepless night, for it was bitterly cold.

Charles was already inside, so he followed him, and a minute later Beatrice was rushing down the stairs, her skirts flying. She launched herself into her brother's arms, and then into Daniel's.

He was almost overcome as he held her, and she whispered in his ear, 'You're my cousin, Daniel, if anyone should ask. That's what I've told them.'

'All right,' he croaked, and thought that this

192

might be the only time he would ever feel her in his arms.

'How wonderful to see you both,' she said, and her cheeks were flushed and her eyes bright as she took a hand of each. 'We'll go into the common room; there won't be anyone in there at this time.'

She was speaking quickly and excitedly, not at all in her usual manner. Then she addressed the maid. 'Thank you, Jeanne. Will you go to the kitchen and ask Cook if she can rustle up some supper for my brother and our cousin? Perhaps some soup, and some of that sausage and potato dish she makes?'

She led them into a room off the hall, which was furnished with comfortable sofas and shelves of books and a bright fire burning in a stove.

'Oh!' She flopped on to a chair. 'I've been waiting and waiting for you. I thought you were never coming!'

'It's a long way,' Charles protested. 'I had no idea that you had to come so far. Do our parents know how long it takes to get here?'

'No,' she said, 'I don't suppose so. But it takes me less time than it has taken you, as I don't linger in Paris!'

How brave and clever she is, Daniel thought, gazing at her. She was calmer now, her excitement on greeting them abating, and she smiled at them both.

'I'm so pleased to see you,' she said. 'I asked Madame Carpeoux if you might have a room when you arrived and she said that you could.'

'Oh, how very kind of her,' Charles said. 'We thought we might have to sleep out again.'

Beatrice raised her eyebrows. 'Sleep out?'

They explained what had happened in Montreux and she laughed. 'The Swiss wouldn't want you making the town look untidy. It will be ready for the tourist season.'

'Shall we be able to meet Madame Carpeoux?' Daniel asked. 'To thank her?'

Beatrice hesitated. 'She isn't here at present. She's gone to visit a sick relative and won't be back for a few days, but the housekeeper was aware that you were coming. There's a room ready for you. It's kept for parents who might come to see their daughters.'

'You've never mentioned that before,' Charles quizzed her.

Beatrice smiled. 'I haven't, have I?'

She seems tense, Daniel thought. What is she up to?

'What's going on, Beatrice?' Charles voiced Daniel's question.

'I don't know what you mean,' she answered.

'Yes, you do. Don't think I can't read you,' Charles said.

'I don't know what you're talking about.'

Jeanne knocked and entered, carrying a laden tray, and Daniel got to his feet to take it from her and place it on a table. 'Thank you,' he said. 'Thank you very much,' and the maid beamed, dipped her knee and left.

'You've made a conquest there, Daniel,' Beatrice remarked lazily. 'Jeanne doesn't often get the chance of seeing handsome young men.'

'She didn't smile at me,' Charles complained.

'That's because you didn't say thank you.' Beatrice set out the dishes of soup, bread and pie. 'Daniel is always polite, no matter who he's talking to.'

Daniel opened his mouth to say something, but then thought better of it. I should know by now that these two have a special banter going on between them that no one else can understand, he told himself.

After they had eaten, Beatrice showed them to their room on the ground floor; it had two beds with a blanket on each, washstand with a jug and basin, and a separate cubicle with a flush lavatory.

'It's quite basic, I'm afraid,' Beatrice said, prowling about. 'But it's only for one night before we move on, isn't it?'

'*We?*' Charles said. 'Are you going to show us the area? We thought we might like to see the Jungfrau, if you're allowed the time off.'

'Of course I'm allowed,' she said. 'I've special privileges. I didn't have to come back, you know.'

'So why did you, Beatrice?' Daniel asked quietly.

'Because you two were coming,' she said. 'I knew Papa wouldn't allow me to come back once I'd left the academy and I wanted to meet you here. So that – so that I could spend some time with you,' she finished lamely.

Charles yawned. 'Let's talk in the morning. I'm dead tired. What time should we be up?'

'About eight o'clock.' She stood. 'I'll give you a knock, shall I?'

Daniel opened the door for her. 'Thanks, Beatrice, for arranging for us to stay.' He hesitated. 'It's really good to see you again.'

She moistened her lips. 'You too, Daniel,' she

said softly. 'Good night.'

The two young men undressed and fell into their beds. Charles was asleep immediately, but Daniel tossed and turned, his senses churning at seeing Beatrice again. I think that after this journey it'll be as well for my own peace of mind if I don't see her too often, he decided. Before long she'll be married off to some toffee-nosed arrogant aristocrat who'll be given short shrift if he doesn't do what's expected of him. She'll make his life a misery, and quite right too, the pretentious conceited braggart.

For some time he considered what he would do to this unknown contender for Beatrice's affections if he should fail her, but at last he fell dead asleep, only to be awakened by someone knocking softly on the door. He put his bare feet to the floor, and wrapping a blanket around himself he staggered to the door and opened it.

Beatrice was outside with a tray in her hands. They stared at each other, lips apart. 'I've brought you breakfast.' A flush spread over her cheeks and she thrust the tray towards him.

Tentatively he put out one hand, but then he realized that he couldn't take the tray without revealing his nakedness beneath the blanket.

'I'll – I'll put it down here.' She averted her eyes and bent down to place it on the floor, and saw his bare feet, his straight toes and ankles. 'I'll – I'll come back in ten minutes,' she said, and hurried away.

Charles grunted and leaned up on one elbow. 'Who was that?'

'Beatrice.' Daniel hastily slipped into his trousers

196

and shirt and went back to fetch the tray. 'She's brought us breakfast.'

'Bea has? Incredible.'

'She's coming back in ten minutes. We'll have to get washed and dressed before then.'

'She's seen me in my underwear plenty of times. Mmm, coffee and muffins. Wonderful.'

'Not me she hasn't,' Daniel disputed sharply. 'And it won't do if she's found in here when we're in a state of undress, brother and cousin or not.'

'Oh, all right, grumpy,' Charles said, taking a sip of coffee. 'But I'm going to partake of this fine breakfast first.'

When Beatrice knocked again some fifteen minutes later, they were both washed and shaved and dressed with their rucksacks repacked.

'Are we ready for off?' Charles asked, for Beatrice too was dressed for walking in a short coat, a plain skirt, a fur hat and sturdy boots.

'Yes,' she said, 'and there's a trap waiting outside to take us down the valley. You did say you wanted to see the Jungfrau?'

'Oh, yes!' Daniel said enthusiastically. 'Charles is going to walk up to 'summit.'

'Do you know how high it is?' Beatrice said incredulously.

'Oh, come on!' Charles picked up his rucksack and Daniel grinned and ushered Beatrice forward. She too picked up a rucksack from where she had left it outside their door and Daniel took it from her.

'This is heavy, Beatrice. There must be more than enough here to last the day.'

She didn't answer him but led the way outside.

Jeanne was waiting by the door and said, 'Good-bye, Miss Beatrice.'

Beatrice kissed her on the cheek. *'Auf Wieder-sehen*, Jeanne. Thank you.'

Puzzled, Daniel followed her to the waiting open-top chaise where Charles was talking to the driver, the chandler who had brought them the evening before. He turned and took their bags and Beatrice got in. There was just room for the three of them on the one seat.

Beatrice turned to look back and wave to Jeanne, who was still standing by the door.

'Why is she seeing you off?' Charles asked. 'Does she always do that?'

'No.' Beatrice lowered her head and smoothed out her skirt. 'Only when saying goodbye.'

Daniel looked at her, taking in her sturdy boots, her fur hat and the sensible coat. 'Beatrice?'

She looked squarely at him and then at her brother and then faced straight ahead, breathing in a deep breath. 'Didn't I say? I'm coming with you. You don't mind, do you?'

CHAPTER TWENTY-FOUR

'Honestly?' Daniel was astonished and elated. 'You're coming with us? You mean to 'Jungfrau, or,' he could hardly dare to hope, 'to Italy?'

'Beatrice!' Charles, shocked, looked at his sister. 'What do you mean, you're coming with us?'

'What I said; Daniel won't mind. Will you, Daniel?' Her voice dropped a little as if she had over-stepped the protocol expected of the uninvited.

'Of course I won't.'

'But...' Charles began, and Daniel prepared himself to defend Beatrice against any objection that Charles might raise.

'...what will Father say? He'll be furious!'

'Only with me,' Beatrice argued. 'And I've written – at least I've written to Madame Car-peoux, and she's sure to write home for con-firmation, so they'll know.'

Charles huffed out a breath. 'I'm quite happy for you to come if Daniel is, but I'm thinking of you, Beatrice. What will people say?'

'Which people?' Daniel broke in. 'We don't know any people, and if we did, what has it to do with anybody else?'

Beatrice smiled gratefully at him. 'I know what Charles means, though, Daniel,' she said. 'It's because I'm female and travelling with two men without a chaperon. People might consider it indecorous, and that's why I described you as my cousin.' She gave a little laugh. 'No one would believe that you were my brother.'

'Of course they wouldn't,' he said. 'You're so very fair, fairer even than Charles.'

'Yes, yes,' Charles said testily, 'but nevertheless–'

'You sound just like Papa!' Beatrice told him. 'I never thought you would be so very proper. Women are travelling all over Europe without an escort and I don't see why I shouldn't too if I want to, and I do,' she added petulantly. 'And be-sides, if Daniel doesn't mind, and it is his journey after all, then I don't see why you should object.'

'I don't think Charles is objecting, Beatrice,' Daniel said mildly. 'He's onny thinking of 'consequences.'

'You see?' Charles said grumpily. 'Daniel understands.'

They were heading down the narrow twisting road and the driver was slowing on the sharp bends. He spoke to Beatrice, far too quickly for either Daniel or Charles to understand.

'He says that he'll take us to his premises. I have some things to collect that he's been storing for me.'

'What things?' Charles asked. 'I hope you're not bringing a sack of fripperies. We've to carry everything on our backs, you realize?'

'Of course.' Beatrice turned up her nose. 'I am prepared, but I wanted to make a suggestion. You must say if you don't agree.'

'We will, don't think that we won't,' Charles retorted, but Daniel said nothing. He was just happy that Beatrice was going to travel with them.

When they reached the town the chandler pulled into a stable yard at the back of his shop and they jumped down and unloaded their belongings. Beatrice followed the chandler into his premises by the back door.

'She's been here before,' Charles commented. 'I'm a bit bothered, Daniel. Beatrice is used to comfort; what if we have to sleep out under the stars as we did before?' He ran his hands through his hair. 'Father would be horrified.'

'Then don't tell him,' Daniel said. 'He'll assume we've stayed in lodgings, which we will be doing most of the time. It's not as if you'd be lying;

you'd be protecting him from a truth he wouldn't like, but which isn't doing any harm.'

Beatrice came out again and waved from the doorway. 'Will you come in?' she called. 'Henri has an idea for us, and there's coffee and cake too.'

'We're being softened up,' Charles muttered, and Daniel laughed. It was going to be unpredictable and fun with Beatrice travelling with them.

They were led into a small room behind the shop where the chandler's wife had set out a pot of coffee and a delicious-looking cake. She chattered to Beatrice as if she knew her well. The chandler was attending to someone in the shop but came in and sat down at the table with them as they drank their coffee.

'I know Henri and his wife fairly well,' Beatrice explained. 'I've often borrowed a mount from him to ride along the lakeside.'

'Alone?' Charles questioned.

'Sometimes,' she said. 'Or sometimes with a companion. Madame Carpeoux hasn't objected. She knows I'm proficient.' She paused. 'And the last time I was here, I told Henri that you were coming and that we were all travelling into Italy. That's why he was happy to drive you up to the academy last night.'

Charles sat back and folded his arms with a resigned sigh, and Daniel hid a smile. It seemed that Beatrice had been planning for some time.

'He asked how we were travelling and said it was quite expensive to take a carriage, for there isn't yet a train from here that goes through the mountains. Obviously it's much too far to walk, so he said why didn't we go on horseback.'

Daniel leaned forward and clasped his hands together. 'That'd be marvellous,' he said. 'But 'cost of hiring would be far too much.'

'Ah, well. Let me explain. Henri has three mountain ponies, Haflingers, that he's been hiring out to the summer tourists, and he was planning on selling them and buying others. They would be perfect for going over the mountains,' she said eagerly. 'And we could sell them ourselves when we were ready to go home.'

Reluctantly Daniel shook his head. Much as he would like to, he could not afford to buy a horse. He couldn't even consider it.

'Haflinger?' Charles said. 'Never heard of them.'

'They're from the Tyrol originally,' Beatrice told him. 'I've ridden one of Henri's and they're very steady and good-natured–'

'I'm sorry, Beatrice,' Daniel interrupted, 'but I can't possibly. I haven't got that kind of money.' And there, he thought, is the great difference between us. Beatrice and Charles don't have to think twice about 'cost; we're a world apart.

'Let's take a look at them.' Charles rose from the table. 'I've got an idea, even though I haven't ridden a pony since I was twelve.'

Somewhat reluctantly Daniel followed Beatrice and Charles and Henri back outside. He'd been so eager to travel, but it seemed now that without money it wasn't possible. Unbidden came the thought that perhaps he should have come alone on this journey, sleeping out under the stars and going at his own speed, tramping on foot and resting when he was tired, eating when he was hungry.

Henri brought out one of the ponies, a mare,

and walked her towards Beatrice. She was a light chestnut with a flaxen mane and tail and a star on her nose, and Daniel heaved a breath at the sight of her. Then the next one was brought out, again a chestnut, with a strong back and a flowing mane and a blaze down his nose, and finally the third, small but powerfully built and handsome, with two white socks on his forelegs.

Daniel breathed out; they were beautiful and he could see by their strong sloping shoulders that there was a strain of Arab in them.

'They're a family,' Beatrice said. 'Mother and two sons, and I suspect that's why they haven't been sold before. Henri is sentimental and doesn't want to split them up.'

'Can I try?' Charles asked. 'They're very handsome, but rather smaller than anything I've ridden in a long time.'

'But sturdy,' Daniel commented. 'They'd carry your weight and more.' But again he shook his head; this wasn't an option for him. 'I'm sorry, it's a grand idea, but–'

'Hang on a minute,' Charles said. 'You haven't heard my suggestion. Beatrice is quite right. It would be quicker and more practical to ride, especially as we're all competent riders, and,' he added swiftly as Daniel opened his mouth to speak, 'what neither of you know is that Father was so concerned that Daniel and I were only bringing a small amount of money with us that he insisted on giving me a banker's draft to be cashed in case of emergency.'

'This isn't an emergency,' Daniel protested. 'It's a convenience.'

'Exactly!' Charles said triumphantly. 'So what I suggest is that we use some of the money to buy the ponies and then at the end of the journey we sell them and put the money back. Can you see anything wrong with that idea, Daniel?'

And try as he might, Daniel couldn't. Finally he shook his head and nodded in acceptance.

They broke out in wreaths of smiles. They all had a love of horses and were skilled and experienced, Daniel probably more so than the twins, and how much more satisfying, they agreed, than travelling on foot or train.

Charles and Beatrice discussed the price with Henri and he suggested that for an extra fifty francs they might also buy one of his donkeys to carry their luggage.

'Oh, yes,' Beatrice broke in enthusiastically. 'And then we'll be just like Robert Louis Stevenson in *Travels in the Cévennes!*'

Daniel looked bemused and Charles said, 'the poet?'

'Yes,' Beatrice laughed. 'He went on a hiking holiday in France and bought a donkey to carry his sleeping sack and other baggage. The donkey, Modestine, was very stubborn and would only go at her own pace or not at all. He wrote a book about it and we read it last year at the academy.'

'And you're suggesting that we take one?' Daniel said humorously. 'Is that a good idea?'

Henri said that all of his donkeys were very obedient and placid and would be no trouble at all, and on the strength of that, Beatrice went off to a local shop and bought herself a small tent to sleep in. This, with the tent poles and sleeping sacks, was loaded on the donkey, who Beatrice insisted should be called Modesty, a name similar to that chosen by the poet.

The price agreed included bridles and saddles and Henri gave them used but serviceable rugs for the horses in case the nights were cold; and then they were ready and it was almost midday.

They decided to take Henri's advice and follow the well-travelled route towards the Jungfrau to get the feel of the ponies, and after that head towards the town of Brig-Glis where they could find accommodation before travelling over the Simplon Pass into Italy.

As they neared the high Alps Daniel felt that he was entering another world; above them was ice and snow, beneath them flower-strewn meadows, and around them air so sweet and clean and crisp that he could taste it. He filled his lungs and felt rejuvenated. He glanced at Beatrice, who was riding alongside, and smiled at her. Her long fair plaits hung beneath a wool hat covering her ears, her cheeks were flushed, her skin was gold and rose and her eyes were bright as she turned towards him. She too looked other-worldly, he thought, a goddess from another sphere, ethereal and yet strong as she sat, not sidesaddle, but astride in her divided skirt, flesh and blood, living and breathing.

'What do you think, Daniel?' she asked softly. 'Isn't it beautiful?'

I love you. His lips didn't move as he breathed the words. He swallowed. 'Yes,' he murmured. 'So very beautiful.'

205

CHAPTER TWENTY-FIVE

The Humber rippled beneath a bright sky. Harriet pinned up a line of washing that flapped in a gusty breeze, then gazed down the hillside towards the estuary and wondered where her eldest son was now. She'd received postcards from Rouen and Paris and a place she had difficulty pronouncing, when Daniel had crossed the border into Switzerland. She was thrilled for him. Her nervousness over his travelling such a long way had dissipated since the first postcard had arrived, telling her with great enthusiasm what he and Charles had seen and done, and now she eagerly awaited others as he continued on his journey.

Fletcher said all along that he'd be fine, she reflected, and of course he was right. What a wonderful adventure. I can hardly believe that a son of mine – there, she thought, I'm doing it again. Why shouldn't a son of mine do anything he wants to do?

It was his unknown grandfather that had excited Daniel's curiosity, and Granny Rosie had encouraged him, Harriet thought, because she wanted to know what had happened to Noah's father.

Maria called her from the back door. 'Ma, I think this cake is done. Do you want to check it?'

'Smells good.' Harriet carefully opened the oven door. She took out the fruitcake that Maria had made and placed it on the table, and then pierced the top with a fine skewer. 'Perfect,' she said, pulling the skewer out clean and dry. 'This is a recipe that your Granny Tuke showed me. It's quite easy to make and keeps well in a tin.'

Harriet always took care to give praise where praise was due, and it was true that Ellen Tuke had taught her a great deal about baking and house-wifery, as well as teaching her to milk cows and keep poultry and other things that every country wife needed to know, and of which she had been completely ignorant when she married Noah. But Ellen's bitterness and resentment had soured any kind of relationship she might have had, not only with Harriet, but with her and Fletcher's children too.

'There's somebody coming.' Maria lifted her head to look out of the kitchen window, and they both heard the clatter of wheels and hooves on the cobbles in the yard.

'It's Mrs Hart,' Maria said, 'driving her trap. Are you expecting her?'

'No, but she knows she's always welcome to drop in at any time. There are no calling cards expected here.'

Maria laughed. Mrs Topham had always ex-pected a note or a card before receiving a visitor, and would not have liked anyone to call without being forewarned. But her mother hadn't been brought up in that way and welcomed anyone who came.

'I apologize for calling without notice!' Mrs Hart exclaimed, entering through the back door, which Harriet was holding open for her. 'Is this your kitchen? Have I come in the wrong way? Oh,

207

but it's lovely – so inviting, and such a glorious smell of baking.' She unbuttoned the collar of her coat. 'What a good thing it's you, Harriet,' she murmured. 'I would be ostracized if I had done this to anyone else. They would think I was out of my senses.'

She did seem to be out of her senses, Harriet thought, taut and anxious and insisting that she didn't want to be a nuisance.

'Maria, would you put a match to 'sitting room fire, there's a love. Mrs Hart and I will sit in there.' Harriet was proud of her neat and cosy sitting room, where she sometimes did her mending or sat peacefully with Fletcher if everyone else was busy at the kitchen table.

'I don't want to be a nuisance,' Mrs Hart repeated.

Maria assured her that it wasn't a bother, and asked if she would take a pot of tea or coffee. Her time at Mrs Topham's had taught her the gracious art of receiving visitors and guests and she knew how to behave.

The fire soon flickered into life and Harriet invited Melissa to take a seat whilst Maria was making coffee.

'This is nice, Harriet. Is this your own room, as my sitting room is mine?'

'Mainly it is,' Harriet said. 'But all 'family are welcome in here. Sometimes if 'bairns want a quiet chat they'll come in to talk to me or to Fletcher. 'Kitchen is a hubbub of activity when we're all in. You seem a little on edge, ma'am,' she ventured. 'Has something happened to upset you?'

'How intuitive you are, Harriet.' Melissa folded

her hands on her lap. 'Do you miss Daniel?' she asked suddenly.

'Oh, yes, I do. All 'time,' Harriet said. 'I expect you're just 'same with Charles and Miss Beatrice, and all your children, o' course,' she added, remembering that Stephen and George were away at school until the summer holidays.

'And have you heard from Daniel recently?' Melissa leaned forward as if eager for information.

'Not for a couple of weeks; they'd crossed into Switzerland by then.' Harriet chuckled. 'He told me about them sleeping out by 'side of 'lake. That was funny, wasn't it?'

Melissa hadn't heard of the escapade, so Harriet laughingly told her of the night in a public garden. 'Charles wouldn't tell us that,' Melissa sighed. 'He would think that his father would be shocked. Which he might have been, or anxious, anyway, that they might have got into trouble, whereas I think it quite hilarious.' She didn't laugh, though, and paused for a moment before adding, 'Except that I'm anxious, Harriet.'

Harriet clasped her hands tightly together. 'About– What about?'

'Yesterday I received a letter from Madame Carpeoux, the principal of Beatrice's academy. She informs me that Beatrice has left the academy and has gone travelling with her brother Charles and their *cousin.*'

Harriet was astonished. 'And Beatrice didn't tell you?'

Melissa shook her head. 'I dare say she will write and explain, but she wouldn't tell us of her intentions beforehand as she'd think that her father would forbid it.'

'She'll be perfectly safe with Charles and Daniel,' Harriet assured her, 'but I wonder why 'headmistress thought that Daniel was their cousin?'

'Because Beatrice will have told her so,' Melissa said wryly. 'It would be considered unacceptable for her to travel with a young man who wasn't related. Beatrice would have been aware of that, the minx.' She gave a grim sigh. 'I know my daughter better than she thinks.'

They both sat silently until Maria brought in a tray with the coffee pot, and Harriet gave a quiet smile as she saw that she had also brought out the best crockery and a plate of shortbread biscuits.

'I haven't yet told my husband,' Melissa admitted. 'I don't want to worry him as he's going through an anxious time. Our bailiff has told him that he would like to leave his position as soon as there is someone to replace him. He's not in good health and doesn't feel that he can continue for much longer. It's a blow to Christopher, as he relies on him totally, and...' She paused. 'Well, if I may confide in you, Harriet, my husband cannot cope with anything more. If only our sons were older, they'd be able to take over some of the tasks on the estate. But that's foolish talk, for they're not, so that's that.'

'I'm so sorry,' Harriet said. 'Can we help in any way? I'm sure Fletcher would be glad to...' Her voice trailed away. Melissa might not want Fletcher at Hart Holme Manor. Although they had never spoken openly of the tangled relationship between Fletcher's mother and Christopher

Hart, it was there like a festering sore.

'That's very kind of you.' Melissa drew herself up straight. 'I will remember your generous offer if we should need it. But what of Beatrice? Your advice would be that I shouldn't worry? That she will be in good hands?'

'I'm sure she will be, and I think that Miss Beatrice is perfectly capable of making her own decisions.'

'You are right, of course, but I wish that she would ask before embarking on these exploits. She's so headstrong. I do wonder whether Charles or Daniel knew about her plan or if she kept them in the dark too.'

After Melissa had left, Harriet returned to the sitting room and pondered on the quandary of Beatrice Hart. She was convinced that Daniel hadn't known that Beatrice intended travelling with them; if he had, Harriet was sure that he would have mentioned it. Did her brother know, and keep it secret from their parents? But then he'd have been keeping it secret from Daniel too and she didn't think Charles would've done that. This was Daniel's journey, after all.

She got up from her chair and placed another piece of coal on the fire, then gazed into the mirror above it. Life, she thought, looking at her reflection, is so very complex, and we all have to cope with it in our own way. Miss Beatrice will have her own reasons for joining the two young men, and whether they want her there or not is something they'll have to deal with themselves. She turned away and put the guard in front of the fire. Whatever her plan, the girl won't be deterred from it, no matter that it's considered *unacceptable* by society. Harriet gave a wry smile. She'll get what she wants, will Miss Beatrice.

She told Maria what had happened and Maria raised her eyebrows and said she didn't know how Beatrice dared to be so far from home and travelling with only her brother and Daniel. 'Although Beatrice has always known what she wanted. Ever since she was sixteen, anyway. I remember when I went to 'twins' sixteenth birthday party – do you remember, Ma, when I didn't want to go? And Beatrice told me...' She hesitated. 'Beatrice said...'

'Yes?' her mother asked. 'What did Beatrice say?'

'Oh,' Maria faltered, 'I can't recall exactly. Something that she wanted or intended to have.'

Harriet always knew when Maria was uneasy and she was uneasy now; whatever Beatrice Hart had said had stayed with her even after so long. It must have been something so momentous that she'd been sworn to secrecy. Harriet smiled. It was probably nothing much, just schoolgirl secrets and of no consequence at all.

Later she told Fletcher the news that Melissa Hart had brought regarding Beatrice, and then about the Harts' bailiff who had given notice. 'I mebbe spoke out o' turn,' she confessed, 'but I asked if we could help at all and said that I was sure you–'

'You didn't! No. It's not that I wouldn't be willing, but you know that I can't! How can I? Mebbe Tom could help if they're really stuck, but not me. Can you imagine what my mother'd say if she found out? Anyway, being 'bailiff is a job worth having. There'll be plenty o' men glad to tek it on.'

212

He seemed anxious and Harriet wished she hadn't told him. 'You're right, of course,' she said. 'And Mrs Hart is probably worrying over nowt much. As you say, they'll soon get somebody else.'

CHAPTER TWENTY-SIX

At Hart Holme Manor, Christopher Hart had arrived home late for luncheon. 'So sorry,' he said to Melissa. 'My apologies to Cook.'

'Why are you so late? Not that it matters too much, as it's a cold meal today.'

'I've been talking to the bailiff and I've sent him home, because he's still unwell. I'm afraid that he might not stay on until November, so I must make more of an effort to find a replacement. Pity. He's been a good man, very reliable.' He sighed. 'No use wishing, of course, but if only the boys were older. I'm in two minds as to whether to let Stephen finish school as he wants to.'

'Not a good idea,' Melissa said. 'But you might enquire about agricultural college; that's what he really wants. They might take him now that he's seventeen and especially in view of the circumstances.'

'What circumstances?'

'The fact that you want to retire from an active part in running the estate and wish to have only an advisory role. And of course, Stephen would still need an older, more experienced man to help him for quite some time, even after being at college.'

'He would, and I must confess, Melissa, it's all getting too much for me.'

After luncheon Melissa gazed at her husband as he dozed off in the chair in her sitting room. She had not yet told him that Beatrice had gone adventuring with her brother and Daniel, for she knew it would worry him. He looked tired, and she realized that the prospect of interviewing for the position of bailiff was also worrying him, as few good men would consider moving to another estate until Martinmas, unless there was an issue with a present employer.

She considered what Harriet Tuke had said about her husband's helping out, but Melissa did not like the idea of that. If what she thought were true, then she didn't want Fletcher Tuke here on the estate, or his daughters either, charming and sweet though they were. But what was to be done over that situation? She was very fond of Harriet and considered her to be a friend in spite of their social differences, yet they had only skirted round the edge of the matter for twenty years. Christopher, she thought as she gazed at her husband, was unaware of any rumours concerning him. Melissa had never told him of her fears even though, she thought bitterly, there was someone who could tell and ruin all their lives if she chose to do so.

As far as she knew, Christopher never saw Ellen Tuke. There was no reason why he should; the bailiff took care of rents from tenant farmers and cottagers and handled any complaints or requirements, and it was foolish, she realized, to fret over what the woman might say or do when she had

214

kept silent for so many years. But fret she did, not always, but from time to time, and it was like having an ominous, threatening cloud hanging over her.

She debated whether or not to go out into the garden. It was a lovely day with barely a breeze, and she was thinking that the fresh air might dispel the malaise that was troubling her when one of the maids knocked softly on the door.

'Beg pardon, ma'am.' She spoke in a whisper when she saw Christopher sleeping. 'Mrs Crossley said would I give this to 'master. Bailiff Thompson came back with it. He said he'd forgotten to mention something.'

Melissa took the envelope that was handed to her, saying she'd give it to her husband when he woke. It was only lightly sealed and there was no name written on it; she guessed that Thompson must have recalled something he had meant to mention to his employer during their discussion. Should I open it? she thought. Then I might be able to resolve the problem, if that's what it is, without troubling Christopher.

The envelope opened easily without recourse to a paper knife and she pulled out a scrap of paper on which Thompson had scribbled a few words.

Sir, I forgot to mention that Jewitt said a fence is down adjoining his land but that he's happy to mend it temporarily until we can get one of our carpenters to renew it. The other thing is that about a week ago I saw Mrs Tuke, her who has the cottage by Brough Haven, and she asked would you call. Nothing I could handle, she said, as it was a personal matter.

215

Sorry I forgot to mention it afore.
Thompson.

'There's another postcard from Daniel, Ma,' Maria called up to her mother. 'Is it all right if I read it?'

'Of course it is. It's for all of us, isn't it?' Harriet shouted down from upstairs where she was changing the bedding. 'I expect everybody in 'district has read it.' She came into the kitchen with an armful of sheets for washing. 'It's not in an envelope, is it?'

'No,' Maria said. 'It's a card. He says ... mm, I can hardly read it, he's crammed so much on to it. He says they're in Switzerland, and going to see 'Jungfrau, and planning 'next part of their journey into Italy on horseback, and that Beatrice is going with them, which of course we knew already. She's so brave, isn't she? Though I expect she'll feel safe with Daniel and Charles.'

She hesitated for a moment, wondering whether to break a confidence, but then thought better of it. Beatrice had probably had a schoolgirl crush on Daniel, she thought. He was very handsome, after all. But Daniel was also honest and caring and would never do anything to besmirch a young woman's reputation, she was certain. Besides, the Hart family were out of their class and therefore out of their reach. She'd told Stephen as much some time ago, when he'd asked if they could be friends. He'd pooh-poohed the idea and said he'd live his life how he wanted to and wouldn't be hidebound by old traditions. But Maria had been brought up with old-fashioned values, and when her mother had told her that Stephen was destined for a different kind of life from theirs she had listened, and reluctantly avoided meeting him as he had wanted her to.

Fletcher looked in. 'I'm going down to Brough,' he said. 'Is there owt you want, or would you like to come?'

'I won't, thank you,' Harriet said. 'Maria, do you fancy a ride out?'

'I thought I'd slip in to see my ma,' Fletcher said. 'Whilst I'm there, you know.'

Harriet smiled and shook her head at him. 'You don't have to mek excuses about seeing your ma. Not to me.'

'I know,' he said sheepishly. 'But I allus come away in a bad mood when I've been to visit her, so I'm warning you.'

'I'll come with you, Da. We can tell her about Daniel; another card's just come. I'll get my jacket.'

Whilst Maria ran upstairs Fletcher read Daniel's card. Harriet leaned over his shoulder to see. 'He's having a great time, isn't he?'

He nodded. 'What's this about Beatrice going with them? I thought she was at school.'

'A finishing school in Switzerland. She's tekken it into her head to leave and travel with them.'

'How do you know? Do her parents know?'

'Mrs Hart's had a letter from 'headmistress. I don't know if she's told her husband yet.'

'A bit risky, isn't it? For people like them, I mean. It's all about reputation, isn't it, especially for a young woman. Mightn't it be frowned upon?'

'Possibly by some and mebbe even by her

217

father, but Mrs Hart is more of a free spirit. I reckon it's 'sort of thing she might have done, given 'opportunity.'

'Well, she'll be safe enough with our Daniel,' he said. 'And her brother too, I expect, although she seems to be a feisty sort of young woman. I reckon she could give anybody a run for their money.'

On arriving in Brough Fletcher went first of all to pick up some equipment at a farrier's shop and then headed towards the Haven. The water was calm, with only a slight breeze to ruffle the surface. Climbing up the side of his mother's cottage door were some early yellow scented roses, planted by the previous tenant, and first Fletcher and then Maria put their noses to them to smell the perfume.

'Your roses are lovely, Gran,' Maria said in an attempt at conversation after their initial cautious greeting. 'Are they early this year?'

'No idea,' Ellen Tuke said brusquely. 'I didn't plant 'em. Mrs Marshall did. They come up every year regardless. Shall I put 'kettle on,' she asked Fletcher, 'or are you dashing on somewhere else as usual?'

Fletcher sighed. 'We've time for a cup o' tea, Ma. Maria came specially to see you.'

'Did she?' his mother said. 'Well, there's a thing. Nowt better to do, had you?'

Maria blushed, not knowing what to say. 'I, erm, I'm not in service now,' she said. 'I'm helping Ma at home. Dolly's doing my old job.'

Her grandmother grunted. 'Your da must have plenty o' money to keep you at home. Doesn't

218

need your wages. Or mebbe your ma can't manage?'

'She can manage,' Fletcher interrupted. 'And if Maria wants to work elsewhere she can, and she can keep her wages or she can work at home for her keep. We're managing to keep 'roof over our heads.'

Ellen gave another grunt and made a pot of tea. 'Do you see much of Master Hart?' she asked.

'No,' Fletcher said. 'Why would I? He's nowt to do wi' us. I own 'land we're farming – at least Tom and I do. It's not Hart land.'

'Ma sees Mrs Hart sometimes,' Maria commented. 'She drops in to see her if she's in 'district.'

Ellen frowned. 'Who does?'

'Mrs Hart. She calls on Ma sometimes.' Maria began to wish she'd never mentioned it when she saw her grandmother's scathing expression.

'Trying to climb up 'ladder, is she, your ma?' She gave a scornful snigger. 'She'll not get further than 'bottom rung.' She pushed a cup and saucer towards Maria. 'Not wi' her background.'

Maria stared at her and her eyes filled with tears. But she drew herself up straight and pushed the cup and saucer back to the middle of the table. 'Thank you,' she said, as politely as she could, 'but I won't have tea after all and I'll wait outside until you're ready, Da.' She left the table and walked to the door, and then, turning, she said to her grandmother, 'I won't be calling again. My mother taught me to be polite. What a pity that yours didn't. Goodbye.'

'Why?' Fletcher said dismally as Maria went

out of the door, closing it firmly behind her. 'Why do you always have to be so controversial and upset everybody? Maria is 'sweetest girl you could ever wish to meet.' In truth he was astonished that his daughter had stood up to her grandmother. 'She'd never do or say owt to hurt anyone, but she'll stick up for her family, I'm pleased to hear, and especially Harriet. How dare you?' he went on, anger suddenly rising. 'How dare you insult her mother in that way?'

'She's not good enough for you,' Ellen said prosaically. 'You could've done better if you'd listened to me.'

'We've been married nigh on eighteen years and I've never met anyone I'd rather be with.' Fletcher's voice became heated. 'I love Harriet. She's 'onny woman I've ever loved and I'll be with her until 'day I die, and,' he added, 'I don't know why you think you're such an expert on marriage considering 'success you made of yours!'

Ellen's lip curled. 'Aye, well that's another story entirely,' she sneered. 'And it's fortuitous that you called today because I've made a decision and tekken steps to rectify a few things.' She pushed Fletcher's tea towards him. 'Tea's getting cold.'

'I don't want it. It'd choke me. And I'm leaving.' He looked at her. He was coming close to hating her, and thought what a terrible thing that was to think of his own mother. But if it came to a contest between her and Harriet, it would be no hardship to walk away from her.

'Please yourself. Mebbe you can afford to waste good provisions, but I can't.' She eyed him narrowly. 'But before you go I'll tell you what I've decided on. I spend a good deal o' time on my own–'

'That's your own fault,' he broke in.

'And I spend most of 'time thinking,' she went on. 'And so I thought I'd put things right and tell 'truth, bring it all into 'open you might say, 'stead of keeping it hidden as I have done all these years.' She lifted her chin. 'Which is why I asked if you saw owt of Christopher Hart.'

Fletcher swallowed. Dismay filled him. She wasn't still going on about this crazy idea that he should be Christopher's Hart's heir?

'I thought that if you did see him you could be the one to tell him, but no matter. And I suppose it'll be in your favour when he sees that you're capable of running your own farm.'

'Get to the point,' he said in a low voice. 'What have you done? What mad scheme are you planning?'

She gave a self-satisfied smile. 'Not mad. Just 'truth. It's time my story was told. So I've asked 'bailiff to tell him to call. Tell Christopher to call. Telled him to say that it's a personal matter. I'm expecting him any day now. He'll know that it's important.'

CHAPTER TWENTY-SEVEN

Melissa left Christopher sleeping in the chair and went out into the garden to wander around the rose beds. The new young gardener understood perfectly what she wanted and had recommended

221

various types of sweet-smelling roses that lasted all summer long. She paused to breathe in one particular deep carmine rose with a fragrant scent. The previous year she had often gathered one or two blooms to take into the house, even though she knew they wouldn't last so long as on the bush. But she didn't pick them now; there were many buds still to open and she decided to wait.

She was uneasy, and had come outside to calm herself. The note from Thompson, which she had left on the side table next to Christopher's chair, had disturbed her, and she wondered what Ellen Tuke wanted and why she should say it was a personal matter. Should I tell Christopher what I suspect? she thought. And yet if I am wrong about his former relationship with Ellen Tuke and the question mark over her son, would he be angry that I had distrusted him? Would our marriage suffer because of it?

She walked slowly back to the house and saw her husband with his back to the window, his head bent as if reading something. He's found the letter, she thought, and was thankful that she had come outside. It will give him time to assimilate the contents, and I'll know by his expression whether or not he is disturbed by them.

When she walked into the sitting room Christopher was pacing the floor, the note in his hand. 'Have you seen this?' he asked irritably. 'If it's not one thing it's another.'

'It's from Thompson, isn't it?' she wavered. 'Something he forgot to mention – about a fence? Not like him; he's obviously not at all well.'

'Not that!' he said edgily. 'That's easily fixed.' He

waved the note about. 'Ellen Tuke wants me to call on her. As if I haven't enough to do without trailing down to Brough Haven! It will be nothing that Thompson couldn't deal with, except that I've sent him home and told him to rest.'

Melissa felt a sense of relief. Christopher had nothing on his conscience after all. Ellen Tuke was merely an irritant to a man who had too much to do.

'Can I help?' she offered. 'Shall I go to see her? I could tell her that you are very busy just now with Thompson being ill.'

He considered for a moment and then sat down. 'No, that wouldn't work. She seems to think that because she's known me for so long she is owed my personal attention.' He sighed. 'I'll go in a day or two. Blasted woman,' he said beneath his breath.

When he did decide to visit it was three days later. He had attended to several things that Thompson would normally have dealt with, including sending a carpenter to fix the broken fence, and drafted out an advertisement for a bailiff or farm manager to go into local and national newspapers and farming magazines. 'I could do with a secretary as well as a bailiff,' he had complained to Melissa.

He left the horse and trap at the end of the lane and walked to Ellen Tuke's cottage. The door was firmly closed, and he cursed beneath his breath. Don't say she's out when I've come especially, he thought impatiently. He knocked firmly on the door and when there was no response he knocked again.

'All right, all right, I'm coming. Don't knock 'door down,' a peeved voice called out, and then came the rattle of a door bolt. Christopher remembered how when old Mrs Marshall was here she always had the door open in the summer, and often sat in her doorway looking out at the rippling water of the Haven.

'Yes?' Ellen opened the door. It took her a moment to realize that it was Christopher Hart standing there. 'Well,' she said, 'I'd given up on you. I thought 'bailiff hadn't given you my message.'

'He did, several days ago, before he went home sick. I am extremely busy and came as soon as I could,' he said bluntly. She was the only one of his tenants who spoke to him in such a discourteous manner. 'He didn't say anything about its being urgent.'

'Come on in,' she said. 'I suppose it's waited so long that a few more days won't matter, but I want it out in 'open.'

He refused her offer of a drink, muttering that he had a lot to do, but he sat down at her bidding. She sat opposite him and folded her hands across her apron. 'It's good to see you, Christopher. I've not seen you in a while,' she said, her voice becoming girlish in a way that made him wary and was at odds with her initial greeting, her lined grey face and her old-fashioned hand-made pleated bonnet. She looks very old, he thought, older than she should, for she's younger than I am. Her face was deeply etched with lines, not of laughter but of what looked like a lifetime of bitterness and spite.

'No,' he said uneasily. 'Thompson normally

224

handles the tenancies and rentals, but he will be leaving soon. As soon as I get a new manager I'll inform all the tenants that someone else will be calling.'

She looked sharply at him. 'I don't want a stranger visiting me,' she said. 'You can call for 'rent when it's due.'

He gave a nervous cough. Why did he always feel vulnerable in her company? 'It's only due once a year, Ellen. Surely you don't mind that? Or you can send it with someone. But in any case, I'll expect the new agent to call to make sure all is well with the tenancy and the property.'

They stared at each other for a moment and then Christopher cleared his throat. 'So what was it you wished to speak of that Thompson couldn't handle?'

'I said it was personal,' she snapped. 'We don't want other folk knowing our business, especially not when I've kept it close to my chest all these years. Fletcher'll be...' she paused, pressing her lips together as she considered, 'what, forty-five, won't he?'

Christopher stared at her. 'I have no idea,' he said, wishing that she would get to the crux of the matter. 'Look, Ellen, tell me the problem because I really must be going. I have a lot to do.' He pushed his chair back as if to stand up.

'No,' she said abruptly. 'I haven't even started. We can't put this off any longer. I want it settled afore I die.'

'Wh– Are you ill?' he said, startled.

'No, I'm not. I'm hale and hearty as far as I know, but we're neither of us getting any younger

225

and I want my son to have his rightful place.'

'Ellen,' he sighed, 'I have no idea what you're talking about and I am so very busy; can you please tell me what it is that's troubling you? Is your son in difficulties? You know that he's not one of my tenants, don't you? But if he's having problems he's welcome to come and discuss them with me and I'll try to advise him.'

'He's not having problems,' she said. 'Not that I'd know if he was.' She leaned towards him and lowered her voice. 'But it's Fletcher we must discuss. I've kept quiet all these years, not disturbed you in any way, have I? Not wi' your mother – she wouldn't have been pleased, I knew that – nor your first wife either?'

Vaguely he stared at her and shook his head. I think she's failing, he thought. She seems to be rambling. Perhaps I ought to get the doctor to call, although her son should be doing that.

'I waited, you see, for 'right time.' She gazed into space and whispered so that he could barely hear her. 'But somehow 'right time never seemed to come, and then you had sons wi' your second wife, but they don't really count.' Her eyes narrowed. 'It's 'first son that matters in society, so it's got to be now. I don't want to leave it any longer.'

This time he did get up; he'd send a message to her son telling him that his mother was unwell.

'You can't go yet,' she said. 'You've got to hear me out. Face up to your responsibilities.'

'What responsibilities?' he said irritably. 'I have given you a roof over your head, Ellen, re-housed you as I try to do with many of our long-term tenants. What more do you want?'

'Don't you understand?' She gazed at him fiercely. 'I want our son – Fletcher – to be given his rightful place before I die. The place that he deserves. *Our* son; your eldest son and heir to Hart Holme Manor.'

Christopher stared at her. Had the woman gone off her head? What was she talking about? She had a triumphant smile on her face as she folded her arms in front of her and waited for him to respond.

'I – I don't know what you mean,' he said, both indignant and confused. 'My eldest son is Charles. What are you implying?'

'I'm implying nowt,' she said, lifting her chin. 'I'm *telling* you that Fletcher is your son.' She pointed a stabbing finger at his chest. 'You've onny to look at him to know.'

'Don't be so ridiculous! How can you accuse me of all people of such a thing? You and I had a friendship of a sort when we were both little more than children, but as for anything else...' He looked back over the years. He had been fond of her when he was young, it was true, but nothing more than that. He'd been lonely, the only son, remote parents and no close companions, and he'd spent much time down in the kitchen with the servants, but as for any impropriety–

'Denying it, are we?' Ellen said slyly. 'Are you telling me you've conveniently forgotten that night of your coming of age party?'

'What?' He gazed at her in bewilderment. 'You've just told me that your son is forty-five years old! How the blazes am I supposed to

227

remember so far back? It takes me all my time to think what happened yesterday! What on earth has put this into your head?'

But he recalled other times when she had made comments that he hadn't understood. When her husband Nathaniel and their younger son had perished in the estuary he had offered his condolences and she had murmured to him, 'It's come at last,' as if there were something significant in their drowning, and he hadn't known what she meant. But good heavens, he thought, even that tragedy was twenty years ago.

'You were drunk,' she said. 'Drunk as a lord. You were drunk and we went down to 'bottom of 'garden, and...' She paused for effect, and Christopher shuddered at the idea of her suggestion. 'It was there,' she added, with an odd kind of expression on her face. 'I could tek you to 'exact spot.'

I don't think you could, he thought. Not since Melissa transformed the garden. *Melissa!* She's bound to ask what Ellen Tuke wanted, and he heaved a silent relieved breath that she hadn't come on his behalf to ask what was troubling Ellen, as she had volunteered to do. But whatever was he going to tell her? How was he to explain the accusations of this crazy woman?

Ellen frowned. 'You're not telling me that you can't remember? It was 'servants' and 'tenants' party, not your official one.'

'I don't remember either of them,' he said. 'As you say, I was drunk. I wasn't a drinker and somebody had given me something strong. I didn't remember anything until I woke up in my own bed the next afternoon. You're mistaken, Ellen. It wasn't me. I wouldn't have been capable.'

'But you were!' Her voice rose in fury. 'There wasn't anyone else. I never went with anyone else!'

'Tuke?' he queried. 'You married him before I married Jane, and you had a child straight away.'

'That's *why* I married him.' She began to rain blows on his chest. 'I was carrying *your* child! Cook – Mrs Marshall – said I'd have to leave 'manor, that I couldn't stay on cos your parents were planning to marry you off, so I had to marry somebody and there was onny Tuke and I *hated* him; hated him for all of his life!'

Tears were streaming down her face. Tears of anger, he thought, not sorrow or regret, and he took hold of her thin bony wrists to hold her back.

'You're overwrought, Ellen,' he said. 'I think you've had some kind of brainstorm. You have been imagining this all these years and it's built up so much that you think it's true, and it's not.' He released her wrists and stood back. 'I'll ask the doctor to visit. He will no doubt give you a sedative to calm you, and I'll send a message to your son and suggest that he calls.'

Ellen stared at him, rubbing her wrists where he had held her, and whispered, 'You don't believe me?'

Christopher shook his head and gave her a gentle smile. 'No,' he said. 'If it was the night you say it happened, it wouldn't have been possible, not in the condition I was in.'

'But *I* remember,' she said in a small, whiny voice. 'I'd planned it. I took you down there beneath 'trees. I wanted to have your child and I knew you'd look after us.' Her eyes narrowed to slits. 'It was Nathaniel Tuke who spoiled it for us, allus being there, not giving us a chance to be together.'

'We would never have been together,' he told her. 'Not ever, and especially not after I married Jane.'

'Wouldn't we?' Her voice dropped to a mere croak. 'Didn't you – didn't you love me? Did you not love me 'same as I allus loved you? And still do!'

He gave a small frown. How was this possible? He never thought of her. Hadn't thought about her in years except as a former servant and tenant, and yet she was still hankering over those long-ago years when they were young, giving them a romance when there was none.

'No, I didn't,' he said, as kindly as he could. 'I didn't know about love then; I was far too young. Not even with Jane. I learned about love when I married Melissa.'

He picked up his hat and made a resolve never to come here again. I'm too old for dealing with a situation such as this. I need a quiet life, not accusations. How could I ever hold my head up against such allegations?

'Goodbye, Ellen.' He trembled and suddenly felt ill, and desperately wanted to be at home with his wife. 'Try to get some rest.'

He turned at the door and saw she was still staring after him. He touched his hat and left.

CHAPTER TWENTY-EIGHT

Fletcher and Maria had driven away from Brough in near silence, but once they had left the town Maria murmured, 'I'm sorry if you thought I was rude to Granny Tuke, Da, but she was saying things about Ma that I didn't like. Why does she say such things, and why do they never meet?'

Fletcher was silent for a moment, and then said, 'It's a long-standing issue from before you were born. It goes back to when Noah brought your ma home as his wife. And then, after his death, when we discovered that he wasn't my brother after all and we could marry as we wanted to, your granny turned completely against her. She had other plans for me, she said, as if I was just a bairn and not a grown man capable of mekking my own decisions about my life.'

They trotted on for a while, neither of them speaking, Fletcher pondering whether he should tell Maria the truth about his mother's irrational and perverse temperament. Should he describe the neurotic and stubborn behaviour that had caused such discord even when he was a boy? Was he never to be rid of the gnawing anxiety he felt whenever he visited her, which was so completely at odds with the happy home life he enjoyed with Harriet and his children?

'So didn't she want you to marry my mother?' Maria asked eventually. 'Was it because of

Daniel? But why did she say that about Ma climbing up 'ladder?' She frowned. 'And why did she ask about Mr Hart? What's he to do with us?'

'Nothing to do wi' Daniel,' he said, 'and mebbe I'll ask your ma to tell you the rest. It's a bit embarrassing for me to talk about.'

'All right, Da, I'll wait till we get home. But it's worrying you, I can see. Will Ma tell me? I'm old enough to know about any problems that need to be shared.'

He smiled. 'Of course you are. You're my grown-up little girl.' Then he grew serious and shook the reins to move the mare along more briskly. 'But there's just one thing; when we've explained matters, I don't want you to discuss it wi' the others, not yet, especially not Dolly. She's a bit of a scatterbrain and I don't want her getting any fancy ideas.'

Maria was intrigued, and after they had finished their midday meal and she and her mother had cleared away, she broached the subject of her grandmother. 'Da said you'd tell me 'reason why she's so grumpy and doesn't seem to like anybody.'

'Come and sit down,' Harriet said. 'It's a long, rather sad story. Granny Tuke is bitter and aggrieved and has been for as long as I've known her, because she's disappointed that life hasn't come up to her expectations.'

As she gazed at her daughter, she hoped that the thought of the prospects she might have had wouldn't affect her in the same way. 'Granny Tuke maintains that your father is Christopher Hart's son.'

'What!' Maria exclaimed, and then laughed. 'But that's ridiculous! And she's only just said?' she asked incredulously.

'Oh, no. She told your father years ago, before we were even married, but to our knowledge she's never told Christopher Hart. And that's why she thinks I'm not good enough for your father.' She gave a wry smile. 'I don't know who she thinks he might have married, seeing as he was from 'wrong side of 'blanket, but she's convinced that as 'eldest son he's 'true heir to the Hart estate.'

Maria mulled over the information. 'But ... but if it's true, then – then it means that Da is brother to Beatrice and Charles and – and all of 'Hart children.'

'Yes, it does, or half-brother at least.'

'Do you believe it, Ma?'

'Well,' Harriet's voice dropped on a sigh. 'As a matter of fact, yes, I do. It wouldn't be 'first time that a gentleman has tekken advantage of a young maidservant, and I dare say it won't be 'last, but I'm of a mind to think that she was willing. Your granny thinks that 'sun shines out of Christopher Hart's head, allus has done, and she wouldn't think that way if he'd – if he'd committed an outrage.'

She gently squeezed Maria's hand. 'And if she really loved him, I don't suppose she would think that there might ever be repercussions for anybody else, if you understand what I mean, Maria?'

'Oh, yes,' Maria murmured. 'I understand perfectly.'

'What on earth has happened?' Her husband's

face was white and strained as he came into Melissa's sitting room. 'My dear,' she said. 'Are you ill?'

Christopher dropped into a chair and closed his eyes. 'No. Yes. I don't feel well.'

Melissa rang the bell and asked for hot sweet tea immediately.

'What is it?' She knelt beside his chair. 'Do you need the doctor? You're so white.' He was short of breath, as if he'd been running.

'No. No, I've had a shock, that's all. Quite knocked the wind out of my sails. I'll be all right in a minute or two.'

The tea was brought and Melissa dismissed the maid and poured it herself, putting a spoonful of sugar into the cup. 'Just take a sip or two and try to relax, and then tell me what's happened.'

'I can't,' he groaned. 'I can't. I – I don't know what you'll think – you'll be horrified. I daren't speak of such a thing. It's too dreadful to contemplate.'

'Has anyone died?'

'No. No, no one has died, it's just–' He broke off. 'I'm sorry, Melissa. I don't know what to say ... if it's true ... but how could it be?'

'If no one has died, it's not the end of the world,' Melissa assured him. 'Drink your tea – or would you like a small brandy?'

He nodded and muttered, 'Please,' and she got up and poured him a small glass, warming it between her hands. She watched him anxiously as he sipped it, and wondered fearfully what had disturbed him so much. He'd been out most of the morning; he'd told her that he was meeting a tenant farmer and then going on to see Ellen Tuke in response to her message. Ellen Tuke, she thought. What was the personal matter she had wanted to discuss?

He drained the brandy glass and put it down on a side table, then sat with his back bent, his head lowered and his hands clasped between his knees. 'I can't believe she could accuse me of such a thing,' he mumbled. 'How dare she? If it should get out – and what will the children think?'

Melissa watched him. He seemed to be talking to himself and not to require a response from her. 'I've always done my best for her, seeing as she was in our employ, just as I did for Mrs Marshall.'

But Mrs Marshall was the cook in the kitchen for many years, from your mother's and Jane's time until we met and married, Melissa thought, whereas Ellen Tuke was a maid for only a short time before her marriage to Tuke. Yet Christopher had given her the tenancy of the old farm and then the cottage at Brough Haven. Melissa felt shaken and uneasy as she considered the possibility of her worst fears coming to light.

'Are you speaking of Mrs Tuke? Has she accused you of some misdemeanour?'

He looked up at her, running his fingers over his face, and nodded. 'I can't speak of it, Melissa. I need to think of what to do.'

'Two heads are better than one,' she said softly. 'And if she has made an accusation against you, then I need to know, so that I am prepared if we have to do battle.'

'You know that I would never do anything to hurt you,' he said imploringly. 'I'd rather die than

235

do that, but this – this...' He cast a glance around the room. 'What she's saying goes back to when we were very young, and ... I can't remember. And surely I would? I was so naive, so immature, surely I would remember?'

I have to say it, Melissa decided. He can't, dare not, so I must be strong. 'Has she accused you of fathering her son?'

'Yes,' he gasped. 'That's what she's saying. Nearly fifty years on and that is what she's saying. The woman is off her head!'

'Have you never thought that her son bears a striking resemblance to you?' Melissa asked quietly.

'What? No, never! Why would I think such a thing? He's tall and fair, but so are many men. Why should she blame me?' He was furiously indignant. 'She said it happened on the evening of my coming of age party, and that she had planned it! Someone had given me ale and I wasn't used to strong liquor and I was drunk; I was so ill that I barely remember the next day either.'

'So in effect she seduced you, Christopher, if she said that she'd planned it.' Melissa looked at his face and saw that he was sunk in misery and shame. 'What did you say to her?'

'I told her that it wasn't me, because ... surely, Melissa, I would remember if it were my first time?' He reached out to hold her hand. 'I was quite incompetent when I married Jane,' he confided, and she turned her head away, not wanting to know.

I should speak to Harriet, she thought. We have always known that there was something but have

236

never spoken of it; perhaps now we should, especially as we have our children to protect. She recalled the twins' sixteenth birthday party, when Stephen and Maria Tuke seemed to be getting along so well. Such a sweet girl, and she looked so much like the twins.

What an unholy entanglement! It will be up to us mothers to sort it out, for the men will be incapable of doing so. Christopher is so shocked that he can't think straight, and Fletcher Tuke will be too embarrassed to speak of it, although I feel sure that his mother will have told him. And that, she thought, might be the saving grace, for he hasn't confronted Christopher, which must mean he wants nothing from him.

But there was still the enigma of Ellen Tuke, who had thrown down the challenge. Why has she waited for so long before confronting Christopher? Does she feel that time is running out? What does she expect from him? Some declaration of love, perhaps? An acknowledgement that he still thinks of her? It's so very sad. Poor disillusioned woman.

From her doorway, Ellen had watched Christopher walk away, his head bent and his shoulders stooped, and she felt a pang of remorse. Have I upset him, made him unhappy? I didn't intend that, although, *yes*, I wanted revenge. Revenge for his rejection of me when for all those years I thought that one day he'd value me, that he'd accept Fletcher as his own. But he doesn't believe me! It's as if there'd been nothing between us.

She brought a chair to the door and sat staring

at the waters and thinking of the past, of her time at the manor when she was a young maid, and of marrying Nathaniel, and telling him that Fletcher was his. Ha! He believed me at first and was thrilled that he'd sired a son, but then he began to suspect that I'd lied. Fletcher grew to be 'image of Christopher, anybody with half an eye could see that, and that's why he brought Noah home, to get his own back at me. And I was so angry. I didn't want him. She thought of Noah's own son, Daniel. You're not my blood, I told him; you're nowt to do wi' me. Mebbe I shouldn't have said that. Mebbe that was cruel and uncalled for, poor bairn, and now he's gone to far-off lands in search of his own forebears. Though I doubt he'll find 'em.

A wind began to blow and the sky darkened. The Haven waters became choppy and rushed against the narrow bank and she considered, as she often did, that one day if there was a very high tide the water would spill over into her cottage. She got up from the chair and without thinking, began to walk along the path, something she rarely did unless she had an errand in Brough.

She shivered. It was colder than she had thought and she hadn't brought a shawl but she walked on, thinking of what she had done and what she might do. Will Christopher tell his wife 'news I've given him about our boy? What will she mek of it?

She forgot Fletcher's age and began to think of him as a young man, imagining him living up at the manor house with Christopher's other child-ren. I shan't want him to be considered inferior; he's just as good as they are, and I'll mek sure they realize that he's 'eldest son, she thought, as if she too would be there to make decisions.

A storm began, a sudden squall of needle-sharp sleet that instantly soaked her, yet she didn't think of turning back even though she had no clear idea of where she was heading. She continued on until the path narrowed and she had to push her way through a thicket of bushes, scratching her arms and legs. It was wet underfoot and she felt her feet sinking but still she plodded on, catching hold of reeds that were strong and tough and cut into her hands. Mebbe I've tekken 'wrong path in life, she thought, mebbe I should go back, p'raps call up at 'manor and tell 'em that there's no need to mek too much of what I said. I could tell Christopher that Fletcher is able to tek care of himself, that he doesn't need them; they're different from us, any-way. And at that point her twisted ambition raised its head again. *But he has to acknowledge that Fletcher's his son.*

That's what I'll do. I'll tell him it's just that I loved him – Christopher – and allus will, but I've kept that love hidden in my heart all these years, and it's gone sour, mekking me resentful; yes, and why not? I've not had 'man I wanted and had to put up wi' second best, so it's not been fair. She stood holding on to the reeds, her legs in water, contemplating. I'll go back, she decided, and clutching the reeds she started to turn round. But her feet were stuck in the squelchy mud and she stumbled up to her armpits in water.

'It's so cold.' She hauled herself up on to the bank, slipping and sliding on the mud, and crawled on to the path, her clothes, arms and legs covered in river mud and green slime. 'Must get home,' she muttered. 'Back to Marsh Farm. Hope 'fire's still in; nobody will think o' mending it, not Mr Tuke or Noah. Fletcher might; he's a good lad. Breeding will out.'

She reached her cottage and wondered who had left the door open. The fire was almost out; she dripped water as she reached for some kindling to ignite it, then went down on her knees, trying to find warmth, and lay down on the rug. 'Soon get warm,' she muttered, 'when 'fire teks hold; lads'll be in soon and mebbe they'll mek me a hot drink. Aye, that'll be 'day, when pigs fly.'

Mebbe Christopher'll come back, she thought. He'll realize I'm telling 'truth. He'll remember if onny he casts his mind back. I should ask him to call again and explain a bit better than I did. I was ... what? Hostile. But I wanted to tell him afore it was too late. I'm not young any more and I suppose he's not either, so he had to know. She smiled. I still think of him as a handsome lad. I should tell him that. I was allus afraid afore to tell him about how I felt.

She began to call 'Christopher,' but her voice was husky and sore. She was cold and shivery; someone had left the door open and the wind was blowing it and banging it against the frame. 'That door'll be off its hinges if somebody doesn't shut it,' she muttered angrily. 'But I can't do it, I'm stopping here in front o' fire. Christopher!' she called hoarsely. 'Christopher! It's me, Ellen. I'm sorry. It was my fault, but I loved you.'

CHAPTER TWENTY-NINE

Three figures stood atop a high peak looking many miles down a twisting ribbon of a road leading into a deep and sunny valley. The sky was sapphire blue, the air crisp and cold for there was still snow on the mountain tops, so bright and white they could only gaze at them with narrowed eyes. Daniel stood in the middle of the group and put his hand on Charles's shoulder, then turned and smiled at Beatrice, who had slipped her hand into his, gently squeezing it.

'Nearly there, Daniel,' she murmured. 'Italy. Your homeland?'

'No,' he said softly. 'Perhaps my beginnings, but England is my homeland.'

'It's incredible,' Charles said, his voice breaking with emotion. 'So beautiful, so awe-inspiring. I wish I could paint,' he said for the hundredth time.

'We should make camp soon,' Daniel said. 'It's cold up here and it'll get colder when 'night comes on. Let's drop down and find a sheltered spot so 'ponies can rest and we can eat.' Throughout the journey, Daniel had insisted that the animals should rest and feed before they did; at midday they grazed on the lush mountain grass, and were walked through running streams to drink and cool their feet. In the evenings, after lighting a small fire, he checked their feet and made sure they were not saddle sore.

They had ridden towards the Jungfrau and admired the lofty mountain from the base, but had gone no further as there were hordes of tourists in the region: serious walkers, riders, holidaymakers arriving in carriages to have their photographs taken with the towering peaks in the background. It was time to move on.

On the way to Brig-Glis they had been fortunate enough to find cheap accommodation in several localities, where villagers were pleased to offer them beds for a few coins and gave Beatrice the consideration of a separate room, sometimes no bigger than a cupboard, but sufficient for her privacy. Mostly, however, they slept outdoors as the nights at those lower altitudes were warm, and after a simple meal of eggs, if they had managed to buy any, bread and sausage eaten by the light of the flickering flames of the fire, Daniel and Charles climbed into their sleeping sacks and Beatrice into hers inside her tent and fell asleep to the sound of nocturnal creatures, the nickering of the ponies and the donkey as they grazed.

When they reached the city of Brig they had decided to find lodgings and stay a day or two to rest themselves and the animals.

The municipal town hall held records for trade and community organizations and Beatrice, with her understanding of German, enquired of a desk clerk about the road into Italy over the Simplon Pass. He told them that a new road had been built to replace an ancient one that had been used in the past by smugglers and traders carrying salt from the Mediterranean; but, he suggested, as they were on horseback they could use the Stockalper mule trail on the south side of the pass, which would take them less than three days, including a rest in Simplon village itself.

'What do you think?' Daniel had asked the other two. 'Sounds exciting, but it might be demanding.'

'We should do it,' Beatrice said.

'Are you sure, Bea?' Charles asked in some concern. 'It could be tiring.'

'We'll be fine,' she said. 'As long as we rest the horses and Modesty and don't overtax them.'

It was Beatrice Daniel had been thinking of when he asked the question; she seemed to be tireless, but looking at the map they were given he came to the conclusion that the route might be exhausting for them all. And it had been, for there were times when they had to walk in single file, leading the ponies with Modesty following behind, especially when passing through the narrow Gondo Gorge with its stony path, steep granite walls and rickety wooden bridges over the many rushing mountain streams. High above them was the route built originally by Napoleon to transport his army and supplies; occasionally they caught glimpses of a post-chaise carrying tourists and locals across the pass to Domodossola. They met hikers carrying packs on their backs and stopped to greet and exchange information on the perils to look out for, and both Daniel and Charles said how much Beatrice had contributed with her language skills, for there were Italians, Germans and Swiss travelling the same route.

'You're a treasure, Beatrice,' Daniel told her. 'How would we have managed without you?'

Beatrice had simply shrugged her shoulders and said wryly, 'I knew you would need me.'

When it rained, as it did suddenly and torrentially several times, they had sought and found accommodation in mountain hamlets; these settlements were now taking on a look of Italy with their slate roofs and some Italian-speaking residents. But on this last day, as they rode by the rushing waters of the River Diveria that ran between Switzerland and Italy, they found a sheltered grassy spot beneath a group of larch and stone pines where they could erect Beatrice's tent; they made a fire and tethered the animals to a nearby tree.

That night Daniel lay sleepless in his warm sack with the hood pulled over his head and wondered what tomorrow might bring as they dropped down into Gondo and crossed the border into Italy.

It was a large country with a language he didn't understand. It's a fool's errand hoping to find anyone with the name of Orsini, he thought. Young George said we must go to Rome, but he only said that because it's 'capital. Or he mebbe meant that we might find information. But Rome was a long way off, and after an earlier discussion with Charles and Beatrice he had agreed that Milan, being nearer, would be an easier target for their enquiries.

If I don't find anything, he mused, I'll try to be content, for if nothing else it's been a wonderful journey and one I might never have taken but for this obsession with finding my grandfather; but most of all I've been with my good friend Charles and – best of all – with Beatrice, the only woman

I'll ever love, and 'memory of that will last me all my life. I know, deep down, that she can never be mine, for I can never, ever, be deserving of her.

He woke at dawn, when a sliver of daylight touched his eyelids just as a nutcracker somewhere nearby began its morning call. As the insistent *tra, tra, tra* pulled him into full wakefulness, he realized he had come to a decision overnight: *not Milan!* Granny Rosie said Marco was a seaman, so why not head for 'nearest port? He sat up, leaned out of his sleeping sack and rummaged in his rucksack, which he always kept close by him. He brought out the map and opened it, and by the movement disturbed a mountain hare that had been feeding close by. He watched it for a moment until it took fright and sped away.

They would cross the border into Domodossola, a frontier town that linked the two countries. His finger moved slowly down the leg of Italy. Milan, if they went there, was to the east, but instead they could head south to the port of Genoa. Yes, he thought, feeling a sense of excitement in the pit of his stomach. Is it instinct that's telling me that's what we should do?

A sound disturbed him and he looked up to see Beatrice coming across the meadow towards the camp site. She was fully dressed, wearing her boots, a warm jacket, her fur hat and a cream silk scarf.

'Good morning. You're up early,' he said.

'Yes. I woke whilst it was still dark so I got up and dressed and sat on a high rock to watch dawn break.' She crouched down beside him. 'It was so beautiful when the light lit the mountain peaks. It coloured them rose,' she murmured. 'I saw a lynx, and what might have been an ibex, but it was too high for me to be sure, and the flora is so lovely, edelweiss and deep blue gentians and so many other alpine plants whose names I don't know, their flowers just unfurling.'

Daniel watched her as her face glowed with pleasure. 'I saw a hare outside your tent,' he said, for something to say, and she nodded. She had seen it too.

He cleared his throat. 'Beatrice, I couldn't get to sleep last night, I'd so many things running through my head, but this morning I woke up with a different plan.' He told her why he had decided against Milan and wanted to head towards Genoa instead.

'Of course,' she agreed. Leaning towards him, she traced her finger down the map, a wisp of her hair tickling his face. 'It makes perfect sense. Genoa is a principal port, and the travelling time must be about the same.'

'What's happening?' Charles sat up and leaned on his elbow, yawning. 'Why are you up so early, Bea?'

'Watching the dawn, slugabed,' she laughed, her eyes bright with merriment. 'But now I suggest we set off and head down the valley and have breakfast in the village.' She pointed up the rocky hillside to where she had been sitting. 'From up there I could see signs of habitation and smoking chimneys, so everybody is up.'

Whilst she packed her rucksack and dismantled her tent, Daniel fed the animals and Charles

246

spread the ash from the fire. In half an hour they were on their way on the final leg of their journey through Switzerland, down the valley towards the village of Gondo.

A resident offered them smoked ham, sausages and eggs for breakfast, with rye bread just out of the oven and a plentiful supply of piping hot coffee. As they ate, they were told that Domodossola, the border town, was approximately two miles down the valley. Their host suggested they visit the caves of Gondo and the deep water canyon where the young men might like to swim; they politely declined, saying that they still had many miles to travel to reach their destination, Genoa.

Their host opened his mouth in astonishment and said it was a long way and that he had never ventured so far. He looked curiously at Beatrice and called his wife to come and take a look at her and seemed to be explaining something to her. She looked at Beatrice and then Charles and nodded as if understanding that they were brother and sister, but had a questioning frown over Daniel.

'Erm – cousin,' Beatrice told her.

'Ah!' the woman said. 'Italiano?'

'No.' Daniel shook his head. 'English.'

'Nein.' She too shook her head and smiled. 'Italiano!'

'You do look Italian,' Charles commented as they said goodbye and *Auf Wiedersehen* to their hosts. 'Especially now you're so suntanned.'

'Do I?' Daniel hadn't looked in a mirror recently, though his hands and arms were brown, whereas Charles and Beatrice had kept themselves covered in fear of burning in the hot sun. 'Then I'd better start practising Italian.'

And as they reached Domodossola and crossed into Italy Charles and Beatrice agreed that he should, for the officials at the border addressed Charles and Beatrice in German and English and Daniel in Italian. *'Bentornato in Italia.'* Welcome back to Italy.

CHAPTER THIRTY

It was Saturday and a market was in full swing in the medieval town of Domodossola. They bought sausages, cured ham, pastries and juicy tomatoes to top up their supply of food; they also bought oats for the ponies and carrots for the donkey, who had proved to be an amiable animal, sweeter perhaps for the company of the horses and rarely obstinate or complaining when being loaded.

Beatrice and Charles bought large straw hats and Daniel a peaked cap like the ones some of the local men were wearing.

'You look even more Italian now, Daniel.' Beatrice adjusted it on his long dark curls at a jaunty angle and took the silk scarf from her neck and knotted it around his. 'There, most definitely *italiano,'* she laughed.

'I might never take it off,' he murmured, glancing at her, and she smiled as if suddenly shy and looked away.

They estimated that a week's travelling should

put them in Genoa. It didn't seem so far on the map, but previous experience now told them that travelling on the smaller cross-country roads added extra miles, and they wanted to have the pleasure of riding at a leisurely pace through Italy to get to know the landscape and the people. They decided that early morning departures would be sensible as the heat during the day would be intense now they were into June; they and the animals would rest over midday and continue on at about four o'clock, when it became cooler, until almost dark.

'I was thinking about home,' Charles said, as they rode down a steep valley, 'and wondering what everyone was doing. Stephen and George will be away at school, of course. Father will be doing paperwork, I expect, or occasionally accompanying the bailiff round the estate, and Mama will be entertaining friends or being entertained by them, and life will be progressing as normal.' He sighed. 'After this adventure I can't think that I'll ever be able to settle down to such a mundane existence where nothing much happens. What about you, Daniel?'

'Well, I know that everybody'll be busy as usual. We've a different kind of life from you, Charles,' Daniel said. 'We've all got a job to do and somebody, probably Fletcher, will be looking after 'hosses while I'm away. Ma will be cooking and baking and looking after 'hens and milking 'cows, as well as doing housework and 'laundry, and Maria will be helping her wi' those jobs now that she's back home again.'

'You and your family are so industrious,' Beatrice broke in. 'We have someone else to do those things for us, and I feel – I feel that we have empty lives in comparison with yours. I wish that I could do something worthwhile, something important.'

'Do you, Bea? Really?' Charles seemed surprised. 'It wouldn't be expected of you. It's up to the men of the family to earn a living in business or running an estate such as ours.'

'No, it's not,' Beatrice said rather sharply. 'Daniel has just said that his mother and sister work in the house and on the farm, and isn't Dolly in service too? So she's earning her keep. We – you and I – are simply people of leisure and it doesn't seem right. We're not contributing anything.'

'You're giving work to people,' Daniel interjected. 'To 'farm labourers and servants in your house and–'

'Yes, I know,' she answered. 'But sometimes it doesn't seem enough.'

After a few miles when they hadn't spoken much, Charles suddenly continued with the conversation. 'I still think what I'd really like to do, if Father will agree, is go to university after all and study art; after visiting the Louvre as Daniel and I did, I think I could make a career of being an art critic, or maybe writing papers on the culture of art by studying, say, Michelangelo, or the new young artists like Pissarro or Monet or Renoir. They're only just beginning to make a name for themselves and the old school don't care for their style, but I do.'

'You'd need to read English too,' Beatrice told him, 'if you're going to write articles for publication.'

'You wouldn't mek much money either,' Daniel said practically. 'Not at first. You'd still have to depend on your father's support.'

'I would, wouldn't I,' Charles agreed thoughtfully, 'and as I'm the eldest son it would be up to me to safeguard the family fortunes.'

Beatrice butted in. 'It might be better to let Stephen do that if your heart isn't in it.'

Daniel stroked his pony's neck. He and Charles had taken it in turns to ride the mare and the larger stallion, whilst Beatrice had ridden the smaller one, whom she had named White Socks; the mare was Mama, the other stallion Blaze. 'I know what I'd like to do if money was plentiful,' Daniel said. 'I'd like to breed hosses. I love these Haflingers. Do you realize that they were bred not far from here? But although they wouldn't be suitable for our flat countryside back home, there are hilly areas where they might be.'

'They're lovely animals, I agree,' Beatrice said. 'But we already have mountain ponies in England: the Welsh cob, the ponies in the New Forest and on Dartmoor and Exmoor.'

'I know,' he sighed. 'It's onny a dream.'

The road to Genoa took them through steep alpine valleys into mossy tree-lined glens where they rested and camped, for the weather was good, and five days later they were approaching the outskirts of the great port. They rode in on busy roads packed with post-buses and carriages and carts bearing commercial goods and private passengers, and found accommodation with stabling in a lodging house; after a night's sleep and a hearty breakfast they set off on foot to explore the city.

They were thrilled and overawed by it, although Daniel wondered how he would ever find any information about the Orsini family, even if it was here to be found. The old town was built around the port and was a conglomeration of ancient buildings dating back many centuries, narrow twisting lanes leading into wide piazzas with market stalls, and one that took them into the larger medieval piazza dei Banchi, which was still a commercial and banking centre where men stood in doorways exchanging information.

They judged that Genoa was a great trading centre as the port itself was crowded with shipping; they noticed also the many races, not only Italian but dark-eyed and dark-skinned North African and fair-haired Swiss and German. They heard French spoken too, though they didn't hear any English voices.

By midday they were flagging as the heat became intense; they looked for a place to eat and found somewhere suitable with tables outside overlooking the quay. They ordered food, Beatrice speaking in Swiss-German as she knew only a little Italian, and they were brought a dish of olives and bread and a jug of local wine.

Daniel leaned against the back of his chair and gazed out at the ships. He put his face up to the sun. 'This is the life, isn't it? I was just thinking that Fletcher and Tom will be attending to 'lambing and calving and Lenny will be farrowing 'pigs, and here am I living a life o' leisure.'

He leaned forward again, putting his elbows on the table, then took a sip of wine, drawing in his cheeks at the rough dry taste. 'How am I going to find out about 'Orsini family?'

Charles folded his arms. 'Well, do you recall when we were in Paris?' He grinned. 'Doesn't that sound very cosmopolitan?' he said, and Daniel and Beatrice agreed that it did. 'Well, we wanted somewhere to stay and we asked in the café and – what was his name...'

'François,' Daniel said, 'and he spoke English. Are you suggesting that we ask this waiter?'

'Well, why not? If he speaks English.'

'Yes, we could,' Beatrice said. 'I'll ask him when he comes back with our meal.' She took off her hat and put her face to the sun for a moment, enjoying the warmth.

Another waiter brought the food she had ordered, a course of pasta with pesto sauce followed by a fish dish with prawns and fat ripe tomatoes. Presumably his colleague had told him that Beatrice was German; he spoke to her in that language, warning her against getting burned.

'*Danke schön*,' she replied. '*Bitte – sprechen Sie englisch?*'

He raised his eyebrows. 'A leetle,' he said in a strong Italian accent. 'I 'ave not much chance to speak wiz ze English.'

Beatrice smiled and Daniel could see that the waiter was charmed by her. 'We were wondering if you know whether any of the Orsini family live in this district?'

The waiter looked astonished, then laughed. 'You know they were ze most noble family in Italy? They lived in Roma. Popes, cardinals, noblemen. I learn 'istory in school. Not all were good men. They like ze power.'

253

'Oh!' Beatrice looked at Daniel.

He sighed. 'Young George was right. He said we should go to Rome.'

'I think ze family is gone long long time ago.' The waiter shrugged expressively. 'But, I 'ear the name sometimes.' He broke off to shout 'Federico!' to a colleague, an older man, maybe the owner, and called out a question to him. Federico came over and the waiter asked him something they couldn't understand.

Their waiter looked them over. *'Inglese?'* His eyes lit on Daniel. *'Italiano?'*

Daniel shook his head. 'English.'

Federico spoke rapidly to their waiter, who said, 'Federico say that sometimes an Inglese he come 'ere. He may know.'

'Long odds, I'd say,' Charles murmured. Beatrice agreed. 'Bare improbability, but,' she added, 'a chance.'

'Why would an Englishman know about an Italian family?' Daniel frowned.

Federico spoke again to the waiter, who told them, 'Federico, 'e say this Englishman 'as lived in Genoa a long time. He may know who to ask. If 'e come, 'e come on a Friday.'

'We could ask, I suppose,' Daniel said gloomily. 'If he doesn't know, then it's a dead end. Rome's too far for us to go.'

They finished their meal, paid the bill and left the table to walk back to the lodging house. Beatrice paused and said, 'So what day is it today?'

They had lost track of the days, but Charles said, 'I think it might be Friday.'

'So, shall we go back and wait?' Beatrice asked.

'We've come all this way, Daniel.' She looked at him anxiously, as if she guessed that he was feeling downcast. 'We can't give up at the first hurdle.'

'Mebbe later then,' he said. 'Mebbe tonight when it's cooler.'

They had gone only a few yards and were standing by the waterfront looking at the ships when they heard someone whistle. They ignored it, but then someone shouted 'Inglese!' and they looked back towards the café. Their waiter stood with his arm held up, beckoning to them.

'We did pay, didn't we?' Daniel asked.

'We did,' Beatrice was watching the waiter. 'But he wants us to go back.'

'The Inglese, he come now, we see 'im,' the waiter called, and pointed down the waterfront.

Federico stood inside the café doorway with his arms folded across his chest, looking in the same direction. A man of medium build wearing a straw Panama and a cream jacket and trousers was walking towards the café talking to another man, who by his clothing of wide trousers, blue shirt and a dark navy cap looked as if he might be off a ship. They shook hands, saying *'Grazie'* and *'Arrivederci'* before separating.

'Milo!' Federico called out. *'Potete aiutarmi, per favore?'*

'Can you help, please,' Beatrice translated and Daniel glanced at her admiringly.

The man threaded his way between the tables outside to the café door. He and the owner shook hands and greeted one another.

Then followed a short conversation too fast for Beatrice to understand, but they all heard the

255

words *'la famiglia Orsini'*. Both men looked to-wards them.

'I think Federico's saying that we're asking about the Orsini family,' Beatrice explained. Daniel and Charles nodded, as that's what they had gathered too. 'He's coming over,' she said softly. 'He doesn't look English, does he?'

'Neither does Daniel,' Charles commented.

Milo lifted his hat, showing hair more grey than dark, and gave a short bow to Beatrice, murmuring, *'Signorina.'* He turned to Daniel and Charles. *'Buongiorno.'* Then, in English with a trace of an Italian accent, he said, 'Good day to you. How may I assist you?'

CHAPTER THIRTY-ONE

Anger had been eating away at Fletcher since the day he'd argued with his mother and he barely slept at night, tossing about in bed and keeping Harriet awake too. He had told her what had happened and she understood his feelings, but after three sleepless nights she had had enough.

'This is no good, Fletcher,' she told him on the morning of the fourth day. 'You'll have to go back and have it out with her. Tell her that even if you believed what she's saying about Christopher Hart, you wouldn't do anything about it. You're never going to settle if you don't.'

'I know,' he sighed. 'But I could do without this. We're in 'middle o' lambing and we're a man short wi' Daniel away–'

'If Daniel had been here, you'd still find a reason not to go,' she said gently. 'But you must, once and for all; I'd offer to come with you but she wouldn't have me in 'house.'

'And that's another thing!' His voice rose and she hushed him in case the family should hear; she'd heard Maria and then Lenny go down and that meant Joseph and Elizabeth would be awake too. 'I won't have her saying things about you. If it came to choosing–'

'Hush,' she said. 'It won't come to that. But you must go and see her, Fletcher. Do your morning jobs and then go.'

Harriet was preparing vegetables for the midday meal. Fletcher had gone again to see his mother, Elizabeth and Joseph were at school and Maria and Lenny were busy elsewhere so she had the house to herself. Like Fletcher, she had his mother on her mind and was trying to think of a solution. How pleased I am to have someone like Rosie in my life, she thought. She's the way my mother was, no grudges or ill-will towards anybody, unlike Ellen, who if she did but know it is 'onny one who can be blamed for her own unhappiness.

There was a timid knock on the door and she took a cloth to dry her hands before opening it.

'I'm sorry, Harriet,' Melissa Hart faltered, looking distressed.

'Please come in, ma'am,' Harriet said. 'I'm on my own; there's no one else here.' Automatically she swung the kettle over the fire. She saw that Melissa was trembling as if she were cold, al-

257

though it was a beautiful sunny day. 'Come and sit by 'fire.'

'You know why I've come?' Melissa said.

'I can guess. Tea or coffee, ma'am?'

'Oh, erm, tea please. Weak, no milk. I'm so sorry,' she said again, sitting down. 'Your husband must be very angry, and shocked by the news?'

'With his mother, yes. But he's known for years. She told him even before we were wed. But we don't understand why she should tell your husband now. I suppose she has told him? She told Fletcher she was going to.'

Melissa sipped the tea that Harriet had placed on a small table beside her chair. 'She sent a message by the bailiff that she needed to see Christopher about a personal matter.' She took a deep shuddering breath. 'He's been so busy that he only went yesterday, and – and she confronted him.' She lifted her head and looked at Harriet. 'I've tried to be strong, but today – today I feel so weak and helpless. I – I persuaded Christopher to go back and see her. He was so shocked when he came home that it made him quite ill, but I said he must go back and ask just what Mrs Tuke wants from him. Your husband is not the kind of man who – who...'

'Wants anything from your family,' Harriet finished for her, and sat down opposite her. 'No, he doesn't. Never has done, and you needn't worry that we'll shout it from 'house tops. If we'd wanted to do that we'd have done it years ago.' She considered for a moment, and then said, 'But truth to tell, if Ellen thinks that she's kept a great secret all these years, I think she'll find that she hasn't. Folks

258

round about have always had suspicions that Nathaniel Tuke wasn't Fletcher's father.'

They both sat silently for a moment, then Harriet asked, 'So when will Mr Hart visit her again?'

'Oh, he's gone this morning. That's why I came. I couldn't bear the waiting and I wanted to speak to you. I think it is up to us, the mothers of our children, my sons and your daughters, to make sure that they are safe and that they understand.'

'I've explained to Maria already,' Harriet said. 'I was mostly concerned about her.' She put her hand to her mouth. 'Your husband will be there now?'

Melissa nodded. 'Yes. I said he should get it over with.'

'Yes, of course,' Harriet agreed. 'That's what I told Fletcher. He'll be there too.'

Fletcher's senses were in turmoil as he pulled the trap to a halt at the end of the lane, jumped down and tied the horse securely. He didn't want to fall out with his mother, but neither did he want any more aggravation from her. All our lives, he thought, mine and Noah's, we had to tread carefully so that we didn't say or do anything to upset her or Da. At least, I did; I don't think Noah was bothered and now we know why. Poor lad, he was unwanted right from 'off. Little wonder he turned out to be so belligerent.

There was a cool breeze down by the Haven and he shivered, though not so much because of the chill as because he was worried about the forthcoming battle of wills. He was almost at the cottage when he heard his name being called, and turned to see Christopher Hart walking towards him. Christopher lifted his hand and called in a croaky voice, 'Wait, please!'

Fletcher walked slowly back to meet him. He was not confrontational and had no wish to get into an argument with the man his mother insisted was his father. He wondered if Hart already knew what she was claiming, or if this was his first visit since she had decided to break her long silence.

Christopher was breathing heavily and his face was grey.

'Are you all right, sir?' Fletcher asked.

Christopher shook his head. 'No,' he panted, 'not really. This – business with your mother has distressed me; I can't believe – still, if she says it's true, then...' He took another breath. 'Then I suppose it must be. Why would she lie? But on the other hand, why has she waited so long to speak of it? If I'd known before ... then I would have supported her in her difficulty.'

I believe he would, Fletcher thought. He couldn't have married her, but he might have provided for her and the child – me. But that wouldn't have been enough for my mother; she would still have wanted him to acknowledge that I was his son, and would Nathaniel Tuke have married her if he'd known 'truth? No, he thought, remembering the ill-tempered man he had assumed was his father, he wouldn't.

Christopher Hart gazed at him through bloodshot eyes. He looked drained, as if he hadn't slept either. 'I'm so sorry,' he said. 'So very sorry.'

Fletcher put out his hand and patted Christopher's arm. 'It's not 'end of 'world,' he said mildly. 'Life is a tangled web sometimes.'

Christopher nodded. '*O what a tangled web we weave...*' he quoted, then sadly shook his head. 'I never thought that it might apply to me.'

'It doesn't, sir,' Fletcher assured him. 'Not to you, if it's true that you didn't know or weren't aware of it. But there could be implications for our children if we're not careful.'

Christopher frowned. 'I don't understand.'

'Now's not the time. Let's go together to see my mother and let her know that we have an understanding, and the understanding is that no matter what she says I expect nothing from you, no inheritance, no apology. My accidental birth has no bearing on the lives we lead now.' Fletcher kept his hand on Hart's arm as they walked towards the cottage; he seemed so shaky that Fletcher feared he might collapse. He's not a young man, he thought. He's as old as my mother and this has brought him to 'verge of collapse. I'll have to keep 'peace between them. Like a dutiful son, he thought wryly. Just like I did when I was a lad living at Marsh Farm.

The first thing Fletcher noticed was that the cottage door was open and swinging gently on its hinges. He frowned; it wasn't like his mother to keep the door open. He pushed it wider. 'Ma?' he said, and then saw her lying on the rug in front of a dead fire. He rushed inside and Christopher followed more slowly, not having seen Ellen lying on the floor until Fletcher bent over her.

'Oh, great heavens,' he said. 'What's happened? She's not–'

'She's still breathing.' Fletcher had his ear to his

261

mother's chest. 'She's soaked through and covered in mud; her skin is cold. Can you move 'blanket off 'bed and I'll lift her on to it.'

Christopher did as he was bid. Fletcher picked Ellen up easily and thought how thin and bony she was. He put her on the bed, took off her boots and stockings and covered her with the blanket. He put his hands to his head. 'I'll have to fetch a doctor,' he faltered. 'Will you stop with her?'

'I'll go,' Christopher said quickly. 'My driver brought me; my wife insisted. The carriage is in the lane and our doctor lives in Brough. It will take no more than ten or fifteen minutes. Pray God he's in.'

Fletcher nodded. 'Please, if you will. Tell him to hurry. I'll get 'fire going – it's cold in here and we'll need hot water.' He had in mind to fill the stone water bottle that his mother always used to warm her bed. But Christopher was already on his way out of the door, galvanized into action whereas previously he had seemed weak and vulnerable.

There was kindling in the hearth and Fletcher placed it on top of the ash and looked on the mantelpiece for matches. He found them and with trembling hands struck one, but it blew out immediately and he looked about him for scraps of paper, which he found in the coal scuttle and pushed beneath the kindling before striking another match.

This time the flame held, the twigs took hold and he carefully added more, whilst still keeping an eye on the bed. He heard a low moan and jumped to his feet. 'Ma, it's me. I've sent for 'doctor. You're not well. What happened? Did you fall in 'water?'

She didn't answer but moaned again. I must tek her wet clothes off, he thought, or she'll get pneumonia, if she hasn't already. He lifted her up, unfastened and removed her blouse and skirt, but hesitated over removing her undergarments, even though they too were wet. He wrapped her in a shawl that was on the back of a chair, took off his own jacket and put that round her, and then replaced the blanket on top. The kindling was now burning brightly and he added more wood and then a lump of coal. The kettle was hanging from a hook and he shook it. There was some water in it but not much, and he knew it would take an age to boil.

He knelt down by the bed and waited, wishing that the doctor would come soon. What if he was out? What would Christopher Hart do then? He tucked the blanket closer to her. 'Ma. Can you hear me? We've sent for 'doctor,' he repeated. 'Christopher Hart has gone to fetch him. He'll be back in a minute.'

Ellen exhaled, but said nothing. He put his hand to her forehead. She was still icy cold, and although he didn't want to admit it, he didn't think she would survive.

He got up again and went to attend to the fire, carefully feeding in twigs and small pieces of wood and coal so as not to smother the flame, and then turned as he heard her say something. He went back to the bed. 'What did you say?' He heard the sound of scurrying feet on the path. 'I think 'doctor's here, and Christopher; we came together, Ma. Everything's all right.' His voice was choked

263

as he lied. 'We've come to an understanding – about me being 'eldest son, just like you wanted.'

He thought she gave a small smile, though he could have been mistaken; it might have been a sudden pain that twisted her lips. She breathed some words and he bent his head, and like a faint rustle or a sigh he heard, 'Tell him – I'm sorry.'

The doctor and Christopher came into the room and Fletcher turned to them. 'It's too late.' Tears streamed down his face. 'She's gone.'

CHAPTER THIRTY-TWO

Milo introduced himself as Leo Milo, adding that most people of his acquaintance called him Milo. Charles gave him a short bow and held out his hand. 'Charles Hart,' he said. 'How do you do? And my sister, Miss Beatrice Hart.'

Beatrice dipped her knee and Milo took off his hat and bowed.

'Daniel Orsini-Tuke,' Daniel said, putting out his hand. The Englishman gave an astonished start at the name, but he didn't comment.

Instead, he led them back to the trattoria, taking them inside because of the heat. There were several small tables and a bar with a kitchen behind it, and he asked if they would like to have lunch. They thanked him and explained that they had just eaten.

He clicked his fingers to their waiter and asked for something. The man brought over a bottle of red wine and four glasses, and a plate of bread and olives.

'Signorina,' Milo addressed Beatrice. 'Perhaps you might prefer something lighter? A glass of Puccino, or Prosecco as it is also known?'

Beatrice hesitated; she wasn't really used to drinking wine. Milo smiled. 'Most ladies like it. The bubbles tickle their nose.'

'Then a small glass, Signor. Thank you.'

He poured the red wine and waited for a bottle of Prosecco to be brought, poured Beatrice a glass and then raised his in a toast. *'Salute.'*

The others raised their glasses and Beatrice pronounced the Prosecco delightful.

'It's produced in this region,' Milo explained. 'Now, I must first of all apologize. I speak so little of my own tongue that I sometimes lapse into Italian. I've lived here for a long time. My wife was Italian and my daughter has been brought up as an Italian.' He paused, and then said, 'Federico said you were enquiring about 'Orsini family, and' – he turned to Daniel – 'you introduced yourself as Orsini, so you must have Italian blood?'

'So I believe, sir. My background is rather a mystery. I never knew my father, he died when I was a baby, but according to my mother it seems that he didn't know much about his father's past either.' He hesitated. 'My grandmother, my father's mother, said that – that my grandfather's name was Orsini and we thought that was an Italian name.'

'Only thought?' Milo asked with a puzzled frown. 'And why did you think he might be from Genoa? The Orsini family originated in Rome.'

'I didn't,' Daniel admitted. 'But Granny Rosie told me he was a seaman, so after we'd crossed Switzerland, where we were meeting Beatrice, we headed towards 'nearest Italian port, which happened to be Genoa. They, erm...' He flushed. 'My grandparents didn't marry. My father was born out of wedlock.'

'It happens.' Milo shrugged. 'It won't be 'first time. But what's left of 'Orsini family – and there aren't many – will mostly be in Rome.'

Charles gave a little frown and glanced at Beatrice, who was listening intently.

'However,' Milo went on after a short pause, 'the reason that Federico called me over was not only because he thought that as an Englishman I could help you find information, but also because he knows I'm related through marriage to an Orsini.'

'*Oh,*' Daniel breathed. 'Really? That's incredible.'

'Goodness,' Beatrice said. 'How very extraordinary! What an amazing coincidence. But earlier, the waiter told us that the Orsinis were a noble family, so does it not follow that there would be several blood lines from the original?'

'Oh, yes, most likely, I'd say.'

'Where does your relative live? Would he be willing to meet me?' Daniel asked eagerly. 'He might be able to help track down my grandfather – if he's alive, that is. I must admit I thought it'd be like finding a needle in a haystack. I didn't expect to find someone wi' same name on 'first day!'

'You're from Yorkshire, aren't you?' Milo asked him. 'I can hear it.'

'Aye, I am,' Daniel said, 'and proud of it even though I might have a drop of foreign blood.'

'More than a drop, I'd say.' Milo poured them all another glass of wine. 'Anyone looking at you would think you were pure Italian. Yes, I'll take you to see *la famiglia*. Where are you staying?'

They explained that they were in lodgings just outside the town, and after considering for a moment Milo said that as Signor Orsini lived outside Genoa in the village of Vernazza, on the Cinque Terre coastline, it was too late for him to take them today.

'I'll tell him about you,' he said, 'so tomorrow morning meet me here at eight thirty and I'll take you to visit him. We'll go by ferry, much easier and quicker than by road or rail. He's sure to invite you to stay, so tell your *padrona* – landlady – that you might be away for one or two nights. Signor Orsini leads a quiet life nowadays but enjoys having company.'

'That's really good of you, Mr Milo,' Daniel began, but Milo interrupted him.

'Just Milo will do.' His brown eyes were merry, appraising him. 'Not my real name, but ... well, not now. I must dash if I'm to catch 'ferry back. It's been good to talk to you. Folks from my own country.' He looked pensive. 'My own county too.' He saw their raised eyebrows and questions hovering. 'More of that tomorrow. Don't be late, the ferry won't wait.' He picked up his hat. *'Arrivederci.'*

They all stared after him as he departed. *'Well!'* Beatrice breathed. And *'Oh!'* Daniel said feelingly. 'I can't believe it.' And Charles added, 'Did you hear the way he spoke? Beatrice, did you notice?'

'Yes,' she nodded. 'I did.'

267

'What?' Daniel asked. 'What about it? He said he isn't used to speaking English now.'

'Not only that,' Charles said, as they again said goodbye to the waiter and made their way outside into the heat of the afternoon. 'Gosh, I feel rather woozy with the wine.'

'What do you mean?' Daniel persisted.

Charles blew out his cheeks and hooked his arms into Daniel's and Beatrice's for support. 'I mean that he has an accent similar to yours, Daniel.'

'What Charles is trying to say,' Beatrice explained, 'is that Milo sounds as if he's from our area of Yorkshire. From the East Riding, just as we are, except that Charles and I don't have the local accent as you do. Yours is the true and old accent of the area, whereas ours–'

'Is toffee-nosed!' Charles gave a snort of laughter at his own joke, and added, 'I do believe I'm slightly drunk.'

'I do believe you are, *old fellow*,' Daniel mocked spontaneously. 'Come on.' He took the lead. 'It's too hot to be out. Let's get back. I think we might need a lie-down!'

Charles snored throughout the afternoon as he slept off the effects of the wine, but Daniel sat on his bed, wide awake, anxiety washing over him as he considered the day's events. It is such a coincidence. I don't suppose this Orsini will know my Marco Orsini – it's probably a popular name just as Joseph Smith or William Brown or Thomas Jones are at home. He thought then of his half-brothers, Lenny and Joseph, and felt guilt yet again that he was here in Italy while although

Joseph was still at school Lenny was contributing to the family finances with his pigs at– Oh, it's his birthday this month. He'll be fourteen.

He got up and looked in his rucksack for his supply of cards, searched for a pencil and began to write. He first of all wished Lenny a happy birthday and apologized that he might have missed the date.

I know we're in June, he wrote. But sometimes we even forget what day it is. We've arrived in Genoa in Italy and by sheer coincidence have tracked down someone who married into the Orsini family. But tell Granny Rosie not to get her hopes up yet as it might be a dead end. **It was an ancient noble family,** he outlined in bold letters. *And I hope to meet one of them tomorrow. I'm missing you all. Your loving son and brother, Daniel.*

He went back to lie on the bed. And it's got to be a fluke, he mused, if Milo comes from our neck of 'woods. Odd sort of name for a Yorkshireman, Leo Milo, though didn't he say it wasn't his real name? Why would he change it? Or mebbe it was too difficult for 'Italians to pronounce. He began to feel sleepy and confused as thoughts rushed through his head and, as he did so often since being in her company every day, he thought of Beatrice, her smile, her fair skin and the blonde hair that was bleaching whiter in the sun. Sun-kissed, he dreamed as he fell asleep. I wish that I could kiss it too.

The next morning they were on the quayside by eight fifteen, not wanting to be late. They'd had to pay their hostess a further deposit to keep their rooms, even though, as Charles grumbled, they were not likely to go off and leave the ponies behind. Daniel said he didn't mind paying as it meant that the animals were being looked after and grazing every day on a grassy area adjacent to the guest house with access to shelter from the afternoon sun.

'It's coming.' Beatrice pointed out the ferry boat heading towards the harbour, a pall of smoke erupting from its tall chimney, and they moved towards the landing stage. As it came nearer they saw a group of passengers waiting to come ashore and in the midst of them Milo, wearing his hat, which he lifted and waved.

Daniel huffed out a breath. 'That's a relief. I half thought he might not come!'

'He must be as curious as we are.' Beatrice smiled at him. 'Are you nervous? I would be in your place.'

'I am,' Daniel admitted. 'I wonder what he's told Signor Orsini – if he's told him anything.'

'We'll find out shortly,' Charles said, narrowing his eyes against the sun, already very bright, though a strong breeze was blowing across the water.

'*Buongiorno!*' Milo greeted them. 'Come aboard. I've already got your tickets.' He came to the gangway and put out his hand to help Beatrice on board. 'I thought you'd like to sit on deck to appreciate the scenery. This is considered to be a most beautiful coastline.'

Solicitously he handed Beatrice a blanket to wrap around her knees, and although she wasn't cold she appreciated his consideration.

'How did you travel here?' he asked as the ferry

got under way. 'By train from Brig, then Domodossola and Milan, I suppose?'

They all shook their heads. 'We rode,' Daniel said.

'Horseback,' Beatrice added.

'Camping,' Charles concluded. 'It's a long way.'

Milo looked astonished. 'No, I meant from Switzerland.'

'So did we,' Daniel told him. 'Charles and I sailed from England to Le Havre then took 'train to Rouen and then to Paris, where we spent a few days before going on to Montreux. Where was it next, Charles? Oh, I can't remember.' He wrinkled his forehead. 'But then across Lake Thun to Interlaken to see Beatrice.' He grinned. 'And then horseback – well, mountain ponies. I can't believe we did all that and finally got to Genoa.'

'You came across the Alps on horseback?' Milo shook his head. 'And you've never been before?'

'I've been living in Interlaken,' Beatrice told him. 'I was at a finishing school for *young ladies*,' she added, laughing.

'Well, I'm sure they prepared you thoroughly for such an adventure,' Milo said, his eyes merry.

'I wasn't going to miss it,' she declared. 'If my brother and...' She hesitated. She was quite sure that this Englishman wouldn't be deceived into thinking Daniel was her cousin. '...and our good friend Daniel could do it, then I saw no reason why I couldn't.'

'I'm very impressed,' Milo said. 'Bravo! But you all came for what reason? To do the Grand Tour?'

'We came because Daniel wanted some answers about his past,' Charles said, adding, 'I wasn't

271

going to let him come without me, although we hadn't reckoned on Beatrice coming too. She tricked us.' He gave an ironic grin at his sister and a heavy sigh. 'As she so often does.'

By the time they had talked and Milo had pointed out the position of Cinque Terre, the five villages nestling in small coves and meandering up the steep mountainside, they were nearing Vernazza with its small harbour, olive groves and terraced vineyards that appeared to be plummeting down into the sea that lashed lazily beneath its feet.

'It's a steep climb up to 'house,' Milo told them when they disembarked. 'If you look up you can see it on that promontory.'

Above them on a rocky shelf stood a tower-like building with a terrace overlooking the sea.

'How lovely!' Beatrice said. 'Do you live there too, Milo?'

He took Beatrice's rucksack from her and put it on his own back as they began the uphill trek. 'I do now. My wife and I used to live in Genoa and after she died I stayed for a few years, but the port is getting busier and busier and I worried about my daughter's safety, so we came to keep her grandfather company.'

'Oh,' Daniel said. 'So Signor Orsini is your father-in-law?'

'He is,' Milo answered. The hillside was very steep, as he had said, and the path so narrow in places that they had to walk in single file and were unable to converse. Eventually Milo said, 'Nearly there. Five minutes or so and you can catch your breath.'

They were all breathing heavily by the time they reached the wooden gates which stood wide open to greet them. The path went higher up the mountain and on each side the vineyards stretched on, as did the sweet-scented lemon groves. They walked through the gates towards the house, which was much bigger than it seemed from below. From the rear it was castle-like, with stone terracing and lows walls and a piazza with stone jars and seating beneath olive trees and trailing vines.

'Come,' Milo said. 'We'll go in from the front and you can look at 'view over the sea.' He led them to the front of the house, where they came to the terrace they had seen from below. They followed him towards the terrace wall to look down at the panorama of steep hillside and vineyards; beyond the small harbour and cluster of houses the deep blue Mediterranean threw up spumes of white spray on to the rocky coastline. They didn't notice the figure sitting at the other end of the terrace.

'*Buongiorno.*' A deep voice made them about-turn and walk towards a broad-shouldered man in his late sixties, with a thick white moustache but dark eyebrows, and a straw hat on a head of white hair. He sat comfortably in a basket chair, a white jug and a cup and saucer placed on a low table beside him. There was a pungent aroma of coffee.

'*Buongiorno,*' they replied. Charles and Daniel bowed and Beatrice dipped her knee graciously.

'*Babbo,*' Milo said, and only Beatrice knew that this was an affectionate term for Father or Da. 'These are the English people I was telling you about.' He spoke slowly, in English. 'Miss Beatrice Hart, her brother Charles, and Daniel...' he hesitated, 'Orsini.' He turned towards them. 'My father-in-law, Signor Orsini.'

'*Caffè*.' Signor Orsini snapped his fingers in the air. 'Tell Sophia she bring *caffè* for our guests.'

Milo went inside and called to someone, and Signor Orsini beckoned to the three of them. 'Come, forgive me for not standing; my legs are not good today.' He beckoned again to Daniel and Charles. 'Bring chairs, *per favore*.' Then, turning to Beatrice, he said, '*Signorina*. Leo no say you are so beautiful.'

He invited Beatrice to sit next to him, murmuring, '*La mia giornata é più luminosa*. You understand, yes?'

'No, *signor*.' Beatrice blushed.

'Explain, Leo,' he said to his son-in-law, who had come back out on to the terrace.

'He says that his whole day is brighter,' Leo translated, adding, 'My father-in-law is a terrible flirt.'

'You're very kind, sir,' Beatrice smiled.

Daniel, listening, thought, I wonder if I could remember that? But then, what's the use? I'd never be able to say it to her.

A pretty dark-haired woman with a flower in her hair and wearing a crisp white apron over her colourful dress brought a tray of coffee cups and another jug of coffee. Leo took it from her and said, 'This is Sophia. She is a good friend of ours and helpmate of Signor Orsini.' She glanced at Beatrice, then Charles, but her eyes lingered on Daniel as she smiled and bobbed her head before she left them.

'So.' Signor Orsini took a sip of coffee, whilst Milo poured for the guests. 'You are in search of your ancestors?' He looked directly at Daniel. 'And your name is Orsini, yes? You perhaps do not know that once there were many Orsinis; some in years past were popes or cardinals and in time their lines disappeared, but others, they intermarry with other noble Italian families and the lines were split into many others.' He shrugged. 'I 'ave not ever heard of an Orsini marrying into an English family.' He sighed. 'I don't, of course, enquire any more. I lead a very quiet life.' He smiled mischievously. 'As a young man I was more adventurous.' He raised his dark eyes towards Milo, who wasn't sitting but standing to drink his coffee. 'As Leo once was, also.'

Daniel answered nervously, 'I'm trying to find out about my grandfather. My English grandmother bore him a son. She knew his name was Orsini, but she wasn't sure where he came from. When I was very young I promised her that one day I'd try to find him for her.' He thought affectionately of Granny Rosie. 'She expects nothing from him, but only wanted to know if he'd had a good life, and I suppose to tell him about 'son she bore him – my father Noah,' he added. 'Who, sad to say, I don't remember, as he died when I was an infant.'

'Ah!' Signor Orsini exclaimed. 'You never knew him? That is most unfortunate. Every son should know 'is father, as a daughter should know her mother.' He lifted his hand towards Milo. 'Leo's daughter doesn't remember her mother either.

275

She 'as aunts but it is not ze same, especially when they live so far away.'

He sat silently, shaking his head and sighing. 'I 'ave no sons or grandsons, but,' he lifted his head, 'I 'ave Leo who is as good as a son to me.'

Daniel nodded. 'I have a stepfather who is 'same as a father to me; he's 'onny one I've ever known. But I've never known a grandfather either, so I don't know what it'd be like to have one, but I want to do this for Granny Rosie, if I can – if it's not impossible, which I think mebbe it might be. But it'd make her very happy.' His voice dropped, and he flushed slightly. 'He was her one true love. She's never forgotten him, even after so many years.'

CHAPTER THIRTY-THREE

A poignant silence descended as Daniel finished speaking. Signor Orsini appeared to be sunk in contemplation, but after a moment Milo said, 'My daughter will be here soon. She's looking forward to meeting you and speaking English. Sometimes I forget to speak my own language and it's important that she doesn't forget that she has English roots, even though she's never been to England. Last time I was there was well over twenty years ago, before she was born.' He seemed nostalgic. 'Like you, Daniel, I was trying to find my family.'

He shrugged in the Italian manner as his father-in-law did. He seemed more Italian than

English, even rolling his R's like the Italians, and yet they could all hear a slight Yorkshire accent.

'And did you?' Beatrice asked. 'Find them?'

'No, I didn't. I left my home town when I was very young and went to seek my fortune.' He grinned. 'Many young men were doing that; I suppose they still do. I went to sea for quite a few years, going home from time to time, but then decided to go to America.'

Daniel nodded. That was what Fletcher did before he married my ma.

'And how did you come to be in Italy?' Charles asked. 'It's hardly a short cut to America.'

'I did go to America and worked there for several years, but I'd the wanderlust and decided to travel back to Europe. I went to New York and signed up with an Italian freight ship – I was a seaman, after all – and after about a year calling at various ports we docked in Sicily.' He smiled at his father-in-law. 'And it was there that I met 'Orsini family.'

'We were visiting our daughter Giovanna; she is married to a Sicilian,' Signor Orsini explained, and flourished a hand for Milo to continue his story.

'I met, by chance, and fell in love with Signor Orsini's youngest daughter, Francesca,' Milo went on. 'She was only sixteen, but I knew she was 'onny one I'd ever love.'

'And...' Beatrice asked softly.

'I followed them back to Italy and stayed here, learning 'language, learning about Italian culture – because I wasn't an educated man – so that in time I could ask her to marry me.' A shadow crossed his face. 'My wife died after giving birth to our daughter,' he continued, his voice low. 'She was nineteen.' He seemed to give himself a mental shake. 'But here I am, telling you about myself, when we are here to find out about this young man's relative. Where do we look, Babbo?' He addressed his father-in-law. 'How do we start?'

'I am just thinking about it,' Signor Orsini said vaguely. 'Where did you say your grandmother was from?' he asked Daniel.

'She came from Hull and then went to live in Brough, further up on 'Humber estuary.'

'And how old is she, your grandmother?'

'I'm not sure,' Daniel said. 'She said she was young when she gave birth to my father. She's probably about sixty-three or four; I don't really know. She doesn't like to talk about that time, because she wasn't married, you see. She thinks it's a blot on her character, but,' he spoke firmly in her defence, 'she was very young when her parents died and she was left destitute.'

'Leo,' their host said abruptly. 'Help me inside, *per favore*. I must speak to this young man alone. And where is Calypso?' he added impatiently. 'Why is she not here to entertain our guests?'

'She'll be here soon. She had to visit someone in Prevo.' Milo spoke kindly and calmly as he helped Signor Orsini out of his chair and gave him his stick. Daniel cast a puzzled glance towards Beatrice and Charles, and followed Milo and Signor Orsini into a light and airy room with large windows overlooking the terrace. Milo drew up a chair for his father-in-law.

'*Ci lascia, per favore*, Leo, leave us, please,' the older man said. 'I need to know more. I need to know more about this Granny Rosie.'

278

As the others disappeared into the house, Beatrice and Charles wandered across to the rail and gazed down the mountainside.

'There's something–' they said simultaneously, something that they did occasionally, tuning in to each other's thoughts. 'Did you notice–' Beatrice said.

'Yes,' Charles answered, even though Beatrice hadn't finished speaking. 'I did. The way Milo blinked when Daniel mentioned Hull.'

'He's from there, I'm sure of it,' Beatrice agreed. 'He has the same accent as Daniel.'

'He'll tell us eventually,' Charles said, and they both turned as they heard running feet coming up the steps just as Milo came back out again.

A girl of about seventeen ran breathlessly on to the terrace. She was small and petite, and her hair was dark, shiny and straight, hanging down almost to her tiny waist. 'I'm so sorry I'm late, Papa. I ran all the way.' She turned as her father indicated they had guests and went towards Beatrice and Charles. The two young women smiled and dipped their knees, but Charles stood as if struck dumb, his blue eyes gazing into her dark brown ones.

Beatrice nudged him, and recovering, he put his hand to his chest. 'Forgive me, signorina. Charles Hart.' He turned to Beatrice and opened and closed his mouth.

She arched an eyebrow. 'Beatrice,' she whispered wryly.

'Ah, erm – yes. May I introduce my sister, Beatrice?'

'This is my daughter Calypso,' Milo said. 'Beatrice and Charles Hart, visitors from England.'

Calypso laughed, glancing at Charles. 'I am very pleased to meet you. You are twins, yes?'

'We are,' Beatrice answered, since her brother seemed to have lost all power of speech. 'Charles is the elder by about fifteen minutes.'

'I have never met any twins before.' She spoke good English with an attractive lilt.

'Calypso is a lovely name,' Beatrice said as they walked towards the chairs to sit down. 'Is it Latin or Greek?'

It was Milo who answered. 'There are many stories about Calypso, but I think that 'best one tells of the Greek goddess who entranced and captivated Odysseus, and that's what our newborn child did to us.' He smiled tenderly at his daughter. 'She's named Calypso, but also Francesca after her mother and Maria, which was my mother's name.'

They sat talking and answering Calypso's eager questions about their journey, and their home and family in England. Beatrice moved to a seat under an umbrella as the sun became hotter, and Calypso took a fan from her pocket and passed it to her.

'Calypso helps at the village school in Prevo,' Milo said. 'She teaches the children basic English.'

They chatted for about twenty minutes or so, and then Daniel emerged from the doorway, blinking in the bright sunshine. He was introduced to Calypso, Milo giving her full name of Calypso Francesca Maria.

'One of my sisters is called Maria after my

mother's mother,' Daniel murmured vaguely. He pressed his fist to his lips; he seemed confused and emotional. 'And – and it seems...' He stopped for a moment and glanced at Beatrice and then at Charles, before his eyes alighted again on Calypso and he went on in a choked voice, 'It seems that we share a grandfather. We – that is, Marco...'

Calypso was puzzled. 'I don't understand.'

Marco Orsini hobbled out of the house. 'I have asked Sophia to bring out Prosecco. We must have a toast.' He looked at Milo. 'It is a most amazing thing, my dear Leo. It seems that I had a son after all. Rosie, whom I met when I was...' he shrugged, 'when I was only a boy. Perhaps the age of these young men.' He glanced at his granddaughter and Beatrice, and intuitively they realized that what he was about to say was not intended for their tender ears. They drifted away to the terrace wall, murmuring softly as Beatrice told Calypso the whole story.

Marco was helped to sit, for he seemed quite shaky and unsteady. 'It was my first time with a woman,' he whispered to the men. 'Rosie too was just a girl, too young to be in such an establishment, but it was as Daniel has said, she was desperate, poor and homeless.' He clasped his hands to his head. 'I cannot believe that I left her to such a fate.' He looked up imploringly at Daniel and Milo. 'Believe me, I meant to go back, for I was quite – quite *besotted* with her, but when I returned to Italy my parents had arranged a marriage for me. It was the way it was done in those days.' He heaved a breath. 'I never went back to England. Had I known – but then, what would I have done?'

He gave a slight shake of his head. 'I don't know.'

Daniel sat down close by him and put his hand on his arm. 'History would've been changed if you'd gone back,' he said softly. 'My father, Noah, wouldn't have met my mother, who gave birth to me; he wouldn't have drowned in 'estuary, Ma wouldn't have met my stepfather and I wouldn't have had any half-brothers or sisters. It would've been a different life for everyone.'

Marco gave a winsome smile. 'How blessed am I? My grandson is a philosopher, and my granddaughter is beautiful.'

Sophia brought out glasses and olives and bread, returning with the chilled wine, and they all sat together in the sunshine and raised their glasses. Daniel was shocked and astounded at the swift discovery of his grandfather, finding him so easily after a mere mention of the name Orsini to a Genoese waiter. He kept glancing at Marco and then at Calypso, who he supposed was a cousin of some kind, and thinking that it was too far-fetched and extraordinary to be true.

She too kept looking at him, and then leaned towards him. 'You are my only male relative,' she murmured. 'Both my aunts have daughters. Aunt Giovanna has two, and Aunt Amalia has one.' She gave a dimpled smile. 'It is so good to meet you. Perhaps now my papa will bring me to England as he promises always to do.'

'I hope so,' Daniel replied. He felt dizzy, unable to comprehend what had happened. 'And then I can introduce you to my family.'

Beatrice began to speak. 'This is so extraordinary. Incredible, even. And I'm also intrigued,

Signor Milo. You told us that you were from the county of Yorkshire, as we are, and Charles and I think we can guess from which area. We think that you were from a port town not far from where we live.'

Daniel looked at Milo and nodded. 'I think so too. My ma has a similar accent and it's a bit different from other parts of Yorkshire.'

'Well then I'll tell you,' Milo said. 'It's no secret. I'm not Signor, but plain Mr, and I was born in 'town of Hull.'

'There!' Beatrice was triumphant. 'That's just what we said, isn't it, Charles?'

'We're all from the East Riding of Yorkshire,' Charles grinned.

'So we are,' Daniel agreed, adding jokingly, 'except that you're both gentlefolk, not a man of the soil like me.'

'Daniel!' Beatrice objected, and turning to Milo she said, 'But Leo Milo is not an English name.'

'It isn't 'name I was given,' Leo said, 'and I'm a plebeian too, but not a country one like Daniel. I was born in 'back streets of Hull where we had to eke out a living 'best way we could, which was why I went to sea as a young lad, as my father and brothers and so many men did before me, and lost their lives into 'bargain.'

'And still do,' Daniel told him. 'There are still many fishermen who go down wi' their ships. My ma's father and brothers were lost at sea.'

All but one, he was going to say, but was suddenly struck by a thought that sent hot and cold shock waves jangling throughout his body and he heard Leo's voice as if through a November fog. He gazed at him, dumbstruck, until his senses slowly returned.

'And so,' Leo was saying, 'when my wife and I married, Marco began to call me Leonardo instead of Leonard, which was then shortened to Leo.' He laughed, 'and my surname, Milo–'

'Had been Miles,' Daniel finished for him.

All eyes turned to him and he stood up, his face flushed. 'Mr Miles,' he croaked. 'Leonard. My middle name is Miles. My mother Harriet gave me her family name so that it wouldn't die out. She told me about her brothers who were lost at sea and one, Leonard, who went to America and never came back. She named one of her sons after him.'

Daniel's eyes were moist. 'Was it you? And if it was, why didn't you get in touch with them? My ma and her mother were destitute, and then her mother died just before she married my father. She's allus wondered what happened to her favourite brother.'

The colour had drained from Leo's face and he gave a small gasp. 'Harriet? My sister Harriet is your mother? *O mio Dio!* I can't believe it.'

Calypso left her seat and knelt by her father's side. 'What does it mean, Papa?'

Leo put his hands to his face, covering his brimming eyes. Then he took a breath and gazed at his daughter. 'It means, *cara mia,* that you have another aunt and,' he looked across at Daniel and gave a hesitant trembling smile, 'more cousins.'

He went across to Daniel and clutched his shoulders with both hands. 'I did go back,' he said urgently. 'Back to 'same house where we'd once lived, but they'd gone. I asked a neighbour, who told me that my mother had died only a few weeks before, but she didn't know where Harriet was. Didn't know her, she said.' He gave a grim laugh. 'Harriet had lived there all her life but her neighbour said she didn't know her. Frightened of who I was, mebbe. I enquired at 'flour mills and other workplaces, hostelries, inns – so many of them – and then finally at 'workhouse, but she wasn't there either. And so I left. I'd been offered a ship and I daren't miss it, but...' He hesitated for a moment. 'I always meant to go back and try again, but once I met and married Francesca, and then lost her, I never did.'

He put out his hand. 'Will you shake my hand?'

Daniel swallowed hard and did so. 'I'm so glad to have found you, Uncle Leonard.' He gave a watery grin. 'A grandfather, an uncle and a double cousin in 'space of a couple of hours.'

Marco struggled to his feet and Charles dashed to help him. 'Well,' Marco said. 'Who would have thought it: *la famiglia*. We are all related.' He looked at Charles and Beatrice. 'And you, fair young Englishman and lady. Are you also related to ze Orsinis?'

Charles gazed adoringly at Calypso and from beneath her eyelashes Beatrice glanced at Daniel. 'Not yet,' they said in unison.

CHAPTER THIRTY-FOUR

Harriet knew something was wrong as soon as Fletcher came through the door. His face was grey beneath its tan.

'What's happened?' she said, and Maria, rolling out pastry, put down the rolling pin and gazed anxiously at her father. 'Was your ma angry with you?'

Fletcher shook his head and sat down by the fire, putting his hands to his face. He said nothing for a moment, as if composing himself.

What's she said to upset him this time? Harriet thought. Or mebbe Christopher Hart was there at the same time and there was a confrontation between the three of them. But Fletcher cleared his throat and stood up.

'Ma's dead,' he said flatly. 'She must've fallen into 'Haven.'

'Oh, dear God.' Horror shot through her. Had Ellen taken her own life? She put out her hand to him. 'She didn't – did she drown?'

'No.' He heaved a breath. 'She was alive when I got there. She was lying on 'floor at home but soaked through as if she'd fallen into 'water. There was no fire. She must've been there all night.'

'Oh, Da.' Maria came and put her arms round him but he just stood there stiffly. She began to weep. 'I'm so sorry. I'm so sorry if I was rude to her.'

He kissed the top of her head, then moved her gently away from him. 'You weren't rude, you were sticking up for your ma. My ma often said things she shouldn't, though I must not speak ill of...' He turned and walked towards the window that looked over his farmland. His land and Harriet's and his friend Tom's too. Land that one day would belong to his children, for Tom had none. Yet his mother had never asked about it, never shown the slightest interest; had never come to look at how successful they had been in developing a thriving farm by the strength of their own hands.

He swallowed tears of anger and sadness and struggled to stop them overflowing into a flood. Why, he thought. Why-why-why? What revengeful parasite had burrowed its tortuous being into her spirit to inflict such malevolence, such hostility on everyone she knew, even her own family? He thought of poor sad Noah, and Nathaniel the angry man he had known as his father, until she had told him otherwise.

Harriet came to him. Standing behind him and putting her arms round his waist, she rested her head on his shoulder. 'She's at peace now, Fletcher,' she murmured. 'Her anguish, all her disappointments, are at rest. Think of her kindly.'

He turned to face her, and looking into her eyes said harshly, 'How can you say that, Harriet, *you* of all people, who took the brunt of her hatred without just cause?'

She put her hand against his cheek. 'She had plans for you,' she said, her voice low. 'And I got in 'way of them.'

Tears ran down his face and this time he was

unable to stop them. 'She was fooling herself! All those years since 'day I was born or even before, she was scheming and plotting, fantasizing and imagining a situation that would never happen, not in a million years.' He rubbed his nose on his sleeve and gave a sobbing derisive laugh. 'She thought that one day I'd be 'lord of 'manor! That's what it was all about. Ha! I think Christopher Hart barely remembered her from 'old days.'

'Was he there?' Harriet asked, and glanced at Maria, indicating that she should make tea.

'Yeh.' He took a large handkerchief from his pocket and blew his nose. 'We arrived at 'same time. Went in together and found her. He's all right. We met at 'top of 'lane and he told me he was sorry, that if he'd known he would have supported her. I think he would have done, if onny she'd told him. Ha,' he said again. 'Everybody knew but him.'

Harriet nodded. She had heard years ago and believed it. 'Yes,' she agreed. 'I think that everybody probably did. But no one would have thought of telling Christopher Hart. Not even his wife.'

The three of them sat and drank tea, and then Fletcher said to Maria, 'Will you fetch Lenny in, and Tom too if he's about? We'll give Joseph and Elizabeth 'news about Granny when they get home.'

Maria slipped out, giving her father a sympathetic pat on his shoulder.

'She's a good girl, isn't she?' he said. 'She's like you. No fancy airs or graces, no yearnings for things out of reach, not like Dolly.'

288

'Oh, I think she might have had yearnings,' Harriet said, thinking of her talk with Maria about the implications of Christopher Hart's being Fletcher's father. 'But she's strong enough to resist them.' She smiled. 'But she's also like you. She's kind and forgiving.'

'I'm not forgiving,' Fletcher said bitterly. 'I can't forgive my mother. I don't mean for having a child out of wedlock, but for blaming everyone but herself, and for her malicious hypocrisy towards someone like Rosie, who gave Noah up because she thought he'd have a better life.'

Harriet recalled Ellen's bitter and scathing remarks about Noah's unwed birth mother; remarks from a woman who was living a double life with a child that wasn't her husband's.

'You must try to forgive and forget,' she said softly. 'In time perhaps you'll realize that she thought she was doing it for you.'

Melissa Hart had paced about her sitting room for nearly an hour. What was keeping Christopher? Had he and Fletcher and Ellen Tuke had an argument? What are we going to tell the children? she fretted. *Should* we tell the children? Is there any need? But if we don't tell them, are we being dishonest?

She walked to the window and was reassured to see the carriage coming up the drive, but it stopped short of the house and Christopher got out before it continued round the back towards the stable block. She watched as Christopher walked across the lawns to the rose beds, stopping now and then as if examining the blooms, which was strange, for he rarely took an interest in them. Then she saw him look towards the house and she drew back so as not to be seen.

Whatever is he doing? Should I go down, or wait? Shall I ring for coffee so that it's here waiting for him if he is in need of it? But as she continued to watch from behind the curtains, he straightened his shoulders and drew himself up, and as if he'd made a resolution he strode towards the front door and a minute later she heard the peal of the door bell.

She made herself sit down and picked up her sewing, trying to appear quite calm as he entered the room, but then she saw his face.

'My goodness, what's wrong? Was it so dreadful?' He seemed to be sunk in misery. Or was it regret?

'It is dreadful, but not in the way you might think,' he said wearily, sitting down opposite her.

'Did you see Fletcher?'

'I did. We met on the river bank. We were both on the way to his mother's cottage.' He paused. 'He seems a decent fellow,' he muttered, and Melissa's lips twitched. That's because he's like you, she thought, and nothing like her.

'I told him I was sorry to hear of the claim his mother had made against me and that I would have supported her, had I known.' Christopher put his hand to his forehead. 'But that's not the worst of it,' he faltered. 'She's dead. We found her lying on the floor. There was no fire in the grate and she was soaked to the skin, but still breathing. But only just. I went off to fetch Chambers, but by the time we got back she was gone. Pneumonia, I suppose.'

Melissa flinched and licked her lips. 'But what had happened? Had she fallen in the Haven? Is the cottage close to the water – or had she...' The question remained hanging on her lips. Was Ellen capable of taking her own life?

'I don't know,' he muttered. 'She was covered in mud and algae. She must have hauled herself out of the water and managed to make her way back.' He gave a deep sigh. 'There'll have to be an inquest,' he said. 'I wish I'd never gone. I'll have to be there as a witness.'

It's my fault, Melissa thought uneasily. I suggested he should go back. But then, if he hadn't, he would have regretted it for the rest of his life. 'It was just as well you did,' she said. 'It would have been dreadful for her son to find her on his own.'

'That's true,' Christopher murmured. 'At least I was able to fetch the doctor, even though it was too late. I don't know what to do or say,' he admitted. 'I feel to blame somehow.'

'That's ridiculous,' his wife said sharply. 'You mustn't think like that and certainly never say it. Ellen Tuke, it seems to me,' she added bitterly, 'was the maker of her own misfortune.' She frowned in thought. 'Do you think that her mind was wandering? Because it seems so very odd that she chose to wait all these years before making accusations against you. I'm not suggesting that she was lying, but why wait?'

'I don't know,' he said again. 'Perhaps she felt that her days were numbered, as we all feel as we get older.' Melissa held back a gasp of concern as he went on, 'Perhaps she wanted to have everything out in the open before it was too late.'

Melissa had held lunch back to await Christopher's return and a maid knocked to ask if they should serve it now. Melissa gazed at her husband and made a decision.

'Tell Cook I'm so sorry, but Mr Hart is unwell. He's caught a chill, we think, and is going to bed. Would you serve him a light lunch on a tray? A bowl of soup and whatever meat is prepared. It's ham today, I think, is it not? Yes, so that and some thinly sliced bread and butter, please, and a pot of coffee. And yes, I'll have mine in here on the small table.'

That done, she rose to her feet. 'Come along, my dear. You've had a shock. Don't think about anything now. Have your lunch and a sleep and we'll talk everything over later.' She held out her hand and dutifully he got up and kissed her cheek.

'What would I ever do without you, Melissa?' he said. 'I am so very tired. Everything seems to be going wrong. The bailiff leaving, this business over Ellen Tuke. I don't want to think about anything.'

'You don't need to,' she said softly. 'It will all be resolved one way or another.'

She saw him to bed and sat with him while he ate his luncheon, and leaving him to sleep she went back to her sitting room to have her own. However, she found she wasn't very hungry, and although she finished the soup she only picked at the rest of the food.

She was worried about Christopher, and although she didn't think he needed to see the doctor, she did feel that he needed to rest. It was disheartening that their bailiff was leaving, but she didn't consider that he could be asked to stay on when he wasn't well enough to do the job, and so far there hadn't been much response to the advertisement that had been placed in the newspapers and farming journals. It will be November before anyone remotely suitable will be available to change their employment, she thought, so will we be able to manage until then? Are there any problems at the moment? The rent for the tenanted farms and cottages will be up to date, I expect. Perhaps I will ask Thompson before he finally leaves if that is so, and ask him too if there is anything outstanding or urgent that needs to be done.

If there isn't, then we have a breathing space, and if there is, well... She poured herself a cup of coffee and leaned back in her chair. She had never had to know about the accounts or the farms and Christopher had rarely discussed the estate with her, except in general terms. But if there is anything to deal with, she decided, I'm quite sure that I am perfectly capable of attending to it myself.

Upstairs, cosy in the bed that had had the warming pan swept over it and with a fire blazing in the grate, Christopher had pretended that he was sleepy in order to mollify Melissa, but in fact his mind was running amok as he thought about the events of that morning. What on earth had possessed Ellen to make such a claim against him? And then, because he had denied it, she had ... had she... Had she walked into the water in her distress? And then had she changed her mind when the water began to close over her? Or had she walked along the path and slipped, dragged herself out and gone home to think things over? But if so, why didn't she build up the fire and get dry?

He gave up. There were so many possibilities that he couldn't solve. But, even so, the accusation was there. Her son had known about it but hadn't confronted him with the knowledge. He closed his eyes and thought of his childhood. He hadn't made many friends at school or among other landowners' sons when they had occasionally met on social occasions; he had been more at ease with the kitchen staff. Most of them had known him from the time he was an infant, when the nursery maid or his nanny had taken him downstairs for some company, and he had continued to visit the kitchens until the time he was sent away to school. Mrs Marshall the cook, he remembered, had wept when he went down to say goodbye, dressed in his new grey uniform and a white wing-collared shirt. What was it she'd said? Something strange – *poor bairn*, she'd said. Fancy sending away a young bairn like that, and some of the kitchen maids had laughed, for they didn't think I was at all poor.

He began to feel sleepy; but Ellen, he thought, became my friend when she came to work here. We used to ride together on my new horse, Sorrel, when no one was looking. He smiled as he huddled under the blanket. It was a secret, he remembered. We thought it exciting to trick Cook and the other servants. We were not much more than children and yet I would have been admonished had we been found out, and she would have been dismissed.

Am I as strict with my children, he wondered. Am I a stern father? I think perhaps I am. There are so many responsibilities when you're caring for a family. Melissa is such a good mother, he mused; she loves our children. She's much better than mine, who didn't really know me.

But as he slipped into sleep, he recalled other things: a shadowy memory of Ellen baking him a cake, and on the night before his birthday being found lying drunk on the lawn, and Ellen's white face as she slipped away into the darkness as somebody half carried him back across the lawn and helped him upstairs to bed so that his parents wouldn't know. And then, some months later as his engagement to Jane was about to be announced, Ellen telling him she was going to marry Tuke.

He breathed deeply and evenly. So was that it? he reflected. If it happened at all, was it on that night, as Ellen had said? He tried to add up the years from his coming of age, but he couldn't, as slumber took hold of him and gently bore him away.

CHAPTER THIRTY-FIVE

Daniel woke the next morning with a hangover; they had consumed copious bottles of wine as they celebrated the reunion of families. The sun was already hot and shone brightly through his window. He looked out and saw that Marco, Leo and Calypso were having breakfast on the terrace below; they appeared to be talking seriously.

I wonder if Marco is having second thoughts about Granny Rosie and me, he considered. After all, it seems incredible, impossible even, that I should turn up out of the blue and he'd agree that we're related. Yesterday they had planned visits, and although Marco had said that he wouldn't be able to come to England as his arthritic legs couldn't withstand the long journey and the English weather was too cold and damp for him, he'd suggested that Daniel might come back and bring Rosie.

Leo had said that he and Calypso would come to England but that they couldn't leave Italy until after the grape and olive harvest, which began in mid-September, and that would mean travelling in the winter months.

Daniel washed and dressed and marvelled at the luxury of this lovely old house. It had been a fortified castle, Marco had told him, and he had bought it forty years ago for his wife and himself and their daughters when they were infants. Over the years he had extended and transformed it from a rather gloomy place to the beautiful home it was now, building the terrace on the rocky mountain-side, widening windows to catch the sun and fitting wooden shutters and marble floors to keep the house cool in the heat of the summer. Daniel tapped quietly on Charles's bedroom door, which was next door to his, but on receiving no answer he went down the stairs and outside to the terrace.

Marco was sitting alone, and after greeting him

jovially he told Daniel that he had just missed Leo and Calypso, but that Calypso would be back soon. Leo had gone up the mountain to check on the grapes and would be home for lunch.

'We are up early at this time of the year, before it becomes too 'ot,' Marco explained and rang a small silver bell to summon Sophia. 'But you are a farmer, you will know 'ow it is.' His English wasn't quite so good this morning and Daniel guessed that he needed to speak the language more often, as he had done yesterday, to be more proficient.

He sat down at the table facing Marco and with his back to the door. 'We're always up early,' he told him. 'But not because of the heat.' He grinned. 'That's hardly ever a problem for us, but when it is hot we have to move fast to bring in 'harvest. Have you heard 'saying, make hay while the sun shines?'

'Ah, yes, I think so.' Marco invited Daniel to help himself to some thinly sliced ham as Sophia came out with a pot of fresh coffee that was hot and strong. 'Or fruit,' he suggested. 'The melon is good. In Italy we do not eat much breakfast. Per'aps you like a brioche or sweet croissant?' He spoke swiftly to Sophia before she went away, and then added, 'What you eat for breakfast in England?'

Daniel laughed. 'Porridge, to start with, then mebbe bacon and eggs with bread. And a big pot of tea, very strong. We have to eat well in a morning, especially in winter when it's cold.'

'Of course,' Marco said. 'I do not 'ave to rise so early now, although when the grapes are ready for picking I go along to watch, and also I like to

297

be sure that they are ready. Old 'abits, you know.'

'I hadn't realized that you were a wine maker,' Daniel said, sipping his coffee. 'I've always thought of you as a seaman.'

'No, no. I 'ave never been a seaman.' Marco put his face up to the sun as he contemplated. 'When I left school I asked my father if I could travel to England and learn English before joining him as a vintner – a wine maker. It takes a long time to learn about wine, and although my father was well known in the business and had brought me up to know some, I felt, like many young men, that I should see something of the world before I, ah, settled down, you know.'

Sophia brought out some fresh sweet bread and placed it in front of Daniel, who said a shy *'Grazie'*. She smiled, and patted the top of his head, murmuring, *'Prego, bell'uomo,'* which he didn't understand.

Marco glanced up at her, raised his eyebrows and then continued, 'He agreed that I could, and as he know ze captain of a ship, he arrange the voyage and say I must work my passage – you know the meaning of this, yes?'

Daniel nodded that he did.

'But I was not a good sailor,' Marco said, and demonstrated being sick by holding his stomach and blowing out his cheeks. Daniel laughed. He knew just what he meant.

Marco poured them both more coffee. 'So we sailed to the south coast of England and then to the north, and the seas there were much worse, very rough, and ze captain he took us to the port of Hull, which you know very well, and 'e told some of the other seamen to take me ashore and come back in three days.' He shook his head. 'I didn't know where we were or 'ow we got upriver, but these men,' he looked around him and lowered his voice, 'they took me to a house where there were lots of young women – you don't mind me telling you this? It is no – what you say, *reflection* on your grandmother.'

Daniel didn't; whatever Marco said, Granny Rosie would still be, in his opinion, the best grandmother anyone could have.

'And I met Rosie,' Marco said softly. 'She was so lovely, and very shy, which was surprising for ze kind of place she was in, and I vowed I would rescue her.' He sighed. 'I went back ze next day, but I know – *knew* no English and so I couldn't tell her. The day after, we had to leave to catch ze ship and sailed back to the London docks, and then we left to come back to Italy.'

He told Daniel again about his parents' decision to arrange his marriage. 'What could I do?' His voice softened. 'But I didn't forget Rosie. You must please tell her that?'

'I will,' Daniel promised, and thought how pleased Rosie would be to know that he was still alive. And he's handsome still, he thought, and his eyes are dark like mine. 'Sir,' he said. 'Can I ask you a question – erm, I don't mean anything too personal.'

Marco shrugged. 'I 'ave no secrets,' he said. 'Not now.'

'It's just that, well, your eyes are very dark, as mine are, and when I was at school sometimes other children would say that I was foreign, which

I suppose I am. But not all Italians have such dark eyes, and I wondered – well, I wondered...'

'Ah!' Marco exclaimed. 'I will tell you, Daniel, why it is. Italy is very close to Sicily and Sicily is close to North Africa. My mother was Sicilian, but you will know, yes, that over many centuries Sicily 'as been ruled by many nations including the Romans, the Spanish and the Greeks, and my mother's grandmother had Moorish blood from when the Arabs were also there many centuries before.' He sat back and surveyed Daniel, and then smiled, his eyes crinkling, and Daniel could see the vibrant young man that he had once been. 'And this is why we are so 'andsome, you and I, just as Sophia said. You understand what she say, yes? I knew the minute I saw you that you had inherited ze same bloodline as mine.'

Daniel laughed, embarrassed. 'So how did your family come to be living in Italy?'

'Ah, we 'ave always intermingled, but my father was pure Italian, and when 'e married my mother he brought her back 'ere to Italy. There has been much fighting in Sicily; even today there are – ah, *leetle* revolutions.' He rubbed his fingers together significantly. 'Pirates, you understand, and corruption too, and my father didn't want to become involved. He was a very ambitious man and there were many temptations.'

Daniel contemplated all he had been told. So I'm a mixture of nationalities. I'm English through my mother and Granny Rosie, but Italian and Sicilian through my grandparents and great-grandparents and whoever else went before.

As if he could read his mind, Marco went on, in

300

his halting English, 'You should be proud. You are ... multi-layered, a true citizen of the world. An Englishman as well as a descendant of a noble Italian family, which is what ze Orsinis were.'

A noble family, Daniel thought. I can't begin to contemplate that.

'And so,' Marco glanced towards the door into the house, where they could hear voices, 'when you come to choose a wife you may tell her father you have excellent, erm – what you might say – *providence?* No, not that, *provenance* I think is ze word. Or *pedigree,* perhaps.'

He broke off as Charles and then Beatrice came out on to the terrace and Daniel wondered if what Marco was saying was sheer coincidence or if he had seen Beatrice through the glass doors.

'Come, come,' their host called to them. 'You must 'ave some caffè and biscotti.'

They came towards them, and to Daniel's surprise Beatrice bent and kissed Marco on the cheek before sitting down. 'Thank you,' she said sincerely. 'Thank you for making us so welcome.'

'Yes, thank you, sir.' Charles gave him a short bow. 'We are total strangers and yet you have welcomed us to your lovely home.'

Marco lifted his hat, which he seemed to wear constantly when he was outside.

'You are very welcome – indeed, as any of my grandson's friends are.' He indicated Daniel and said huskily, 'You are good friends, I think?'

Daniel's lips quivered and he blinked rapidly as he realized that Marco was making a public declaration of his acceptance of him as his grandson.

Beatrice looked at him and gave a trembling

smile, her eyes glistening, whilst Charles gave a wide exultant grin. 'I think I can speak for my sister as well as myself,' he pronounced, 'when I say that Daniel is the best friend *anyone* could hope to have.'

They sat silently as Sophia brought in more coffee, brioche and biscotti. Last night there had been a celebration, but in the clear light of day Daniel, Beatrice and Charles all wondered if the knowledge of Daniel's background would make any difference to him.

Daniel knew for certain that there would be no changes for him when he got home, and he doubted that Granny Rosie would ever come to Italy. It would be too far for her to travel, but he thought that she would take great comfort from knowing that Marco accepted that she had given birth to his son and without any question had acknowledged Daniel as his grandson.

How trusting he is, he thought. I could have been anybody, a fraudster worming his way into his family, though I suppose the coincidence of being Leo's nephew must have added to my credentials. But he felt satisfied that he had found out about his grandfather, and for the first time ever he wished that his birth father, Noah, could have known what he was doing. Neither could he wait to give his mother the news that he had found her long-lost brother and his daughter.

Although Beatrice felt light-headed this morning – too much sparkling wine and sunshine yesterday – she was scheming and planning. Father wouldn't want me to marry for money alone, she thought, for he's kind and not mercenary by any means, and in any case would not require a prospective husband to be rich. He has money of his own he could give as a substantial dowry, but perhaps he would like to think I was marrying into a family of status: a noble family, no less. A small smile played around her lips, but an involuntary sigh broke through. The barrier is Daniel himself, for I know for a fact that he won't declare himself to Father. He's far too proud, and yet so very humble. And, she thought, perhaps I'm wrong, perhaps he won't declare himself even to me, because he thinks of me only as his friend.

Charles kept glancing towards the staircase, hoping that Calypso would appear. I wish I could remember what Signor Orsini said to Beatrice. Something about the day made brighter? Something *lumino?* I'm in love. I haven't met many young ladies, it is true, but it doesn't matter how many one might meet, I just know that Calypso is the only one for me. She is the most beautiful creature I have ever seen, and she seems kind and gracious too. I will come back to Italy. I shall ask my father – *tell* my father that my chosen profession is art and that I would like to study in Italy. Where else? He continued to debate in his mind. Where else would anyone wish to study art? Except, yes, I agree, I'd first thought of Paris, but I was wrong. Italy is the only place.

'We must move on soon,' Daniel was saying to Marco. He wasn't sure what name to give him. *Grandfather* seemed to be very personal and he didn't think he yet knew him well enough, but he couldn't call him Signor Orsini when they were related, while just Marco was, he thought, perhaps impolite.

'No! Not yet!' Marco said. 'Why? Why must you go?'

'Well,' Daniel fidgeted, 'I don't mean today, but perhaps tomorrow or 'next day. We must collect 'hosses and then make our way back home to England.'

Marco frowned. 'Your horses? You have horses? Where are they?'

'They are being well looked after,' Daniel assured him, 'and they were in need of a rest after their long journey.'

Marco was astounded, just as Leo had been, to hear that they had ridden across the Alps. 'And you will ride back?' he asked.

Daniel looked at Charles. 'We'll sell them,' Charles said. 'Although we'll miss them. They are beautiful animals, Haflingers, but we used the emergency fund and Daniel insists we must put it back before we go home.'

Daniel stood firm. 'Well, I must sell 'one I'm using and put 'money back, no matter what you and Beatrice do with yours.'

'And, erm, this emergency fund,' Marco asked. 'This was given to you, yes?'

'Yes,' Charles admitted. 'My father said we should have it in case we got into difficulties.'

'I see, but instead you decided to ride across ze Alps rather than take the train, yes?'

'There was no train from where we started, and we couldn't afford to come all the way by carriage,' Daniel told him. 'We're travelling on a shoestring.' He broke into laughter at Marco's bemused expression. 'On very little money,' he explained. 'But we haven't spent everything, so we can go part of 'way back by rail.' He glanced at Beatrice. She hadn't said what her plans were, but he was fairly sure she wouldn't be going back to the academy, even if they would have her back after this escapade, and he added, 'Mebbe as far as Switzerland. We haven't talked about it yet.'

'We didn't expect to find any clues about Daniel's beginnings so quickly,' Charles said. 'We half expected we'd have to travel to Rome.'

'Well, why not do that?' Marco suggested. 'It is not only a beautiful city but also Daniel's ancestral home.'

The three of them looked startled, Daniel with astonishment and wonderment written on his face.

'Oh, yes, do let's, Daniel,' Beatrice pleaded excitedly. 'We can go home and boast about Signor Orsini living in a castle by the Mediterranean and seeing the family palaces in Rome.'

Daniel frowned and lifted his hands in an almost Italian gesture, she thought.

'But who would I boast to? And why would I want to? I onny wanted to find 'Orsini family and tell Granny Rosie that I'd found Noah's father. On 'other hand, I suppose we might ... seeing as we're here. I might not ever get 'chance to go there again.'

'Ah! Tsk, tsk,' Marco said. 'I 'ope that you will be 'ere often.'

'I didn't mean...' Daniel chose his words carefully, not wanting to offend. 'I want to come back and see you, Grandfather.' The designation slipped out without intention. 'And I'll come back when I can, but I'm a working man and if I'm not there on 'farm, pulling my weight, then someone else has to tek my place.'

'I understand,' Marco nodded, 'and it's Nonno,' he added mildly. 'It means grandfather. But let me think. There must be a way round this.'

He gazed at Beatrice and then Charles. 'I think you also understand, but sometimes forget, that Daniel has to make a living, yes?'

'I'm sorry,' Beatrice said, her cheeks flushed. 'Yes, we do forget, and we forget also how spoiled we've been and take it for granted that we can do what we want, more or less; yes we can, Charles,' she admonished him, seeing the dispute in her brother's expression that said that he couldn't. 'At least as far as finance is concerned. Of course, there are times when we have to do what is considered to be socially correct. To conform.'

'We have to toe the line,' Charles added gloomily.

Marco laughed heartily. 'Toe ze line, and travel on a string, these English expressions I do not know until now. You must write them down for me, *per favore*.'

Then came a clattering up the steps and Calypso appeared on the terrace, followed by her father.

'More caffè,' Marco shouted towards the house, and in response a long stream of unfathomable Italian words from Sophia came spilling out through the doors. Marco ducked as if something was being thrown at him, and Calypso and Leo laughed uproariously.

CHAPTER THIRTY-SIX

It was decided that they would go back to Genoa by ferry, collect the ponies and bring them back the same way. In the meantime Leo would arrange terms with a local grower who had a small acreage of land down near the village and would allow them to let the ponies graze, so that they could stay on for a few more days.

'Oh, Papa. Can I go to Genoa too?' Calypso pleaded. 'It's such a long time since I was there.'

'No,' he said. 'I'm too busy to come with you right now.'

'She'd be perfectly safe with us, sir,' Charles said eagerly. 'We'd look after her; Beatrice has travelled all this way with us and felt perfectly at ease, haven't you, Bea?'

Beatrice put on a frail and winsome expression that fooled no one as she agreed she had felt quite safe and not at all threatened, with such strong and capable male escorts to take care of her, and privately wondered what her father would have to say about it once she arrived home.

'It's different in Italy,' Leo argued. 'It wouldn't look good, even though Calypso has more freedom than most unmarried young women.'

'I think it wouldn't hurt, Leo,' Marco broke in. 'She would be travelling with a cousin, after all – your nephew who is also my grandson!'

'How would you get to and from this lodging

house,' Leo asked briskly, 'if it's not in Genoa but outside in the hills?'

'Well, if you'd agree,' Daniel offered, 'the Haflingers are very strong and Calypso could ride behind me. It's not a long journey from our lodgings, fifteen minutes at most. We walked into the town on two occasions.'

'*Please*, Papa.' Calypso pouted her lips. 'I do so want to ask Beatrice about English ladies.'

'Oh, very well.' Leo realized that he had been overruled and admitted also that his views had changed since he had lived in Italy. Had he lived in England and in the same circumstances he'd once known, his daughter would probably be working for a living, unlike the fair gentlewoman Beatrice, travelling with her brother and Daniel. How has that been allowed? he mused. She must have very liberal parents.

Calypso gave her father a smacking kiss on his cheek. 'Thank you. I'll get my hat,' she said, jumping up to dash into the house. 'It will be very hot in Genoa.'

'Whoa, whoa!' her father and grandfather chorused. 'You're not thinking of going *now?*'

'It will be too hot for Beatrice,' Daniel said, flushing slightly. 'She's so fair, as is Charles,' he added.

Calypso turned back. 'Oh, of course,' she murmured. 'I'm so sorry. But Papa, you won't change your mind, will you?'

'No,' he promised, 'I won't. You could go later this afternoon and catch 'last ferry back.'

'But then we can't look at Genoa,' Calypso objected. 'Tomorrow morning then,' she decided, 'and I will show you the sights of Genoa.' She smiled at Beatrice. 'And we'll catch the late ferry home.'

During the hottest part of the day they all adjourned inside. Beatrice chatted to Calypso and Charles hung on to every word that Calypso uttered, and whilst Marco went to his room for an afternoon nap Daniel answered as many of Leo's questions as he could, about his mother and how she came to be living in a country district and married to a farmer.

Daniel only knew that his mother had married Noah in Hull, and he had then taken her to live with him and his family by the marshy estuary land near Brough.

'Harriet was a town girl,' Leo said. 'I can't imagine her living on a farm.'

'Ma told me she was on her uppers when she met Noah,' Daniel told him. 'She'd lost her job – at a mill, I think – her mother had just died, and then Noah offered her marriage. He said he needed a wife.' He paused. 'I gather that, erm, well, I don't think there was any love between them. It was convenient for them both.' He paused, and wondered how anyone could marry without love in their lives.

'Ellen Tuke, who'd adopted Noah, showed her how to milk a cow and look after 'hens, and taught her to cook and bake, but after I was born and when Noah died, my ma left, cos she felt she wasn't wanted, and went to live with a friend in her cottage.'

Daniel had always wondered what had gone wrong between them for Granny Tuke to take such a dislike to his mother. There had always been a mystery that his mother was unwilling to talk about. 'It's history,' she used to say.

'And your brothers and sisters,' Leo said. 'They're your stepfather's children?'

Daniel frowned. He never thought of them in that way. 'Y-eh,' he replied reluctantly. 'But I've onny ever known Fletcher as my father, so there's never been any difference between us. They're all fairer than me, except for Lenny.' He smiled. 'Ma has allus said that he looks like you, wi' same dark hair and brown eyes.'

'And she named him after me?' Leo had a catch in his voice, as if overcome that he hadn't been forgotten after so many years.

'Yeh.' Daniel laughed. 'I can't wait to tell them all that I've met you.'

'I was thinking about that onny this morning before you were up,' Leo said. 'I was talking to Marco and Calypso and trying to plan when I – that is Calypso and I – could come to England, and we thought that December might be best. Marco wouldn't come, as it would be too cold for him. Probably too cold for me, too, after living in this climate. But the olive harvest will be over apart from some of the pressings, and that can be left to the locals, who know more about it than I do, being a mere newcomer. I negotiate the sale of the products.'

'So you really will come?' Daniel was overjoyed. He had nurtured doubts.

'Of course.' Leo expressed surprise at the question. 'But I had to think it through, and think also about Marco. Sophia has said she'll stay with him. Her father's an old friend of Marco's, which is why she's so familiar with him: she's known him all her life. She also says that her parents will watch over him or even come to stay, though don't tell Marco I said so. He's very spirited and independent, but his legs let him down. Still, I'm sure he won't mind us leaving him, and maybe one of his daughters might come to stay too. He could be inundated with friends and family.' He hesitated. 'But just in case ... I have been wondering, might it be better not to tell Harriet – your mother – about me just yet? Then if we can't leave Marco for any reason, she won't be disappointed, and if we can come over it will be a wonderful surprise. What do you think?'

Daniel pondered. Harriet would be so happy to know that Leonard was still alive – would it be fair to keep the news from her for even a day? On the other hand, Leo's reluctance to risk disappointing her was understandable too. 'What about this?' he said slowly. 'I tell her that I've met you and that you're planning to come to England at some time in 'future, and *then* you can write to me and arrange a date and then we could surprise her, without worrying that she'll be terribly upset if you do have to cancel.'

Leo beamed. 'That's perfect. We don't catch her on the hop, and we don't risk letting her down either. So – we plan for December!'

The next morning they were up early to catch the first ferry back to Genoa. Calypso was thrilled to be going and Daniel, Charles and Beatrice again promised her father that they would take great

311

care of her. However, once they were on their way down the hillside and heading towards the harbour, they discovered that she was perfectly capable of looking after herself.

'Papa treats me like a child,' she complained. 'He doesn't know that I often come down to the town and meet friends.'

'Oh,' Charles said. 'Do you have any special friends?' Male friends, he wanted to say, but thought better of it. It would be prying.

'Oh, lots,' she said gaily. 'We sit on the harbour wall and discuss so much. If we see any of them, I will introduce you. They will be intrigued by you, Beatrice, and the girls will fall in love with Charles,' she said slyly, looking at him from beneath her lashes. 'But my cousin Daniel, they will think he is Italian and will want to know if he is promised.'

'Promised?' Daniel repeated. 'How do you mean – promised?'

'Promised in marriage, Daniel,' Beatrice broke in lightly. 'The same as in England. You're not, are you?'

He gazed back at her and slowly shook his head. 'Nothing to offer, I'm afraid. I'll have to stay single all my life, like Uncle Tom.'

'Ah.' Calypso shook back her long dark hair. 'But you are an Orsini, yes? We will find you a *reech* Italian woman who won't mind about you being poor if she can have your name.'

'And what about you, Calypso?' Charles cleared his throat, and dared. 'Are you promised?'

'No.' She laughed. 'My papa won't let me go.'

She was so much merrier and more lighthearted away from her father and grandfather, had so much more to say when out of their earshot, that although they were not so very strict with her it was obvious that she was expected to conform as a young lady should.

'The ferry it is coming, see.' She pointed. 'I am so looking forward to being with you. What would you like to see? The Duomo, of course, and the Sottoripa galleries when we get to the waterfront – oh, and you must look inside the San Giovanni church. It was a – what you call, a Knights Hospitaller of St John; pilgrims on their way to Rome and the Holy Land would rest there.'

'You're very well informed, Calypso,' Charles said, paying for the tickets as they boarded.

'Oh, I was at school in Genoa,' she explained. 'And our teachers take – took us to see all these places. It was our history lesson. And then I will show them on a tour of the city whilst the morning was still cool, Calypso and Beatrice walking in front with their arms linked, Daniel and Charles close behind. They attracted much attention and curious glances were directed at them; Beatrice with her fair skin and elegant demeanour and Charles, so obviously her brother, tall and slim, with the bearing of a gentleman, and a neat beard and sideburns, for he had paid particular attention whilst using the blade this morning, and his fair hair tucked beneath his hat. Calypso, vivacious and *'italiana'* like the young man behind her, who was an inch shorter than his male companion but broader in the shoulder and lithe as a cat, hatless, with dark curls falling about his face and a silk scarf knotted around his neck.

Calypso guided them down narrow and ancient winding streets, bringing them out to face the church of San Giovanni. 'It is a most ancient church,' she told them. 'Two churches – Romanesque.' They had a look inside, at the statuary and the wide hall with black walls and arches and the wooden ceiling that once sheltered the pilgrims, and admired the bell tower.

Then she led them on to the ducal palace, and showed them the *palazzi* built by bankers and rich traders, until by mutual consent they stopped to rest their legs and drink coffee.

When they had finished, she urged them on uphill to see the villa where she and her father had once lived. It was set high on the hillside, a tall house with shutters at the window, and she told them it had a private terrace at the back. She led them towards an open area next to the villa, where from a low wall they looked down over a panorama of the city below them; the Duomo and the ducal palace and in the distance the busy waterfront and ships from the world over, the jetty where small boats were being unloaded and, standing tall, La Lanterna, the old lighthouse, that was said, she told them, to have been built by a relative of Christopher Columbus.

'I love it here,' Calypso said softly. 'Of course I love my nonno's house too and the mountains, and Rome where Papa took me a few years ago.' She turned to Beatrice. 'But, do you not think, Beatrice, that women should be allowed to travel more? I would so like to see more of my own country, as well as others.'

Beatrice nodded. 'It will come in time,' she said. 'English women are travelling more. Independent women who perhaps don't have husbands, who dare to travel alone or with only a female companion.'

'Not yet in Italy,' Calypso murmured.

'Perhaps,' Charles suggested, hoping to plant the idea of himself in her mind, 'you will find a husband who wants to travel too, and you can go together.'

'Yes,' she agreed. 'It would be very nice to find someone compatible.'

'But are you not too young yet, Calypso?' Daniel asked anxiously.

'No,' she said firmly. 'Soon I will be eighteen. Perfect marriageable age.'

CHAPTER THIRTY-SEVEN

From the top of the hill they walked down to a restaurant where Calypso's father was known. Calypso was greeted effusively and volubly by the proprietor, who kissed her on both cheeks and tapped the top of her head to indicate that she had grown since he had last seen her. She laughed and introduced her *inglese* companions, telling them breathlessly that Giuseppe Cerutti didn't speak any English.

He invited them to sit down and eat and brought them a small carafe of wine, touching the side of his nose as if to say to Calypso, *Don't tell your father.* Then he brought water and fresh warm bread and olive oil, a dish of sliced tomatoes, and cloves of garlic that Calypso showed them how to eat, peeling and slicing, then pouring the olive oil into a dish, dipping in a piece of bread and rubbing the garlic on to it.

'Delicious!' she said, and they smiled and tried it and the oil dripped down from their lips to their chins.

Giuseppe brought them pasta with tomato and olive oil and salad, and after eating they all lifted their hands and said, 'No more, Calypso.'

'We have to fetch the ponies,' Beatrice reminded her.

'It's a good walk from up here,' Daniel said.

'Pah!' she said. 'I know a quick way. Giuseppe will be upset if you don't eat another course.'

But she told Giuseppe to bring only a small dish, and he brought cold meat with salad, saying something to Calypso that they couldn't understand, and shaking his head and waving his hands in a decided negative.

'He say we must not pay,' she laughed. 'That the English have an appetite of sparrows!'

'He's very generous,' Beatrice said, and murmured, *'Grazie mille, signor,'* which Daniel and Charles repeated.

Giuseppe kissed Calypso again on both cheeks and Beatrice on the hand, and shook hands with Daniel and Charles, talking loquaciously as he did so.

'Grazie,' they repeated. 'Most enjoyable,' Charles added. Daniel grinned and to outdo him said, *'Molto grazie,'* vowing to himself that one day he

would learn to speak Italian.

Charles was lost in admiration as Calypso led them down and across the hillside, through side streets and then back up the hill again.

'She must have known this area since she was at school,' he told Daniel. 'How else would she know the way? She is more than capable of looking after herself, and Leo is quite unaware of it.'

Daniel agreed, and commented that they were heading more or less in the direction of the lodgings. And so they were. Ten more minutes and they were standing at the gate to the meadow where the Haflingers and the donkey were placidly grazing. 'Let's see if they recognize us,' he said, and putting his fingers to his lips blew several piercing whistles. The mare looked up and shook her thick flaxen mane, and the stallions followed suit, snorting. The mare kicked up her heels and began to trot towards them, the stallions following, leaving the donkey braying at them.

'Come on, old gal,' Daniel crooned to the mare and she snickered at him, nuzzling his hair, whilst the two stallions jostled for position behind her.

'Oh, but they're beautiful,' Calypso murmured. 'How can you think of selling them?'

'How can we get them home?' Daniel answered, thinking that he would love to take at least one of them back to England if only he could. 'Besides, we must sell them and put back the money.'

'I shall ask Papa if he will buy me one.' Calypso ran her fingers through Blaze's mane. 'He has hair like yours, Beatrice,' she giggled.

'When would you use him?' Daniel asked.

'I would ride in the mountains, or to Prevo, or

317

even to Genoa. It's a good road for riding.'

He shook his head. 'That's not enough, Calypso. They're not onny for pleasure-riding. They're working hosses; they need to be used.'

They went to search out the landlady, the *padrona*, and told her they were moving on and wished to pay her what they owed. She asked them in and gave them coffee and cake and then went to wake her husband, who was having a sleep. When he came in he said he'd like to buy the donkey and the mare. Calypso negotiated a fee for the donkey but shook her head over the sale of the mare.

'I have told him we need three ponies now, but that you might be willing to sell one of them before you return to England. But I don't think he has enough money for them. He does not seem like a rich man.'

'We onny want what we paid for them,' Daniel said practically. 'No more; they've worked well for us.'

Charles laughed. 'You're too honest to be a horse dealer, Daniel.'

'Aye,' he said, 'I suppose I am. But I'm not a dealer. I'd try for more if I were.'

They all patted the donkey goodbye and rode back into Genoa, Calypso behind Beatrice. It was very hot but the sky had darkened. 'We will have rain,' Calypso said. 'We must look for shelter before it starts.'

'It will be a relief to have rain.' Beatrice took a deep breath. 'I don't mind getting wet. It will cool us down.'

'I think you will,' Calypso said, and suggested they shelter beneath the old portico of Sottoripa, the wide covered galleries that held shops selling fruit and spices and art. 'Come quickly,' she urged, digging her heels into the pony's flanks. 'The rain, it comes.'

They were no sooner beneath the stone shelter than the storm began, torrential rain thundering on the road, a drenching deluge that fell like a curtain – and had they been out in it would have soaked them in seconds.

Ten more minutes and it had stopped, and the shoppers who had taken shelter with them came out and went about their business. The sun shone anew and the road began to steam. 'Goodness,' Charles commented. 'I've never seen rain like that before.'

'I have, in Switzerland.' Beatrice wiped her forehead with the back of her hand. 'But I've never been out in it. Still, it's cleared the air; it's much fresher and cooler now.'

Daniel glanced at Beatrice and then up at a clock on a nearby building. 'What time does 'next ferry leave?' he asked. 'There's one coming towards 'harbour. I think we should try to get on board.' He'd noticed whilst they were sheltering that Beatrice had looked ill, and he thought that they ought to be getting back to Marco's.

They rode swiftly towards the landing place, and when the ferry had docked and passengers disembarked they led the ponies clattering up the gangplank. Charles said he and Calypso would stay with them and Daniel found Beatrice a seat; she leaned her head back, catching the breeze as they steamed out of the harbour and turned towards the Cinque Terre.

'Are you all right, Beatrice?' Daniel asked. 'You seem unwell.'

'Y-yes, I am,' she said in a breathless whisper. 'Just very hot, that's all.'

He sat beside her whilst Calypso and Charles stood near the stern holding the ponies' bridles, she pointing out various things which seemed to be of great interest to Charles.

Beatrice gave a small smile. 'Charles has fallen in love,' she said.

Daniel nodded and turned towards her. 'I believe he has. But Calypso is too young to realize.'

'She's not much younger than we are,' she said softly.

'She's been sheltered by her father and grandfather,' he answered, thinking that it was just as well that Beatrice couldn't read him as easily as she could her brother, or that would be the end of their friendship.

Beatrice didn't answer but closed her eyes and Daniel stood looking down at her, at her fineboned face, flushed now because of the heat, and the wisps of hair that strayed from beneath her hat and wafted gently, tickling her face until she brushed them away with her fingertips.

Abruptly she opened her eyes and found him gazing at her. 'You were watching me,' she whispered.

He swallowed. 'I was. I – I thought that you were not well.' But that wasn't the reason, he thought. I merely wanted to feast my eyes upon her, to register her face so that I never forget it, because once we are home again she'll be gone from me. We'll never get another opportunity of being together like this, ever again.

She sighed. 'Why?' she said wearily. 'Do I look terrible?'

He gave a sudden laugh. 'Beatrice, you could never look terrible!'

She shook her head, not believing him, and closed her eyes again.

When they reached Vernazza, Daniel and Beatrice were amongst the first of the passengers to disembark, and Calypso and Charles, leading the ponies, were last. Beatrice held on to Daniel's arm as they waited for them and he thought that she trembled.

He bent and cupped his hands to give her a leg-up to mount White Socks, but she hesitated. 'I'm not sure that I can ride,' she muttered, swaying into him. 'I feel dizzy.'

'Oh, Bea, what's up, old thing?' Charles said. 'It's not like you.'

'Too much heat,' Daniel said. 'Calypso, are you happy to ride White Socks so that Beatrice can come up with me?'

'Yes, yes,' she said eagerly. 'I can do that. He's not too big for me.'

'Bea can come up with me,' Charles suggested.

'You'd be better riding alongside Calypso,' Daniel told him. 'She might be headstrong and the road is rocky. We'll go ahead at a steady pace.'

'Of course,' he agreed. 'If that's all right, Beatrice?'

'I think so,' Beatrice uttered through pale lips. 'Though I do feel rather sick.'

Calypso looked about her and saw a kiosk meant for the ferrymen to sit in when they came ashore. 'This way,' she said. 'Out of the sun.'

Daniel lifted Beatrice off her feet and into his arms and followed Calypso, who had already commandeered a seaman's seat inside the kiosk where he gently put her down.

'I'm so sorry,' she said. 'How silly of me.'

Daniel turned to Charles. 'See if you can get some water. Mek sure it's clean!'

'*Limonata!*' Calypso shouted, and was off down the quayside with Charles running after her to a small café, returning a few minutes later with a jug and a cup.

'Just a drop at a time,' Daniel told Beatrice, holding the cup for her. 'We're not used to this kind of heat and we haven't drunk enough water today. Onny wine and coffee.'

Beatrice took a sip and screwed up her mouth. 'Sour!' she shuddered. 'Try it!'

'No thank you,' he smiled, putting the cup to her lips again. 'I could murder a pot o' tea. Strong, a drop of milk, with sugar like we have at home.'

She took a few more sips and gave a weak laugh. 'Pale with a slice of lemon for me,' she said. 'How English we are.' She took a deep breath. 'I feel a little better.'

'We'll wait another five minutes,' he said, 'and see if you're fit to travel.'

'Yes, doctor.' She smiled at him. 'Thank you, Daniel.'

He shrugged. 'I do it all 'time,' he joked. 'Helping maidens in distress. It's 'onny way I can get them into my arms!' Then, because he thought she might think him presumptuous, he said, 'Sorry, Beatrice, I didn't mean...'

'You don't have to apologize to me,' she said softly. 'I know already what a gentleman you are and that you'd never take advantage of any young woman.' She saw his embarrassment and joked back. 'And I'm quite sure that there's many a young lady who'd be pleased to be swept into your arms if you did but know it.'

He stood up. 'I reckon you're fit to move on now,' he said. 'The old Beatrice is back.'

As if they had both overstepped the mark, there was a diffidence between them as Daniel lifted her on to the saddle and, with Charles's hands to his foot, hoisted himself up behind her and took the reins. In a chivalrous manner he asked if she was comfortable, and taking the scarf she had given him from his neck he placed it round hers to keep the sun off her skin.

Beatrice adjusted her hat so that it covered her forehead. 'Perfectly,' she said graciously, taking hold of the pommel. 'Thank you.'

They moved steadily up the mountain path. The sun was lower in the sky and with a cool breeze blowing off the sea it wasn't as hot as it had been. They rode right on to the terrace rather than leave the ponies at the gate, so that Beatrice wasn't put to any further exertion. Calypso went to ask Sophia to bring cold water for Beatrice to drink, Daniel tied the ponies in the shade and then, with the others, went into the cool and dark living room with its closed shutters.

Sophia brought a large jug of drinking water and a bowl of cool water to bathe Beatrice's forehead, tutting at Calypso and speaking rapidly as she did so. Calypso sat with her eyes lowered.

'I'm in trouble,' she said, pressing her lips together. 'Sophia says that I should know better than to take you out in the heat of the day, and that with your fair skin you can soon burn. I am very sorry. I was so excited at taking you out on my own. I wanted to show you everything.'

'It wasn't your fault,' Beatrice and Charles said together. 'It was my own,' Beatrice added. 'I have known hot days in Switzerland and been warned about going out in the heat. It was entirely my own foolishness.'

'Sophia says that you should go to bed, to rest,' Calypso said. 'That I have worn you all out.'

'I will go to bed for an hour,' Beatrice agreed. 'I do feel rather tired.' She looked at Charles and Daniel.

'I won't, thank you,' Daniel said. 'After seeing to 'ponies, I'd like to write home if I could ask for some writing paper?'

'And I'd like to take a look at the vines, please, Calypso,' Charles said. 'If you'd agree to show me.'

'Oh, of course.' Calypso jumped up, grateful to be absolved. 'It will be my very greatest pleasure.'

CHAPTER THIRTY-EIGHT

Fletcher wore a black felt bowler hat and a black armband over the sleeve of his grey jacket, as did Lenny. Harriet wore a dark brown dress, jacket and hat. She hadn't wanted Joseph or Elizabeth to come to their grandmother's funeral as she thought they were too young, but Fletcher said it was better that they should know what happened when someone died.

'Besides,' he'd muttered, 'there won't be anybody else there but our bairns and 'parson. Ma was hardly what you might call popular.'

There had been an inquest; the verdict had been pneumonia following an accidental fall into the Haven. The funeral was to be held in Brough parish church.

'Do you think that Christopher Hart'll be there?' Harriet asked hesitantly.

'No reason why he should be,' Fletcher said briskly. 'I doubt he'd be at any other tenant's funeral, so it'd look odd if he was at hers.'

Harriet nodded and wondered if Ellen Tuke would have wanted her there, could she have known, but, she thought, it would seem odd if she stayed away.

Maria, Dolly, Elizabeth and Joseph were waiting in suspense, for none had ever attended a funeral. Then Elizabeth piped up. 'I'm going to sit with Granny Rosie in 'church, cos she said she'd hold my hand.'

'She's going to hold mine as well,' Joseph said, 'and I don't care if it's sissy cos I'm a lad.'

'It's not sissy,' Fletcher told him. 'Your ma's going to hold mine, aren't you, Harriet?' he said.

'We'll all hold hands,' she said. 'It'll show that we're comforting each other.'

'I don't really mind that she's dead,' Joseph said, 'cos I didn't really know her, but I'm sorry for you, Da, cos she was your ma, and I'd hate it if you died, Ma.' He screwed up his face and pressed his lips together. 'I expect I'd cry, even though I am a lad.'

Harriet patted the top of his head. 'Well, don't worry, Joseph,' she murmured. 'I'm not planning on dying just yet.'

'Tom's here,' Lenny said, looking out of the kitchen window as he heard the rattle of Tom's trap. 'I'm going with him. We're picking Granny Rosie up.'

'I'm coming as well then,' Elizabeth said as she stood up. 'Will you, Joseph?'

Joseph nodded. 'I wish our Daniel was here. He doesn't know yet, does he?'

'He doesn't, and we can't tell him, cos we don't know where he is except that he's in Italy,' his mother said. Fletcher muttered that he'd bring their trap to the door and through the window she saw Tom greet him, punching a friendly sympathetic fist on his shoulder. She breathed her thanks for Tom's support. He'd been a loyal friend to Fletcher and all of them throughout their lives.

Tom and Lenny, with Elizabeth and Joseph, drove off to collect Rosie. They would all meet at the church. Because Fletcher and Harriet didn't want the children distressed, arrangements had been made for Ellen to be brought to the church by the undertakers in whose premises she had been lying since the inquest. The undertaker and his men were dressed completely in black, with top hats, and had employed a mute to walk in front of the carriage.

Fletcher looked at Harriet and raised an eyebrow. He imagined what his mother might have

326

said. *Wasting good money* was what came to mind, but he felt he had to show an outward respect even though she had been so controversial throughout her life for as long as he could remember; and for reasons that he couldn't begin to describe he was glad that she wasn't to be buried in the same churchyard as Noah, who had always been the butt of her anger and frustration.

To Harriet's surprise, Mary, the Hart children's nanny, was waiting outside the church door. 'I didn't think that many folk would be here,' she whispered. 'I thought I'd mek 'numbers up.'

She beckoned Harriet closer as the undertaker, Fletcher, Tom and Lenny lifted the small coffin on their shoulders. 'Mrs Hart brought me when I said I'd like to come. She's waiting in 'carriage just up 'lane.'

'Oh, that was good of her,' Harriet whispered back, before bringing up the rear with Maria and Dolly, both looking pale and tearful. Joseph and Elizabeth clutched Rosie's hands as they entered the church door, the parson intoning, 'I am the resurrection and the life, saith the Lord.'

'I think she'd like a word after,' Mary continued, not hearing him. 'Master's not well.'

The question of what Mrs Hart wanted a word about occupied Harriet's thoughts throughout the service, which fortunately wasn't long as Ellen hadn't attended the church. The parson, who had never been welcomed at her door, apparently deduced that as there was only family, and Mary, who sat in a pew at the back of the church, there wasn't anything he could say that they didn't already know. He concluded the

327

service at the graveside with a hymn, 'Oh, God to know that thou art just; Gives hope and peace within.' And finally a verse from Psalm 39. 'I held my tongue and spake nothing; I kept silence, yea even from good words; but it was pain and grief to me.'

'Amen,' Fletcher and Harriet breathed in unison, and she squeezed his hand as she saw a tear run down his cheek as he threw soil on the coffin, before turning away.

Melissa Hart was waiting at the gate for Mary, her carriage discreetly further away from the church. Fletcher touched his hat but didn't speak, but Harriet dipped her knee and walked with Mary to meet her.

'I'm very sorry for your loss, Harriet. Please convey my condolences to your husband,' Melissa said quietly. She hesitated, and, turning her head and murmuring so that Mary wouldn't hear, said, 'My husband is unwell and confined to bed, otherwise he would have come.'

'I'm sorry to hear–' Harriet began, but Melissa waved away her sympathy.

'When it's convenient I'd like to speak to you, Harriet. I – need some advice – from your husband, if he wouldn't mind? Not yet, of course, whilst he's in mourning, but whenever it would be convenient – if it's not an intrusion.'

'Of course it's not,' Harriet assured her. 'Fletcher will be back at work tomorrow. Why not come on Sunday afternoon?'

She saw the relief on Melissa's face. 'Thank you,' she said. 'I do appreciate... I – I need to make some changes whilst Christopher is ill. He – it's exhaustion, the doctor says. He's very troubled – Christopher, I mean – and I must help him all I can. Thank you,' she said again. 'I won't keep you now. You'll want to get home.'

'What was that about?' Fletcher asked when she reached his side.

'She'd come to collect Mary,' Harriet told him, 'but she also said that her husband would have come except that he's ill; 'doctor's been to see him and he's suffering from exhaustion.'

Fletcher gave a wry grimace.

'And she wants to come and see us. I suggested Sunday.'

'Why?' he asked. 'Why so pally?'

'We've allus been able to talk to each other,' Harriet said softly, realizing that he was tense. 'Always able to confide. But she wants to talk to you as well.'

'I want nowt from them,' Fletcher said brusquely. 'Just because there was an accident of birth, he needn't think he has to compensate me.'

'I don't think it's that,' Harriet said slowly. 'I don't think it was about him. It sounded to me as if she wanted something from us, or at least from you.'

Maria picked up the post that had arrived whilst they were out; Dolly swung the kettle over the fire and put the cloth on the table, setting it with cutlery and condiments and crockery. Harriet didn't comment but saw how Dolly did these things without prompting and thought how she had settled down since working for Mrs Topham; she had grown up since leaving home.

Harriet had prepared food in advance so that they could eat straight away. Fletcher, Lenny and Tom would want to change into their work clothes and go outside as soon as they had eaten. Tom had said he would take Rosie home later.

'Here's a letter from Daniel,' Maria squealed. 'At least – it's got a foreign stamp on it.'

'Can I have it?' Joseph jumped to snatch it.

'No!' Maria held it out of reach. 'It's not addressed to you.'

'I meant 'stamp,' Joseph objected. 'I'm collecting foreign stamps.'

His mother held out her hand for the letter. 'It won't be much of a collection. We onny know Daniel who's sending to us from abroad.'

She turned the envelope over in her hand. 'It's a proper letter,' she said, feeling the thickness. 'Not just a card this time. We'll wait for your da to come in before we read it.'

Rosie sighed. 'I miss that boy. I hope he didn't go just on my account. I know you're a man short on 'farm now he's not here.'

'He needed to go, Rosie,' Harriet observed, still turning the envelope over and over. 'How else could he find out his ancestry? He'll be sorry not to have been here for Granny Tuke, though.' Even though she regarded him as nothing to do with her, she reflected. How cruel she was to treat him so coldly, just as she had his father. She gave a deep sigh that came from the bottom of her heart. I hope that one day I'll be able to forgive her.

Fletcher came in from putting the horse and trap away. 'Hoss is going lame. She's cut herself on a fence post or summat. Needs a poultice on

330

it; what do you think, Joseph? Are you up to doing it?'

Joseph averted his eyes from his father's. 'Don't know. Can't our Lenny do it?'

His father shook his head. 'You've got to start sometime.'

'We've got a letter from Daniel, Da,' Maria broke in, averting attention from Joseph, who was still not happy around horses.

'Oh aye. What's he got to say?'

'We waited for you,' Harriet smiled, relieved that the letter would be an antidote to the gloom of the funeral. She slit it open with a knife from the table. 'Oh, two letters,' she said, pulling out a folded sheet of notepaper with *Granny Rosie* written on it. 'One for you, Rosie.'

Rosie took it and stared at it. 'I daren't read it,' she whispered.

'We'll read ours first.' Harriet suddenly felt happy. Daniel had been so constant in keeping in touch, even if there had been only a few hastily written words on a postcard. But this was a long letter, two pages of tightly written lines, as if he didn't want to waste the paper. She rubbed a page between her fingers. Good paper too, she thought, and wondered where he'd got it from.

'"Dear Ma, Da and everybody,"' she began. '"You must have thought that we'd got lost as it's a few days since I wrote to you, but there's so much to tell you and I don't know where to begin, except to say it might be a good idea if you read this letter first before giving Granny Rosie hers."'

'Don't open your letter yet,' Harriet interrupted the reading to tell Rosie. 'We've to hear

331

this one first.'

She continued reading aloud. '"I told you we were in Genoa. I can't recall whether I told you how we got here from Switzerland, although you might have heard from Mrs Hart. I think Beatrice has written to her."'

Daniel went on to explain about the Haflingers and the donkey, but not how they had bought them, and Harriet looked up at Fletcher. 'How's he been able to afford to do that?' she said.

Fletcher just shrugged and indicated she should continue. Tom came in and sat down quietly to listen. Dolly made a pot of tea and poured it for everybody.

'"And so we came down into Genoa and found lodgings where we left the ponies so that we could explore on foot. This is such a wonderful place but I'm going to save that for when I come home–"' Harriet breathed a relieved sigh. So he's coming home after all. Of course he is, she chastised herself, and continued reading about going into a trattoria by the harbour and asking if anyone had heard of the Orsini family.

She read on to herself and then gave a shriek. 'Rosie! He's found someone related to 'Orsini family.'

'Never!' Rosie struck her hand on her chest. 'Oh, my word!'

Harriet scanned the letter, hardly believing what she was reading. 'Daniel says – he says that he's sitting in the house of his *grandfather, Marco Orsini,* on top of a hillside in the small town of ... Ver-nazza.' Her voice dropped to a whisper and she handed the letter to Fletcher, because she couldn't read on when she'd seen Rosie's shocked expression.

Rosie whispered, 'I must be dreaming. Is Marco alive? Does he remember me? Does he say if he does?' Her eyes filled with tears and her voice became husky.

Harriet stood up and went to sit on the arm of Rosie's chair. 'I think that's why Daniel's written to you separately,' she murmured. 'He mebbe thought you'd want to read it privately.'

'I've no secrets from any of you.' Rosie began to sob. 'I've no secrets at all. You're my family.'

Harriet put an arm around her shoulder. 'Of course we are, and you are ours.'

'Harriet.' Fletcher had continued reading the letter, but to himself, not out loud. 'Harriet, there's more,' he said quietly. 'And not onny about Marco Orsini. This concerns you.'

Harriet put her hand to her mouth. 'It's not bad news, is it?'

'No, far from it. You've waited a long time for this.' He passed the letter back to her. 'You'd better sit down in 'chair. Dolly, mek your ma another pot o' tea, strong wi' sugar!' He gave an odd kind of ironic grimace. 'What a strange sort o' day. First a funeral and then a discovery.'

Tom got up, and taking the kettle from Dolly, who was looking from her father to her mother in some bewilderment, filled it up from the tap and hung it over the fire.

Harriet glanced at Fletcher and then at all the children. 'Maria,' she said, 'best get 'food out of 'pantry. It's getting late.'

'Leave it, Maria,' said Fletcher. 'There's no

333

hurry. This is more important.'

What can be more important than finding Marco Orsini and knowing that Daniel will be coming home, Harriet thought. He seems to have been away for such a long time. He *has* been away a long time.

She sat down again. '"But even more amazing, Ma, is what I have to tell you next and I hope you're sitting down. You're not going to believe this, for not only have I discovered my grand-father, Marco Orsini, who is a perfect gentleman, but also an uncle and a cousin. How, you might be asking and trying to fit the connection. But you'll find it impossible until I tell you that your long-lost brother Leonard was married to one of Marco's daughters, who died giving birth to a girl called Calypso Francesca Maria. Leo, as he's known here, and Calypso are sitting next to me as I write.

'"Ma, I'm as stunned as you must be, but he'll write to you himself in a day or two, now that he knows where you are. He says he came to look for you twenty odd years ago, but couldn't find you; he onny knew that your mother had died. Tell my sisters and brothers that they have a beautiful Italian cousin.

'"I'll write again before we leave for our journey home via Rome, the *ancestral* home of the Orsinis.

'"Your loving son and brother,

'"Daniel".'

CHAPTER THIRTY-NINE

By the Sunday, Harriet was still reeling from the news that Daniel had given her. 'I can't believe it,' she kept saying to whoever happened to be near. 'Leonard is alive and well, and prospering too by 'sound of it. Fancy him being in Italy all this time, and I might never have known but for Daniel going on another mission entirely.'

It was Maria who was on the listening end of the conversation as she and her mother cleared up after the midday meal. Dolly had gone back to work at Mrs Topham's after having had time off for the funeral. Joseph was outside doing jobs for his father; Fletcher was determined that the boy would get over his fear of horses and had set him to sweeping out the stables. Elizabeth was dusting the sitting room, where a fire was already burning in anticipation of Mrs Hart's visit.

'I'll finish in here, Ma,' Maria told her. 'Why don't you go and sit down and wait for Mrs Hart? You could mebbe start a letter to Uncle Leo.'

'That sounds strange.' Harriet put down her washing up cloth. 'I can't think of my brother as Leo.'

'But we've already got a Lenny,' Maria said. 'We can't have both with 'same name.' She put her head on one side. 'I quite like 'sound of Leo – and Calypso! Isn't that lovely!'

'It is,' Harriet agreed. 'What was it? Calypso

Francesca Maria! I'm so glad that he chose our mother's name for his daughter.' She smiled wistfully. 'Just as I did for you.'

'I wish we could meet them,' Maria said longingly. 'Perhaps they'll come, although I suppose it'd cost a lot of money, but it would be so nice to meet a cousin, especially an Italian one. Could I – do you think I could write to her? She'll be able to understand English, won't she?'

'I expect so,' her mother said. 'Surely Leonard – Leo – will talk to her in English. I can't believe it,' she repeated. 'My brother with an Italian daughter. Poor Leonard. To lose his wife in child-birth, that's so very sad.'

'No sadder than for you, Ma, when you lost Daniel's father,' Maria said sensibly. 'Go on,' she urged her. 'Go and start a letter to him. There'll be so much to say after so many years; about Daniel's father, and our da, and he doesn't know about any of us, except for what Daniel will have told him. It'll take for ever to tell. And while you're talking to Mrs Hart, I'll start one to Calypso.'

Harriet sat thinking about her life as she tried to decide what she would say to her brother. That she was so pleased to know that he was alive and had a daughter Daniel said was beautiful, that would be easy, but how to explain her own life since coming to live out at the other end of the estuary in an attempt to escape from poverty and destitution? She rarely visited Hull, although she was often tempted to return to her home town to see if it was much changed, but there never seemed to be time; she was fully occupied with being a farmer's wife and mother of six children.

How that will surprise him, she thought, although Daniel will have told him something of my life, as much as he knows anyway, but not all; none of our children knows everything about our lives, mine and Fletcher's, and why should they? They have their own lives ahead of them, their own history to make.

She hadn't written a single word when Maria brought in Mrs Hart. She hadn't heard her horse and trap come into the yard or her knock on the kitchen door, for Melissa always preferred to use that door now, never the front one.

'Harriet, I'm disturbing you,' she said, seeing the writing paper, ink bottle, pen and blotting paper on the table.

'No, ma'am, you're not.' Harriet rose and invited her to take a seat. 'You'll mebbe have heard some of our news? We didn't receive a letter from Daniel until 'day of Ellen's funeral, which he doesn't know about, of course.'

Melissa shook her head. 'I'm afraid the twins are not prolific letter writers, as Daniel appears to be, although Beatrice did say that there might soon be something to tell us about Daniel's quest.'

'Miss Beatrice wouldn't want to say anything until we'd heard from Daniel first.' Harriet sat opposite her. 'That was very considerate of her, but I can tell you while we're waiting for Fletcher to come in and Maria to mek 'tea. In fact, I was trying to write a letter when you arrived, but didn't know where to start. You see, Daniel has found not only his grandfather, but also my brother, who I thought was lost.' Tears sprang unbidden to her eyes, not for the first time since receiving the news.

'And I'm – so happy,' she gasped, before bursting into a fit of weeping.

By the time Fletcher had come in and swilled his hands and face and Maria had served a tray of tea and cake, Harriet had told Melissa everything she knew about Daniel's grandfather, his uncle Leo – her brother Leonard – and his cousin Calypso.

'Rosie is quite overcome,' she said, wiping her eyes as tears started afresh, 'and she is thrilled that Marco Orsini has accepted Daniel without question. Seemingly, he said that he knew Daniel was of their bloodline as soon as he saw him.'

'How remarkable!' Melissa exclaimed. 'And so extraordinary that your brother should be related to him. It must be true when it is said that fact is stranger than fiction, for you couldn't make up such a story.'

Fletcher came in as they were speaking, and she rose and offered her hand. 'I'm sorry about your mother's death, Mr Tuke,' she said softly. 'You must have taken it very hard, especially under the very sad circumstances.'

He nodded. 'Aye, I did,' he agreed. 'Although I should've expected she wouldn't go peaceably to her maker like most folks. She had to be awkward and troublesome right up to 'end.' Melissa was taken aback. It was what they were all thinking about Ellen Tuke, but only her son had the wit and the strength to say it. She licked her lips. There didn't seem to be any answer she could make.

'It's true,' Harriet said. 'She'd be mekking sure we didn't forget her.'

'We'll not do that,' Fletcher said philosophically.

'That's a fact.' He took a gulp of tea, and putting down his cup said, 'I understand from Harriet that Mr Hart isn't well. I hope it's not summat serious? So what can we do for you?'

He's direct, I'll say that for him, Melissa thought. And I like that in a man. He'll call a spade a spade. He's a man I could trust.

'I'm sure it's not serious,' she said. 'But he's become very worried and anxious, and not only about this – this issue over your mother, which has upset him greatly–'

'Well,' Fletcher interrupted, 'let's get this out of 'way here and now. We've been skirting round it for years, nobody wanting to mention it but everybody knowing – at least, not everybody, but those of us it concerns. We've told Maria cos we've been worried about her, or Harriet has, and we'd hoped that you'll tell or mebbe have already told your children?' He heaved a breath. 'Told them that I'm their half-brother.'

There it was, out in the open, and the three of them looked at each other and were relieved.

'Who'd have thought,' Fletcher continued, 'that summat that happened all those years ago would have such repercussions – *could* have,' he corrected himself. 'But might not, now that we're all aware of it.'

'Fletcher,' Melissa said. 'I can call you Fletcher? Seeing as I'm – I'm,' she smiled, 'your step-mother!'

Harriet put her hand to her mouth. That was one aspect she hadn't considered.

Fletcher gave a sudden grin. 'I hadn't thought of that.'

'Nor I until recently.' Melissa paused. 'I haven't told the children anything yet, but I will explain in time.' She hesitated again, as if not sure how to continue. 'As I said, Christopher is very troubled about the circumstances and feels that he has let everyone down, and it has made him quite distressed. But it's not only that. He's feeling that he can't cope with running the estate alone; our bailiff has left before his contract is up – the poor man is very ill and can't continue – and although Christopher has advertised for someone else there has been little response, and those who have responded he considers unsuitable.'

'So you want me to ask around, find out if there's anybody willing to tek on 'job?' Fletcher queried.

'No,' she said quickly. 'I'm asking you to help us, if you will, by acting as a temporary bailiff, talking to the tenants, ascertaining what needs to be done and so on, which is what Thompson did. They won't want to talk to me and neither do I want them to think there's anything amiss, but we're coming up to harvest time and although I'm quite sure you are very busy yourself, perhaps you could advise me on what should be done. It will only be until November,' she pleaded. 'We'll surely be able to get a bailiff at the Hirings Fair.

'I'm afraid that Charles will not want to come into the estate when he returns, but Stephen will be home for the holidays next week and he's very keen to enrol at an agricultural college and then work on the estate. I've written to him to say that his father is not well and that I'm hoping he'll be able to take on some of his duties. I know he'll be

340

pleased to help, but he'll need guidance and I don't think that his father is in any fit state to do that at the moment.'

Fletcher considered. It was true that the tenant farmers would be anxious if Mrs Hart started *interfering* in men's matters, which was how they would see it, and besides, did she know anything about running a business, which was what farming was? She was a feisty kind of woman, intelligent, and probably well able to do it, but she was a lady and had never had her hands dirty – and that would be the first thing the farmers would think of. Now Harriet, he thought, they'd listen to her all right, for they'd realize she knew what she was talking about.

'All right,' he said. 'We'll do what we can to help out. It'll not be easy with Daniel being away, but we allus get help with harvest in any case. First off I'll speak to your foreman and mek sure he's up to scratch, then when Stephen comes home I'll go with him to visit 'tenants and tell them that he's learning 'business. We'll say that 'master's temporarily under 'weather, that, erm, he's picked up an infection but 'doctor doesn't think it's catching, but best stay away just in case. They need to be told to pay 'rent as usual and to keep everything in order, which is what 'bailiff would do. And mebbe ask them to keep a lookout for poachers, too, seeing as there's no bailiff. But what about keeping 'books? Harriet does ours.'

'Well, in that case, I'm sure that I can too. It's only numbers, isn't it?'

Fletcher and Harriet both laughed. 'Yes, it is,' Harriet said. 'But it's also buying and ordering

341

and knowing where to get 'best deal at 'market. Who does that? Mebbe bailiff?'

'I suppose so,' Melissa said slowly. She had taken so much for granted. It was time for change.

Stephen came home midweek. After receiving his mother's letter he asked permission to leave early; when it was given he packed his belongings and caught the first train, and rather than asking for someone to pick him up from the railway station he walked home from Brough and rang the front doorbell.

He grinned at the maid who opened the door. 'Hello, Milly. Is Mama at home?'

He dumped his bag on the landing and knocked on the door of his mother's sitting room, which was where Milly had said she was, and looked in. His mother was sitting on the floor surrounded by files and ledgers and piles of paper. She looked up, startled, and then, lifting the hem of her skirt, scrambled to her feet.

'Oh, a miracle!' Overjoyed to see him, she put her arms about him. 'Just when I was wishing the week away until you came. Were you given time off? How did you get here? Is George with you?'

'Yes, train and walked, and no,' he said. 'I told George he was to stay on until the end of term and he was happy to do so. I also told him to make his own way home. Seeing as he's so very clever it shouldn't be too difficult!'

Melissa gazed at her second son. He seemed to have grown up so suddenly, able to take control of his life. She thought of the task in front of her, that of telling him about Fletcher Tuke, and was fairly certain that he could cope with the news.

'How is Father? he asked. 'He's not seriously ill, is he?'

'No,' she said. 'But he's very tired, and – and, well, he's had rather an upsetting time lately, and it's set him back. He – he needs to rest until he comes to terms with what has happened.'

She saw the query in his expression. 'I'll ring for tea,' she said softly, 'and tell you all about it.'

CHAPTER FORTY

'We must think of the best way to get you to Roma,' Marco said. 'It is a three-hundred-mile journey. Too far, I think, on horseback unless you stay in Italy all ze summer.'

'I can't do that, sir,' Daniel said. 'I should be thinking of returning to England. I'll miss this year's harvest, and I already feel that I'm not pulling my weight.'

'But surely,' Leo chipped in, 'your parents knew you wouldn't be home in time for harvest? They hadn't given you a date for your return?'

'No,' Daniel admitted. 'They didn't. It's me, I suppose. Feeling guilty.'

'Knowing your parents as we do,' Beatrice said, 'they'd want you to make the most of your time here. They'll manage the harvest perfectly well without you, Daniel, even though they'll miss you.'

'If you are going to Roma, then you must go *now*,' Marco said firmly. 'Already it is too 'ot.

Especially for Miss Beatrice.'

'And me too,' Charles interrupted. 'But I don't want to miss it.'

'All right!' Marco said decidedly. 'This is what you will do!' He shook his forefinger for emphasis. 'I will buy your 'orses from you. I know someone who will let them graze, and you will use ze money for the train.'

Daniel glanced at Beatrice and Charles, who were both nodding. He smiled. It made sense, he knew; he was so used to a working life, to being a component part of a team, a cog in a wheel, that it was difficult for him to think otherwise; but, he considered, he had done what he had set out to do: his family would expect him to enjoy the rest of his time here and absorb his Italian heritage. He knew now just who he was and where he had come from.

Marco had some distant relatives living in Rome and he would write to them immediately. *'Pronto, pronto,'* he said, adding that he would give Daniel an address and a letter of introduction. 'You will stay with them,' he said. 'And they will show you 'ospitality.'

Calypso wanted to go with them, but Leo refused and Marco agreed with him. 'It will not seem right,' he said, 'for an Italian *signorina* to travel without her parent.'

She'd pouted and argued, but both men were steadfast in their refusal.

'I'm so sorry, Calypso,' Daniel told her later. 'When you come to England you'll have more freedom.'

'She might not,' Beatrice disagreed. 'Not all

344

young Englishwomen do.'

Daniel thought of his sisters, who had more freedom than Beatrice yet were not as independent as she was. It depended on their upbringing, and it seemed that although Leo had been brought up in a poor English family he had risen above it and was treating his daughter as a genteel Italian girl.

Their plan now was to catch an early morning local train from Genoa's Porta Principe railway station to La Spezia along the coast from Cinque Terre, then change trains to travel to Rome. They would arrive very late in the evening and find lodgings for the night before making their way to Marco's relatives the following day.

They stayed two more days with Marco, making the most of their time there, and Daniel wondered sadly if they really would meet again, as from Rome they would journey to France and then across to England.

Charles was distraught over leaving Calypso. 'I love her,' he told Daniel. 'I can't bear to go away from her. She fills me with the joy of life. I never knew that love was like this. I don't know how she feels about me, as we're never alone, but, well, do you think it is too soon for me to speak to your uncle?'

'I do, in all honesty,' Daniel said. They were sitting out on the terrace. Marco had gone inside for his customary afternoon nap, and Beatrice and Calypso were also indoors. 'You've known her for onny a few days. She's beautiful, I can see that, but there must be some other attraction than beauty if you're to be together for life.'

'I shall come back,' Charles said fiercely. 'When

we get back to England I'll speak to my father, ask him to let Stephen take over the estate. It's what he wants and I don't, and then I'll return to Italy to study art. It was to have been France, as you know, but not now. I'll definitely come back to Italy, maybe Rome or Florence, and then I'll be able to travel to see her.'

Daniel wondered if Charles might be dissuaded once he arrived home, but he had seemed sure that his future lay in the arts even before they arrived in Italy, and now that he had met Calypso he was even more determined.

'But only with her father's permission,' he said. 'Would you like me to have a quiet word with Leo? I could drop a hint about your feelings towards her.'

'Oh, would you? Please! And be sure to tell him that I'm honourable and all that, although I suppose I won't be rich if Father cuts me off. I don't think he will; he's a decent old chap really.'

'All right, *old fellow.*' Daniel grinned. 'I'll spread 'compliments on really thick.'

'I'll do the same for you, you know, Daniel,' Charles said seriously, 'if you should meet someone that you care for. Except, of course,' he hesitated as he saw Daniel's smile disappear, 'I think that maybe you already have.'

That evening, whilst Charles stayed behind to talk to Marco and Calypso, Daniel, Beatrice and Leo walked down the mountain towards the harbour, and then across a rocky lane towards a vineyard with a grassy paddock below it. The three ponies were grazing but as soon as Daniel whistled they came trotting towards them. Daniel put his arms around their necks as they nuzzled up to him.

'Oh, how I wish I could tek you home,' he snuffled into their silky manes. 'But it's a long way back to England, and mebbe you wouldn't like our weather either.'

'I don't think they'd mind 'weather,' Leo said. 'They're used to the cold, but we'll look after them, don't worry about that, and when you come back again...' He smiled. 'You will come back, won't you? Marco will be very disappointed if you don't. He's so thrilled that he has a grandson, more than he can explain.'

'And I'm so grateful that he's accepted me. I still can't believe that it's happened, and then to find you as well,' Daniel choked. It was going to be hard to leave, even though he was missing home.

Beatrice was speaking softly to White Socks, her favourite of the three animals. 'I'm just telling them that we'll come back one day soon,' she said. 'Do you know of Daniel's ambition, Leo?'

Leo shook his head and raised his eyebrows in query, and Daniel got a sudden glimpse of his brother Lenny in the gesture. His mother had been right when she said that he looked like Leonard.

'Daniel would like to breed horses, isn't that right, Daniel?' she said. 'An ambition.'

'A dream, Beatrice, not an ambition,' Daniel said. 'Aye, I love my hosses, we can never do without them; even though they're bringing in modern machinery that'll replace manpower, they'll never replace horsepower.'

'I've heard that it'll come, Daniel,' Leo said.

'Fifty years ago people used to say that railway trains would never catch on, but here they are and everybody uses them.'

Daniel sighed. 'You're right. I've heard it too, and that's progress. But I hope it won't be yet awhile, or some of us will be out of a job.' He looked at his uncle. 'Do you miss England? Would you ever come back?'

'I'll come back to see you all as I promised,' he said. 'And especially to see your mother. I want to see where Harriet lives and meet her husband and your brothers and sisters so that when I return home to Italy – for this is my home now – I'll be able to picture exactly where you are and what you're doing.' He turned to Beatrice. 'And I hope to meet you and Charles again too, Beatrice.'

She smiled. 'Be sure that you will.' She raised a questioning glance at Daniel.

'Yes. As a matter of fact,' Daniel hummed and hawed, 'I've, erm, I've been entrusted with a mission on Charles's behalf as he feels it's too soon to speak of it himself.'

Leo let out a great bellow of a laugh. 'Don't tell me – he's fallen in love with Calypso!'

'It's very obvious, isn't it?' Beatrice said. 'But it is the very first time he has been in love.'

'He's completely smitten,' Daniel added. 'And I've been charged with advising you of his good and honourable intentions.'

'He's only known her five minutes,' Leo bantered, 'and she's still a child, spoilt by me and her grandfather – a butterfly!'

'That's why he's fallen in love with her,' Beatrice told him. 'He's never met anyone like her, and

Charles is so serious. She lightens up his life.'

'Well,' Leo said, 'I didn't expect this.' He laughed again. 'My little girl! But I suppose it's something I must get used to.'

'Charles wants to be 'first in 'queue,' Daniel grinned. 'And I heartily recommend him for my cousin Calypso.'

They were ready to move off at six o'clock the following morning in time to catch the first ferry to Genoa. Leo was coming with them to the railway station. Calypso wanted to come too but her father refused, as he was staying in the city to conclude some business. She'd sulked, but Daniel had appeased her by saying that it wouldn't be long before they met again.

'Come up 'hillside and watch the train go past,' he suggested. He'd checked out the rail system and seen that the train passed above or through all of the five villages, although it didn't stop every day at all the stations. 'We'll look out for you.'

'Oh, I will,' she said eagerly, her moodiness quickly disappearing. Daniel saw why her father called her a butterfly and wondered how Charles would cope with that if indeed they began a courtship.

He said a tearful goodbye to Marco; both were emotional and Marco reminded him that he was not a young man so Daniel must return soon. 'And bring Rosie too,' he added. 'Is she in good enough health to travel?'

Daniel thought of Granny Rosie trudging up the hill to visit them at Dale Top Farm, which was not as steep as the hills on Vernazza, but replied that she was bonny and robust.

Charles was very quiet on the ferry, and Daniel asked Beatrice whether he'd spoken to Calypso before they left.

'Yes,' she murmured, 'he did, and took her hand. She seemed to grow very still.'

Is that all it takes, Daniel wondered. Just a simple gesture to tell someone you love them? Or do they already know, or are they unaware, no matter how long they've known someone? He looked back at Vernazza as the ferry pulled away. So much had happened in such a short time that it seemed impossible. Meeting his uncle Leo and discovering his grandfather, and most of all having Beatrice in such close proximity. This was something he would lock into his memory until he died.

They had said goodbye to Leo at Genoa, and Daniel had noticed that Charles had shaken hands with Leo with a firm grip, although neither of them had mentioned Calypso. The small local train steamed along the coastal track towards Vernazza and La Spezia, the Mediterranean below them a shimmering, dazzling blue with dashing white-crested waves. They gathered by the window ready to wave to Calypso if she had climbed the mountain path as promised.

'There she is,' Charles shouted and waved a handkerchief, but Daniel's gaze was on the white-haired old man waving his straw hat, whilst behind him two men stood with a sedan chair.

'Look,' he said, waving a hand but barely able to speak or see through his tear-filled eyes. 'It's Nonno! They've carried him up the mountain to say goodbye.'

He felt a soft hand close over his. It was Beatrice's, and she was smiling and weeping too.

CHAPTER FORTY-ONE

It was very late in the evening when they arrived in Rome, but it seemed that the Romans didn't retire early to bed. The streets were thronging with people, either strolling along or sitting in their doorways chatting.

'We must be careful,' Charles said as they stood on the concourse wondering which direction to take. 'There's a good deal of poverty here and we probably look like rich foreigners.'

'We are rich foreigners,' Beatrice murmured, 'in comparison with some of the people here.'

'No wonder that so many are emigrating,' Daniel said. 'There are people without shoes on their feet!'

Marco had told them of the vast emigration of the populace who had scraped together enough money to buy a ticket to America and look for a new life. Weary of the political upheaval that had reigned until Italian patriots Giuseppe Mazzini and Giuseppi Garibaldi spearheaded a revolution, thousands had left even before the unification of Italy, when Victor Emmanuel II was pronounced king a mere twenty years ago. In 1871 Rome was declared the capital of a united Italy and there came to be a kind of peace.

Once more they looked for a café or trattoria where they could take refreshment and enquire about lodgings. They found one on the Via Giulia and ordered bowls of fettuccine with grated cheese and butter. As they waited they were brought a basket of bread, a dish of olives, a bottle of dry white wine and the addresses of two recommended lodging houses.

The first house they tried they rejected as there was only one room available, but in the second there were two rooms and the use of a bathroom which had no bath but a wash stand with a jug and bowl and the promise of hot water, and a water closet.

'It's clean and homely,' Beatrice said, on inspecting the rooms, 'and quite adequate. I'm so tired I could happily sleep on the floor.'

She didn't have to, as the beds were comfortable and the rent was cheap, and as it was only for the one night they elected to stay. Their host, Enrico, spoke little English but they managed with their few words of Italian and sign language to make their requirements clear.

Their windows overlooked the narrow street and they could hear music playing and voices singing and talking, and then the sound of church bells ringing out the hour, which lulled them to sleep, but all felt the lurch and roll of the train and heard in their dreams the whistle and screech of the engine.

They awoke to hear their host singing, not well, but pleasantly. Beatrice, fully dressed, opened her door the better to hear just as Daniel and Charles came out of their room.

'Bravo,' they all said, entering the small dining room, which they guessed also served as a living room.

'You lika ze opera? *La Traviata* – Brindisi – they drinka.'

'The drinking song, I think,' Beatrice explained. 'We were to read *The Lady of the Camellias* at the academy but then it was banned. Madame Carpeoux said it was considered immoral so it was not suitable for us young ladies.' Her eyebrows twitched provocatively. 'But we managed to obtain a copy. It wasn't immoral at all, it was about love, and I think that's what the song is about. They're drinking a toast to love.'

'Well, I'll join them in that.' Charles raised his cup of black coffee.

Daniel laughed and raised his cup too. 'You never cease to amaze me, Beatrice! What a lot you know.'

She smiled. 'A little about a lot of things,' she said. 'That's what happens at finishing school. We're told many things about lots of subjects so that we are able to have conversations with...' she hesitated, 'young people, particularly young *gentlemen,* who will then be dazzled by our wit and intelligence!'

Daniel nodded sagely. 'I think it just might be working, don't you, Charles?'

Charles leaned back in his chair and said nonchalantly, 'Difficult to say as Bea's my sister, but I might ask her to coach me when we arrive home and find out if it works in reverse.'

Enrico told them that they could leave their belongings there until the evening in case they wanted to stay another night. Daniel suggested they should, as they were not certain that they would be offered accommodation with Marco's relatives. Enrico helpfully gave them directions to the Colosseum, from which they would be able to find the Orsini home on their map.

He had seemed impressed when told the district they were looking for was near the Parco del Colle Oppio, and rubbed his fingers together to indicate wealth. Then he studied Daniel closely. *'Italiano? Come ti chiami?'*

Daniel smiled. Are you Italian? What's your name? He was getting used to this question and now knew what it meant and how to answer. 'English,' he said. 'My name is Daniel Orsini.'

'Ah!' Enrico threw up his hands and talked volubly and at great speed and they couldn't understand a word, and then he took a piece of paper and wrote on it *Teatro di Marcello*. 'Palazzo Orsini,' he said. 'You go.'

But first they made their way to the address near the Colosseum, and this was easy to find, the Colosseum being recognizable from a great distance. There were many shops and businesses down the busy street, which was packed with carriages, carts and hundreds of pedestrians. On the top floors of the buildings were apartments rather than the houses they were expecting.

The door number they wanted was outside a bank, a building with many floors and windows, and down the side street they found an entrance with a mosaic floor and a stone staircase with an oak stair rail leading to the top floor.

'Take a deep breath,' Daniel said. 'It looks like

354

a long walk up.'

Beatrice was hampered by her skirts, but telling Daniel and Charles to go ahead, she hitched them up above her ankles and set off behind them. The apartment they required was on the third floor, and from behind the door they could hear the sound of a violin playing.

Daniel raised the brass knocker and gave two sharp raps; the door was opened almost immediately by a young maid, and he put his hand to his chest and said, 'Daniel Orsini, signorina.'

She indicated that they should enter and they followed her through a lavishly decorated hall also with a mosaic floor and with walls dressed with tapestry hangings; a marble table with a large display of scented lilies was placed in the centre. The maid tapped on another door before ushering them into a wide withdrawing room set with sofas and side tables and large oil paintings where an elderly man, white-haired and bearded and probably Marco's age, was standing by the window with a violin in his hand.

Daniel gave a short bow. 'Signor Rosso, my name is Daniel Orsini. My grandfather, Marco Orsini–'

'Ah! Come in. Come in, welcome.' He embraced them all with wide arms and Daniel bowed again, as did Charles, whilst Beatrice gave a graceful dip of her knee.

'I have a letter from Marco to expect you. Come, meet my wife.' He led them into a smaller sitting room where a tiny woman dressed in black was sitting on a velvet chair. She rose to meet them and again they were welcomed. Her name was Isabella and they were told she didn't speak any English. She gave Daniel a small white hand that looked too fragile to hold, but he bent over it in what he thought an appropriate gesture, and Charles did the same. Beatrice dipped her knee again and Signora Rosso came towards her as if to examine her more closely.

'*Inglese*,' she murmured, '*bella bella*,' patting each of her own cheeks as if to demonstrate Beatrice's fair skin. '*Flavia*,' she added, indicating Beatrice's blonde hair.

The three of them were invited to be seated and in halting Italian Beatrice asked if Signor Rosso was a musician. Instantly he denied it, exclaiming that he played only for himself, for his own and his wife's entertainment.

The maid brought in coffee and biscotti and after a moment's silence Signor Rosso said, 'I did not know that Marco had an English grandson. He and I, our fathers were cousins, perhaps you know that? My father, he was from the Bracciano line, and Marco and I were good friends when we were young men, but have not met in over twenty years. He went to England and had a son, yes? Or a daughter?'

'A son, sir,' Daniel told him. 'My father. He died when I was young. I don't remember him.'

'Ah!' Rosso nodded. 'Marco, he came back to Italy and his father had chosen a wife for him; she was a good woman but she no give him sons, only daughters.'

'Erm, yes. My grandmother was an English-woman.' Daniel didn't quite know how to continue the conversation, but Signor Rosso had no such reservations and with a quick glance at Beatrice he said, 'My wife she no understand English so you need not worry on her account, and signorina,' again a glance at Beatrice, 'I think you understand ze situation?'

'I do, Signor,' Beatrice assured him. 'I have known our good friend Daniel since childhood. We've grown up together; there are no secrets.'

'Well then, I tell you.' He leaned forward and lowered his voice. 'Marco, he tell me when he come back to Italy that he 'ad fallen in love wiz a beautiful English *signorina*.' He glanced at Daniel. 'That ees your grandmother, yes?'

'Yes, so I understand, sir.'

'And so you come to claim your heritage, yes? You 'ave found your family.'

'Oh!' Daniel was shocked. 'No, signor, I haven't come to claim anything, only to find 'truth of my blood. My father was adopted; he didn't know his birth mother or father.'

'Ah, I understand.' Rosso nodded wisely. 'You wish to know how you, wiz your Italian blood, came to be born in England, yes?'

'Yes,' Daniel said reluctantly. 'Something like that.'

'It's so very interesting, isn't it?' Beatrice put in. 'And important to know who we are.'

'Indeed.' Rosso smiled at her. 'But anyone can tell who you and your brother are. You are pure bred *Inglesi*.' He shrugged, shaking his head from side to side and his mouth making a little moue. 'Or perhaps Swiss or Scandinavian, who knows? We will never be sure of who our forefathers are.' His eyes gave a merry twinkle. 'Perhaps we should not ask, eh?'

Signor Rosso went to fetch his coat and hat and said he would take them out for lunch and show them some of the important sites of Rome. His wife would not be joining them as she didn't go out in the heat of the day, and she warned Beatrice in sign language that she should be careful. Then she lifted a finger and scurried away, returning a moment later with a parasol and a fan which she gave to Beatrice, indicating that she should keep them.

They walked in the shade of the buildings but even so the heat seemed to bounce off the walls. Daniel and Charles, following Rosso who had taken Beatrice's arm to escort her, quietly discussed their preference for staying in the lodging house rather than with the Rossos.

'I agree, Daniel,' Charles murmured. 'It might seem rather an intrusion for the three of us to stay even if for courtesy's sake we were asked.'

'Just what I was thinking,' Daniel said. 'He doesn't know us, after all. I'm a relation of a relation and nothing to do with him.'

They hadn't gone far before Rosso turned into a building that housed a restaurant. He was obviously well known as he was greeted profusely by the waiters and the owner, and he seemed to be explaining who the three English people were.

He pointed out Daniel and they heard the name Orsini; the owner came and shook Daniel by the hand and then Charles, and put his hand to his chest and gave a bow as he greeted Beatrice.

Rosso ordered food and wine for them, and

whilst they waited he began a long explanation of the Orsini family that completely lost them except for the fact that it was an ancient *famiglia* going back to Roman times. He lifted his shoulders and hands as he told them, 'There were popes and cardinals and many noblemen and many broken lines wiz intermarriage and so on. I show you ze Teatro di Marcello, it is a ruined place, very old, two thousand years old, even more old than ze Colosseum, it become a ruin and then noblemen, they begin to build a beautiful 'ouse on top, which then ze Orsinis live in and make it their palace,' again came the shrug of his shoulders, 'I don't know, maybe two hundred years ago.'

Daniel was beginning to feel dizzy with information and knew he wouldn't remember half of it; he gave a slight smile as he recalled George Hart saying solemnly that he should go to Rome. And here I am, he thought, and completely, incredibly, overwhelmed.

'And also,' Rosso was still talking, 'you might like to go to Nerola and see ze Castello Orsini, it ees a ruin, or even Lazio and Taranto, but I don't know them, there are too many to visit and I am old. Older even than Marco who 'as such great spirit.'

They shared a platter of *antipasti misti* with many thinly sliced meats including prosciutto, baby artichokes and slices of tomato and garlic drizzled with olive oil and served with freshly baked bruschetta; then came dishes of pasta, a speciality of the house, followed by a platter of roasted lamb flavoured with spices and herbs. A bottle of Frascati was ordered to drink with the lamb, and just as they were beginning to think

359

they might not want to eat again for a week, Signor Rosso signalled to a waiter and said to Beatrice, 'You musta try ze *crostata di ricotta,* how you say, cake with cheese and eggs and *limone,* and for drink you must have Marsala.'

'Cheesecake?' Beatrice suggested, and said she would like to try it.

Daniel gazed at it when the dish was brought. It looked delicious, a thin slice of pastry holding the light concoction. 'It looks good,' he said. 'And nothing like my ma's Yorkshire cheesecake.'

By the time they had finished eating and talking in the cool restaurant it was three thirty and the heat outside had abated slightly as the sky clouded over.

'But you must still be careful,' Signor Rosso told them. 'Keep under cover. Now,' he said, 'I will tell you where to find ze Orsini palace, because you must excuse me, I go now home to rest.'

Of course they quite understood, and they thanked him sincerely for the meal and his company and hospitality.

Rosso shook hands with Daniel and welcomed him into the Orsini family, shook hands with Charles, bowed and kissed Beatrice's hand.

'*Arrivederci.* Come back to Roma again,' he said. 'It ees your ancestral home, Daniel. Always you are welcome.'

'*Arrivederci.* Thank you,' Daniel said fervently. '*Mille grazie.*'

None of them felt like going very far after the meal they had eaten, so they walked slowly, Beatrice holding the parasol to shield her face.

Within fifteen minutes they came to the rear of the Colosseum, where they saw ancient statuary, ruins of antiquity and vestiges of old walls with orange trees growing between them, and what looked like another smaller Colosseum with open ruined walls and arches and stone columns, except that another occupied floor had been built on the very top. They could see the windows dressed with curtains and flower pots on the sills.

'This is like an ancient arena,' Charles said, looking round the vast area surrounding them.

'Or an auditorium,' Beatrice added. 'Perhaps it was used for music and entertainment.'

'Or gladiatorial battles,' Charles said, his eyes gleaming.

But Daniel had his eyes glued on the edifice before him. 'And this,' he said quietly, 'is the Orsini Palace, home of the Roman Orsinis.' He took a huge breath and exhaled. 'I've seen enough,' he said. 'Now I want to go home.'

CHAPTER FORTY-TWO

Stephen sat silently, not asking any questions as his mother explained the connection between his father and Fletcher Tuke. She concluded by saying, 'Ellen Tuke died not long ago. Her funeral was last week.'

'So was that when it all came out?' Stephen asked. 'Did no one know about it before?' He wrinkled his heavy eyebrows. 'I can't believe that

361

no one knew, not in such a small community as this.'

'Fletcher and Harriet Tuke have known for over twenty years, and I – I guessed that ... yes, I did harbour suspicions that ... that...' How to say to your son that you suspected your husband had had a liaison with a servant girl who had given birth to an illegitimate child? '...that Fletcher Tuke looked very much like your father when he was a young man.'

'So did my father support her and the child?' Stephen's voice was brisk and quite grown up. 'And why didn't he confide in you before you were married? Or perhaps he thought you wouldn't marry him if you knew.'

'He didn't support her because he didn't know,' she replied softly. 'And she never asked for anything, or accused him. It seems that your father was probably the last person to know. She – Ellen Tuke – passed off the child as her husband's until she decided to tell.' When it suited her, Melissa thought bitterly. She bided her time for greater effect and in the hope that Fletcher would inherit the estate; for I am certain that is why she did it.

'I don't believe it,' Stephen said with the wisdom of youth. 'How could he not know?'

But then he became silent again as he remembered he was speaking to his mother, and then the implication seemed to hit home and he muttered, 'So Fletcher Tuke is my half-brother, is that what you're saying?' He looked down at his feet. 'And does that mean ... as the eldest son...'

'No,' his mother said. 'Let's be quite clear on

that. He will *not* inherit, and more to the point, Stephen, he doesn't want to. He's quite determined about that. He's a self-made man, a farmer who has succeeded without the help of anyone else. I've had conversations with him and Harriet, and I have asked him if he will assist us on the estate, show you the ropes so to speak, until such time as your father recovers and we can employ another bailiff, which is proving difficult at the moment. I'm assuming that you are still intent on attending farming college? And if you are,' she said, as Stephen nodded in assent, 'then we need to have a discussion with Charles when he comes home.'

Stephen mulled it over. 'I've always liked Fletcher Tuke, but now, well, I don't know if I can see him in the same light.'

'It's not his fault.'

'I know,' Stephen acknowledged. 'But there's something else to be considered.'

Melissa shook her head. She had known the subject would be mentioned. Stephen was a straight-talking boy – no, young man, she thought. But he was young, young enough to recover.

'You know what I'm going to say?' His voice faltered and cracked a little.

'Yes,' she said sadly, 'and I'm sorry, Stephen, but you must now consider the Tuke sons and daughters as your nephews and nieces.'

He was shocked when he went up to see his father. A fire had been lit in the bedroom and he was sitting in an armchair with a blanket over his knees. His face was grey, as if the colour had leached out of it. He seemed to have aged by years.

'Stephen!' he said croakily. 'Are you home already? Has term finished early?'

'Mama sent for me, Father. She seemed to think you needed some company and help on the estate. It's only another week to the end of the term in any case.'

'Oh, nonsense.' Christopher made a stab at being positive. 'I'm just a bit down at the moment. Things don't always go well when you're running a place this size.'

Stephen sat on the edge of the bed. 'It's all right, Father. Mama has explained everything.'

'Has she?' Christopher answered quietly. 'No, I don't think she has. She can't explain why a young man such as I was, shy and reserved, could get into a situation like this. Or how an incident nearly fifty years ago could cause such a reverberation.'

'An incident!' Stephen said incredulously. 'Surely it was more than just an incident?' I might be young, he thought, but I'm not totally naive. I know how these things can happen.

Christopher sighed. 'I wish I could explain it,' he said, 'but I can't. I remember Ellen Tuke very well. We were about the same age and I was often in the kitchen chatting to Cook and the other servants, and I admit I was at fault in making a friend of her. I was lonely, I suppose,' he said softly. 'But I'm as much a victim of circumstance as everyone else, and I'll speak frankly, Stephen, man to man, when I say that although it should have been a momentous and profound experience for me as well as for her, I can't recall a damned thing about it!'

The next day, Stephen saddled up his horse and rode off towards Elloughton Dale, ostensibly to meet Fletcher Tuke face to face so that there was no embarrassment between them when they started to work together. His mother had explained what she had agreed with Fletcher, and his father had said he knew nothing about the arrangements but would go along with whatever Melissa had decided. He'd added that he and Fletcher had had a discussion to clear the air before Ellen Tuke had died, but he hadn't seen him since.

But Stephen's visit was really to see Maria. He had admired her and thought her a sweet girl when he'd met her at the twins' party all those years ago, and on subsequent occasions when he'd seen her at the Tukes' house. He remembered the time he'd gone especially to see her and found that she had left home to work in Brough. He'd thought it odd at the time, for surely she hadn't needed to work elsewhere, but now he wondered if the Tukes had sent her away deliberately so that they wouldn't meet.

He knocked on the door but no one answered; he tried the sneck and looked in. A fire was burning merrily and there was an appetizing aroma of meat and onions, but no one was there. He tied up his horse and went looking for someone, and heard men's voices from far down a field. Haymaking, he realized. Then he heard the clatter of a metal bucket from one of the sheds and followed the noise.

'Hello,' he called. 'Is anyone there?'

'I'm in 'cowshed,' a female voice called back. 'I can't stop, we're in full flow.'

He put his head round the door; there was a sweet smell of hay and milk and Maria was sitting on a low stool with her back to him milking a cow, the milk flowing in a fast stream into a white bucket.

She half turned towards him. 'We can't stop, as you'll see. Who is it?'

Stephen quietly stepped inside, not wanting to disturb the cow. 'It's me. Stephen.' He moved so that she could see him. 'I didn't know you could do that.'

She gazed up at him from beneath her lashes. 'Been milking for a while,' she explained. 'Ma showed me how. She said it might come in useful one day, if I ever...' Her voice tailed away. 'Are you looking for my da?'

'Not really,' he said, continuing to watch her as she rhythmically squeezed the animal's teats. 'I was looking for you.'

He saw alarm shoot across her face. 'It's all right,' he said quickly. 'I know – about what's happened.'

A slow flush crept up his neck and he saw that Maria's cheeks flushed too. 'I, erm, I just wanted to ask if we could still be friends, you and I, even though...' He shrugged. 'I mean, just because we're – well, sort of related...'

'Yes,' she murmured. 'I'd like that.' She kept her face turned away from him, her head bent against the cow's belly as she concentrated on the milking. 'I'd like that very much. To be friends.'

'Oh, good,' he said. 'That's good. Thank you. I was hoping that's what you'd say. All right, I'd better go and look for your father after all, so – well, goodbye then. I'll see you again soon, I expect?'

'Yes, I expect so,' she said softly, her eyes on his. 'Goodbye, Stephen.'

'Goodbye,' he said, and afterwards wondered how he had plucked up the courage, for the first and probably the last time, to bend down and kiss her gently on her cheek.

CHAPTER FORTY-THREE

Beatrice and Charles were in agreement with Daniel about going home. Beatrice felt that she should return soon and face her parents after having taken the unprecedented step of coming on this momentous tour with her brother and Daniel without their approval or permission.

'I don't know if they'll be angry or not,' she said, as they walked back to the lodging house. 'But I do know that I would not have missed this experience for anything.'

'And I must go home and tell Father that I definitely won't be going to university in England, but mean to study in Italy,' Charles said uneasily. 'We'll have to have a discussion about the estate too, of course. I hope there won't be too many complications, because I'm fairly sure that Stephen will be pleased to take over the running of it in time, though not yet of course. And, I don't know whether or not to tell Mama that I've fallen in love and want to get married.'

'They'll say you're too young,' Beatrice told him. 'You'll have to wait until you're twenty-one in any case, because that's when you'll get your inheritance, unless of course Papa disowns you,' she said smugly, raising her eyebrows, which made Daniel hide a smile and mouth *Cruel*.

'He won't, will he?' Charles said anxiously. 'Of course, he'll see things differently because he's from another generation entirely. He married his first wife because it was expected of him, not because he loved her but because she was suitable.' He sighed dramatically. 'He will probably think that Calypso is totally unsuitable, being foreign.'

'Here, hold on,' Daniel said in mock severity. 'You're speaking of my cousin, *old chap*.'

Charles glanced at Daniel, ready to apologize until he saw his lips trembling with laughter, as were Beatrice's. 'Gosh, yes.' He grinned. 'Do you realize, Daniel, that when Calypso and I are married, you and I will be related?'

'Yes,' Daniel agreed. 'I had realized that, but have *you* thought that you haven't asked her yet?'

Beatrice didn't comment, but her sharp mind was busy calculating, assessing and planning.

They spent two more days in Rome looking at the ancient sites, admiring St Peter's from afar, gazing through the locked gates of the Vatican where the Pope and his cardinals had resided since the unification of Italy; they visited museums and the Colosseum and read some of the history; but as there was so much and it was so hot and Beatrice and Charles had to take cover so often,

368

they decided that it was time to move on.

'When I come to live here,' Charles said, fanning himself with his hat, 'you'll be able to come and stay for a longer period during, say, spring or autumn.'

Daniel laughed. 'Thank you, Charles,' he said. 'How very kind of you. But you're assuming that I'll have no work to do, and will be able to take time off whenever I want to.'

'Ah, yes,' Charles said, glancing lazily at Beatrice. 'Yes, sorry, so I was.'

They had taken a unanimous decision that as they had money left to travel by train they would do so for part of the journey, take a coach at other times, and occasionally, when the mood took them, walk. They all had good walking boots and Beatrice wore her divided skirt, which she said was comfortable for walking in as well as riding. They all wore hats, Beatrice carried her parasol all the time, and both Daniel and Charles acquired stout sticks for walking.

Their first train journey was to Florence, the city of art and culture, where they spent two days. They were able to get about quite easily, as it appeared that the locals took to the hills in the summer to escape the heat, and so they visited the Duomo, walked across the medieval Ponte Vecchio, where Beatrice stopped to gaze into the enclosed shops selling gold and silver, and viewed the art galleries, where they stood in awe before the paintings and sculptures of Michelangelo and da Vinci.

The next rail journey took them through Genoa

on the way to Turin, and Daniel gazed out of the windows down towards the Mediterranean, wishing that he might have seen his grandfather just once more; he wondered what he was doing, inspecting the grapes or the olives and assessing the quality, or sitting on the terrace drinking coffee with his straw hat over his eyes.

From Turin they took the coach to Bardonecchia and up to the entrance of the Fréjus rail tunnel, which would carry them through the Alps and into France. Beatrice was nervous and said she didn't like to be enclosed. The alternative would be to travel by coach, a perilous journey on the narrow and steep roads over the Alps, hire horses, or walk, all of which would take them much longer.

'It's up to you, Beatrice,' Daniel said. 'We can walk or ride, which we've done already, or we can take a short cut through the Alps, and even then we still have a long journey ahead of us.'

'All right, I'll be brave,' she said. 'I'll close my eyes and pretend to be asleep. But you must both hold my hands.'

'Gladly.' Daniel smiled. That would be a bonus, he thought, for he was longing for the experience of travelling deep below the Alps on a railroad that had only been built ten years before.

As it happened they were all very tired after the days of travelling, and as the train entered the tunnel and the sunshine disappeared, with Daniel and Charles sitting on either side of Beatrice holding her hands as promised, one by one they fell asleep, Daniel gently stroking Beatrice's hand with his thumb as she slept and thinking he had never been happier.

They awoke as the train rumbled to a halt in the border town of Modane. The sun was still shining but it wasn't as hot as it had been in Italy; the clusters of houses were painted in bright colours and potted plants adorned the balconies.

'It's lovely,' Beatrice said. 'Shall we stay a day or two?'

'I think that's a good idea,' Daniel agreed. 'We could rest and then mebbe walk a while down the valley. 'Weather's good for walking.'

They could also write postcards home, they all agreed, and let everyone know they were on the homeward journey.

After two days they ventured forth again and rode for many miles through the mountains on hired horses; they caught local omnibuses or rode in carriers' carts from village to village and finally decided to travel by train to Lyon, then by boat down the Loire from Roanne, spending lazy days gazing at the *châteaux* and wildlife along the banks. Daniel and Charles in the prow steered the barge under the casual eye of the accommodating captain, or drifted slowly along the canals while Beatrice lounged in a deck chair in warm sunshine with a hat over her eyes and wrote a letter home to her mother, until they reached Orléans ten days later.

They shook hands with the captain, who had sung in a hearty voice for most of the journey, had fed them on French bread and ham and strong local wine, and spoke no English, so that they had once more had to rely on Beatrice to translate. He wished them a cheery *au revoir et bonne chance,* goodbye and good luck, as they set off to catch the train to Paris and Le Havre on the final leg of their journey.

The sight of the English Channel both cheered and deflated them. All three knew that their freedom would be curtailed once they returned to a normal life. Daniel was eager to see his family again and pass on the messages from Leo and Marco. Yet it all seems like an improbable dream, he thought, and once I'm back working on 'farm again it'll seem as if it happened to somebody else. I'll miss those lovely ponies too, and much as I love my Shires I wish I could have brought the Haflingers home.

His thoughts were also on Beatrice; he knew full well that she would be lost to him once they were home. She would live a life that wouldn't include him. She would do whatever a young woman of her status did, which was unknown to him; visiting other young women, he supposed, going to parties and balls, meeting eligible young men who might seek her hand in marriage. He was not a contender for that, the son of a small farmer, a ploughman who knew nothing but farming, horses, farrowing, sowing and reaping.

He swallowed hard and leaned on the ship's rail, letting the cold wind blow into his face as if it could prepare him to accept his lot. Come on, he told himself, you've had 'pleasure of her company, heard her laughter, held her hand; nobody can take that away. And surely he would still have her friendship, the friendship they had shared from childhood.

He felt a small hand on his shoulder. Beatrice. He turned and looked at her.

'What are you doing out here all alone?' she asked. 'Charles is in the saloon fast asleep and you have deserted me.'

'No,' he said, 'I'd never do that; I was just looking out to sea and thinking of all that we'd done and seen. It's been a chance in a lifetime for me, and now it's back to real life. Not that I'm complaining,' he said with a forced laugh. 'I've a good life, doing what I like doing.' He smiled at her, seeing how the breeze caught her hair and flushed her cheeks. 'And it'll be good to see everybody again and hear what they've been up to while we've been away. I wonder if Da – Fletcher – brought in another lad to help out with 'harvest? They'll be turning 'stock out to graze in 'fields now, if they've got harvest in, that is; if they've had good weather.'

He was talking for the sake of it, he realized. Talking of everyday things so that he didn't make a fool of himself and say what he really wanted to say, which was that he'd miss her, miss seeing her every morning with her face freshly washed and glowing and her hair hanging down her back before she plaited it. And seeing her every night, languid and sleepy before she retired to bed. But of course he couldn't say any of it.

CHAPTER FORTY-FOUR

The ship docked in Dover as dawn was breaking and they rushed to catch the early train into London. They took the train to Hull and steamed into Brough station just as the sun was setting. They collected their luggage and stood on the station platform, looking round as if uncertain what to do next.

A railway porter saw them, and recognizing Beatrice and Charles, came towards them. He tipped his hat. 'Good evening, sir, good evening, Miss Hart.' He glanced at Daniel, but didn't appear to recognize the dark-haired, sun-browned stranger. 'Will you require a cab, sir?' he asked Charles. 'I can arrange one in ten minutes.'

Charles and Beatrice both glanced at Daniel. He smiled. 'I'm walking. We've been sitting for hours.'

'We're walking,' Charles and Beatrice both said. 'Thank you,' Beatrice added.

The porter seemed startled, but nodded politely and moved away.

'We'll be home before dark,' Daniel said. 'I'd like to see 'sunset.'

'So would I,' Beatrice agreed. 'And it's only a short walk home compared with what we've done.'

They hitched their rucksacks and sleeping sacks on to their backs and set off, the railway man gazing curiously at the young gentleman and lady from the manor as they left the station dressed like peasants and accompanied by a foreigner.

They walked together for a short distance, then coming to the parting of the ways they stopped to gaze over the Humber, gleaming with a dark intensity as the sun sank lower. Beatrice and Charles were to take the lower Broomfleet road to the manor whilst Daniel headed up to the top of the dale. They were all unsettled and tense, unable to say goodbye.

Finally, Daniel put out his hand to shake Charles's. 'See you again soon, eh, *old chap?*' he said.

'I hope so,' Charles answered quietly. 'It will seem strange not seeing you every day.'

Beatrice stood on tiptoe to kiss Daniel on his cheek. 'We shall meet again before long,' she murmured. 'Sooner than we think.'

He gazed at her and saw that her eyes were moist. He put his hand to his bristly cheek and joked, 'I won't ever shave again.'

He raised his hand as he set off up the footpath that took him through a meadow and towards the top road; he paused to turn round and watch them and saw Beatrice turn too and wave. None of them had said goodbye.

On the top road he looked down and they were lost to view; the Humber was still visible, a dark ribbon dividing east Yorkshire from Lincolnshire, with the last ferry steaming towards Brough from New Holland and other ships and barges like smudges on the water. He cut through Elloughton village but didn't stop to call on Granny Rosie as her house was dark and the curtains drawn and he didn't want to disturb her. Besides, he wanted to get home and give all his news there first.

As he strode on upwards he could see the rooftop of the farmhouse partly hidden beneath trees, and smoke issuing from the chimneys. He sniffed and could smell apple-wood and felt a heart-warming sense of coming home. Sheep were grazing in the harvested fields, and in one of the meadows where the piggeries were kept someone was closing them up for the night. Lenny! Daniel gave a piercing whistle and Lenny looked up, putting his hand to his forehead the better to see. Then he gave a sudden wave as he recognized him and set off at great speed towards the farmstead to announce that Daniel was home.

Lenny, Fletcher, Maria, Joseph and Elizabeth were in the yard to greet him, while his mother was at the open door, waiting to welcome him home. Smiling, he put down his pack and opened his arms wide to embrace them all. 'Oh,' he said, 'it's so good to be home.'

Granny Rosie was there too, busily making tea and bringing out cake; she had been staying at the farm to help Harriet during the harvesting.

Daniel looked round the kitchen. Nothing had changed. The big table in the centre of the room, the lamp in the middle of it casting a cosy glow, enough chairs to accommodate them all at one sitting, easy chairs by the fire for those who had five minutes to spare to sit in them.

'Have you missed me, then?' he asked.

'No, not a bit,' Fletcher, Lenny and Joseph said in unison. 'But your ma has,' Fletcher grinned. 'Cried every night.' He patted Harriet on the shoulder as she wiped her eyes. 'She thought you were never coming home.'

'Not true,' Harriet objected. 'Once I got that first postcard from France, I was much easier in my mind. I knew you'd come back when you were ready.'

'We've been a long way, Ma,' Daniel said softly, and sipped his tea. 'And it took us a long time to get home from Italy.'

'You hired horses?' Fletcher said. 'How come? Did you have enough money to do that?'

Daniel shook his head. 'Bought them,' he said, helping himself to a slice of cake. 'I didn't know when we left that Charles's father was worried that we might get stranded and had insisted on giving Charles a banker's draft as well as making some sort of arrangement with his Swiss bank, so Charles came up with 'idea...' he paused, 'or come to think of it, it might have been Beatrice's idea – she's full of ideas, is Beatrice – that we buy the ponies rather than hire them and then sell them on before we came home and put 'money back.'

'And did you?' his mother asked worriedly. 'You don't owe anybody?'

'I don't owe anybody, Ma, I've even brought a copper or two home wi' me.' He took a deep breath. 'But don't you want to know about Leo or Marco?' He glanced at Rosie, who was perched on the edge of her chair as if ready to take flight, and then at his mother who was screwing up her handkerchief into a tiny ball. 'Where would you like me to start? With finding, without intending to, an uncle and a cousin, or meeting my grand-father who is from one of 'oldest and most noble families in Italy?'

He grinned at the expressions on their faces. 'Questions, please, and then I want to know what you've all been up to while I've been away.'

They all listened without interruption as he told them of travelling across France and Switzerland, of meeting Beatrice and her decision to come with them. 'We couldn't have stopped her,' he explained. 'She was set on it, and as it turned out it was 'best thing ever; cos of her being able to speak other languages, you see,' he finished lamely. Then he told them about travelling over the Alps on horseback and down into Italy, and there meeting his mother's brother. 'Without Leo we'd never have met Marco. We'd never have thought of going to Vernazza and might never have gone to Rome either.'

They were all getting tired and Harriet insisted that Elizabeth and Joseph should go to bed, and that there was plenty of time to hear more the following day. At some time during the evening Harriet and Fletcher had tactically agreed that although they would tell Daniel about Granny Tuke, they wouldn't discuss the relationship between Christopher Hart and Fletcher in front of Joseph and Elizabeth, as they hadn't yet been told. However, as Elizabeth was saying goodnight, she blurted out that Granny Tuke had died and they had all been to her funeral. 'She fell into 'water,' the little girl said, her bottom lip trembling.

'How did that happen?' Daniel was aghast. 'I'm so sorry, Da.'

'We don't know,' Fletcher said. 'She must have

slipped. Off to bed now, Lizzie.'

'I'll go up and read her a story.' Maria stood up. 'She'll have bad dreams otherwise.'

Lenny also decided to go to bed as he had to be up early. 'I've a couple of sows about to farrow,' he said. 'I'll catch up wi' 'news, about Uncle Leonard in 'morning.' He grinned. 'I wouldn't mind being called Leo.'

'We'll talk more tomorrow, Daniel,' Fletcher said. 'I'm tired too. We've had a busy time recently, what with 'harvest and 'funeral and other things too. I'm going up to Hart Holme some time tomorrow. If you want to come wi' me, I'll tell you then what's been going on.'

Daniel turned a questioning glance on his mother after Fletcher and then Rosie went off to bed. 'There's too much to tell tonight, Daniel,' Harriet said. 'Tomorrow is soon enough.' She put both hands to his face and kissed him on the forehead. 'Your bed's made up as usual. Get a good night's sleep. I'm so pleased that you're home.'

'I hope you're not too cross with me, Mama,' Beatrice said anxiously. 'I thought that … well, I thought that if I asked you if I could travel with Charles and Daniel you might say no, or at least Papa would say no; he would have been anxious, I know.'

'And did you think that he would be less anxious once we heard from the academy that you'd gone without leaving a forwarding address?' Melissa was determined that her wayward daughter would not get away scot free even though she wasn't angry with her and wished that she had had some of her adventurous spirit when she was young.

Beatrice was penitent, or at least partly so. 'I'm sorry,' she said. 'And it wasn't Charles's fault either. I'd planned it in advance, ever since he and Daniel discussed travelling abroad. I didn't want to be left out.'

'But you are a female,' her mother said patiently. 'Your father would have thought that you were destroying your reputation by travelling abroad without a female companion.'

'I did think of that, as a matter of fact, but for one thing I didn't know of anyone who would have come, and for another it would have been embarrassing for Charles and Daniel. After all, the three of us have known each other for ever, and I knew they would look after me. Not that I needed looking after,' she said in a sudden surge of pique. 'I was actually very useful to them.'

'I'm sure that you were,' her mother agreed, 'but they could hardly refuse you, could they? However, what's done is done.' She smiled. 'I'm quite sure that you all had a wonderful time and I'm looking forward to hearing about everything you did. When Charles comes down we'll talk.'

Charles had gone up to speak to his father, who had gone early to bed.

'Is Papa ill, Mama?' Beatrice asked anxiously. 'What's happened?'

'Not ill,' Melissa said, 'but he's a little frail at the moment. I'm sure he'll recover quite rapidly now that you and Charles are home again. He's had a worrying and anxious time,' she added as she saw another question hovering on her daughter's lips. 'It's something that needs to be discussed, but perhaps we'll wait until the morning. Stephen and George are eager to see you. Stephen has something special to tell you and George particularly wants to hear about Rome. He seems to think that you followed his advice!'

The following day Fletcher and Daniel set off together for Hart Holme Manor, Fletcher saying that there were things they needed to discuss and Daniel hoping that he'd also see Beatrice and Charles.

'Get on with them all right, did you?' Fletcher asked as they jogged along in the trap.

'Yeh, of course,' Daniel laughed. 'I allus have done.'

'I suppose you were all on an equal footing, travelling as you did. But how did Miss Beatrice cope? Was that difficult?'

'Not for Beatrice it wasn't. To begin with, she introduced me as their cousin, but after a while there didn't seem to be any need, and in any case once we were travelling across 'Alps we didn't see many folk and those we did, hikers and travellers like us, didn't seem to think it strange that we should have a woman with us. There are more women travellers nowadays, Da, they're becoming very independent.'

Fletcher nodded. 'And rightly so,' he said. 'I found when I was in America that there was a certain kind of freedom for women, but there were some who stuck strictly to the rules of what women could or couldn't do.'

Daniel smiled. 'They obviously hadn't met Beatrice, had they?' He hesitated, then added, 'I think she's a bit nervous about what her father will say about travelling with us without his permission.'

Fletcher cleared his throat. 'I think she'll find that he won't have much to say about it, not in view of recent happenings.'

Daniel turned to him. 'Why? What's been going on?'

Fletcher didn't meet his gaze. 'Several things,' he said. 'Beginning with Granny Tuke. Although I've known 'full story for years, as have your ma and seemingly many other folk, Christopher Hart didn't, even though it concerns him more than anybody, and that's why I wanted to talk to you, to have it out in 'open. Maria and Dolly know and so does Lenny. Now it's your turn.'

Melissa had suggested to Christopher when she went to his room to say goodnight that they discuss the issue of Ellen Tuke with Charles and Beatrice the following morning. Christopher demurred slightly, but when Melissa pointed out that they didn't want it hanging over them whilst the twins were telling them about their journey, he agreed. 'It's just that I'm so embarrassed about it,' he explained.

'I don't think that they will be,' she said. 'They'll think of you differently, perhaps.' She gave a little smile. 'More human.'

'Are you suggesting that I'm not?' he harrumphed.

She kissed his cheek. 'I know you are,' she said. 'But they'll know that you haven't always been as proper as you appear to be now.' Her cheeks dimpled. 'They'll love you for your weakness, especially when I tell them that you were seduced.'

'Don't you dare,' he said, with some of his old spark. 'I'll tell them myself, or at least I'll tell Charles that I was drunk and that will keep *him* out of mischief.'

'Yes,' she agreed. 'Unless he's already been into mischief, although I rather think that Beatrice and Daniel would have seen to it that he hasn't.'

When the maid knocked on the sitting room door to announce Fletcher and Daniel, Christopher was leaning with one arm on the mantelpiece, Melissa was standing by the window where she had seen them arrive and Charles and Beatrice rose from where they had been sitting to greet them. There were a few hesitant strands of strained conversation and then Charles went across to Fletcher and put out his hand. 'I thought there was a likeness,' he said. 'I first saw it that time I came to your harvest.'

Fletcher shook his hand. 'Yes, Tom told me that you seemed to have noticed a similarity that day.'

'So he knew, did he, or had you told him?' Christopher asked.

'No, sir, I hadn't, but apparently he's known 'connection ever since he was a young lad.' What Fletcher didn't say was that Tom's Aunt Mary, the Harts' nanny, had also known.

Christopher sighed and shook his head as if he didn't know what to say.

Beatrice came across to Fletcher and gave him her hand, and then impulsively kissed his cheek. 'I hope you won't tease me in the way my other brothers do,' she said quietly, and glancing at

Daniel she gave a small huff of breath. Thank goodness Fletcher wasn't Daniel's natural father, or all of her plans would come to nought.

'Will you have coffee?' Melissa reached for the bell.

'No thank you, ma'am – Melissa,' Fletcher said. 'I've come to collect Stephen. We're meeting some of 'tenant farmers this morning so we'd better get off, if he's about?'

Charles looked questioningly from Fletcher to his father.

'We've lost our bailiff,' his father told him. 'Fletcher has kindly agreed to help out temporarily whilst I've been out of commission, but,' Christopher smiled and it seemed as if a great weight had been lifted from his shoulders, 'I'm feeling much better now, and Stephen has taken to farming like a duck to water. When he comes in later we've several things to discuss, so Charles, if you are still keen to do something other than manage the estate, then we'll talk about that too.'

The twins glanced at each other and then at Daniel. They all smiled. So that, Beatrice thought, is one hurdle over.

CHAPTER FORTY-FIVE

During the following months there were many letters written and sent between England and Italy. Daniel wrote to Marco; Harriet came to terms with her brother's change of name and addressed her letters to Leo. Maria and Dolly wrote to Calypso welcoming her as a cousin and hoping, they both said, to meet her soon. Indeed, Dolly was already planning to use her wages on a visit to Italy, although she hadn't yet worked out how she would get there. Rosie wrote to Marco, and all of them received letters in return.

Charles wrote requesting literature from various Italian universities and colleges of art and culture, for his father had agreed that if that was what he really wanted to do he should start making enquiries immediately; he wrote to Leo and Marco too, assuring them of his best regards and intentions at all times, and asked Leo if he might write to Calypso. He also began Italian lessons.

Beatrice had long and ardent conversations with her mother, drew up plans and wrote to Marco thanking him for his hospitality and advising him of some of her proposals for Daniel's forthcoming twenty-first birthday in December.

'I don't for one moment think that Daniel has even considered the event to be of any significance,' she wrote. 'But I do not wish it to pass unnoticed.' She asked him to be discreet and not to mention anything of her ideas to Daniel.

She wrote too to Signor Rosso in Rome, who, although distant, was also a relative of Daniel's and, she felt, should be informed of the special occasion about to be celebrated in this noble family.

By mid-November life was almost back to how it had been before they had gone abroad, with one or two exceptions. Stephen had secured a place as a first-year student at the Royal Agricultural College in Gloucestershire and had begun that term.

George had gone back to school and informed his parents that he wished to study science and law, not farming.

'Which means,' Christopher said gloomily, 'we have only one son prepared to take the reins.'

'Which Stephen will do admirably,' Melissa said, 'especially if you get a good bailiff, and Fletcher has promised he will find someone suitable, has he not?'

Christopher agreed that he had and admitted that he didn't know how he would have managed without Fletcher and would be sorry when he returned to his own farm duties. Fletcher in turn had realized whilst Daniel was away that he wouldn't have been able to help out at the manor if it hadn't been for Tom and Lenny taking on extra work, so when Tom had suggested they employ another lad, the son of one of their former school friends, he had agreed at once.

'You remember Bob Taylor, don't you?' Tom said. 'He was hopeless at reading and writing but could mek anything grow. He married Betsy, a lass from Brough, and took on a tenancy over at Ellerker; he died a few years back, and Betsy brought up both their lads on her own. 'Eldest, Adam, teks after his da for having green fingers.'

Fletcher remembered Bob Taylor, but there was something in Tom's voice that made him take notice. 'Hey!' he said. 'A widow woman?'

'Aye,' Tom said sheepishly. 'I've met up wi' her once or twice; she meks an apple pie nearly as good as your Harriet's.'

Now that Daniel was back and resuming his work with the horse team life was a little easier, although they had decided to keep Adam on for the foreseeable future; neither Fletcher nor Tom wanted him to go off to the November Hirings, which were coming up in a few weeks' time. He was a good all-rounder, handy with the nuts and bolts of machinery, and was teaching Joseph, who had also found an aptitude for all things mechanical.

Daniel, however, had seemed rather morose of late and Harriet put it down to the fact that he was missing the company of Charles and Beatrice.

'He'll have to get used to being without them,' Fletcher said as he undressed, washed and slipped into bed beside her. 'Charles will be off abroad soon. He's starting at some university or other in Italy in January.'

'It's Beatrice that Daniel is missing,' she murmured, then, 'What have you been doing up at 'manor? I can smell brick dust in your hair!'

'Mrs Hart – Melissa, I mean – I can't get used to using her first name,' he grumbled. 'Her and Beatrice have got a building project on 'go, building on an extension to 'stable block. Beatrice is getting another hoss, seemingly.' He yawned. 'I just gave them 'benefit of my advice and suggested what they should do. I built this house, after all.'

'So you did.' She snuggled up to him. 'I've been wondering if we should extend out at 'back. All our bairns are growing up; suppose Lenny meets somebody and gets married. He wouldn't leave his precious pigs so he'd want to bring his wife here, and young people need their own place.'

'Heavens,' he said. 'He's onny fifteen! You

387

women, thinking so far ahead! And what about Daniel? Won't he want a place of his own as well? We're likely to have a house as big as Hart Holme if we provide for them all!'

Harriet sighed. 'No, not Daniel,' she said. 'And not Maria either. I believe their hearts are already broken.'

'Mm,' he said sleepily, 'I don't know owt about that, but I expect they'll mend.'

'Beatrice,' her mother said. 'It's time you spoke to your father.'

'I'm nervous,' Beatrice said. 'What if he refuses?'

'He won't,' Melissa smiled. 'But if he should, then you'd have to wait.'

'I don't want to upset him. He's such a dear.'

'Nevertheless,' her mother insisted. 'Time is of the essence.'

'That's true,' Beatrice began, but broke off as the door opened and her father came in for his morning coffee.

'What's going on down at the stables?' Christopher asked. 'There's a great pile of brick and stone and one of the men said they were working on Mrs Hart's orders.'

'Ah, yes,' Melissa said, and looked at Beatrice.

'It was me actually, Papa,' Beatrice said. 'I was going to ask you but the delivery came sooner than I expected.'

'Delivery? What delivery?'

'Of bricks,' she said. 'It's – it's temporary, but it will prove useful afterwards, I'm quite sure.' She laughed nervously. 'It's extra storage space.'

'It looks like an extension to the stable block to

me. What are you up to, Beatrice, and you too Melissa?' he said, in mock severity.

'Do come and sit down, Papa,' Beatrice pleaded. 'I need to talk to you.'

He sat down and folded his arms, and Melissa thought how much he seemed like his old self again, his self-assurance restored.

'When I was away in Italy, Papa, I resolved that when I returned home I would tell you of a secret I've been keeping for a long time; years, in fact,' Beatrice started.

Christopher smiled. When Beatrice was a child she often whispered secrets into his ear, cupping her hand so that her mother or her brothers didn't hear, but then telling them afterwards. 'Did you, darling?' he said, so pleased and proud that he was still her confidant. 'And are you going to tell me now?'

'Yes.' She bent her head as she felt tears welling. 'I'm in love, Papa. Well, no, not *in* love, but love somebody with my whole heart.'

Startled, Christopher looked at Melissa, who gave a grave and silent nod.

'Do I know this somebody? Is he worthy of my daughter?'

'Yes, Papa, he is. He's of noble birth from an ancient line, much older than ours.' She took a breath. 'But you might think that he's poor in comparison to us because he doesn't own land and he isn't rich, but I want to marry him and if you forbid it, then I shan't ever marry anyone!'

Her father's lips twitched and he raised his eyebrows. Here was the Beatrice of old, dramatic and determined. 'So does that mean that if I

389

don't approve, then I should turn you out of my house and never see you again?'

Melissa hid a smile. Beatrice often sparred with Christopher when she wanted something, never realizing that her father would always indulge her.

'Oh, Papa. You'd never do that, would you?'

Her father appeared to consider. 'Mm! So you would be marrying this poor but noble man for love?' he murmured. 'Just as I did with your mama. And has he asked for you without coming to me first?' He frowned.

'I think that what Beatrice is trying to tell you,' Melissa interjected, 'is that Daniel won't ask you for her hand in marriage because he doesn't think he's good enough for her, notwithstanding his newly discovered pedigree.'

'Yes.' Beatrice's voice broke. 'That is what I'm saying – Mama! I never mentioned Daniel! How–'

'My dear Beatrice.' Melissa glanced at her husband, who seemed rather perplexed. 'It has been perfectly obvious, to me at least, for a long time, and your father and I were young once; we do know the signs.'

'Oh, you're both so wonderful,' Beatrice proclaimed. 'But how are we going to convince Daniel?'

'Am I missing something?' Her father gazed at her in astonishment. 'Do you mean to say we're talking about Daniel Tuke? Fletcher Tuke's son?'

'Stepson, Papa,' Beatrice said. 'Not a blood relation. Daniel Tuke Orsini.'

Christopher put his hand to his forehead. 'Forgive me. Of course.' His face cleared. 'I first met Daniel when he was only an infant, a babe in arms. Do you remember that fateful day, Melissa, just before that dreadful Christmas when his father drowned in the estuary?'

'I do,' she said softly. 'We have all had much happier days since then.'

'We have,' Christopher agreed, and with a subtle shift of mood said, 'So what indeed do we do to convince the noble Daniel that my daughter must have him for her own?'

Beatrice smiled. 'I have a plan, Papa.'

There were letters from Leo to Harriet telling her that he and Calypso were hoping to come to England very soon. 'The grape and olive harvest is over and the fruits of our labour have gone off for processing,' he wrote, 'and I can now begin to make arrangements for someone to stay with Marco and make plans for our journey. I hope it will be convenient for us to come. I'm ready for the cold weather and have bought Calypso warm clothing.'

Harriet broke off from reading the letter. 'They're coming!' she said excitedly. 'He doesn't say when, just that they're definitely coming.'

Daniel grinned. That's what Leo had written to him too, except that he had given him a date. 'Yes,' he said. 'I suppose you'll want to scrub 'house from top to bottom?'

Harriet nodded. 'I'll get Maria to help me.' She put her hand to her chin. 'I wonder if I should bring Dolly home.'

They did indeed clean the house from the bedrooms down to the ground floor. Rugs were beaten, floorboards polished, curtains that had been washed in the summer taken down, shaken well and put back up again. Windows and mirrors were washed and polished and the house smelled of beeswax as chairs and tables were burnished.

'I wonder if they'll come for your birthday, Daniel?' his mother said. 'That would be really nice, wouldn't it, as it's a special one. Twenty-one!' She came over and gave him a hug. 'I can't believe that it's nearly twenty-one years since you were born.'

Her eyes grew misty and her throat tightened as she recalled her joy at his birth and the trauma of Noah's death shortly afterwards.

'I didn't tell them about my birthday, Ma. I never thought to. But, well, it's special to you and me, but not–'

'And us,' Maria interrupted.

'And me!' Fletcher came through the door. 'What? What's special?'

Daniel laughed. 'Nowt much, Da. Just somebody's birthday!'

'Oh, yeh?' Fletcher said blithely. 'Who's having a birthday?'

Daniel shook his head. 'Nobody I know. Oh, of course,' he added hastily, 'Charles and Beatrice will be twenty very soon.' To cover his disappointment that he hadn't seen either of them for several weeks, he said, 'Look at you, Da. What've you been doing? You're covered in brick dust.'

'Yeh, I'm going to have a swill under 'pump, but 'job at 'manor is finished, thank goodness; it's bigger than I expected it to be, but I can now go back to being a farmer rather than a builder, because 'new bailiff has started. A bit later than expected, but he's arrived and he seems promising!'

392

Daniel took Maria and Lenny into his confidence and told them when Leo and Calypso were expected. 'You'll have to shuffle 'bedrooms round, I expect, won't you?' he asked Maria.

'That's already organized,' she said. 'Me and Dolly are going to share and Calypso can have my room, and Uncle Leo can have 'spare bedroom. We've lit fires in there already and all 'bedding is aired.'

'I'll need you to come to 'station with me in 'trap, Lenny,' Daniel said. 'Or mebbe we should tek 'waggon for their luggage.'

They discussed various aspects of getting the family to the house without their mother knowing, and apart from Harriet baking a cake and other provisions Daniel's birthday seemed to be rather overlooked, which was fine, he thought, for it was only a number and nothing special to celebrate; he'd had the best year he could ever expect to have and would never in his life forget, with Beatrice and Charles as his constant companions as they travelled across Europe, and meeting his grandfather for the first time.

On the twins' birthday, Daniel went to the manor with small gifts and cards from everyone; the young maid who answered the door took them, saying that everyone was out and she would leave them on the hall table for when they returned.

He was extremely disappointed, and supposed that they had gone off on a family outing, but as he was driving the trap back down the drive Beatrice rushed round from the back of the house and called to him to stop.

'Oh, Daniel, I'm so pleased to see you,' she said breathlessly, and he felt somewhat mollified. 'I wanted to tell you that Charles and I are not celebrating our birthday today, because it's only a twentieth, isn't it, and nothing has been arranged...' Her words tailed away at his expression. 'Oh, Daniel, you look sad. What is it?'

'No. No, not sad at all,' he blustered. 'As a matter of fact I'm really quite happy. Can you keep a secret, from my mother, I mean?'

She nodded and glanced away. 'Of course.'

'It's just that Leo and Calypso are coming to stay. They'll be here in just a few days.'

'Really?' she said. 'How wonderful! I'm so thrilled for you.'

But as he drove away, he thought she seemed rather preoccupied. Knowing her so well, he wondered what exactly she had on her mind – and why, he wondered, was she coming from the back of the house?

On the day the visitors were due, snow began to fall and Daniel whispered to Dolly to build up all the fires; she had arrived unexpectedly, cheerfully claiming that she had felt unwell and Mrs Topham had said she must come home immediately.

At midday they ate a meal of thick soup and fresh bread and then Maria insisted on cooking a ham and chicken pie and told her mother that she might as well make two seeing as there were two chickens in the larder and the oven was hot; and as the apples in the store room needed using up she would make an apple crumble as well. 'We can eat one pie tonight and save 'other one for tomorrow,' she said.

'There's enough here for an army,' Harriet objected, and Fletcher, who was also in on the secret, said that he thought there were enough of them to make their own army anyway and that he for one was ravenous.

Tom popped his head round the door. 'Shall I go and fetch Rosie?' he said. 'Snow's coming down fast. Better today than tomorrow.'

'Yes, all right,' Harriet agreed. 'Seeing as we're going to have plenty of food. Maria's preparing for a siege by 'look of it.'

'Aye.' Tom winked at Maria. 'Best to be prepared. Winter's setting in.'

Just after three o'clock, before the sky darkened, Daniel came in and slipped upstairs to his room. When he came down he'd brushed his hair and changed into a warm coat, not his working one. 'Just popping out, Ma,' he said. 'Won't be long.'

Harriet stood with her arms akimbo. 'What's going on?' she said suspiciously, for as Daniel disappeared in one direction, Lenny dashed in, in the other and ran upstairs, he too reappearing in another coat and cap before going out in Daniel's wake.

'Don't know,' Maria said vaguely. 'Why don't you put your feet up, Ma, and I'll mek you a cup of tea.' She glanced at her mother. 'You look nice,' she said. 'But your hair needs brushing.'

'Let me do it.' Dolly hurried to the drawer where her mother kept her hairbrush.

'Now I know something's going on,' Harriet said, as she allowed herself to be gently pushed into a chair, while her hair was unpinned and brushed and then neatly coiled again. Her apron was taken off and a cup of tea put into her hand. She drank it steadily, and as she handed it back looked questioningly at her daughters.

'It's a surprise,' Maria said, smiling. 'You'll like it,' Dolly added.

Shortly afterwards, Tom arrived back with Rosie, who said she hadn't expected to come today, and then Joseph and Elizabeth came home from school.

Joseph gave an appreciative sniff. 'Summat smells good, Ma. Is it ready?'

'I don't know, Joseph, it's not my kitchen any more,' his mother said. 'It's been tekken over. Where's your da?' she asked anyone who might have been listening. 'Has he gone off somewhere as well?'

'He's outside in 'yard,' Elizabeth told her. 'He's talking to Daniel and those people in our trap.'

'What people?' Harriet half rose from her chair and gazed at Maria and Dolly, who were both beaming, and then suddenly the room was full as Fletcher ushered in a man with dark greying hair and dressed in a warm overcoat, who seemed to be struck by a strong emotion as he looked at Harriet; a beautiful dark-eyed young woman dressed in furs, escorted by Lenny who had a great grin on his face, and, holding firmly on to Daniel's arm, a white-haired elderly gentleman, who by his liquid dark brown eyes and long lashes could only be Marco, Daniel's grandfather.

CHAPTER FORTY-SIX

Harriet and her brother talked and talked. He told her about his visit home when he had not been able to find her, although he had been told that their mother had died. 'I always intended to come back,' Leo shrugged, 'but you get caught up with life, and when my wife died I had my baby daughter to consider. It was a very difficult time.'

Harriet told him some, but not all, of her life since moving away from Hull. Much of it could be dripped into conversation for some time to come.

Marco and Rosie were reintroduced and she was shy, as he recalled she always had been, and he told her that he had decided he must make an effort to come to England with Leo. 'For who knows what is in front of us, Rosie, or how much time we have left?' He added softly, 'I am so sorry about our child.'

She wiped her tears and gently squeezed his hand.

Calypso was kidnapped by Maria and Dolly and taken upstairs to the room Maria had vacated for her, so that they could question her and admire her beauty and listen to her lilting accent, and Elizabeth and Joseph pressed their ears to the door so that they could listen.

'It must be *lovely* to live in Italy,' Dolly said in envy.

'You must come, both of you,' Calypso said. 'I will introduce you to my friends. They will be so envious of your beautiful blonde hair and English skin – what you say, complexion – and the Italian boys,' she made kissing noises, 'they will want to be your friends.' She leaned forward and spoke softly. 'You know this young gentleman, Charles, he is Daniel's friend?'

They both nodded, their eyes glued to her. 'He is 'andsome, yes? He wants to marry me. He 'as asked my papa if he can write to me. He is good family, is he not?'

'He is,' Maria said fervently.

'He's our father's half-brother,' Dolly told her, 'but I think you'd be all right to marry him.' She frowned. 'I can't really work it out!'

They all talked through the meal that Maria and Dolly dished up, and Harriet smiled at her daughters, knowing now why so much food had been prepared, and they talked past midnight until Fletcher, seeing Marco tiring, suggested that they go to bed now and continue their conversation the following day.

'Yes, we've much more to discuss,' Leo said, 'and Marco wants to chat to Daniel, don't you, Babbo?'

'I do,' Marco agreed. 'But tomorrow. We have had a very long journey but already it has been so agreeable.'

There was a shuffling round of beds; Marco took Fletcher and Harriet's room, Harriet slept with Maria, Dolly and Elizabeth, head to tail which she said she used to do when she was a child as they only ever had one bed; Fletcher

398

slept in the boys' room with Daniel, Lenny and Joseph. Rosie had her own little room, and Tom, who had come in to be introduced, said he would drop Adam off at his mother's house and then go home, and Fletcher gave him a quizzical glance that made him blush.

'It's a good thing it's Sunday,' Fletcher yawned the next morning when he came downstairs to find Harriet proving dough for bread making. He poured himself a cup of tea and headed outside, then came back in. 'I like your brother,' he said.

Harriet smiled and nodded. 'Yes,' she said. 'So do I. And I like Marco too, even though it seems very strange to me that he's Daniel's grandfather.'

The visitors all came down to breakfast at different times except that Harriet took a tray of tea and toast to Marco for him to have in bed, but they were all downstairs at eleven when the skittering and clattering of hooves was heard in the yard.

'It's Beatrice and Charles – and Stephen.' Maria's voice faltered when she saw Stephen coming towards the door with the twins.

There was a great commotion of kisses and hand shakes and more tea making, and then Calypso's lilting voice was heard above the others when she said, 'Maria – Dolly, how very strange, but you look so much like Charles and Beatrice. What was it you say?'

There was a second's silence and then a murmur of laughter from the Tukes and the Hart family, which grew louder until Fletcher said wryly, 'That's a subject for another day.'

'We've come to invite you all to tea,' Beatrice announced after a while. 'Three o'clock, before

399

dark. Do say you'll come. Our parents are eager to meet you. We'll send the carriage.'

'How did you know they'd arrived?' Daniel asked her. 'I didn't say which day.'

'Didn't you?' she said vaguely and put a finger to her cheek. 'Oh.'

'Beatrice?' Daniel laughed, his mood lightening as it always did when he was in her company. 'You're up to something.'

'Something, perhaps, or nothing,' she said impertinently. 'But I can't tell. It's a surprise. Look,' she said, to divert his attention. 'See how besotted Charles is with Calypso. He has told Mama and Papa that he doesn't think he's good enough for her.' She gave a deep sigh. 'I wish that someone special loved me in the way he loves her.'

Daniel took a breath. She was standing so close, and although the room was crowded it was as if there was no one else there. 'Beatrice,' he murmured, taking her hand, 'someone does love you, but he's not special, not in any way.'

She removed her hand from his. 'Then he should tell me so,' she whispered. 'For how else will I know?' She gazed directly at him, her blue eyes into his dark ones. 'And I will be the judge of whether he's special or not.'

Charles then lost Calypso to Lenny, who was captivated by his cousin and dewy-eyed over her, much to Dolly's amusement. Charles looked towards Beatrice, and then at Stephen who was talking to Fletcher, and then at the clock on the wall. Beatrice followed his gaze.

'Mrs Tuke,' she said to Harriet, 'forgive us for dropping in uninvited, and I do hope you will all

400

come this afternoon, but now we must leave. Charles – Stephen – don't forget we have to be at home for midday.'

'She is lovely, is she not?' Marco said after the Harts had left, sitting down comfortably and at ease and accepting another cup of coffee from Rosie. 'Impulsive, yes, and – well, I expect there will be a lucky young man to capture her one day, unless of course someone has already done so?'

Daniel glanced round and wondered why everyone was, but pretending not to be, looking at him.

The snow began as they all headed off towards the manor. The Harts' carriage had picked up Harriet, Rosie, Marco and Calypso and squeezed Elizabeth and Joseph in between them. The rest, Fletcher driving, Leo beside him, Daniel, Lenny, Maria and Dolly, all squashed up in the trap, all laughing and jolly and already with snowflakes settling on their heads and shoulders.

'Just as well it's not far,' Fletcher joked. 'You'll like 'house, Leo, and so will Calypso.' He smiled as he said it. Any young woman would, he thought, and it will give her and Leo an insight into what kind of family the Harts are.

As they drove up the long drive with the house at the end of it, Leo murmured, 'Never in a million years would I have imagined I'd see my sister Harriet so close to people living in a house like this.' He immediately told Fletcher, 'I don't mean that your house isn't substantial and cosy, it's the kind of house I would like for myself, but this – this is impressive!'

'Yeh!' Fletcher said softly. 'This is – old money,

this is grandeur. Is it, do you think, 'reason we've been invited to tea, for Charles to show it off to Calypso?'

Leo smiled. 'No, I don't think so. From what I've seen of Charles and Beatrice in 'short time I've known them, I don't think that would have occurred to either of them. I think they're quite oblivious of 'differences between us. I mean,' he said, turning to look at Fletcher, 'the sort of lifestyle we – you and I – were born into.'

Fletcher laughed. 'Remind me to tell you a story when we have an hour or two to spare, Leo. I reckon you'll find it interesting. But if you don't think it's to impress Calypso, then there's summat else going on.'

'You are right, my friend,' Leo agreed. 'But I'm not at liberty to say. It's not really my secret.'

The skies were darkening and more snow was threatening, and Beatrice seemed a little agitated when they were all gathered in the withdrawing room. She went to whisper something to her mother, who nodded, murmuring, 'Very well.'

'Erm, before we take tea,' Beatrice said, glancing round at everyone, 'does anyone object if I steal Daniel away for ten minutes or so? It's getting dark, you see, and I'm afraid we might have a snowstorm.'

'Started already,' her father said, looking out of the window, where there was a veritable blizzard blowing.

'I don't think we should be too late getting back,' Fletcher said and glanced at Daniel, who shrugged his shoulders and lifted his hands, indicating he didn't know what was happening.

'We'll start tea without you,' Melissa said. 'That's all right, isn't it?'

'Yes, of course,' Daniel told her, adding, 'Is this one of Beatrice's schemes?'

'I rather think so,' her mother smiled.

'You should go, Daniel,' Marco insisted. 'We will save you a piece of cake.'

Daniel followed Beatrice into the hallway. 'What are you up to, Beatrice? I thought this was supposed to be a tea party.'

'It is,' she said, putting on her coat, which one of the maids was holding for her. 'But I hadn't planned for snow, so we must go whilst there's still light to see.'

'To see what?' They ran down the steps and he followed her as she led him to the back of the house.

'You've forgotten that it's your birthday in two days' time, haven't you?' she said, taking his arm.

'No, but my coming of age is of no real significance,' he said. 'I can do most of what I want anyway. Where are we going?'

'To the stables,' she said. 'I know that your parents will want you with them on your birthday, so I've got you an early birthday present and I had to put it in the stables so that no one would find it, except for Aaron, the stable lad, and he's to be trusted.'

Daniel gave a great sigh. 'I give in,' he said. Then, 'But wait, Beatrice. I have to tell you something.' He stopped and pulled her to a halt too. 'You said earlier that you wished someone loved you in the way that Charles loves Calypso.'

403

'I do,' she said, 'but it has to be...' She paused, as if not knowing what to say, and besides he was standing very close.

He looked down at her and saw snowflakes on her lashes, and tenderly he brushed them away. 'I know we've been good friends all our lives, Beatrice, and you've probably accepted that that is what we've always been, just that. Friends.' He swallowed. 'But it's not true; for me it's always been more and I can't even remember when it was that I knew I loved you; and it's nothing like how Charles loves Calypso because his is a new love, whereas mine,' he hesitated, 'mine is an old strong love and one that will last for ever, even though ... even though–'

She put her hand over his mouth. 'Don't say that you're not good enough, because you are more than I deserve,' she said softly. 'I've known that I wanted to be with you since I was a child, and I even told your sister I intended marrying you. Ask her, ask Maria, and she'll tell you. I've been waiting for you, Daniel, all my life. And please don't say that your coming of age isn't significant because it is, it is to me and it is to your parents and everybody else who loves you, and it should be to you.'

He bent his head and kissed her mouth, closing his eyes, and still not convinced that he should make a commitment. Would he spoil her chances of marrying someone from her own background, someone richer, a gentleman descended from a family with a fine lineage and ancestry–

He opened his eyes and found hers smiling at him. 'That's me, isn't it?' he exclaimed.

'What?'

'A fine lineage! Descended from a noble background – but not rich.'

'I don't need riches, Daniel, I've already got them. Papa and I are agreed on that.'

'Oh!' He huffed out a breath. 'You've spoken to him!'

'Well, I thought you were never going to.' She stood on tiptoe and kissed the end of his nose. 'Do you want to see this present or not?'

'Yes.' He felt dizzy; was this really happening? 'What? Erm, wait, Beatrice.' He pulled her towards him once more. 'I'd like to kiss you again.'

'All right,' she breathed. 'But let's stand inside.' She took his hand and led him towards the stable block. 'I want you to close your eyes.'

He did so and could smell sweet straw and hay and hear nickering and whinnying. He opened his eyes briefly and saw that they were in the new stable that Fletcher had said they were building, but he closed his eyes again as Beatrice was kissing him, on his cheeks and on his lips.

'Beatrice!' he whispered and opened his eyes fully, and in the dim light saw a young pony looking back at him over the wooden stall. A pale chestnut pony with a flaxen mane and with alert and intelligent eyes, who nickered and snorted at him.

'Who's this?' Daniel drew away from Beatrice but kept hold of her hand.

'We haven't given her a name yet,' she said. 'We thought that you might like to choose. She's a three year old, unbroken as yet; we thought that you might like to do that too.'

Daniel slowly moved closer to the pony, so as not to startle her. He put out his hand for her to sniff. 'She's beautiful. She's a Haflinger! Whose is she? Where's she come from?'

'She is beautiful,' Beatrice agreed, 'and she is a Haflinger. She's yours and she comes from the Tyrol.'

He turned to look at Beatrice. 'Mine?'

'Yes, she's your birthday present, from me and from Charles too.'

'But – how?'

'I discussed it with Marco before we left Italy: Marco chose her and he and Leo arranged her transport. She only arrived yesterday, so that's why she's in here resting. We had the stable extended for her until–'

'Until?' Daniel asked.

'I wasn't sure if you would accept her, or even go along with my plans.'

He gazed at her. 'Your plans?' he said huskily.

'Yes,' she smiled. 'But I can't tell you what they are yet. She's only half the present, you see.'

'Beatrice! You are so unpredictable. What kind of life am I going to have with you?'

'A wonderful one!' she said. 'Come on, let's tell your parents and mine.'

'In a moment,' Daniel said, and sliding back the bolt on the door he entered the stall, holding out his hand to the pony. She was wearing a warm wool blanket and the straw was deep, and a hay bag was hooked firmly on the wall. She nudged him with her long nose and tried to search his pockets. He stroked her neck and, remembering Signora Rosso's name for Beatrice, murmured to her, 'I'll call you Flavia, and I think *somebody* is going to get her nose pushed out of joint, for I've fallen hopelessly in love with you.'

CHAPTER FORTY-SEVEN

They were breathless when they arrived back in the drawing room, their hair wet from the driving snow, and all who looked at them knew that the glow on their faces wasn't only because of the cold. Daniel's eyes were drawn to his mother's and saw the wistfulness in hers.

Harriet, giving him a trembling smile and blinking rapidly to keep the tears at bay, thought, Have I lost my boy? But no, as she saw him so happy, she knew she was sharing him with someone else who loved him too. She looked at her other sons, Lenny and Joseph, who would be with her for a long while yet, and at her three daughters who would always remain close.

She glanced at Marco, in deep conversation with Christopher, and Melissa, who was talking to Maria and gently patting her hand. Maria will always keep a place in her heart for Stephen, Harriet thought, but she is young, she will find another love. Leo was talking to Charles. Charles had broken off his conversation with Leo to shake hands with Daniel and then impulsively given him a bear hug, and while he was gone from his side, Leo seemed to be in a contemplative mood.

'You're thinking of Calypso, aren't you?'

Harriet asked him, when he came to talk to her, balancing a cup and saucer in his hand, for afternoon tea was quite informal.

'No, as a matter of fact I'm thinking of someone else and realizing I'm missing her.'

'Your wife?' she said softly.

He shook his head. 'I think of her every day; but no, this is someone else. Sophia, the daughter of friends of Marco. She's a treasure, looks after Marco and has been a good friend to Calypso. She's a lot younger than me; she's fiery and lovely, and – and yes, I'm missing her.'

Daniel announced that they were keeping the pony quiet for the next few days, and that after that Mr Hart had kindly agreed that he might bring anyone to inspect and admire her.

'I hope that I can be one of the first to look at her,' Christopher joked. 'No one, except for the horse lad, has been allowed near her.'

'Aaron,' Beatrice murmured. 'He loves her already.'

Daniel thanked Marco and Leo for arranging to bring the pony over on the long journey and was intrigued by the complicit glances they gave each other. Later, as teatime was drawing to a close, he went across to Christopher Hart to ask if he might come to see him in two days' time.

Christopher raised an eyebrow. 'You may come whenever you wish, Daniel,' he said. 'Can you imagine the furore my daughter might make if I laid down stipulations on when you might visit?'

'It's just that in two days' time I will have reached my majority, sir, and I'm led to believe that it's important to mark it.'

Christopher gave a slight nod. His own coming of age had certainly been remarkable, although he hadn't realized it at the time. He looked across at Fletcher, who caught his glance and gave a crooked grin, an acknowledgement of an understanding between them.

Daniel rose early on his birthday and found his mother putting finishing touches to a cake. 'Mm, smells good.' He put his arms round her waist, resting his chin on her shoulder. 'Somebody said today was a special day. Do you know owt about it?'

'Me? No!' she said. 'Can't think what it might be.'

'Me neither,' he grinned. 'Except that I've to go up and see *'maister,* and have a word about marrying his daughter.'

'Watch your p's and q's, then,' she said, with a crack in her voice.

'You don't need to think I'll be leaving home just yet,' he said, sliding his arm across her shoulder. 'I haven't enough money to give Beatrice a home yet, and we're a bit crowded here, and besides,' he added, 'I've a pony to keep as well.'

His mother laughed. 'So you have. Well, mebbe you'll have to choose between 'pony and Beatrice.'

'I don't think that will be necessary.' Marco had come into the kitchen and overheard some of their conversation.

'I was going to bring your breakfast up.' Harriet wiped her hands on her apron. 'You didn't have to get up so early.'

'Ah, but I did, my dear. Today is a special day,

which of course you know already, but I wished to help my grandson celebrate.' He held out his hand to Daniel and shook his warmly and then kissed him on both cheeks. *'Buona fortuna,* as we say in Italy, and many congratulations.'

He sat down at the kitchen table, quite at home in his surroundings. Harriet gave him a cup of coffee; he hadn't changed his preference to English tea. 'Now,' he said, 'where is everyone? We must talk about this special day.'

'Everyone will be here in a few minutes,' Harriet said. 'Fletcher and Lenny are feeding the animals and everyone else will be down as well.'

'I need to see to 'hosses,' Daniel said. 'I should have been up earlier.'

'Fletcher's seeing to them,' Harriet told him. 'We decided that you should have a day off today.'

Leo came wandering down in a warm dressing gown. 'Am I late?' he said.

'No. What's going on?' Daniel asked, as one by one his family started to appear, Maria in from milking, and then Dolly, who still hadn't gone back to work, Rosie, and the last to appear, Joseph and Elizabeth, dressed ready for school.

'We had to be up early,' Elizabeth said. 'Otherwise we'd miss—'

'Ssh,' Joseph said. 'It's a secret. I wish we could have a day off school, Ma.'

'You can't, but you break up at 'end of 'week,' she said, and smiled at Calypso, who had also come down, looking sleepy and lovely; the morning was still very young, and still dark outside.

Fletcher came in and hugged Daniel and was followed by Tom, who shook hands with Daniel and gave him a thumbs up and said congratulations.

'It's like a meeting of the clans,' Daniel said, as they all sat round the big table. 'I thought this was going to be an ordinary day, with cake this afternoon.'

'There will be cake this afternoon,' Harriet said, pouring tea from a huge brown teapot and then putting a jug of coffee in the middle of the table for those who wanted it. Then she came and sat next to Daniel.

'Can I say,' Fletcher began, 'that this is a special day for us all. Our son, Harriet's and mine too, has reached his majority, and first of all I'd like to raise a toast to Noah, Daniel's birth father, who made it possible by marrying Harriet and bringing her home.' He glanced at Harriet and then at Rosie, who gave a winsome smile. He lifted his cup and everyone else followed suit. 'And who, because of a tragic accident, allowed me to marry Harriet and become Daniel's very proud stepfather.' His voice suddenly broke and it was a second before he could continue to say, '...as proud of him as I am of all my sons and daughters.'

'Well said,' Leo murmured, and Marco nodded and blew his nose loudly.

'And so to a second toast.' He lifted his teacup again. 'To Daniel, many congratulations and may you always have love in your life.'

Whilst everyone was shaking hands with Daniel or kissing him, Harriet reached into her apron pocket and brought out a small box, which she pushed towards him.

'Daniel,' she said. 'Here is a small present from

us all to show how much we love and care for you.'

'Oh, you shouldn't have,' he said, feeling really choked as he opened the box. 'I never expected– Oh, that's so– Thank you!' He put his hand to his face to stem his emotion, and then with a great intake of breath took out the gold signet ring with the three initials inscribed in italic script: *DTO*. Daniel Tuke Orsini.

He slipped it on to his finger, a perfect fit. He hadn't expected a gift, but only a birthday tea with maybe a glass of home-made wine, but already it was becoming a special time, beginning with him declaring his love for Beatrice and the unthinkable prospect of her father agreeing that they might marry. Of Beatrice and Charles's gift of the Haflinger, he wondered vaguely how he was going to afford to keep her, let alone how he would use her, for she wasn't any ordinary pony, and now this gift from his parents and brothers and sisters. It was all too much.

Then Marco stood up and leaned with his fingertips touching the table. 'I too must offer my congratulations publicly to my newly discovered grandson, of whom I knew nothing until a mere five or six months ago, and I must tell you, my friends, that the discovery has brought joy into my life, to know that my branch of the Orsini line will continue after I am gone. To this end I have made provision for Daniel in my Will and I must assure you that this is done with the approval of my daughters, who also send their good wishes, and of my dear son-in-law Leo and my granddaughter Calypso.

'However,' he continued, 'I do not intend leaving this life for quite some time, especially now that I 'ave met Rosie again,' here a little twinkle in his eyes, 'so until then, Daniel, I 'ave for you made a bank deposit.'

He pushed a sheet of paper towards him, signed and countersigned, naming a sum of money that Daniel gaped at.

I can marry Beatrice, he thought, and maybe her father has a tenancy we could rent with a field and a stable for Flavia, although he couldn't quite see Beatrice in a farm kitchen such as this one, no matter that she said she loved it; and I can still keep on working here with Fletcher and 'farm hosses.

They all left the table after a substantial breakfast and Daniel went to his room to change into his one and only suit of clothes for his visit to the manor.

'How smart and handsome you look,' his mother said when he reappeared. 'My noble son!'

'Oh, give over, Ma,' he said bashfully. 'It's onny me.'

'I think you're handsome too, even if you are my brother,' Dolly said, appearing from out of the larder. 'I'm going to Italy to stay with Calypso next year to catch myself an Italian who looks like you.' She looked him over and brushed away a stray dark hair from his shoulder. 'Are you going to officially propose today?'

Daniel ran his fingers round his shirt collar and cleared his throat. 'Is there no privacy in this house?' he asked. 'Nosy sisters wanting to know 'far end of everything!'

'You'll miss us when you've left,' she countered.

'You just said you were going to Italy!'

'I am,' she said smugly. 'But I'll come back for your wedding.' Then she covered her face with her hands. 'But I'll miss you, Daniel,' she wept, 'when Beatrice steals you from us.'

He put his arms round her. This was so unlike the carefree Dolly. 'I shan't be going far,' he murmured. 'And you know there'll allus be a special place in my heart for all of you.'

She nodded and blew her nose, but he could see she wasn't convinced.

He hitched the mare to the trap to drive down to the manor. There had been more snow overnight and the road surface was thick and white, with animal tracks scattered over it and the hedges dusted with a fine lacy covering. He pondered about what he would say to Beatrice's father if he should ask him about keeping her in the manner to which she was accustomed; well, I can't, he thought. I have this gift of money from Marco and that will keep us comfortably for a year or two, but I think I'll still have to ask Mr Hart for a tenancy. He sighed. Much as he loved the filly that Beatrice and Charles had given him, he was still unsure how he could afford her. Beatrice and Charles had never had to consider finances and wouldn't know how much it cost to keep horses. He did, for he had worked with them from a young age. It was the only thing he really knew about, the training of them, the caring, feeding and cost of them.

He sighed. What will I do if he refuses? Will he ask us to wait a year or two until I have earned more money, although I know that Fletcher and

Tom can't really afford to pay me more; he always had to remember that it was Tom's farm too.

He drew up at the front of the house, climbed down from the trap and was straightening his jacket when the door was flung open by Beatrice. 'Oh, Daniel, I thought you were never coming.' She ran down the steps to greet him. 'Happy, happy birthday,' she enthused. 'Oh, Daniel, I do love you so, and I want to kiss you, but I can't as everyone will be watching.'

'Then allow me.' He was so full of happiness he thought he would explode. He put his hand to his chest and in case anyone was watching from the window he made a formal bow, reaching for her hand and gently kissing it. 'Oh dear, Beatrice,' he said in mock dismay. 'Is this how I must behave from now on?'

She tucked her arm into his. 'No, silly. Of course not!'

He was ushered into the study, where Christopher Hart was sitting at his desk with a pen in his hand and a sheet of paper in front of him. He had apparently been making notes. Daniel, shaking with nerves, said, 'Good morning, sir. I hope I'm not disturbing you,' in a voice he thought sounded rather strained.

'Come in, Daniel. Come in and take a seat.' Christopher indicated a large leather wing-backed chair.

Daniel cleared his throat. 'If you don't mind, sir, I'd prefer to stand.'

'Oh, would you? Very well.' Christopher got up from his desk. 'I don't know about you, old chap,' he said in a voice that sounded just like Charles, which made Daniel smile, 'but I'm rather nervous. I know why you've come, of course, and Beatrice has coached me in what I have to say. That's the thing with ladies, don't you find: a fellow thinks he is in control and finds that he is not.'

'I – I don't know, sir, except – yes, mebbe so, especially with Beatrice.' He thought then that he shouldn't have said that about Beatrice. Christopher Hart probably thought the sun shone out of her; which of course it does, he thought happily.

'So, what do you want to say? Best get it over with and then we can join my wife and Beatrice, and Charles too, I imagine, who are all waiting anxiously, no doubt.'

'I'd like to marry Beatrice, sir,' Daniel said at great speed. 'I realize I'm not her equal, but I love her and always have.'

Christopher rubbed his chin and viewed him seriously. 'Odd, that,' he said. 'That's exactly what Beatrice said you would say – about not being her equal, I mean. But from what I gather your ancestry is medieval, and there have been some very notable characters along the way – popes, cardinals, counts and politicians, I believe – but in my opinion it's the present generation that is important rather than what happened back in history, and having known you so long and now having met Signor Orsini I have no anxiety about that.'

He smiled and offered his hand to Daniel, which he shook with a great sense of relief, until Christopher said, 'What I would like to say to you and Beatrice is, I would prefer it if we might wait until Christmas week for the official announcement. I have my reasons for doing so: I need to speak to my lawyer about Beatrice's dowry and one or two other things. I've rather had the wind taken out of my sails, if you understand my meaning, so if you don't mind...'

'Oh, erm, no, sir.' Daniel was flummoxed. 'I rather feel 'same way and I don't mind waiting, but I didn't – don't expect a dowry, sir. It didn't cross my mind.'

'Well, I dare say it didn't, Daniel.' Christopher gazed at him with a wry expression. 'But that's the way it is done.'

They came to the withdrawing room together, and there waiting for them was Beatrice dressed in blue muslin and in mid-pace between the window and the door; Charles was standing by the window with his arms folded, and their mother was sitting calmly by the fire.

Beatrice turned, her eyes and demeanour eager, gazing at Daniel. 'Oh, what is it to be? Are we to be married? Papa, you did agree?'

She's so lovely, Daniel thought, and impetuous. How can I be so lucky that she wants to spend the rest of her life with me?

'Well?' she demanded, her eyes suddenly anxious.

'You'd better tell us, old chap,' Charles bantered, 'or our lives won't be worth living.'

Daniel laughed. What a wonderful, exhilarating time they were going to have.

'Yes,' he said. 'Beatrice, if you will have me, we are to be married.'

CHAPTER FORTY-EIGHT

Everyone had been invited to spend Christmas Day at Hart Holme Manor when the engagement of Beatrice and Daniel would be officially announced.

Harriet was pleased, for with extra guests at Dale Top Farm, although very pleasant, it was quite exhausting keeping everyone fed and entertained, and she was rather gratified to be invited to dine in such luxurious surroundings. She, Fletcher, Daniel, Lenny, Maria and Dolly were up early to organize their usual duties including milking, collecting eggs, and feeding the cattle and other livestock, and Joseph and Elizabeth were kept busy wrapping presents to take to the manor where they would spend the day at leisure, whilst Marco, Leo and Calypso held whispered conversations whenever they were alone.

Tom had come up on Christmas Eve to bring presents and announced rather bashfully that on Christmas Day he intended to ask the widow Betsy if she would do him the honour of being his wife. Her son Adam had come with him to help Lenny with the pigs and had asked Fletcher if he thought Maria might walk out with him. Fletcher said he thought that she might. He was a handsome and hard-working lad and an asset to the farm.

It had snowed overnight and the meadows were

bright white, crisp and dazzling, and the sky blue with scarcely a cloud as they set off, some of them in the trap, others in a waggon and the Italian visitors in the Harts' carriage.

They were all dressed in their best, Maria, Dolly and Elizabeth in fine wool dresses, warm capes and ribbons in their hair. Calypso wore exotic red with a frilled hem. Harriet had chosen a grey fitted gown with a pleated hem trimmed with white, Rosie was in black and grey with a white cap, and the menfolk were all in their smartest suits with cravats or stocks at their necks. Melissa, in dark red velvet with a ruched bustle, and Beatrice, in cream figured silk, were at the door to greet them.

They toasted each other a happy Christmas in their preferences of sherry, whisky or mulled wine, although Joseph and Elizabeth to their disappointment were given lemonade; after the exchange of simple presents, Beatrice's father made the announcement of the betrothal which was celebrated with champagne; neither Harriet nor Melissa remained dry-eyed. They exchanged glances and smiled. The secret fears these mothers had shared were over; Ellen Tuke had not after all divided their families. All the long years of anxiety and apprehension they had suffered had blown away like gossamer on a breeze.

Before Christmas luncheon Christopher asked everyone to put on their top coats again as they must all venture down to the meadow adjoining the stables where there was something special to see. 'But before we do,' he said, 'I must tell you that my wife and I were at a loss to think of a suitable wedding gift for the young couple, but now,

419

having been informed by Beatrice of Daniel's longed-for ambition, we think we have come up with a solution.'

Daniel's forehead creased. Ambition? I've achieved mine, he thought; what more could I possibly want than to marry Beatrice and find my grandfather? He looked across at Marco and then his mother and Fletcher with a query in his eyes, but all any of them did was smile or nod in a meaningful manner.

'What ambition, Beatrice?' he whispered to her. 'I now have everything I desire.'

'This is for the future, Daniel,' she murmured into his ear. *'Our* future.'

They trooped outside, Marco and Rosie arm in arm, with Stephen and Charles at either side of them to steady them, and Leo walking with Harriet.

'Some of you have seen Flavia already,' Charles announced as they arrived at the stables. 'She's young and very beautiful, rather like all the ladies here today,' he said gallantly, 'but we thought she seemed a little lonely and in need of companions, and so Signor Orsini, Leo and Calypso came up with a splendid idea.' He smiled at Calypso, totally smitten as her dark eyes glimmered beneath the cream shawl she had draped over her head.

'Aaron,' he called, and the stable lad looked out from the stable door. 'Will you bring Flavia out?'

Aaron put up his thumb, disappearing inside again and bringing out the young pony on a leading rein. He opened the gate for her to trot into the field, where she kicked up her heels and cantered around, scattering snow. Then Aaron went back into the other stable, where they could hear him opening the stalls and talking to someone. Daniel and Beatrice walked across to the fence, leaning on it to watch Flavia.

'Daniel, will you whistle?' Beatrice said. 'You know, the way you did to the ponies when we were travelling. Just to see if Flavia will respond.'

'She doesn't know me yet,' he objected. 'As soon as 'snow's gone I'll be here every day to see her – and you,' he added tenderly.

But at further prompting from Beatrice he faced Flavia, put his fingers to his lips and whistled.

Flavia pricked up her ears and started to come towards him, but behind him came an excited nickering and snorting and a clattering of hooves on the cobbled yard as Aaron led out three ponies, Blaze, White Socks and Mama, and had great difficulty holding them in check. Charles and Stephen dashed to help him and together they ran beside the ponies, who were heading straight for Daniel.

He buried his head in their manes, stroked their necks and breathed into their nostrils and wondered what he'd done in his life to deserve so much.

'They're from Marco,' Beatrice explained, seeing how overcome he was. 'They're his wedding present to us, and my parents are giving us a gift of land higher up the dale so that we can build our own farm and start a breeding programme with Flavia and White Socks. It is what you want, isn't it, Daniel?' she said anxiously.

'I can't believe how generous everyone has been,' he said, and turning round to see them all

421

watching from the shelter of the stable he raised his hand in a salute; then, taking a deep breath and putting his arm round Beatrice's waist, he kissed her cheek. Murmuring, 'I love you,' he led her towards the field with the three ponies following and Flavia watching from a safe distance. 'Come on,' he said, in a choked voice. 'Let's introduce them. They're going to be great friends.'

ENDING

I have often found that on finishing a saga such as this, I must be careful to tell my readers all of what I think might have happened to the secondary characters who play a minor but important part in the story – important, for otherwise why would they be there?

And so with the many varied personalities involved I will begin with Maria and Dolly, Daniel's half-sisters. Maria, having had to abandon any notion of a relationship with Stephen Hart, begins to 'walk out' with Adam, whose mother Betsy marries Tom Bolton, and we hope that they will all find happiness in their lives together. Dolly does as she said she would and travels to Italy where she stays with Calypso and Marco and eventually finds herself a rich and handsome Italian gentleman to keep her in the manner she has always desired.

Leo marries Sophia and brings her to meet his sister Harriet and there is much to-ing and froing between Italy and England as the women become good friends.

Rosie too is persuaded to travel to Italy and with their renewed friendship in their older years she spends the winters with Marco, travelling to Vernazza escorted by Charles Hart who, after studying at an Italian university, takes up a career in art and culture. After his marriage to Calypso they make a home in Florence where they become a very popular couple enjoying the finer things in life without too much effort on their part.

Young George Hart becomes a professor, and makes an enormous contribution to the world of science. Lenny changes his name to Leo like his uncle, and with his partner Adam, his sister Maria's husband, he becomes one of the premier pig breeders in Yorkshire. He remains a bachelor all his life.

Stephen Hart doesn't marry until he is thirty, when he meets and marries a widow from a farming background who understands perfectly what he is talking about when he discusses the comparative prices and quality of grain in America compared with England's.

Melissa and Christopher Hart, having given full control of the estate to Stephen and making generous allowances to their other children, decide to travel in Europe whilst they still can, considering Christopher's age.

Elizabeth and Joseph are too young as yet to have their lives mapped out, but no doubt in time they will have their own stories to tell.

Harriet and Fletcher are content to stay at home and don't travel far; they work with their good friend Tom Bolton, buying more land and increasing their farm stock and building on another extension to their farmhouse as Harriet had suggested they should, to accommodate their children and their children's children when they come to stay. Harriet in particular becomes even busier, as, when least expecting to, she gives birth to another daughter who is given the name of Daisy as she was born in springtime.

And as for Daniel and Beatrice, after their marriage which was said to be the Yorkshire wedding of the year as gossip goes, the groom is of noble birth and the bride an heiress, they steal Aaron from the Hart estate and make him farm manager of their stud farm and prepare to begin their breeding programme; two years after Flavia had been brought to England she gives birth to a foal whom they name Freya. There is no conclusive evidence of the thoughts of White Socks as he frolics with his offspring.

Beatrice gives birth to a son twelve months after her marriage to Daniel, the first of four children; he is born with dark curly hair like his father and blue eyes like his mother and is blessed with a warm and happy nature, and when he plays on the rug with Grandmother Harriet's daughter – his aunt Daisy – he knows exactly who he is: Marco Daniel Tuke-Orsini, to be known as Marco, the first son of doting parents Beatrice and Daniel Tuke-Orsini.

AUTHOR'S NOTE

Orsini is a noble Italian name and I do not intend any discourtesy in my use of it. I do not know anyone of that line and have used it as I would any English name such as Smith, Brown or even Wood for my fiction. I did, however, need an aristocratic and eminent name associated with Italian history, and on reading about the family it seemed just perfect. It is true that there are many Orsini palaces scattered around Italy; the Palazzo Orsini in Rome, which resembles a mini Colosseum and was once the Theatre of Marcellus, was for sale in 2012. The price was £26 million and if it has been sold and you were unlucky enough to miss it, then it will probably be another two hundred years before it comes on the market again.

ACKNOWLEDGEMENTS

Thanks are due to my Transworld publishing team for their support over the last twenty-one years and for believing in each and every one of my books. The production of a book requires a dedicated team effort and I am aware that everyone within Transworld plays a vital part. To my editors over the years for their expertise and enthusiasm I say a grateful thank you, as I do to my production editor Vivien Thompson and copy-editor Nancy Webber for their innate ability to spot a misplaced comma, spelling mistake or inaccuracy, and ensure that the whole is polished and honed to as near perfection as possible.

To you all – I thank you.

SOURCES

Books for general reading:

Travels with a Donkey in the Cévennes by Robert
  Louis Stevenson, Chatto & Windus, London,
  1925
*The Ultimate Encyclopedia of Horse Breeds and
  Horse Care* by Judith Draper, Selectabook Ltd,
  Anness Publishing Ltd, London

And general information from various Internet
sites including:

150th Anniversary of Switzerland's Grand Tour.
  MySwitzerland.com

The publishers hope that this book has given you enjoyable reading. Large Print Books are especially designed to be as easy to see and hold as possible. If you wish a complete list of our books please ask at your local library or write directly to:

Magna Large Print Books
Magna House, Long Preston,
Skipton, North Yorkshire.
BD23 4ND

This Large Print Book for the partially sighted, who cannot read normal print, is published under the auspices of

THE ULVERSCROFT FOUNDATION